DARK CHOICES

WILLIAM J. SEYMOUR

DARK CHOICES

DARK CHOICES is a work of fiction. Names, places, and incidents either are a product of the author's imagination or are used fictitiously.

A Book Furnace Publications Book

Copyright © 2015 by William J. Seymour

Originally Published under the pseudonym RJ Seymour

Published in English by Book Furnace Publications, York, Pennsylvania.

ISBN 978-1-943266-09-8

Cover Images: © Pavel Chagochkin | Dreamstime.com

© Oleg Zabielin | Dreamstime.com

 Created with Vellum

Chapter One

1817 hours, Juin 13, 2258
Qrecrathe, Azhana

BULLET SHELLS FELL LIKE RAIN. The sound of brass coins being dumped at their feet sang a melody in the background. Ankle deep and the storm would not cease.

Brett watched the casings fall from the window above him.

Whoever was getting rich from this war, it sure wasn't him or his men. If you accepted a large body count for payment, his team would be kings among men.

"Witch sure is doing a fine job out there!" David shouted from across the three-foot-wide hole they had created in the concrete wall leading to the first floor of the building.

Looking out, Brett watched as six sets of muzzle flashes peppered the windows above them. Smiling, he knew his man was safely bunkered three buildings up the natural amphitheater.

The team had been making their way toward the target since before dawn. Sneaking through the city had been the easy part. Reaching the inside of this one building, was becoming more of a headache than anyone wanted. Dickie didn't help when he knifed a patrol car's driver.

"What was I supposed to do? Fucker came out of nowhere, and a man like me doesn't hide so easily." Dickie argued as he patted his stomach before stowing his knife away.

The man was as wide at the waist as he was at the shoulders. By all regulations, the army should have discharged him years ago, but Brett would not allow a man of his talents to ride off into the sunset. Even if he had to force the army to build a special line for the man in the mess hall.

"Think the others have made it to the back entrance?" David asked as he smiled back at Brett.

His face was covered in black and dark-green paint though the team was armored in neutral colors to help blend with the city's surroundings.

"They had better! We go in two minutes." Brett called back over the constant thunder of the guns above them. "You know one day, you'll learn to stop covering your face with that God damn makeup of yours."

David blew him a kiss as the indicator switch on each of their belts turned from red to green.

Leading the way, David turned quickly into the opening that led them into the building. Being careful not to fall, Brett followed two steps behind. The lower floor was vacant as the men stepped over the concrete pieces that scattered on the floor. Dust filled the air as sparks bounced around from a wire now swinging dangerously from the ceiling.

"There is an elevator at the back," David said as he led Brett out of the first room and down the hall.

Rats scurried past the men's feet as they checked each door they passed. Most were locked; the others led to small closets full of maintenance supplies. Men's voices could be heard through the floor above them as they shouted orders to one another between the pounding cadence of the mounted weapon that continued to fire at targets below.

"Damn that man has them chasing their tails. Boy, they are gonna be angry if they discover there is no one out there to shoot at." David whispered as he looked up the partially opened elevator door. "Don't think we are gonna go up the easy way, Sergeant."

"We never do. Stairs to our right." Brett grumbled back as he now led the way.

The building was a three-story retail store, converted into a makeshift headquarters by a splinter cell of ARA, Azhana's Revolutionary Army, the building had been a good hideaway. From the outside, they made sure it still looked like a civilian clothing store on the ground level. Apartment style rooms filled the top two levels, though, from the constant pounding of gunfire; they had equipped several of them with heavy weapons.

Opening the door slowly to the stairwell up, Brett couldn't see anything that would stop them from making their way to the next floor. No trip wires and no alarms. These men were acting more like amateurs than trained soldiers. It didn't matter. He had his orders, and his men would see them through.

"Up we go," David said as the smile returned to his face.

David took a step in but was cautious to keep his sight ahead and to anything they may have missed. Brett stayed no more than two steps behind as he covered the rear and tried to listen for any signs of danger.

"Second floor, how we going in, Boss?" David asked, placing his back against the wall nearest the door that had a large two painted on it.

"Quick and quiet. They still don't know we are here."

Shouts and gunfire could be heard coming through the wall. Witch was doing a good job; bullets slammed into the exterior wall with such consistency that the men inside only had time to return fire at the enemies on the field below.

Reaching down, David placed a small box over the door-frame and the bolt lock that kept the door closed. Lights on the front console flickered red as the small sound of sizzling mixed with the smell of melting metal as each light slowly changed from red to green. Finished its job, the device fell from the door and into David's hands.

"All clear," David whispered as he slowly removed a flash canister from his belt.

Brett nodded as he gently pressed the handle on the door and inched it open gradually. The voices of the men inside grew louder as the metal door opened, once there was enough room for his arm, David tossed the bomb in and Brett shut the door.

Seconds later, the sound of the device going off was quickly followed by shouts and coughing. The thunder of the mounted guns stopped as the men inside staggered from the smoke and burst of light that filled their world.

Kicking the door in, David was the first to enter as he fired several bursts at the first enemy to stagger his way. Stepping in and moving off to the right, Brett was quick to follow as he sent several rounds into the back of the man still seated on the weapon that fired out the front window.

"All clear," David called as he held up his hand.

The smoke was beginning to settle as the two soldiers checked the rest of the room. Six men laid lifeless on the floor. Thousands of rounds of shells littered the linoleum floor as Brett examined the carnage.

"Nothing here, let's get upstairs. The others should just about be there." Brett ordered as he turned back to the door that would lead them to the top floor.

David, with his painted face, again led the way as he began to ascend the stairs quickly. The shouting on the third floor was intense as both men neared the turn before they reached the next floor.

"What the fuck are they saying?" David asked as he stopped moving forward, his rifle still held up and ready.

"That's nothing I've ever heard," Brett replied as he tried to translate the words one by one.

They were speaking a foreign language, even for these parts. No one had told them there would be foreign mercenaries involved with this group. The ARA didn't hire others to win their war for them; they fought to the last man in every battle from the start. Brett tapped his man on the shoulder, and they went to continue moving up.

Plink, plink.

The sound of metal bouncing on the stairs echoed in the small stairwell.

"Grenade!" David shouted as he turned and threw himself into Brett.

Both men tumbled down the stairs just as the corridor filled with fire and flying shrapnel.

"Ah!" David screamed as they came to a rest one floor down.

Smoke and dust filled the air as pieces of wall and rock rained on them.

"You alright?" Brett asked as he rolled his friend over.

"Yeah, I'm fucking alright." David shoved the Sergeant's hand away and slowly removed the pack from his back. "Fuckers probably destroyed my favorite canteen."

David opened the small pack now shredded and burned from the blast. Water leaked from several holes in its side, the flatten lead now rattled as it moved. Brett noticed two tears in the man's uniform over his arms quickly becoming wet with blood.

"You sure you're alright?"

"Damn straight I am. Let's kill these bastards!" David countered as he pushed himself back to his feet.

Reaching down on his belt, he clicked the green indicator, and Brett noticed it started a countdown from ten. Quickly making their way up the stairs, they noticed the grenade had done little damage to the stairwell. A large crater was blasted out where the stairs met the cement wall, but everything else remained sturdy.

"You smell that?" David asked as he approached the door marked with a three.

The corridor still smelled of dust from the grenade, but behind it something different lingered. Brett looked down as he tried to listen to the room on the other side that was now eerily quiet. Gray smoke began to roll out from under the metal framing. Straining his ears just enough, Brett couldn't understand what they were saying, but it was in whispers, and they were speaking in short quick bursts.

"They are burning something, get in now!" Brett shouted as he stepped back.

Without waiting, the Sergeant kicked at the horizontal handle of the door. Bending the arm-bar with his foot, the door swung open, just as David stepped around and fired at the first man he saw. Papers flew into the air as the bullets tore through the man's back and sent him crashing to his knees. Brett's first several shots slammed into a man piling papers into a small trash can where smoldering black smoke rolled out. Tearing into the man's shoulder and neck, he stumbled backward before crashing through a bullet puckered window and falling to the ground below.

"3 o'clock!" David shouted as he knelt under Brett's raised rifle and sent several more rounds into a man pulling a rifle out from behind a desk.

Looking around, Brett could not see anyone else in the room. Walking over, he kicked the small trash can to the ground and stamped out the small flames struggling to build their way up.

"Where are the others?" David asked as he bent to scoop up some documents on the floor.

Screaming erupted from behind the door at the far end of the room.

"Well," Brett tried to answer before the wall next to the door exploded at the top as three bullets shattered through and into the ceiling.

Crouching, both men readied for whatever was behind that last door. More arguing, then several more explosions of gunfire before everything fell silent. Nodding, Brett pointed to the small brass knob on the door as he readied his weapon. Reaching up, he slowly began turning and pulling on the door.

"You wouldn't sneak up on a lady like that would you? At least not without a camera, right?" Dickie chuckled as he pulled the door open from the other side.

Brett and David stood straight as Dickie turned and waved them into the room. Just as the one they had entered, there was paper spread all over the floor. Four bodies were sprawled across the room while the single remaining enemy knelt next to Ed with his hands pressed against the back of his head.

"They try to burn anything on this side as well?" Brett asked as he picked up a few documents off the floor.

"Nope, but they sure didn't want to be taken alive. Had to tackle that fool before he shot himself. Crazy bastard." Dickie answered as he began rummaging through a small refrigerator behind one of the desks.

Brett looked at the paper in his hand. He couldn't read any of it. The symbols and drawings all looked foreign to him though he had been trained to read the languages of the area.

"What does this say?" The Sergeant asked the man who struggled to get off his knees.

Blood trickled down his pale face from a cut over his right eye. A large black beard and dark bushy eyebrows covered most of his face though the top of his head was shaved clean. His uniform, like the others, matched the ARA's standard blue and gray colors, but he didn't look like them.

Brett bent over closer and pointed to the paperwork in his hand.

"What does this say? You can answer me now, or I'll let one of my men work the truth right out of you."

Words that Brett could not understand spilled from the man's mouth. Looking up for help, Ed and the others shrugged and shook their heads, they were as confused as he was. Rearing back, Brett's fist connected with the side of the man's face. Grabbing the collar of the man's uniform, Brett yanked him from the ground.

"Now, I'm going to ask again!"

The man's eyes grew wide as he looked down at Brett's forearm. His split lip curled into a smile as he rolled his shoulders back in defiance.

"You do not know what death awaits you in this world. Our Lord awaits his calling, and soon his chosen will rule the pathetic excuses for men that you are." Blood spit out as the man replied, red saliva filling the gap between his teeth.

"Enough with you," Brett mocked as he kicked the man's stomach.

Their prisoner's coughs mixed with wheezing as he tried to catch his breath, doubled over where his nose was within inches of the ground. Two shots ended the man's life as the room fell silent. Brett had his sidearm back into its holster before he turned back to the others.

"Alright everyone, take what you think looks important, and let's get out of here," the Sergeant ordered as he folded the papers in his hands.

"Hey, Boss. Look at this." Ed called over as he rolled the dead prisoner over.

"Finally get something out of the bastard?" Brett asked as he walked over.

Standing, Ed held a small gold chain on the palm of his hand. Yellow and rose gold intertwined as they curved to form a small amulet of fire. Picking it up with his fingers, Brett could see the tiniest of gems mixed with the metal as it reflected the light, giving the small piece of jewelry the appearance that it was on fire.

"What do you think it is?" Ed asked.

Brett tried to answer, but his mouth was as dry as a dessert. Cold sweat ran down his back as he found it difficult to concentrate on anything but the tiny flames of light moving across the shiny metal.

"Hey, Sergeant. You still with us?" David chuckled as he slapped Brett on the back.

The sounds around the room rushed back into his ears as his vision cleared, and the world around him became whole again. His men were about finished picking through everything when he squeezed the necklace in his hand before putting it in his pocket.

"Yeah, I'm alright. Let's make our way out of here. Ed, you signal Witch to prepare for departure. He can get the jeeps ready." Brett answered as he took a swig of water to wet his dry throat.

Chapter Two

0857 Hours, Juillet 1, 2258
  East of Fort Frozen Heart, Northwest Azhana

THE FIGHTING HAD GOTTEN WORSE over the last couple of months, and Charlie knew that it would continue like this for the foreseeable future. The Republic had been making intrusions down from the north with sporadic raids, but until now, nothing this sustained. This attack had come out of nowhere. Will and Charlie had been patrolling to the north of their base camp when the first shots had hit the trees they were standing beside.

After a snowstorm had blown through, as it did last night, patrols spent a day or two settling back into their routines. It was the only time they could spend enjoying the beautiful sight of a new day as they made their daily rounds. The harshness of the weather up this far north usually meant neither side was ready to fight again, so soon after nature itself decided to get in on the act. She had such high hopes when she awoke this morning.

"Target to your 2 o'clock!" Will shouted over the gunfire.

Will was hunkered down against a tree not much thicker than himself. His white and faded blue winter-suited armor helped him blend with his surroundings as he positioned himself closer to the snow covered base of the tree. If you weren't looking directly at him and knew he was there, the only thing that did not fade in with the snow was his dark as night skin. Some said it would be a problem for a man of his color to fight this far north. He said they were just jealous because at least he had a tan all year round.

Reacting to his call, Charlie quickly aimed her assault rifle and squeezed off a short burst of three rounds at a target she barely saw.

"Damn these guys are fast," she yelled to her partner as she tried to see anyone else out in the small clearing between the trees.

"You expect them to march in single file right at us?" He fired a burst of his own at what, she couldn't tell.

"It would help you know!"

She didn't like their current situation. They didn't know how many there were. The echoes of gunfire were bouncing through the trees in every direction, and there was no indication if the radio signal they had sent out would get them help in time. Several bullets tore the tree she was kneeling behind, sending pieces of bark into her face and hair.

"We gotta move! On three, get your pretty ass moving!"

Will was off the ground and kneeling but ready to run. Pulling the pin on a grenade, he turned and tossed it out into the middle of the brush and trees between them and the line of forest where they assumed the enemy was. Instead of detonating and tearing everything near it apart, the grenade fizzed and tossed out a bright flash. Anyone thinking of looking in that general direction was now temporarily blinded. If the flash wasn't enough, a white smoke quickly sprayed in all directions from where the canister landed, filling the gaps between the trees with a cover impossible to see through.

Just as they had expected, a typical barrage of gunfire erupted as whomever now stood on the other side of the smoke wall, attempted to fire at them trying to escape.

"Follow me!" Charlie ordered.

She didn't bother looking as she took off in front of her friend. The smoke would last only a minute or two, but that had to be enough time for them to make some ground. Their snowshoes helped stop them from sinking into the shin-high snow, but it did not help their speed. The two soldiers raced as fast as they could through the low-lying brush and thick pine branches still heavy with snow. Their base was three miles away, but neither of them hoped to have to run that far.

As both soldiers ran, bullets crashed into the trees next to them, the ground near their feet or buzzed over their shoulders. Neither of the two was sure who heard it first. The unmistakable sound of a proximity grenade crashing into a tree not far from where they were running caused them to look into each other's face for a second.

Without hesitating, Will crashed right into Charlie, and both rolled as an explosion went off several yards to their left. The blast sent pieces of tree, rock, and earth high into the air, only to rain on where they laid. A large leafless tree crashed down, missing both of them by a few feet. Charlie looked up into Will's eyes as he picked himself off her and surveyed around them. The deep brown color of his eyes made it easy to see the look of concern and determination was hard pressed to his face.

Not wanting to waste any time, the partners picked each other up and began moving again. The time spent rolling in the snow had not helped whoever was chasing them as the shots fired still missed their mark, and they could still not see their enemy. Both knew that eventually this chase would not end well if they did not get help soon. The snow hindered their movement, speed and was tiring them quickly.

"We have to get to cover!" Charlie, breathing heavily between words, yelled as the two kept stumbling through the snow.

"Fine by me. Tell me when you find any!" Will didn't bother looking at her as he knew as well as she did; there wasn't much between them and the base. He kept pushing, knowing their best hope was to keep the distance between them and whoever chased them, as far as possible.

Charlie tried to keep up as she saw her friend pushing her harder. They had both trained daily for years, making sure they were ready when an event like this happened. But in the end, it did not help. He was too strong, had too much endurance, and, damn, he was tall. Each step of his would carry him farther and farther ahead. The cold winter air was tearing at her lungs with every breath she was forced to take.

Where was that damn support?

"Ah!" She let out a bellowing scream as pain tore into her back.

Bright lights flashed in her eyes as the pain and force of the impact threw her forward. Crashing face first into the snow and brush on the ground, she tried picking herself up but the pain in her back weakened the left side of her body. Will was right by her side, firing round after round at an enemy she couldn't see with her face buried in the snow. Lances of pain radiated all the way down her legs as she lifted her face just enough to keep breathing. Will was screaming at the top of his lungs as the casings from his rifle fell to the ground around her. The sound of each bullet exploding forward drowned anything else she could hear.

Stopping her heart in fear, the continued sound of his weapon firing was soon accompanied by the cracks of more rifles. There had to be at least two dozen other men, but her friend was not going down. Using what strength she could to bear the pain, she pulled her face from the snow and into the shadows of the forest.

Behind Will and her prone form stood two dozens of her fellow soldiers. All of them spread out, flanked on both sides by two armored trucks with their rifles going. Whoever was chasing them, was now confronted with a lot more than two scouts. The pain was quickly overcoming her as she sank back to the cold, wet snow.

Chapter Three

2258 Hours, Juin 14, 2258
  Fort Forward Trinity, Edge of Republic Territory

THE FORWARD OPERATING base was full of life and movement as the team arrived in the middle of the night. Built on what was once an airport, the perimeter structures were converted into barracks and mechanic stations shortly after they arrived. Dozens of soldiers moved like worker ants from an anthill as they filtered in and out at all hours. The exterior fence was patrolled 24/7 by guards, dogs, and armored vehicles. Within the relative confines of the small airport, there were more than a thousand soldiers: men and women, thousands of miles away from home, all fighting for various reasons. Some fought for glory, some because it was a job, and many others for reasons all their own.

The men of the Havoc Squad, at least that's what they were rumored to be called, were also here for reasons of their own. Unlike the others, they had a job that took them deep behind enemy lines for assignments that would not find them glory. Missions that only ended with one possible outcome, death: theirs or the target. Tonight it was the latter and another reason to celebrate.

"All right, you shits, it's late, and I feel a late-night steak calling my name. Catch you guys back at the bunks." Dickie jogged off toward his one love in the life of soldiering, the food.

Killing always made him hungry. Turning men into nothing but meat made him, well, crave meat.

"Don't eat all of it, you bum!" David looked at the others, "I'm just hoping there's some left for the rest of the camp for breakfast." David whispered, barely able to hold back the chuckles building. Always the one able to find humor in himself. "I think that will be enough for me. I feel the woman of my dreams calling my name!" He had Dickie's voice imitated perfectly. "I'm gonna get some shut-eye. Catch you guys later."

Not bothering to look back at the others as he walked off toward the small barracks they called home.

"You know, sleep sounds like a good idea to me as well. It's way later than I like to go to bed, so have a good night you guys." Witch was off racing to catch David.

The man tried too hard to act older than fifty. Seven at night was his bedtime if anyone would ever let him. Pretty sure he hadn't seen that in years.

"That was a good job back there, wasn't it Sergeant?" Ed was never one to bring up serious business in front of others if it could wait until they were alone.

"We made it home alive, I'd say that's a win. Tomorrow is always the question." Brett knew he should feel better.

The plan had gone flawlessly, but these days nothing short of a miracle would turn his mood around. It bothered him that again they were sent in for one mission, to find someone or something else there. Wherever this intel they were getting was coming from, it sure found a way to be wrong every time lately.

"Yeah, that brings up another question I wanted to ask you. None of the others were gonna say anything, but how many assignments have we found the wrong people in the right place now? They keep telling us we are taking out high-profile targets, ones that will help end all this. Instead, we find unknown and unranked soldiers carrying these?"

In the man's hand were several ancient-looking books of text.

Witch had insisted on spending some time with the material, but Brett had refused. The thought of discovering more was intriguing, but they had their orders. The overhead lights created long shadows everywhere while the two continued to walk. Bound with expert craftsmanship, the top book in Ed's hand reminded him of something he had seen recently. Reaching for the top book and using the light from the street lamps above, he recognized it. All along the edge, around the spine of the book, and to the back, was gold embroidered stitching. Page side down, the stitching formed a gold flame on the red cloth cover, the same symbol he found on that pendant in the man's shirt. Too much of a coincidence, he'd bring this to the General's attention. They had men for things like this, just as they were the men for the dirty work.

"The mission was to find and isolate the target. Step two was to eliminate all threats and return to base. That's all there was to it. Threat eliminated, and now we are back. Anything unclear?"

He hadn't meant to sound so harsh, lately though, it came out naturally. He felt his team was being used for a purpose they didn't understand. Too many questions, too few answers, nothing of which he was going to talk about right now. Ed's eyebrows scrunched as he looked deep into Brett's eyes for a second. The moment passed and with a shake of his head, Ed quickly replaced it with a half-smile and a nod.

"Aye, Aye, sir! Just wanted to get it off my chest, that's all. I think I will be joining Dickie for his late-night snack. Make sure he didn't eat a recruit accidentally or something. Take care, Sergeant."

The mess hall wasn't far away now that they had spent so much time walking around the base, but Ed turned and jogged off quickly.

Why was he keeping his men, his friends, at bay like they were the enemy? Maybe the others were right? Sleep sounded good. A full night of rest would help clear up some minds. With a promised week of leave, a little time away from the saddle was a welcomed thought.

"Sergeant Giles! Sir! Sergeant Giles!"

He knew it would bring nothing but pain or trouble the second he heard the squeaky voice. Running down the center road was Private Erickson, hand waving as if it wasn't easy to see a single man running alone down the middle of the road. The Private looked not a day over eighteen when he finally stopped, bending over at the waist to catch his breath. His buzzed short brown hair was perfect and at regulation length, his uniform pressed and wrinkle-free as if he had pulled them right out of the instruction manual when he had dressed that morning.

Odd that running should put such a young man out of breath. They needed to get this boy more work. Recruits didn't bother Brett much, but he knew this one. Personal messenger boy of the General. Swallowing hard and taking a deep breath, nothing good could come of this.

"Sir, I was sent the moment he heard you had

returned." Finally, catching his breath, the private was now standing at full attention.

"Who heard we had returned?"

He didn't have to ask.

"The-the General, sir. He insists you come directly to him once you are settled." The boy didn't seem to want to meet him eye to eye.

"Insists?"

"Well, sir. It's an order, sir."

The boy knew him and his men's reputation and was trying to give him as much respect as he could. He could admire that.

"I don't think he'll accept 'never' as my time for being settled. Lead the way, might as well get this over with."

Bad news always preceded good news or was it good news always preceded bad news? Guess he was going to find out.

The General's quarters, if you could call them that, was a palace compared to what the men that surrounded him had to use. It had originally been a hangar for independent aircraft, flown by those with too much money to spend. Outside of the building was a large aluminum exterior with three arching hangar doors. A second-floor office area extended the entire length of the building and was a home and makeshift "throne" for the General.

The primary room where they first entered, which formerly housed aircraft, stretched the length of a sports field with tables set into dozens of stations. Higher ranked officers were set up at each station where they gave orders to recruits, who, judging by their boyish looks, had probably enlisted right out of high school. Brett didn't recognize the silent men who dressed in all black robes with white sashes across their waist that walked around observing. They watched all that was going on with an air of curiosity. Or was it superiority?

Nothing about this strange scene looked more out of place than the tapestry that had hung from the walls. Hangar door-sized flags flapped in the air conditioning over the first and last door. On each was a giant sword with three stars evenly placed over the pommel. In the middle was a large framed photograph of the General himself with the slogan "The God Wants Peace" hanging from a banner below the portrait itself.

Brett shook his head and tried to ignore the scene in front of him.

"Right this way, Sir."

The Private tried to move quickly. Never taking his eyes off the stairs ahead, the young man was nervous and in a hurry to get him there.

The General's office was at the end of a short flight of open stairs that led to the second floor. The entire upper level was gutted out to make what used to be a dozen offices into one large apartment-style room. A full kitchen had been established off to the right with a dining area now covered in maps and other paperwork. At the far end of the room, Brett could make out the appearance of a large unmade bed through a slightly ajar door. In the center sat three plush leather couches, capable of sitting up to nine large men. The little table that sat between them all had empty glassware and half-full bottles of alcohol on it.

"Sir! General, Sir!"

Erickson threw up a perfect salute as the man in charge turned around. Unlike the soldiers stationed on this base, the General felt a black and red silk evening suit, with its wrinkle-less sheen and matching black soft leather slippers, was more to his taste. His hair was a shade of brown, not a spot of gray, which would have revealed more of his age, than the wrinkles on his face. The constant look of anger he showed his men made them think he spent too much time looking in the mirror with that expression. It must have stuck.

He was a career soldier who long ago gave up the dream of battlefield glory and instead traded it in for politics. Whispers had it he was using every victory to get his name thrown into the forefront of the next election. Tonight, the General was not alone. Turning around, he revealed a much younger man sitting on one of the fine couches that lined the outer wall. The man did not stand or look at the two who had entered the room as the General himself had done.

"Ah, there is the man I wanted to see." The General gave a brief smile as he tipped the glass in his hand toward them. "Back from another successful mission."

The way he talked when it seemed they were alone made you think he was your friend, until you felt him sizing your back with his eyes for the knife he kept up his sleeve.

"We made it back alive. I would call that a victory." Brett found no reason to hide his annoyance for being there.

"By God's will, that is great to hear. What of the target? Were you able to locate him?" The General had made his way to the couch he had been sitting on and reached for a half glass of wine.

"No sir, we did not find him. Instead, it was a poorly fortified building, guarded by a dozen men. Where our directive said they would be, we found a ragtag squad of soldiers disguised as the enemy. They spent a lot of effort trying to protect the place, but there wasn't that many of them." Brett kept an eye on the man who had yet to be introduced. "Like the LAST several you have sent us on, wrong place or wrong time. Take your pick."

The smell of alcohol radiated all the way to Brett's nose. He could guess how much the man had already consumed.

"Any information? Anything we can use?" The General seemed more interested in his wine than the conversation as he refilled his glass.

"Sir, if I may. I think sensitive mission information best be left for your ears, only."

The stranger shifted his seat on the couch but made no attempt to introduce himself.

"Oh, pardon me there, Sergeant." The General got himself off the couch, staggering to find his balance. "Wow, this wine can go right to a man's head. Let me introduce you to Father Rondeau. He is a representative of the church, and they are here to help us in any way they can."

So it's the church down there watching everything we do.

"What does the church think it can offer us out here? More bullets, maybe a body shield or two?"

A small smile came to Brett's face at the thought of one of their black cloaked figures torn to pieces by incoming fire. Or maybe outgoing?

"The church is here to offer its guidance and support. The God wants peace among its children." The man stood, dressed in all black and hooded like the others of his order. He was much taller than the General and Brett. He had to look directly down at Brett. "The Church knows it is God's will that we fight these heathens, for they bring nothing but pain and suffering to the people of the world. As we know, THEY started this conflict in the first place."

Brett could remember all too well the events that started this whole bloody thing.

"So, you're saying, that to bring peace to the world we have to kill those whose own 'God' calls for peace?"

The hypocrisy of religion always stirred anger deep in his heart. The only thing you could trust in this world was your weapon, the men you fought beside, and the fact that when your time comes, there isn't any stopping it.

"Those so-called 'peace talkers' are wolves in sheep's clothing. Don't let them fool you, my child, they plot our demise at this very moment."

"Don't call me your child. You son of a bitch."

For an instant, anger flashed across the man's face as his shoulders tensed. Passing quickly, the man relaxed and placed his hands behind his back.

"OK, OK. Let's calm here a second there, Sergeant. Bitching about religion and all other acts of God is not why I called you up here. Private! Get our next guest, will you?"

The General found his way between the two men, the strong smell of alcohol assaulting Brett's nose even more. Until this point, the men in the room had forgotten Private Erickson was still there. Without needing another word, he was down the steps and gone.

The tension in the room hadn't lifted the tiniest when he returned with another soldier right on his heels. The man, tall and stocky like a farm boy, looked fresh out of basic training. His blond hair was buzzed short, and his big blue eyes filled with awe as he took in everything around him.

"Sergeant, I want you to meet Sergeant Kristofer Bowman, your new weapons expert, top of his class. He'll be joining your squad as we turn ourselves to the next stage in our assault on the enemy."

The General sat himself back on the couch, where he prepared himself another glass of wine.

"Sir, I'm ready to serve, sir!" The young man snapped a salute so crisp he damn near hit himself in the face.

"For fucks sake, sir, this isn't frontline infantry here." All sense of restraint was gone. Ordering him around was one thing, manipulating the order of his team was a whole other matter. "You want me to bring this kid behind enemy lines and babysit him while I try to keep the rest of my team alive?"

"There is no babysitting here, Sergeant! Also, there will be no questioning my orders!" The several glasses of wine had gone to his head, and the General's anger was also starting to slur his speech. "We have several crucial missions ahead of us, and it is my opinion that you need another man to succeed."

The General stood to poke Brett in the chest. His coordination was off, and he missed by several inches as he almost stumbled to the ground. Realizing his mistake, he swung his hand out, dismissing the notion altogether.

"Sergeant Bowman here is the man for the job, and he will accompany you. Have I made myself clear?"

The General left no more room for argument, and that was clear enough. The little smile now on Father Rondeau's face made him look like a snake about to devour its next meal. It took everything Brett had to not put a bullet right between those dark beady brown eyes of his.

"Yes, sir! Let's get out of here Sergeant. We have a lot of setting up to do. I have a feeling you're gonna have to learn real fast."

Brett looked at the General before turning to leave. The officer waved him off.

"Oh, how can I forget? Leave any of that information

you found with some of our specialists downstairs. They'll start working on it right away."

The General was already refilling his glass.

"The men of the church will be of service in deciphering any pertinent information sir, and they are at your disposal."

Father Rondeau nodded at Brett with a sly grin as he sat back across from the drunk leader, who on queue lifted a glass in a toast to himself.

Tapping Sergeant Kris on the shoulder for his attention, Brett went to leave. The private snapped another salute and followed Brett out. The General was going to be damned if he'd get a salute this evening or this century from Brett.

Chapter Four

1215 Hours, Juillet 1, 2258
   Fort Frozen Heart, Northwest Azhana

THE SEARING PAIN as the surgeon stitched together the skin had Charlie gritting her teeth. She had to stop for a second to make sure she wasn't catch her tongue as she knew she'd be regretting it later. Sitting on the makeshift hospital bed of tarp stretched between cold metal bars, she looked over at Will as he acted as if he were watching intensely. In honesty, he was probably trying not to laugh at her as she winced in pain. If it were anyone but him, she'd feel self-conscious sitting there naked down to her waist, but they had been sharing more than patrol rounds for over a year now. He was more than just a teammate or a lover. In all the fighting they had seen together, he had become the only family she had in this world.

"All done. Try to keep it as clean as you can." The doctor was taking off her gloves and straightening what tools she had. "The nurses outside will give you what medications they can afford." Charlie jumped off the bed, her knees slightly wobbly from the muscle straining.

"Let me take a look at that scratch of yours." Will stood and walked over. He was a head taller than her, his dark skin a contrast to her pale white complexion. "Nice job there doc, the stitches won't even bother the artwork much." Will used his hands to frame her back as if he were taking a picture of the tattoos that decorated her skin.

Extending from the base of her neck all along the sides and ending just below her pants line were two snarling dragons. The one on the left side was red, the other was blue. The appropriate color fire flared out from each, joining and running directly back up her spine.

"Even if it did, you know I'd just get more." She looked back and smiled at him as she threw her shirt back over her shoulders. "By the time I'm done, you won't be the only colored one around here." With that, she giggled and finished dressing.

He always found a reason to pick on her about her body work. He said he couldn't figure out why such a beautiful woman, his opinion not hers, would cover themselves with ink and needles. Just because he didn't understand that it meant something to her, each picture a part of her life, didn't mean she was going to stop. Plus anything that would push his buttons was something she was going to exploit.

"OK, enough with all this crying you've been doing. The Captain wants to see us." Will led the way out the door.

"Crying! I don't see you with any injuries. Let's see how you do next time you get hurt. Even one word out of your mouth, and you'll never live to see the end of it." She reared back and hit him in the shoulder with her good right arm.

"Injuries, what injuries? You got a piece of tree bark stuck in your shoulder." With a smile, he was holding his shoulder as if it were injured. "You're lucky if you even have ten stitches total. Call me next time you're hurt. Maybe I'll shed a tear." With that, he took off in a small jog toward the far end of the base.

"Oh you'll cry alright, and I won't be there to hold you!" She yelled at him as she watched his powerful figure run out in front.

A smile came to her face as she tried jogging behind him, but realized she didn't have the strength. Fortunate for her, he wasn't trying to get away.

It took them a few minutes to travel to the far end of Fort Frozen Heart. Their location could hardly be called a typical fort. Located to the far north, but as close to the Western front as they could be, it was designed to look like it housed a full company of soldiers. Three layers of razor-topped fencing extended from solid rock walls. Guard towers were at all corners, and to top it off, the men and women inside worked double duty to resemble a fighting body of thousands and not a few hundred that were currently present. All of it designed to try to hold their enemy back over land that would be too harsh to sustain a fight. 'Bog them down where the fighting gets tough' is what their captain always said. To the soldiers, it was just a reason to freeze their asses off. Most men and women of the base hoped he was right. The Republic came with soldiers from lands more suitable for farming or vacationing, not the cold, harsh frozen north. For them, the world warmed up two months a year, the rest was either cold, wet mud or freezing dry snow. For the past two years, Charlie and Will, like many others, called this place home.

The captain's quarters were laid out sparsely as Charlie and Will approached it. Simply built, the structure was a square building with just one door in and out. A solitary window looked out to the base and the men patrolling it. At other times, it would probably be used as a maintenance shed, but now it housed the fort's current highest-ranking officer.

Entering the building revealed an inside just as simple as the outside. The front door immediately opened to the man's office with the back area quartered off for his private bending and washing facilities. Directly under the window was a desk, layered with paperwork so high the act of opening the door sent several layers to the floor.

"Captain!" Will snapped a salute as did Charlie to the best of her ability.

The captain had made it a policy that his door was open to men and women of the direct frontline patrols whenever there was a confrontation. Lately, the man's front door had been used so much they were surprised it still stood.

"Sergeants!" The captain saluted back as he eyed Charlie and her injured shoulder. "I hope that won't keep you from your duties too long, soldier." He pointed to the mound of padding under her shirt.

"Sir, no it won't, sir!" She tried to straighten just that bit more because of the attention he was giving her, regretting it the second the pain tore through her back.

"That's good to hear. I've been over each of your reports. Am I to take it you came under fire less than three miles from this position, and you don't know how many there were?"

The man sat and looked at the map on his desk. Gray hair peppered the military buzzed black hair on his head, and the weight of their world rested on his broad shoulders as they slouched forward.

"Sir, that is correct." Will wanted to make sure the

attention was on him so Charlie could relax. "Counting casualties after they fell back, we estimate there may have been at least a dozen to maybe two dozen. They never got any closer, though." He looked down at Charlie and was glad to see her relax for a second.

"Three skirmishes this week, Sergeant. This one the closest." The officer was drawing a few lines on his map. "You were in sector B340 correct?"

"Yes, sir, we were coming from the west and making our way east when they ambushed us." Both could see the captain marking their location on the map as Will answered.

"Sir, if I may, there are rumors the Graon's may be arming for a full on attack." Charlie looked up at Will quickly before continuing. "Are we going to get any reinforcements if they do?"

The man in charge visibly slumped in his chair as he took a deep breath.

"To be honest with you two, up here this far north we are designed to be a plug for a sinking ship. Tie the enemy up as much as possible. The weather itself was designed to be our best ally."

The man looked as if he had too many things on his mind as his eyes darted over every map and document on his desk. For a second, Charlie thought the man was going to say he was afraid, and then with a deep breath, he raised his chin and straightened his back.

"No way of telling what those over righteous zealots have planned, but I know what we are going to do. Good weather or bad weather, we are going to give them one hell of a fight. With good men and women like you out there, I am certain they can throw whatever they want at us, and we'll throw it back. Coming over the hills, who knows what the weather will throw at them. If they arrive, we'll be ready."

"Sir, yes sir!" Will interrupted; Charlie could see he wanted to leave before this conversation went any further.

Each of them had talked this over a thousand times. It wasn't a rumor that if it came to a full-out fight, Fort Frozen Heart wasn't designed to win. Deception and delaying tactics were their game, but what happens if the enemy had a different game plan?

"Alright you two, you're dismissed. Go take care of that shoulder, so we can get you back out there as soon as possible."

The captain waved them off and went back to his maps. Not wanting to waste another second, both soldiers exited quickly. The man had been right though; her shoulder was killing her, and she had forgotten to grab anything from the nurses. Thinking about it, she didn't which was worse, the pain in her shoulder or the fear growing in the back of her mind.

Chapter Five

0710 Hours, Juin 15, 2258
  Fort Forward Trinity, Edge of Republic Territory

NIGHTS SEEMED SHORTER when you went to bed angry. A good rest was an easy way to release the tension of the misery around you, but the anger won't let it in. The sun had risen to the east when Brett made his way to the area of the barracks his men called home. Unlike the primary population, where rows upon rows of men slept on bunks right next to each other, his men had a small segregated area no one bothered unless asked. Still within the same large quarters as the others, instead of being neatly aligned with the rest, their bunks were turned to form a circle. In the center of the circle rested their gear, cleaned and ready to go at a moment's notice.

His men were mostly awake and at their morning routine when Brett and the new weapons expert reached the circle of beds. Dickie was still in his bed snoring away (still his routine). Witch was reading away in a leather bound book with his pistol on one side of his lap and extra magazines of ammunition on the other. Ed was polishing his boots to a shine though he knew it was a fruitless venture from the damage caused by the sand of their last mission. They group didn't bother looking up when the two men approached.

"Where's David this morning?" Brett asked.

He was the only one missing this early in the morning, and with the new announcements he had to make, it was best if the whole team was present.

"Off for a morning run. It's been his new 'ritual' since that newest recruit squad came in." Ed shrugged it off and looked back down at his shoes. "Heard there's a few women mixed with the bunch, you know how he is with the ladies. Who's this standing with you, Sergeant?"

The recognition that Sergeant Kris was with him got Witch's attention from whatever new book he was reading.

"Uhh," groaned Dickie as he rolled over away from the men talking too close to his bunk.

"I was going to wait till David got back, but we cannot spare any time while he sobers up from the rejection. Standing beside me is Sergeant Kristofer Bowman. Newly assigned to our squad."

The smile on Kris' face looked forced as his wide inexperienced eyes tried to hide his nervousness. It reminded Brett of the new kid in town being introduced to the class on the first day of school.

"Ah, where you from there Kris?" Ed stood to shake the man's hand that was like shaking the hand of a tree branch. "Wow, you're a large fella aren't ya?"

"I'm from Draycott, a small town north of Nolz Lake, sir!" Kris replied while standing at attention.

Ed couldn't help chuckling at the sight.

"Well, I'm Sergeant Ed McCormick, our medical

expert. Behind me here is Corporal James Forest. Witch, if you'd prefer to keep it short. The man is a master of electronics with a specialty in 'ghosting'."

"Ghosting, sir?" The look on Kris' face was a mixture of excitement and confusion.

"It's a technique we developed in the field. It's Witch's baby. With shortwave transponders and as many rifles as he chooses, Witch can fire from different locations as many times and in whatever positions he wants."

"Can't aim worth shit though," Dickie growled as he sat up from his bunk, his shirt rolled up over his belly.

"There in front of you is Sergeant Charles Ramirez. We call him Dickie, mainly because he told us to. I wouldn't go any further into that story if I were you."

"Go piss off then if you don't like it." Dickie was on his feet, looking through his bunk for something to eat. "I've saved your ass a time or two, don't you go forgetting that."

"Oh, I won't be forgetting that anytime soon. You won't let me. You'd better get moving. Breakfast is almost over. Don't need to be pulling you out of the brig again for punching out a cook, do we?" Dickie flipped him his middle finger as he walked off. "The man's a hard-ass, but there are only one or two men in this whole army better than he is at hand-to-hand combat. For as big as he is, the man is as fast as a cat, and will kill you before you realize what hand he hit you with."

Sergeant Kris lost all use for words looking at the men he was now going to call a family. They were such a dysfunctional group to have a history made of legends following them.

He was getting himself settled in his new bunk when a new man came jogging around the corner. His dark skin was covered in sweat as he stopped in front of the rest, his grin covering his face.

"Here we have Sergeant David Cooper. He's our second-in-command or as he prefers it, the ladies' man. Find any to your liking this morning did we, David?" The amusement in Ed's voice was beyond evident.

"Women these days, we are fighting for our lives here and they just don't see a good man when he's jogging right in front of their barracks. What is this world coming to?" The smile never left his face even as he sat and started rummaging through his stuff. "Who's the big oak tree you got sitting next you there, Ed?"

"This is Sergeant Kristofer Bowman. The newest member of our little choir here. Fresh out of qualifying school, isn't that right?"

"Yes, sir!" He stood to shake David's hands.

"Oh, ho, ho, fresh blood. First off there, Oakie. There will be no saluting, or yes, sirs, or any of that horseshit here. It gives you off as a recruit from a mile away. We live by three rules here, and I know you didn't read them in any of your guidebooks on good soldiering. First rule, stay the fuck alive. You're no good to yourself, the team, or for a matter of fact the army if you're dead. You do rule number one by following rule number two. Trust the men in your team; that's us. So, you watch our backs, and we'll watch yours. A lot of rough shit goes on out on the battle-field; sometimes you can't trust your own eyes. The one thing you can trust in is the five of us. We are probably going to be the only five people who give two shits if you make it home alive or in a wooden box." The sudden picture of arriving home draped in a flag sank Kris' heart into his stomach.

"What's rule number three?" Nerves made his voice crack as he asked.

All three battle-hardened men looked at him for a second without answering. A large smile, yet a serious look came over David's face as he lifted one hand and pointed it at Sergeant Brett, sitting alone, writing in a small notepad.

"You listen to everything that man has to say, and you stay the fuck out of his way. Out beyond these fences that man's word is law. He says kill; you kill. He says charge, you charge, and if he says run; you run as if your first girlfriend's father came home and found you with your pants around your feet. Run till your ass can't run anymore, and then you start crawling cause if you for a second doubt that man won't hesitate to kill you for disobeying and endangering this team you are dead wrong. Once the fighting starts, if you aren't helping the team, your life is worth the bullet it takes to end it." Kris looked over at Ed, and all he did was give him a shrug of the shoulders. Looking at Witch, the man had returned to reading his unknown leather-bound book. "Don't worry though, you do everything he says, when he says it, he'll make sure you get home to your family. He's the best killer this army has. There isn't a target he can't get to, and, unless people start getting killed by the walking dead, he'll make sure they are dead before we are."

For what it was worth, and for what David was trying to do, that last statement didn't make Kris feel any better.

Chapter Six

0630 Hours, Avos 2, 2258
    Fort Frozen Heart, Northwest Azhana

THE SNOW SHONE brightly as the new day's sun broke over the horizon and pushed the gray of the dusk out. Charlie stood and watched as the shadows took shape across the fort from her vantage at the top of the northwest guard tower. The newly fallen evening snow made it difficult to tell the difference between the pavement within the fort and the mix of earth and road outside. Looking at the drooping trees with branches bent low under the frozen weight, snow still clung to the branches in the hope of not falling to the earth. Memories of a time before all this fighting flooded into her mind.

Her life, until the war began, had been peaceful and uneventful. She had recently finished school and was looking forward to moving on with her life. Her accomplishment was the talk of the area as women did not normally make it through higher education in this part of the world. The land of her people was difficult compared to others more accustomed to city life and luxury beyond what she knew. In her mind though, tough work and determination was a way of life. Her parents had saved every bit of money and favor that they could to put her through the local university. She had been determined to show them what she could do, that their money and dreams were well spent.

That was before her world turned upside down in a ball of fire. It started a few months after she had finished her last classes, when bombs tore through the center of their capital city of Roenthar. A radical Graon religious group had claimed responsibility in the name of their 'God'. Not long after, retaliatory strikes found their way to highly populated cities on both sides. The all-out war was inevitable, and it felt as if everyone became involved; no matter what their circumstances.

Now, fighting in a war that had consumed the world hadn't been in her original plans for making something of her life. In the end, looking over at Will as he leaned against the frozen railing and spit down on the ground below, she realized things could be a lot worse. She had discovered that somewhere deep inside, she had a knack for survival and scouting. Maybe it was her short, petite stature, or that she had spent most of her early years hunting small game with her father in the day's first light. Whichever it was, she tried to use it to her advantage.

"You know, with what happened to us last time we were out there, I still think I prefer it to this." Will always hated standing around. "At least we got to walk around when we were out there. Shoot, we even got to run."

There weren't too many people she knew that could turn a bad situation, like almost getting killed, into a joke.

"You could always go down and run some laps around

the tower." Charlie waved to the ground below with a piece of apple in her hand. "I promise I won't throw things at you from up here." With that, she flicked the core over her shoulder, and he watched it fall to the snow below.

"Oh yeah, right, like last time. Shit, I swore you hit me with everything you could get your grubby little hands on." Will replied, reaching up to rub the back of his head. "I'm still surprised you didn't include your boots."

She smiled at the memory of that while she coyly walked to him. Looking around and confirming that most of the base was still deep in its evening slumber, she reached up on her toes and wrapped her arms around his neck.

"There's only one way these boots come off, and there isn't enough privacy up here on this tower for that," she whispered into his ear as she nibbled on it gently.

He hugged her back and nearly took her off the ground. They tried to hide their affair, as it was against military rules, but in a sparsely populated fort in such a remote location, most people looked the other way. The captain said she reminded him of his late wife. Sometimes, she didn't know whether that was sweet or whether it bothered her.

Something caught her eye as his arms threatened to steal her to a place far from where she stood. A flock of birds took off all at once a mile or two into the woods. Normally, this wouldn't be such a big deal, but soon after, another flock took off, this one closer and in a direct line with the fort.

"Do you see that?" She pulled Will's attention to the forest.

"I don't see anything, maybe a few birds."

"Exactly, watch for a minute."

Almost on cue, another flock took off and there was

almost a noticeable rustle with the trees. Not wanting to wait any longer, Charlie slapped her partner on the back of his shoulder and ran to the control room in the tower. Inside was a few sets of TVs, all connected to remotely controlled cameras within the forest. Several of them were blacked out, probably from the snow of the previous evening, but others were clear. Typing in a few commands, the monitors started flickering as they changed from camera to camera. Will was busy working the radio, signaling to the other towers of the general direction that concerned them.

"You find anything out there yet?" Will looked over as her eyes moved back and forth over every screen.

"Nothing, but I swear something is out there. I can feel it."

"I've signaled the others, but maybe it's just end of shift jitters. It could have just been a few birds."

"I know, but this feels different. If only I could, wait!" She waved him over, and he didn't hesitate as he nearly jumped to her side. She was now controlling the camera monitors instead of letting them cycle.

"There's nothing there."

"Exactly, see there are at least four cameras down." She turned the monitors to show the four that were out, leaving two still scanning.

"Yeah, that's typical after a snowfall. Becker and Fridgehead probably haven't cleaned them off yet."

"That's not it, look at their locations."

She pointed down to the identification number on the corner of each screen. His eyes got wider as he noticed the same thing that she did, the ones being blacked out were in order as one came closer to the fort.

"It can't be, can it?"

Without trying to answer his question, Charlie took

control of the nearest cameras that she could to those not working. Manually controlling them, each turned to view as much of the area blacked out as possible.

Both soldiers sat in silence as they couldn't find the breath to speak the words. Revealed on the screen in front of them was a line of armored vehicles, each full and surrounded by a dozen armed men. They were trying to conceal their approach, which at this point was working rather well, but now that Charlie had found them it was clear the enemy had arrived on their doorstep.

Chapter Seven

2132 Hours, Juin 22, 2258
  Fort Forward Trinity, Edge of Republic Territory

THE SUN HAD SETTLED to the west and cast its last clear red rays over the base when the soldiers of Fort Forward Trinity were finally able to relax. The past week of intense fighting had pushed the enemy deep into their territory, leaving a large well-guarded swath of territory between them and the base itself. Word had quickly circulated among the men that the end was near as any more pushing would have them knocking on the doorstep of the enemy's capital.

Their success did not change the hopes of Brett and his men. War was sadly natural for human beings, and no matter how many people wished for it, world peace would never be possible. Someone, somewhere, always wanted something that someone else had. After the attacks on both sides, the anger held by the citizens was too deep. This fighting felt as if it would go on for a long time, no matter which side won the final battle. Only something drastic, something world-changing would ever fix it.

The unexpected nighttime meeting with the General did not help anything. He did not usually summon Brett for attendance at such a late-night hour. Doing the dirty work of the army was their specialty, and the other soldiers knew it. It wasn't a secret to anyone above the level of a janitor, so why the secrecy now? Something didn't feel right but without the ability to see an alternative, seeing this through seemed the best decision.

The General's "palace" looked different this evening as he approached. Most lights in the building were out other than a few flickers of lamp light in the upstairs area. Inside, the building was as silent as it was dark. Going up the stairwell, he took notice that again the only others present were the General himself and Father Rondeau. Brett shot both an angry look before throwing up a halfhearted salute.

"General, you requested my attention, sir?" Requested was not exactly the tone the Private had used, but he decided formalities were moot at this point.

"Ah yes, Sergeant come on over here. You remember Father Rondeau don't you?" Seated on the General's couch, the man still had his hood covering most of his face. To him, the little he could see still reminded him of a snake, the bile inching its way up his throat was overpowering.

"Yes, I do though I still do not understand why he is here." Brett stopped there for a second to let the words sink in. "I also do not understand why I am here either, sir."

"You are both here at my request, and that is all you need to know." The General waved off any further discussion on whom was present as he walked to one of his desks and picked up another glass of wine. "We have made tremendous advances into enemy territory lately, no little thanks to the work of you and your men." Lifting his glass as if toasting them by himself. "Now we strike at the head of the dragon and bring it down. We have intelligence that leads us to believe Azhana's leaders are holed up in a temple, a few days travel behind enemy lines, in the city of Miavlaco."

"Would they be stupid enough to remain so close to our forward lines?" The thought seemed impossibly idiotic, but if it were true, this could mean a true possible end to part of this conflict.

"Their heretical belief has them taking refuge in a temple of their gods. They believe they will be protected." Father Rondeau's voice grated at every inch of Brett's nerves. "That is where you and your team will become the instrument of the one true God's might."

"Don't you ever start talking like you know anything about me and my team, you hypocritical…"

"That's enough Sergeant! You may not agree with his advice, but in the end, he is still correct." The General was quickly finishing his second glass since Brett had arrived. "You and your team will leave at sunup tomorrow. You are to travel to the temple and eliminate all high priority targets that you find. Is that understood?" Anger and a small case of swollen tongue mixed with the man's voice.

"So that's our plan? Send us into what will probably be the heaviest guarded building in all their territory and tell us to kill every person there?" This mission had suicide written all over it. "How are we supposed to know who's 'high priority'? What information have we got on possible civilians in the temple as well? Are we expected to go in as blind as you're making it sound? What will be our extraction plan? I doubt they are going to let us walk away after shooting up their temple. I wouldn't be surprised if the whole city rises against us."

Brett found himself scratching at the newly formed rash on his right forearm. Ed had looked at it but had found nothing unusual. David was too eager to point out how it made the dragon tattoo on his arm appear to be boiling his arm from under his skin. Brett hoped it wasn't as obvious that it would bother him when he was under distress, as he felt it was.

"The building will, of course, be empty of all innocent people." Father Rondeau's emphasis on innocent brought an image of a church full of women and children praying just as his team barged in. Nothing good could come of this. "Our information from the inside tells us the military has tight control over the city. When the officials take over the temple for their meeting, they won't have non-essential people around."

The man turned his hooded face back to the General.

"You and your team can then do what you do best." Their leader finished between swallows as he was already halfway done his next glass.

"Kill them all, sir?"

"Yes! Send them a message that we mean to end this, and swiftly. I will not have this world think we are not strong enough to bring peace to its people. We will be the spear that ends this bloodshed."

With that, the man plopped back down on his couch. His shoulders hung low as he struggled to make himself comfortable where he rested.

"The God will see us to victory General, all believers can see that."

Brett bit his tongue, all 'believers'? He wasn't going to believe any of this horseshit. All this felt wrong. He traced his eyes between the two men. Who was leading here? The snake offering 'godly' advice, or the drunk who stank of cheap imported wine.

"Is there anything else, Sir? My men and I will have to prepare. It may take them more than thirty seconds to absorb all this new 'information'." Brett could see the edge of the General's lips curl up though he was mocking the officer.

"Yes go! Bring us back a victory! The histories will always remember us after this my boy!"

Brett quickly turned and left. Yeah, the histories would remember them. A fool general willing to sacrifice every man under his command: too drunk to see the dangers right in front of him, and the men, too naive to stop him.

Chapter Eight

0750 Hours, Avos 2, 2258
Fort Frozen Heart, Northwest Azhana

THE ALARM for the defensive breach went out later than anyone wanted though the response by the men and women of the fort had been quick and well thought out. Moments after Will had sent out the relay message, every man and woman within the fort became active.

Mobile units were brought to bear and broken into three groups. The heaviest armored vehicles moved to the front and were used to plug the primary entrance. Each vehicle could take direct fire from any hand held weapon and could last at minimum one direct hit from a similarly built armored vehicle. The faster and lighter vehicles were quickly sent around the rear exits to prepare for when they got their chance to flank the incoming aggressors. In all, the base mobilized sixteen armored war vehicles and more than three hundred soldiers in less than ten minutes. If the enemy believed they were going down without a fight, they were dead wrong. Charlie hoped the Captain was right and spending all this time up here in this remote station was for more than it seemed, a decoy.

"You ready for this?" Will risked a look over at Charlie stationed on one of the mounted guns at the top of the tower.

"Ready as I will ever be. Why? You scared?" She didn't bother to look, the second she looked away, they would arrive. She knew it.

"Nope, these bastards haven't seen what a real woman can do when she gets angry. I have a feeling before you're done, they are gonna find out."

She smiled at that. He always knew how to calm her nerves at a time like this. When the first row of armored vehicles exited the tree line, she had expected it to either scare her or send her blood into a war frenzy but it didn't. Instead, she sat there for a quiet minute, thoughtless, as she stared down at the approaching wall of death that now looked each soldier directly in the eye. She should have been thinking of the best way to break their line, or worse, how the few hundred men and women that stood by her were going to make it against such odds.

"Oh shit, here we go." The sound of Will's voice was the first thing to break her from her trance.

All the units of warriors stood motionless as nothing happened in what was guaranteed to become a blood-soaked battlefield. The only thing that broke the deafening silence was the shuffling of boots as soldiers anxiously waited in fear or excitement for something to happen.

"What happens now?" Will stopped looking down the scope of his rifle and tried to get Charlie's attention.

"Um…I'm not sure."

Last time she was in a firefight, she had acted on instinct and training. Nothing in the manual said what happened when both armies stood around looking at one another.

"This better start soon, or I'm gonna piss my pants."

As if on cue, the front and center enemy vehicle moved forward, the others quickly filled the gap as their frontline moved ahead. Their intent was now clear and the defenders of the makeshift base opened fire with everything they had.

The front assaulting vehicle took the brunt of the trauma as heavy rounds from armored cannons and bullets from all angles smashed into its armor. It had time to fire a single round before the front suspension and tracks crumbled under the weight of the assault, and it became a smoldering mess of smoke and twisted metal. The one shot it fired though was well aimed as it hit the brick framed wall next to the front entrance of the base. With an explosion that shook the foundation of the tower, Charlie stood on, bricks, smoke, and debris were sent high into the air and crashing down on soldiers and the three front defending vehicles.

The rest of the armored vehicles halted their advance and began to fire themselves. Fortunately for the soldiers of Fort Frozen Heart, the first vehicle, while now out of commission, was heavier armed as the explosives fired from the smaller machines did not do as much direct damage. What destruction they did cause was enough. Small explosions erupted along the wall weakening the structure and maiming any soldier unlucky enough to be close to the destruction.

The defenders of the fort kept their composure as they continued to fire from in the walls and towers of the fort. Shots and explosions erupted on each side as the space between quickly filled with smoke and dust that had been sent up into the air. A small beeping sound vibrated on

Charlie's belt as she continued to fire her mounted rifle at any target she could see out in the open. Looking down at the flashing green light, she realized that she had lost herself in the heat of the moment and was still responsible for an important part of this battle.

Releasing her grip on the rifle, she clicked the response button on the radio and turned the light red. Knowing her message had been sent, she reached for a box stored inside the control room. She grabbed it and kicked it to Will.

"Hey Will, time to light them up!"

Feeling the box hit him in the leg, Will stopped firing and grabbed a canister and loaded it into his rifle.

"Here goes nothing, hope they aren't wearing any sunglasses." Chuckling, he fired the canister in an arc onto the battlefield below.

Before the canister could hit the ground, he was grabbing another and preparing to fire. Each tower along the battlefield wall was doing the same thing as shot by shot the pieces of aluminum landed in the snow. Like clockwork, the devices started spitting smoke and seconds later detonated into a bright flash that blinded all soldiers within sight of the blast.

The sound of gunfire from the enemy began to recede as the light bombs took their desired effect, and the sound of roaring engines rumbled onto the field. The two flanking divisions of armored all-terrain vehicles charged from the shadows of the walls and forest and raced onto the field toward the front line of enemy soldiers.

It only took seconds before the attackers broke rank and tried to run for the safety of the forest. The line of vehicles that they stood behind began to smoke one after another as each fell to waves of ammunition hitting them from three sides.

Seeing the men run or fall where they stood brought a

little relief to Charlie's heart as she released her white-knuckle grip on her weapon. Maybe the Captain was right. Somehow, this little decoy had shown that there was a little bite to them after all.

"Look at those bastards run!" Will was jumping up and down with joy.

Cheers could be heard from the others around the base as soldiers made their way out of cover and began to celebrate. The officers among the fighters quickly came back to reality and started barking orders, as the cries of those who were hurt echoed within the walls.

Several vehicles that had chased the enemy to the tree line had already turned and began making their way back to the fort. A couple remained and began to make a path of patrol along the tree line.

"I can't believe we did it!" Will quickly swept Charlie up in his arms and gave her one of his giant bear hugs.

"Yeah, we did it. Maybe, they'll think better of it next time."

"And we'll be ready for them just as we were this time. WooHoo!" Will was still cheering as he began to circle the top of the tower shouting to friends and others within earshot on the ground.

Something was unsettled in Charlie's stomach as she looked down at the remains of the enemy vehicles smoking and charred on the field below. In all, there were twenty-three destroyed vehicles of war scattered in the snow. The bodies of soldiers littered the field behind the destroyed vehicles, as many had chosen to die where they stood rather than run for the forest.

Why did they stand around to get slaughtered? The advantage in this fight was always going to be to the defenders so long as they remained behind the…

She ran to the railing of her tower and looked down to the men below.

"Captain! Pull everyone…"

Three explosions tore the patrolling vehicles apart that were closest to the forest. The vibrations from everything was strong enough to shake the brick towers that anchored the base. Charlie watched in horror as several more plumes of smoke chased each other from the tree line and smashed directly into the line of disabled vehicles a couple hundred yards away from the base. Charlie turned only to see Will begin to step toward her, horror masking his face and eyes as the world lit up in a flash of light a mere second before everything went black and silent.

Chapter Nine

0547 Hours, Juin 23, 2258
  Fort Forward Trinity, Edge of Republic Territory

THE SUN WAS RISING over the eastern horizon as the team looked over the forest that lay ahead. A few clouds floated deep in the sky, white as the feathers of a new pillow, signaling the coming of a new and fair-weather day. The men and women of the base behind them were awakening, and those who had stood guard were eagerly awaiting the arrival of their relief so they could find themselves closing their eyes for a much-needed rest.

"So Oakie, you ready for your first time out? Going straight to the big show, no minors for you. Ha-ha," David patted him on the back as they stood side by side looking out.

Kris turned his head slightly to look at David. "Well, there is a first time for everything isn't there? Just can't believe we have such a high-priority target."

"Every target for us is a high-priority target. When it's a

fucker's time to go, it's time to go." Dickie said as he sat on his pack a few paces ahead, cleaning off a knife till it had a bright shine to it.

"You gonna eat with that knife later there Dickie? Looks like a steak knife to me." David gave a small wink to Kris.

"Only way I'm eating off this knife is after it has drunk its fill of blood. You fuckers know I hate an empty stomach, and I can't eat till a day's worth of killing is done. Where is the Sergeant, anyway?"

The question brought the same thought to all the team as they looked around and realized he still wasn't with them.

"He'll get here when the time is right, probably getting some last bit of intel we need or something." Ed responded.

Ed was always the optimistic one and believed in the cause. Witch, the quiet one of the bunch, was still tearing away at that leather-bound book of his.

"What intel do we need? If it moves, make it dead. The enemy is that way and the friendlies are behind us." Dickie finished with his first knife and had a second out though no one knew where the first was hidden.

"If it were that easy there, Mr. Anxious-Killer, why don't we send you out ahead and clear the road for us? We'll let the boss know that we can take it easy for the first day or two." The way David said it, it sounded as though he was honest.

A big smile rose on Dickie's face.

"Actually, that might be a pretty damn good idea. I do more than half the work around here anyway. Always having to carry your lazy ass. Can't believe I haven't lost more weight already with all this extra work because of you." The smile now ear to ear on the man.

"Ha, Ha. Good one, Dickie." David turned to walk around, looking as if he were searching for the Sergeant. "Prick."

"You ever killed anyone, son?" It couldn't have been more than the second or third time he'd ever heard Witch say anything since he joined the team a week ago.

"Who, me, sir?" The shock of the question had his answer coming out before he could stop himself.

"No, these other religious, naturally nonviolent men standing right here with us. Of course, I mean you. Have you ever killed anyone?" Witch had now put the book down and was looking directly into his eyes. He was the oldest of the group, his steel-gray eyes, and white hair contrasting his deep tan and leather stretched skin.

"Um, no, I haven't, sir." The question did nothing but strengthen the nerves and doubt he already held deep in his stomach.

"Have you ever killed anything in your life? Maybe a deer or something?" Witch's eyes were locked on his as Dickie was to an after mission steak.

"Oh, of course, I've killed plenty of deer in my life. That's one of the reasons the General said he wanted me on your team."

"The General wanted you on our team because you can shoot a few deer?" David had returned and was standing by his side again. The shock of the questioning behind him almost made him jump out of his boots.

"Um, not actually. I'm not sure, but I think it's more about how far away I have been on some of my shots." Looking around, he noticed all of them were looking at him now. "Father says I'm the best man with a rifle he has ever known. Two seasons ago I hit one in the head at thirteen hundred yards. He was running too." The memory of his father boasting months later at church on Sunday brought a little inner strength for his nerves.

"Well, I'll be damned. We got ourselves a marksman here. Hey Dickie, sounds like you'll be eating some damn good steak tonight! You like venison?" David began chuckling as he finished the question and rubbed Kris' shoulders for a moment.

Dickie smiled and turned back to another knife on his lap.

"I don't think your rifle ability, as good as it may be, is the whole reason you are here with us son." Witch stood, tucked his book into his equipment sack, patted himself off and began walking over. "That man ask you any other questions before telling you the good news of your new assignment?"

"I... I think I remember him asking if my intentions in this war were true." It began feeling like an interrogation more than friendly banter between friends now. "He wanted to know if I felt this mission was God's true purpose for me."

A look of understanding found its way across Witch's face.

"Ah, finally. We have some truth here. So, you're a devout believer, aren't you? There's no shame in it, son, but am I right?"

"Yes sir, I am." For some reason, that answer felt as if it were the wrong one at the moment. "Is there something wrong with that?"

"Wrong? In this army, no, there is nothing wrong with that. On this team, well, I believe you're not here to be our new sniper if that's what you're thinking."

"What are you getting at, Witch?" Ed always the one to want things to the point and honest.

"The kid is a spy though he doesn't know it." Witch

made his way back to where he was seated and pulled out his book again.

"What! I'm not… I swear I'm no spy against you guys." The shock of it made him sick. All the men of the team were looking at him now.

"Oh, I don't think you're a spy in the normal sense of the word. Question is, how much do you know about those religious men walking around the base lately?"

"Those men are from the Church. They are here to give guidance to those in need, help them at their lowest of time, and remind us that the God wants us to push forward to victory." With that, he could see all of them nod in agreement. Witch opened his book and went back to reading. "But…"

"Don't worry about it there, Kris." David had put his arm back around him. "We don't call him Witch because his white hair freaks us out. That man is a philosopher of religions. He could tell you the history of every known religion of this world, then make you believe his gods are real. Get him talking and there is nothing you can do to stop it. It doesn't help we got him some new material to look through. You're the first person to get him away from that book of his since we got back."

"You, believe me, don't you?" He needed assurance from someone, anyone.

"That you're not a spy? Of course I do. Well, I think you don't know you are one." All joking left David's face. "See here Kris, each person has their reasons for being in this fight. These reasons give us all the strength we need. It is obvious now that your belief is in your God, which aligns well with the General and his new 'advisers'."

"If you don't believe in the God, what do you guys believe in?"

David looked as if he had to think about that question for a second.

"Well, Witch as I said, believes in various gods and demons. Dickie over there believes in a sharp knife and a good steak. Ed, no one knows because he's Ed. And me? I believe in the honesty of a bullet, and that man right there. I think in the end, we trust in him." David used his hand to turn the young man around, and coming from the gate exiting the base walked the Sergeant.

As he approached, it was easy to see the hardened look on his face, and the bandage on his right forearm. The man walked with a stride of determination, and it looked like it would take an act of God to change him from his course.

"Hey, Sergeant, Sir!" Private Kris snapped a salute as the other men continued whatever they were doing at the moment.

Brett didn't bother to take his eyes off his target to acknowledge the solute.

"David, we ready to go? We've got a lot of ground to cover, and the day isn't getting any younger." The smile on David's face didn't diminish at all as he looked his leader right in the eye.

"Yes, we are. Just getting Kris over here all broken in for his first mission." David looked over and gave Kris a wink. "Already promised Dickie over here a nice fresh venison steak when we get back. Compliments of the new weapons specialist there."

The mention of his deer story made him feel uncomfortable for having said it at all.

"There won't be any killing of deer where we are going, no matter how far away you can hit one." The Sergeant turned and looked right at Kris. "But there will be plenty of men to kill when we get there. I hope you're up for this."

The last bit of that message was left hanging like a knife dangling from a string above his chest. He looked at the other men for support but didn't see anything but indifference. The thought that his first mission could be his last crossed his mind for what felt like the thousandth time. The question is, who's going to fire the shot that kills him? The enemy, or one of these guys?

Chapter Ten

0815 Hours, Avos 2, 2258
  Fort Frozen Heart, Northwest Azhana

EVERYTHING in the world was black and silent. No feeling of cold or heat, pain or pleasure, the world felt empty and endless. The nothingness was serene in its pleasantness. All of it ended in a wave of spasms and coughs that overtook her body. Opening her eyes as the phlegm and dust spewed on the ground brought her back to the land of the living.

Trying to look around, Charlie rocked left and right as she oriented herself to her new surroundings. A mixture of dust and snow fell to the ground as rocks and soldiers laid sprawled among the remains of what had been the front wall of the base. Everything moved silently and in slow motion as she watched the few that remained on their feet try either running away from the destruction or to those they thought they could help. Neither direction led the survivors to a good reception as several fell to bullets fired from somewhere behind the cloud of dust.

"Hey, you okay over there Charlie?" She thought she could hear a voice, but the silence of the surrounding scene was now being filled with a ringing that threatened to shred her ears bloody.

"I said, can you move Charlie?"

Through the ringing, she could make out that someone was yelling from behind and turned to look. Halfway around, screeching pain shot through her right leg. Taking a glance showed a large piece of wall laying on top of her knee and lower leg. From what she could tell, it wasn't lying in the most natural directions, and now after seeing it, the pain quickly rushed in to fill her consciousness.

"Okay, if you're not gonna answer me, I'm just gonna have to figure you're stupid or deaf." The distant voice was now replaced by a dust-covered soldier as he ran over and started lifting the bricks off her leg.

"Ah!" She knew she recognized him, but couldn't think of it as the pain became unbearable.

"Ssh! We need to move you now!" The man put a bloody, dust-covered hand over her mouth, the distinct metal taste quickly bringing her discipline back. "Look, those fuckers are gonna be coming through that damn hole they just created any second. You can stay here and end up like the rest, or keep your fucking mouth shut, and help me, help you out of here."

The determined look in the man's green eyes left no room for arguing. Gritting her teeth as hard as she could, she allowed him to get her back on her feet. Her right leg felt broken, anchoring himself under her arm; the two soldiers made their way to an unmarked doorway along the sidewall as fast as their three-legged walk would allow.

Stepping in, the man seated her on a wooden box as he

shut the door. They were in a maintenance walkway between the outer wall and inner wall. Hardly used by anything other than the maintenance workers, the hallway was a shoulder width wide and damp from melted water that found its way inside.

Looking around, she noticed that she wasn't the only person there. Three other soldiers laid or sat on the floor in various states of injury. One, she was certain was no longer breathing. Looking each of them in the face turned her state of confusion into one of despair. Everything that had happened over the last few minutes was quickly flooding back into her mind as the feelings within her hit an ultimate low.

"Wait! Where is Will? Have you seen Will?" She tried standing as the others looked at her, and the man who had helped them made his way from the door. The pain in her busted leg quickly put her back onto the box.

"I grabbed every person I could." Looking at the worry and fear in her eyes, he placed his hand on her shoulder. "We don't have much time left. Now, we can all help each other make our way to the end of this tunnel and out the back, or those who want to stay can go right back out that door. I don't feel like dying out in that snow. Be my guest if you want out. I'm going to seal it shut the second we can all get up and get going."

She didn't know what to think. She wanted to cry; she wanted to scream, she wanted to run out that door and take every Graon fucker with her to the burning gates of hell. Even shifting slightly reminded her that if she wanted to, she'd be fortunate to make it to the door, much less out it by herself.

"I...I can't leave him."

"I know, Charlie. I can't say he is even out there." She was amazed how level-headed the man was. The light of the damp hallway revealed the maintenance uniform he was wearing, yet his demeanor felt more like an officer. The shadows and incandescent lighting highlighted the white that grew through his thinning hair and a full career of wrinkles on his face. "Believe me, we aren't the only survivors making a run for it. Maybe he made it out himself. Hell, I was lucky I even saw you within the rubble."

"Just, I can't, he means..." Her sobbing was becoming more than she could control.

"Come on, we need to keep moving. If he has survived, we can find him once we are clear of here. If he's dead, then you know he doesn't want you to die for nothing." She tried stiffening up as she sniffled back into her running nose. "It's your choice. Make the good one, and let's go."

He was right, and she knew it. Using his arm again as an anchor, she got back on her feet. Two of the others were able to do the same. One had a makeshift bandage over his left eye and a bandage that barely hid the fact that most of his left hand was missing. The second was scraped and cut, but his limp was horrible as his leg buckled with every step. His wet and hacking cough grew worse by the minute; she knew it did not bode well for his continued health. She had been correct when the third did not stir as the others got up. Dead, the man was left to be found and forgotten with the rest that remained within the fort.

The maintenance hallway the four survivors followed led a few hundred feet away from where the fighting had occurred, but to Charlie it felt as though it was the last mile to a certain death. Everything she knew and loved was now behind a brick wall and a sealed door. The enemy had come quickly and had acted swiftly.

How many made it out? How many remained behind?

Handled by a force now rumored to do things unimaginable to its prisoners, the thought of it threatened to bring tears back to her eyes.

Resting on her good leg, and leaning against the wall, she watched as the maintenance man unlocked and dislodged the exit door, opening a way through the exterior wall. The cold air rushed in bringing with it a few flakes of snow. Accepting help with every step, Charlie took her first steps away from the battle she barely survived.

Where was Will? Was he alive, and if he were, was he going to be okay?

She had too many questions to answer, but there was one thing she knew. This fight would not end her. Her knee would heal. Her strength would return. The moment she could, she would be the one to put the final nail in the Republic's coffin.

Chapter Eleven

0830 Hours, Avos 2, 2258
Fort Frozen Heart, Northwest Azhana

THE TASTE of dirt and snow filled his mouth as Will rolled over coughing. Dust, ash, smoke, and snow floated in the air as he sat up and looked around. Pain lanced through his shoulder, and every part of him ached as he finally realized that he was no longer on the western tower, but seated firmly on the ground. Scenes filtered through his mind as he worked to remember what was going on around him. Just as suddenly as he tried, the image of Charlie turning to him to scream flashed in his mind.

"Charlie! Oh shit, Charlie!" He started to yell her name as he struggled to get to his feet. Every joint ached and resisted as he succeeded in standing and circling to get his position straight in his mind.

Looking around, he could finally see that he was somewhere close to the center road that split the fort into halves. He must have been thrown away from the tower as it collapsed, but where was Charlie? Fear and emotions ran high as he gingerly jogged his way to the rocky remains of the front corner of the fort.

Giant slabs of concrete laid all over the ground, and the sounds of men screaming for help filled the air as Will tried to catch any glimpse of the woman he loved. The dust was settling, but as he got closer, his heart sank deeper. Nothing was moving around him; the front wall of the fort reduced to a pile of debris and slabs of gray burned black with the fires of war. Lifting a few stones where he could only revealed more crushed stone and debris.

"Help! Help, me please!" A struggling male voice broke the grayness around him.

Through the gloom, he could see there was someone half covered in slabs of solid rock that pinned him to the ground.

"Hold on, I'll be right there." Will struggled, but he made his way over as carefully as he could.

The man was in bad shape. Blood trickled from several cuts on his head. Stone, dust, and snow covered everything from the soldier's abdomen to his boots. Breathing shallowly with a few bits of coughing, the man tried to shift under the rock.

"Just keep still. Let me get some of this stuff off you."

Will went to work on lifting the stone piece by piece. After a couple of bricks, he started noticing that each new one had blood on the bottom of it. Having cleared away enough to see the man's lower body, Will recognized that the thing keeping him alive was the very stone crushing him.

"How…How bad is it?"

Blood now mixed with the man's saliva as he struggled to talk.

"It's pretty bad man, pretty bad."

Will didn't know how to tell the man it was over, and there was nothing he could do. Tears welled up in the fallen soldier's eyes as Will watched him come to terms with his fate.

"Ah fuck, I don't want it to end like this."

The man began to sob, his coughing horse and wet as blood trickled between his teeth. A few moments later he lost consciousness as his lungs filled with blood. Will felt sorry for the soldier for only a moment, but looking at him lying there only brought the fear for Charlie front and center in his mind.

Turning to the rubble where she most likely was, Will started making his way back. He knew other men probably needed his help, but wherever she was, he knew she needed his help more.

Gunfire erupted not long after he started making his way back across the yard. The shots were too far away to be for him, but on instinct he ducked and ran as fast as his beaten body would carry him. A pile of half-settled stone covered him as he sprawled on the ground, crawling forward on his belly so that he could get a better look.

At first, there was nothing he could see. The echoes of each shot bounced around the walls of the fort not allowing him any chance to pinpoint the shooters. For a second, Will thought it was both sides fighting again, but as each new set of rounds fired off, the shots got closer.

"Fuckers are cleaning up their mess," Will whispered to himself as he sorted out the situation in his mind.

He knew the enemy was making their way in, probably killing any survivors they happened to find, leaving him little time to find Charlie and get to safety.

"Charlie, where are you?"

Squeezing his fists as hard as he could, it took everything he had to decide that he had to go without her. As quietly as he could, he made his way to his feet and started to inch away from his cover. If he could stay as close to what remained of the outer wall, maybe circle the backside of some rubble, he could get out before they even knew he was there. In his mind, it sounded like the best chance he had.

Step by step, he crept his way to the broken rock slabs. Every few seconds, he looked over his shoulder to see whether anyone approached, or noticed him. Only a few dozen feet separated him from the broken pieces of the wall with each moment that passed as long as a decade of time. He was a man without a friend and a soldier without a weapon.

Just as he reached the broken stone, two of the slabs inches from his right exploded as bullets crashed into them. Diving and rolling roughly forward, Will tried to find cover behind whatever he could. No longer able to get out without being noticed, he could only try to keep everything between him, and them.

Lifting his head, he still couldn't see the enemy. His shoulder hurt as the rest of his body now protested any further movement after the tumble he took over the broken bits of wall. With no one around that he could see, he tried standing back up and moving again. Each muscle strained as he made it to his feet and began walking along the wall, crouched as low as he could get.

Three more bullets crashed into the wall next to him, and it was off to the races. His adrenaline pumped as he did the best he could running. A lot of ground remained between where he was now, and the rear of the fort. Will's only thought was to get lost among the buildings within the center of the fort, lose them in the sprawl of shacks and buildings that he had once called home.

His lungs were burning, and his legs and back stiffened

the moment he slowed. He had made it to the first alleyway between the infirmary and military library. No bullets were fired in his direction as he ran, from what he could tell, but the blood pounding in his ears was too loud for him to be sure. Now standing with his back against the wall of the mess hall, catching his breath, surviving was his only mission.

He tried listening for the sound of anyone following, but between his deep breaths, and the blood rushing through his ears, it was impossible. His adrenaline was fading the longer he spent resting against that wall. He knew he had to keep moving. Every second he wasted there, the closer death would get.

Slowly, and cautiously, he made his way to the entrance of the alley. Looking left and right, he needed to be certain no one was around. Just as he was about to step out, he could make out the outline of three men walking slowly up the road. As they came closer, he could see they were searching every shadow and hiding spot they encountered as they moved forward.

"How many more you think they got holed up in here?" The male voice had some twang that Will didn't recognize. It didn't matter, he was weaponless and could only hope they passed without stopping.

"How should I know? I'm only here to take orders, I don't ask questions about where they get their information. We can only hope the God is leading us in the right direction." The second male voice sounded angrier.

Will crept back into the shadows and found a pile of old boxes he could hide behind. It wasn't much, but it was all he could do. Flattening himself against the wall and ground, he held his breath as he listened for them to get closer.

The three men's footsteps stopped as they reached the

front of the alley. He couldn't tell without looking, but in his mind he prayed to whatever gods remained in the heavens that they continued their search down the road. Blood trickled over his tongue as his teeth ground into his lower lip, and his lungs burned as he tried to keep his breath held as long as he could.

Pieces of wood and fiber covered him as the men fired several rounds into the boxes he hid behind. Chips of stone cracked as his feet with every bullet that flattened against the wall of the library, only one coming close enough to graze the left shoulder of his uniform before it shattered against the wall.

"Come on, let's keep looking farther down there. This area is as dead as those we found out front." The angry one sounded as though he was giving the orders as the twangy one chuckled. Will had waited several long moments before he stood from behind the shredded boxes.

Cautiously, he made his way to the front of the alley. Escaping was going to be harder now that these men were on both sides of him. He didn't feel any better when he thought about what he would do if he made it outside the fort. Looking left he could see the silhouette of the three men down the street, turning to his right is when everything went black…

Chapter Twelve

2248 Hours, Juin 27, 2258
   Forest Outside of Miavlaco, Azhana

FOUR DAYS PASSED since the team had left the forward
base. The first two days had been easy with travel during
the day by vehicle and relaxed camping at night. They had
crossed into enemy territory after the first night, but the
way was mostly clear and well known to the men of the
group. After night two, things got slower and a lot tougher.
They left the all-terrain infantry vehicle hidden along the
side of an embankment within the forest and headed out
the rest of the way on foot.

The travel became slow and tedious as the good
weather they had left in, quickly turned to rain and humid
conditions. The ground of the forest for the first day held
up nicely as the men marched over the fallen leaves and
avoided raised roots the best they could. On day four, the
rain began to come down in sheets despite the tree canopy
above them. The ground became mush, their clothes

soaked through to their skin, and everyone had the sniffles or a cough.

To make things worse, the closer they got to their destination, the more often they had to stop. Witch, who seemed to have a sixth sense for the things, continually found either trip wires attached to antipersonnel mines or covered holes that lead to a deadly fall below. Each time they found another defense, the team would get angrier and angrier at whoever was the next person to make unwanted noise. Most of the time it was Sergeant Kris.

"I don't think I've been this wet before in my life," Kris whispered as he sat with Ed and Dickie. The Sergeant had decided it was a good place to rest, and that it would be their last rest before sundown.

"One of the things to get used to in this life. You're either: soaked to the bone from rain and pissed you ever joined the army. Then there are the times you sweat faster than you can drink, and your skin boils from exposure. Or the best yet, you're frozen like a popsicle. Every night before you go lay down you consider setting yourself on fire. Build a man a fire and you keep him warm for the night. Set a man on fire, and you keep him warm for the rest of his life," Dickie said with a wink before he began rummaging through his pack. The others were glad when he spoke before he stuffed his mouth. "Can't these pricks ever learn the fighting is better when they pick somewhere pleasant? Fuck, can't we, for once, fight over land on an island resort or something?"

"We going to fight in flower dresses and throw coconuts at each other also, Dickie?" Ed couldn't help chuckling at the thought after he said it.

Kris couldn't figure out how these guys were still so at ease in this weather.

"Now there's probably the smartest thing you've ever

said." Dickie took no time devouring a piece of jerky between talking. "I'd think the rookie here is becoming a good influence on you. Next, you may be thinking of world peace, or maybe even talks of diplomacy. Think these bastards sing campfire songs?"

Ed couldn't help laughing at that. Kris wasn't sure, but it seemed as if they were still making fun of him.

Were these guys that against their God? Am I a spy for the General?

"Peace wouldn't be such a bad thing, would it? I mean, then we wouldn't have to be out here looking for someone to kill."

His question rang on deaf ears.

"Some men search for peace, some men search for love, and some men kill for a living, son. What would those of us, who are the latter, do with world peace?" Dickie gave Kris a quick glance before chomping down on the last piece of jerky.

"Uh, I don't know. You guys have to have skills at something other than war. Right?"

Ed and Dickie looked at one another before returning to him.

"We don't look for people to kill when we are out here." The Sergeant's voice came up so suddenly behind him; Kris nearly jumped out of his seat. "The reason for this mission is to find targets of interest and make use of them the best way we can. Mostly, that means we have to kill them. They don't usually leave us a choice. When we do have a choice, well, sometimes, they are better off dead."

The Sergeant sat right next to Kris.

"Hi, Sergeant. We were just talking about…"

"I know what you guys were talking about, and I know Dickie over here was setting you up for a speech. The one about how the only good man is the man at the right end of a rifle, isn't that right, Dickie?"

Dickie looked as if he had to ponder that for a second.

"Well, there's always the man on the other end of a campfire, you know the one offering you a steak. He's pretty good as well."

Ed, being more quiet than usual, let out another chuckle.

"Enough of this bantering. While you three were relaxing and making yourself at home, the rest of us looked ahead. We have about half a night's march before we reach the city limits. No perimeter fence from the information we have, so, unless things have changed, we should be able to slip in during the dead of night."

Ed and Dickie looked at Brett and nodded.

"Aye-Aye Sir," they said in unison.

Collecting their stuff, they headed off toward their target destination. Kris stood to follow them, but a firm, steady hand on his shoulder kept him in his seat.

"Son, you have anything to tell me before we get ourselves into a firefight?"

The Sergeant didn't need to look him in the face to tell him that there was no way to lie.

"Um, sir, I think there has been a rumor between the men about me being a spy, Sir. I want you to know, to know..."

"That it's true? I already know that son. As Witch tried to tell you, you are what you are, and you don't even know it yet. I knew the day you joined, why you were with us. If there had been any other reason for you to join us, I wouldn't have allowed it." He was now looking at Kris with a look that said listen now or you won't live to regret it. "You would have found yourself inconveniently injured in training, or voluntarily removing yourself from duty.

Anyway though, that is not why I'm speaking to you privately."

Kris could feel the worse coming.

"Then why, Sir? Why are we here?"

"A lot of enemy soldiers stand between us and our target. These men you are with, have followed me through more than six dozen battles. I expect you to follow my commands to the letter. If you do anything, I mean anything, to put my men in greater danger than they already are facing, I will kill you myself." There wasn't an ounce of softness in the man's face or tone. "If you do listen to me, we'll get you out of this as safe as we can. When we return to base, we can talk more about this whole 'spy' thing. Now, get up and get your ass with the rest. We have a long day or two ahead of us."

The talk wasn't what he wanted hours before his first combat mission. Maybe something more reassuring, something about how this mission was for the greater good, or maybe that they had each other's back. Discovering that he had a crosshair on his own back before he could put one on the enemy, did little for his confidence.

Chapter Thirteen

1000 Hours, Avos 2, 2258
East of Fort Frozen Heart, Northwest Azhana

AT FIRST, she had thought he was crazy when he told them they would be crossing the river. They weren't more than a third of the way across, when she decided, yes, this man must have lost something more than blood in the battle. Walking over the snow and uneven terrain with one busted leg and leaning heavily on his shoulder had been risky enough. Now, she was taking one cautious step after another on the ice that threatened to spill her at any second.

The other two men weren't faring as well either. 'Righty' had already fallen twice on his damaged hands. The maintenance man threatened to kill him where he laid if he didn't stop screaming each time. The possibility of being followed through the snow was real and very high. Leaving a trail of blood and screams to follow wasn't going to make their escape any easier. The quiet man's cough was still growing worse by the minute. Charlie was certain that some blood on the ground wasn't 'Righty's', but she didn't want to press the issue.

"How much longer do we have to go?" Charlie tried keeping her voice high enough for the others to hear, maybe keep their hopes up as she was trying to do the same for her own.

"Normally this walk would take an hour, but, with you lot, I guess maybe a week."

She hoped he was joking, but who can find humor at a time like this?

"Now honestly there, jackass. I'm just trying to keep our minds on something other than our injuries." Injured or not, she wasn't going to let him push them around. "Again, how much longer do we have to go?"

The man stopped their progress over the icy river. The two other soldiers didn't notice as they were barely better than walking dead men. 'Righty' made it a step or two past them before he realized and stopped. The quiet one walked right into the maintenance man and damn near knocked all three of them to the ground.

"Let me see here." Just to make a point, he let some of her weight go, forcing her to balance herself. Charlie put some weight on her leg and regretted it the second she did. "If it weren't for me, the three of you would already be dead like the rest. A couple of personal ATV's, hidden not too far from here, are waiting for us not long after we reach the riverbank. We can keep moving, and be there within the hour, or you can all sit here and waste your energy wondering who's gonna die first. Take your fucking pick."

The man's tone and unemotional reference to all they lost back at the base took Charlie by surprise. The pain and weariness had been settling to where everything they left had hidden behind the pure instinct to survive. Now standing here on this road of ice, being reprimanded and reminded, it felt as though the weight of the world had sunk into her.

"OK, I'm sorry. It's just been so much, so fast." She was honest in every way. "Please. We each owe you our lives. Let's just keep moving. We'll go as far as needed."

The others agreed silently, or, at least, they hadn't said any differently. So they turned and continued. In just under an hour, as the man had suggested, the four soldiers reached a small recess along the steep hill that bordered the river. The makeshift shelter was half natural cave finished with pine branches tied close, which blocked the view inside from all but one angle. Up close it was easy to see that the area was man-made, but from a distant passerby, it would look like a dense cluster of trees next to the hill face.

"Wait, how did you come by these?" The maintenance man, till now, had been full of surprises. In front of the weary group sat two like-new personal ATVs, dust free and a lack of use reflected on their painted bodies. Each vehicle had been protected and were more than capable of carrying two people at once.

"Let's just say that on a couple of resource trips into the area for supplies, the team 'accidentally' lost one or two of these." The man couldn't help smiling as he leaned Charlie against one and began preparing them for operation.

"Losing one of these would hardly go over well with the captain." She was amazed at how new and well-kept they seemed.

"Oh, trust me. A demotion or two were given out. But hey, now looking at it, I'd say it was worth it."

Charlie had so many questions she wanted to ask, as hope of survival started to build within her. The other two remained silent, at this point, still barely staying on their feet.

"But why though? How could you have known that you would need a couple of these, and on the opposite side of the river to the base?"

Hopeful feelings aside, the cautious side of her mind was taking over as she tried to put one and one together.

"Why? The whole base was set up as a plug to delay the entire Western military!" Frustration and anger flashed in the man's face as he gripped the wrench in his hand tighter. "I didn't serve this long in the damn military to lose it all holding a damn leak in a defense already starting to fall. A couple of guys from the maintenance crew, myself included, decided that if shit got bad too fast, we'd all breakaway and meet here." For a second, he seemed to get lost in a memory of something or someone.

"What about the others? Should we wait for them then?"

The question brought the man back to the present, and he quickly pointed to the other two men using the other ATV to keep themselves standing.

"Those two couldn't stand for us to wait one more minute. Besides, it doesn't matter. We'd be waiting here a damn long time if we tried. Pete and Jason were in supply tunnel three by the east tower when the front of the fort exploded. When I looked over in that direction, the whole wall had collapsed. I'm gonna bet that second ATV right there, they didn't make it. You're more than welcome to stay and wait if you want to."

Heeding the man's advice, she stayed silent as he finished the preparations for starting the vehicles. At first, they were going to have Charlie and the maintenance man ride together, just as they had been traveling. But, on second thought, they realized that the other two couldn't make it a hundred yards without help. In the end, Charlie would navigate one while he navigated the other. Their passengers would have to hold on for dear life.

After several minutes of unlocking and other preparations, the two ATVs were running, and their passengers were seated and ready to go.

"You know, through all this, I never asked your name. I know I've seen you around the base."

His eyes were hard pressed ahead and ready to go before he turned to look at her with a smile.

"My name is Tyaldir, but everyone calls me, Fiddler. They say it's because there wasn't a thing that I wasn't fiddling with."

The story didn't ring a bell with her, but she knew she recognized his face. She couldn't put a particular time or date to when, but she was damn sure he'd always been around.

"And one last thing!" Charlie shouted over the roar of the ATV engines. Fiddler had started moving but stopped and looked back. "Where are we headed, anyway?"

"There's a small town just down the valley road. Not many people left up there, but I'm certain at least a few old-timers remain. Their ways may be ancient to you and me, but it's the best we can do."

Not wanting to get delayed again, Fiddler sped forward and Charlie was quick to follow. They had miles to go, and for the injured, their time was running out. Charlie didn't know what was in front of her, or how long she could trust this man, but, for now, it was her only option.

Chapter Fourteen

1524 Hours, Avos 2, 2258
Small Unknown Town, Northeast of Fort Frozen Heart

TWO HOURS of straight riding had taken its toll on the four survivors. Through the valley pass, the trip from the hidden supply cave had been cold and bumpy, yet modest, compared to what it could have been in this region. The road, more like an animal trail, was still undisturbed from the previous evening's snow as their tires tore through it with ease. Each side of the road crept closer to their shoulders as the rock of the mountain and the forest that slumbered through the winter closed around them.

When they came within sight of their intended destination, Charlie was shocked and relieved. At first she couldn't understand how a village this close to their base had gone unnoticed. Feeling the jarring pain of her busted leg on the next rock the ATV hit, reminded her it didn't matter. How this village and its inhabitants remained secluded wouldn't matter, so long as someone here could help them.

Her next thought brought to her mind that she hadn't felt the embrace of the man holding on behind her shift in any way as far as she could remember. She hoped 'Righty' remained alive.

Entering the village on what seemed the only path in, the four soldiers looked at the simple one to two bedroom buildings spread in front of them. The path that entered became the main street of the area as buildings reached in all directions from it. The other streets were naturally formed alleyways between the wooden structures. There wasn't very much activity on the street other than the odd passerby walking their dog, or a few children running as they threw snowballs at one another.

"This way!" Fiddler waved his hand forward and sped off down the road. When it seemed they had reached the center of town, he turned them left into an alleyway perfectly sized to fit their ATVs.

"Is there anyone here that can help us?" Charlie asked.

She couldn't imagine that this town had well-trained surgeons, let alone those capable of saving them. She tried sliding her leg so she could get off the ATV but came up short by the pain and the fact that 'Righty' wasn't moving at all.

"Shit!" Fiddler ran to check on the man, who at this point seemed attached to her. "He's still breathing, but barely. Wait here, I'll get someone."

In a flash, he was off to the front. It seemed he knew his way around the area, which bothered Charlie slightly, but at this point it didn't matter. If they didn't find someone, they might be trying to peel this man off her within the hour.

Looking around at what she could see, the village seemed peaceful enough. Secluded as it was, everything was quiet and had a foggy feel to the air. One would think if they hadn't come by to disturb things, everything would settle down and remain as it was for a hundred years. A people lost in time.

Loud hacking coughs brought Charlie out of her trance as she turned and looked at the quiet one as he toppled over in pain. Reacting on instinct, Charlie tried getting off the ATV. Pain lanced straight up her leg and finally got an "Ugh" sound from 'Righty' as he still clung to her.

"They are over here!" The higher pitched voice of a young boy turned her back to the front of the alley as he stood there waving around the corner.

From this distance, and judging by the over-sized clothes he was wearing, he wasn't yet to his teenage years. Moments after he had appeared, Fiddler and a following of men and women came around, all of them dressed in what looked like simple religious attire hastily covered in winter jackets.

"Take these two first," Charlie pushed the first women toward her two companions. "They need a lot more work than I do. I just need someone to help me walk wherever we are going."

Fiddler was quick to jump back into his original role and slipped her arm over his shoulder.

"I told you I'd find some people to help." He had a smile that showed he was over proud of himself.

"Did you have to bring the whole church with you? We need doctors, not prayers." She was glad when she saw that the door of the next building was open and awaiting their arrival.

"Prayers and blessings can go a longer way than you think, young lady," one of the larger men out front with 'Righty' spoke but did not turn around. "You only need to know who to pray to."

Something seemed out of place to her in that comment, but she quickly shrugged it off. As they entered the front door, the pleasant warmth of a heated room was a welcomed guest. She had been so cold, for so long, that she instantly shivered as her body began to warm itself.

The church they walked into wasn't as stuffy and extravagant as she had been led to believe, but she had never been much of a believer in religion or rumors, and the inside comfort was welcoming. From the front door to the back wall, a rolled rug lined the center path between two rows of pews. The rest of the building was hardwood floors that lead to brick walls. Up near the rafters, eloquently crafted stained-glass windows depicted stories of spiritual beings and battles she did not understand, nor recognize.

Only one thing stuck out to her, odd for what little memories she had of the last church that she had seen, there were regularly placed single chairs with small marble covered tables along each wall. Everything in the building seemed to funnel toward the front altar. The crowd of townsfolk ushered each survivor to the front pews. With gentle instructions, each of them was seated comfortably, while several members of the congregation excused themselves to other rooms found within the church.

"Don't worry, these people will take good care of us," Fiddler whispered to Charlie as a gentle faced older women helped her position her leg in as comfortable way as possible.

"They seem nice enough." She looked over after being helped out of her battle jacket, which she realized she hadn't taken off in more hours than she could remember. Most people were ignoring Fiddler altogether. Of the four people brought in, he needed help the least. "How do you know them though?"

"I told you that I and the others spent time scouting the area when we stashed those transports. Now sit back and relax. We'll have time to talk later."

Not wanting to concede that he was right, Charlie gave in and relaxed back into the worn wooden pew. The few villagers who had exited were now reemerging with pitchers of water and clean clothes. They worked over each wound the group suffered as diligently as any experienced nurse Charlie had ever met. There wasn't much they could do for any internal wounds, but she had to agree the treatment made her feel as if things weren't that rough.

"Ah, so this is the reason for all the commotion going on in my temple."

A tall, fat man dressed in a deep blue robe exited from behind a large brass organ at the rear of the front altar. His robes covered him from shoulders to his feet, giving him the appearance of gliding across the floor. If it wasn't for his belly pushing the cloth out so far, and giving him such a large gait, the illusion would have worked. Instead, he reminded her of an extravagant businessman, dressed for cigar smoking and whoring with the best-priced women in town.

"Your holiness, we have done everything we can for these men," a middle-aged parishioner turned bowing his head to the fat man. "Uh, and woman, Sir." The man quickly corrected himself when he stole a quick look at Charlie.

"I see, but just cleaning their wounds will not solve all that aches their troubled bodies." The man was now directly in front of them; all the others had stopped working, and none had their eyes away from the preacher standing in front. "Please, bring each of them some soothing tea. There is so much more work that needs to be done."

The large preacher then made his way to the 'Quiet one' and 'Righty'. She couldn't hear what he was whispering to them over the rustling of the parishioners now picking up everything they had used to help the wounded soldiers. It didn't matter too much as she couldn't take her eyes off the robes the man wore. Within the dark blue colors, a pattern of the faintest gold was etched into the material. Once she could follow it with her eyes, she could finally see what it was. Blue Flames!

"Ah, there she is, my beautiful." Being transfixed by the pattern of the material, she never noticed he had stepped in front of her, his size and girth was far more intimidating than it had been from afar.

"Hi there, Sir." Her words stumbled as she struggled to find something to say to the man.

He had never given her his name. The smell of garlic coming off him had her inching slightly deeper into her seat.

"You can call me, Father Martin, if you would like." He bent at his knees so he was now eye to eye with her. "So what ails you, my daughter?"

She had not been in a church for a very long time, but it only took a second for her to remember how she never liked the way they addressed people.

"My leg got pretty busted up back there. I couldn't walk if I wanted to, Martin."

She watched as the brow over his left eye raised before it softened with a smile.

"A little fire in you. I like that."

By now, several older female parishioners had returned with pots of tea and were handing it out to the soldiers. Taking a sip, the bitterness of the tea was a shock, but having not drank anything for almost an entire day, helped her get past it. After a few sips, a slight sweetness crept in as an aftertaste.

"Thank you for the help that you are offering us. I'm not sure how much you can do here in this small village, but that man over there is in pretty bad shape." She looked over at the quiet one, he was paler than she had remembered him being. "The army will be grateful for the help, in the morning if we could, I'd like to radio in. Maybe even get us to a hospital as soon as possible."

"All things can be arranged, my child. For now, just relax. Too much thinking like an officer won't help that leg of yours heal. Here we can work wonders with prayers and blessings, you wait and see." The man stood himself back up and whispered a direction or two to the nearest woman, who then rushed off to a room to the side of the altar.

"Hey, I told you these people can take care of you. No reason to be asking about radioing back in. You're free now. Enjoy it while you can." Fiddler leaned over and put his hand on her shoulder.

"Look, a lot of good men and women died back at that base. I've lost more than I'd like to think about now." The thought of not getting back at those bastards who did this welled up a ball of anger in her chest that threatened to burst, but quickly defused as she suddenly found herself very confused. "I'm not sure what you're planning but…"

"She'll be taken care of, don't you worry. You were right though, she has a strong heart and fire within her that will do just fine."

The bald, fat man and Fiddler smiled at each other. She tried to say something, but her tongue felt as though it filled her mouth, and the words came out as a gurgle.

Tracing the look between both men's eyes, she tried to see what was going on, but her body was no longer listening to her as she slumped backward and fell into darkness.

Chapter Fifteen

0535 Hours, Juin 28, 2258
Miavlaco, Azhana

THE SUN HAD RISEN in the east, chasing away the darkness of the city, and drying the water that had soaked the land the last few days. A sliver above the horizon, the warmth felt good as the men made their last preparations before moving farther into the city. They sat now in the downstairs living area of an abandoned stone building on the edge of the city. Witch was in the building across the alleyway; this gave him a higher vantage to keep a lookout for any passing patrols.

Within the city, according to their scouting and reports, patrols regularly circulated out from the center of the city to the outer slums in clockwork fashion. Out here in the poorest areas, the patrols would stick to the primary roads, making movement and coordination much easier until they crossed the front lines.

The city itself had seen the conflict from inside and

outside the perimeter. Two years ago, the Republic had pushed this far into Azhana's territory, taking this city and holding it for several weeks. A daring nighttime raid and lack of strong support had pushed the Republic out, and back deep into the forest.

The war over the last ten years had not done much for the population. Dozens of reported bombings and civil unrest scarred the past several years. Rumors had it that someone was financing and stirring up the unrest, but nothing had been brought forward as evidence. That would change today.

"Alright, after we get past checkpoint two, here, Ed and our new 'weapons specialist' will make camp at this bell-tower over the library. There hasn't been much need for books and socialization lately, so it should be empty and remain that way once we get there." Brett looked over a topographical map as the others gathered around. "Kris, we need to see how good a shot you are. Once you're set up, you should have an almost 360 view of the city layout. Keep your eye on our backs, and, if any of these bastards make a break for us, you shoot to kill. Got that?"

Kris took a quick look around and swallowed loudly.

"Yes, Sir!" The urge to snap a salute was overwhelming.

"Witch, Dickie, David, and I will make our way to this temple right here. Usually, the military tries to stay away from such 'sacred' areas, but the price on this target is too high." They knew what was at stake here. If they went with guns blazing, this could turn an already ugly war into something unfathomable. Religion would take an even more front stage presence between the combatants. Everyone wanted to prevent that as much as possible, or at least, feigned wanting to prevent that.

"What about civilians there, Sergeant?" Ed was

studying the map intently. "There is a good amount of civilian housing standing between us and them. Plus, once you are inside, who knows what you will find."

Brett took another long look at the map.

"We do what we can, prevent as much damage as possible. In the end, those in that building are priority number one. The rest, we let fate decide. Any more questions?" He looked around at his men.

Each of them had confidence and strength in their eyes, except Sergeant Kris. The thought of killing unarmed civilians was not settling well in his stomach. He looked ready to vomit, and they hadn't even started yet.

"My only question, Sir, is, will we be home in time for steak night? You know how hungry I get after this." Dickie had a knife out in his hand and an impossibly large grin on his face.

"Remember Dickie, we are having venison on the way home. Oakie here is gonna get us a celebration dinner. Aren't ya?" David patted Kris so hard on the shoulder the man almost toppled over.

"I…uh."

"Enough. The sun is moving higher, and we'd better get moving. Ed signal Witch and let's grab our gear. Time to move out."

The banter between them quickly stopped as they made their way to the door. Witch appeared in the doorway of the next building. Giving the signal that it was all clear, he took point and moved forward. The rest followed in tight formation behind him.

This part of the city was a mixture of broken-down stone buildings and shanty-town houses in a state of disrepair that made them only useful to feral animals. At this hour, Brett knew that they had at least an hour before the first patrol made its way to the outer dwellings. He had the full intention of getting the team inside that line before that.

Keeping to the shadows as best they could, they followed Witch from building to building. Each man covered a different angle; either up, left, right, or forward and backward. They could not afford to be caught this quickly within the city. That would leave them too much fighting ground between them and the target, and at least a hundred men, 'if' their intelligence reports were correct.

Three blocks of travel had them seeing the city change right before their eyes. A distinct visual line separated the poor vacant slums and the upward mobility of the city. The buildings began to rise higher and less, and less of them would be considered uninhabitable. Several of them were recognizable as businesses that had shut down a long time ago, but the buildings remained intact. Knowing that they could not sit for too long, Witch quickly had them running across the three lane road and into the shadows of the next alley.

"OK, Sergeant. We are at location alpha." Witch didn't bother looking back as he crept forward to see what obstacles lay ahead. The rest of the men didn't say a word.

"Ed and Kris, you know what to do. Location Beta is three blocks to our north. We need you there in exactly thirty minutes. Get a move on." The Sergeant nodded at Ed who quickly nodded back.

Reaching to tap Kris on the shoulder, Ed didn't hesitate as he rounded the first corner with the rookie close on his heels.

They had a few hundred feet of ground to cover before they hit the next alleyway. With some quick paced jogging, they got to it swiftly. Hiding in the shadows, it appeared Ed was considering something with his back against the wall and his eyes tracing their steps back and forth.

"What's wrong?" Kris asked, trying to not think about the thousand possibilities running through his mind.

"We haven't seen a single person yet. It may be our lucky day, but this city is way too populated to be this empty."

Thinking about it, he was right. Not finding anyone in the outer slums was to be expected. They were now in what was the old business district and still no sight of anyone, alive or dead.

"Should we warn the others?"

"Hold on, let me just call them on the radio. 'Hey, Sergeant we haven't seen anyone around yet. Just wanted to let you know that." Ed mocked putting his imaginary radio away. "What the fuck? Don't you think they have already figured that out too?"

That was the harshest he'd ever seen Ed get. This must be what they mean when they say 'War brings out the true man inside'.

"Look, there is nothing we can do to help the others, but get to our post on time. We still have two blocks, and there are no more alleyways between us and the library. That is a lot of open ground for us to run." The harshness in Ed's face left, but his tone still spoke of the reality of their situation. "Unless you have some better idea, I think we may have to see how much of this 'luck' we still have left."

Hoping there wasn't a soul in the city to spot them in the daylight, the thought of a dead sprint to the library two blocks away did not put Kris' feelings at ease. Looking around the alleyway wasn't yielding many other options, nothing but trash and a broken down dumpster.

"Time to get moving, follow me closely, and…"

"Wait!" Kris said.

He had found their answer. Waving to Ed, Kris crept to

the back of the building that made up the alleyway. The concrete wall, hidden partly by the dumpster, did not come flush to the back of the store building. Behind was a small walkway that led to a metal ladder used as a fire escape for the occupants.

"Holy shit! Kris, I think you found our answer."

Ed took the lead again. As quickly and safely as they could, they ascended the unused fire escape. The steel frame looked as if it hadn't held the weight of a man, much less two in full battle gear, in several years. It creaked and squealed as they climbed the four stories to the top, but it held.

On top of the building, it was easy to see their destination ahead. From this vantage, the entire landscape opened before them. The land itself sloped downward, giving this part of the city the highest elevation. Just over the row of buildings across the street, everything gave way to a large park laid out in front of their target, the city's temple.

"Let's move. We don't have a lot of time." Ed called back as he led the way.

Ed moved without hesitation as they went from rooftop to rooftop, stepping with caution so they wouldn't alert anyone below.

When they reached the library, the roof was flat and didn't provide much cover. On the north end of the building, the bell tower rose two more stories, which would give them plenty of visual coverage for the men below.

"We need to get you into that tower. I'm going to remain below. You can handle this, right?" The look in Ed's face didn't leave much room for saying no, no matter how much he wanted to.

"Yeah," Kris said as he looked around the deserted library. "I've got this."

"Good." A smile came to his face. "Let's get inside and signal the others."

Just as the alleyway that helped them get to the rooftops, the metal ladder which the library used, was still in place at the rear of the building. Using the first entrance they could, Ed picked the lock on the door and let them in.

Inside the first room, trash and broken pieces of furniture laid all over the floor. Empty bookcases laid on the carpet or leaned against the walls. The shelves inside them were broken and scattered across the room. The smell of dust and urine filled their nostrils as they moved along inspecting the area. On each side, there was a door, neither of them locked. The one on the right led to a spiral staircase that led up to the top of the bell tower. The second doorway was the stairwell downstairs.

"Up you go. Once you're settled, send out the signal on comms." Ed patted him on the shoulders like an older brother would. "I'll keep you covered downstairs. Just send out the message, and then stay quiet. Let the others do their job."

Nerves wouldn't let him say anything, as it got tied up in his stomach. So, instead, he nodded his agreement. With that, Ed turned and made his way across the room and down the stairs. Turning to the staircase ahead, each step Kris took felt as though concrete was solidifying in his boots. Was everything in this mission relying on him? What if I mess up? Just calm down, take a deep breath. These thoughts and others flooded his mind, threatening to prevent him from taking another step. Let alone pulling the trigger and ending the life of another human being.

The top of the stairwell felt miles ahead, but, before he knew it, he was at the top. Releasing the bolt that held the floor door in place, he climbed inside and closed it behind him.

The room was a good size, even for a man of his stature. The white painted wood of the floor had an inch of dust covering it, giving it a charred appearance. The bell no longer remained, its reassuring sound silenced long ago.

Muscle memory took over as he set up his long-range rifle and positioned it with a full view of the temple below. It took a few seconds before the silencing box powered on, signaling it was ready to fire. It wouldn't silence the shot, but unless you were directly beneath the tower, you'd be hard-pressed to know a round had been fired.

His hands were shaking so intensely he almost turned the device back off when checking the meter on the silencer. The moment he pushed the relay button on his radio, he knew it would all start. Reaching into his shirt, he quietly squeezed the three starred sword that hung around his neck, closing his eyes he reached down and pressed the relay button on his belt. The mission was a go.

Chapter Sixteen

2130 Hours, Avos 3, 2258

Small Unknown Town, Northeast of Fort Forward Trinity

THE SMELL of burning wood from the campfire filled everything around Charlie, and a cool breeze flowing through the forest sent shivers down her spine as it brushed against her bare shoulders. The campsite Will had picked was perfect. The fire burned in a small opening of the tree canopy that formed a circle where they had set their tent the night before. If she listened closely, she could hear the faintest rush of water flowing from the river only a hundred yards into the woods.

They were alone for the first time since they had met each other in the army. Their relationship was a secret, one that had been growing harder as of late, and by a lucky chance, getting a solid weekend together had been a blessing. Leaning back against the fallen tree trunk she was using as a rest, she closed her eyes to let her surroundings sink in.

Suddenly, there was a rustle coming from the bushes behind her. With her eyes closed, the sudden sound made her heart stop as the fear of the unknown presence filled her mind. Trying to act as calmly as she could, she slowly lifted her head and turned to see what it was.

Will was making his way out of the brush, struggling with his boot that he had caught on several roots. The man had six fish hanging from a line thrown over his shoulders.

He smiled at her as he noticed she was looking and finally freed himself. The man must have decided to take a swim in the river while he was fishing as he was now shirtless and wet from head to toe. It didn't seem to bother him as he sat next to her. The sight didn't bother her in the slightest bit either.

"Looks like we'll be eating like royalty tonig..." His voice became suddenly distant to her.

"What did you say? I couldn't hear you."

The expression on his face didn't change as he smiled and shook his head. Removing one of the fish from the line, he began preparing it for cooking.

"Looks like we'll be succeeding tonight, are the rest ready?" She thought she could hear him clearly this time, but he didn't bother to look up at her. Why was he sweating so much? The water covering his body had doubled since he had arrived.

"Hey! Are you, OK?" She reached over and tried shaking him by the shoulder. The sweat now on her hand was thick, warm and didn't feel right. She wiped her palm on her leg to dry her hands, looking as she felt the liquid squirt between her fingers. Horror hit her like a punch to the gut as blood covered and dripped from her hand.

"The timing is right, bring forth his holiness. We shall see our father soon."

The look on Will's face was a blank stare as his eyes had gone ghostly gray. Out of pure instinct, she slapped the man she loved right across the face and started to scream. The noise that came out of her mouth sounded oddly distant. Will hesitated before he looked at her once again. The smile she had fallen in love with slowly returned to his face. Opening his mouth as if to let something crawl out, the most horrific scream she could imagine, started to come out like a tidal wave. The leaves of all the trees started to fall as the sound grew in intensity. Limbs started shaking, and the earth around her started to tremble.

Adding to the sound, she started screaming herself but realized she didn't have the strength to shout over him. The fear was overwhelming. She could feel it building in her chest, the need for tears burning behind her eyes. The pressure began filling her chest so much she couldn't find the ability to breathe.

Pain cracked inside her ears as she crumpled to the ground next to the empty fire-pit. She struggled for breath, why couldn't she breathe? She started clawing at her neck, trying to force the slightest bit of air into her lungs. Nothing would work, her muscles wouldn't listen to her. Using what strength she could, she drew herself up into a seated position.

Gasping for air, the feeling of her lungs filling was exhilarating as she looked around. She was no longer in the nightmare that the oasis in the forest had become, but entered another in the reality of the altar she now laid on.

The church, now filled with soft candlelight, remained still. She could hear the soft steps of someone else in the room, but through the smoky haze, she could not find them. Shifting her position, she found herself laying upon the front altar in a clean white dress. Lifting her head to take a look at her right leg, she was amazed when moving caused very little pain. Whoever had dressed her and placed her here, had taken the time to put her knee into a splint.

"What is going on around here?" She asked herself in a whisper as she noticed the strange symbols drawn on her arms and legs. She traced the markings up her legs and across her chest. Wiping the skin of her cheeks, she couldn't see any evidence of the drawings on her face, but assumed they were there as well.

"You're not supposed to be awake." One of the older parishioners from before appeared behind her with a golden chalice in his hand, red liquid splashed as he carried it.

The man dressed in simple gray robes. His shoulders hunched forward with age and the weight of the cup he held reverently before him. Light hazel eyes shift beneath the cotton cowl as he refused to look at her directly, but stood so that he was always facing her.

"I just woke up from a terrible… Hey, why am I up here?" She started to slide herself off the altar as a second person, a younger blond woman, came around from behind the pipe organ.

"No, no, you need to stay up there. Our father is almost ready for you." Both parishioners had similar symbols drawn on their faces as she did her arms. When they reached her, they began gently pushing her back onto the altar.

"Hey, wait a minute. I really don't want to lay."
She attempted to move, but their grips tightened enough to send pain through her arms.
Something changed in their eyes as she again struggled

against their grip. These were no longer the peaceful people who so openly allowed four injured soldiers into their homes. They had something in mind, and it didn't seem as though she was going to like it. Fighting against both wasn't helping, as no matter what she did, their strength held her down; so she relaxed.

When her struggle stopped, she could feel the white knuckle grip of both loosen. It took a minute before she took the chance and yanked her left arm as hard as she could. The effort didn't dislodge the older man's arm, but it did tear him forward. In the same motion, she shot her head forward, and her forehead met his nose.

Blood squirted out immediately as the man fell to the floor screaming obscenities. Not wanting to give the other a chance to react, she balled her fist and swung as hard as she could. By chance, she caught the woman square on the jaw, and she watched as her eyes rolled back, and she tumbled down the steps away from the altar.

"What is going on in here? I told you to have our master's sacrifice ready when I arrived!" Father Martin came out from behind the organ. He still dressed in his exotic blue robes, but this time he had an ornate dagger strapped to the front of his belt.

The white of his eyes tripled in size as he saw his two servants laying on the floor next to where she had slipped off the altar.

"What have you done? He will be furious!"

"Well, tell him I don't give a shit. What the fuck are you doing here?"

She tried stepping away from the altar and realized that though there was no pain, her leg wasn't near its full strength as she tumbled from placing her weight on it. With an outstretched arm, her hand fumbled with the small glass jars on the credence table and finally came to rest around the chalice.

"Wait just one second my child, let us not be hasty." The preacher had his hands open and palms out toward her. "All will be forgiven now. Just come over here, closer to me." The fat man started waving her closer as he would a young child.

"Fuck off. Where are the others? We are getting out of here." The brace on her knee hobbled her horribly, but she moved away from the man as steady as she could. Her hand remained gripped on the chalice as she noticed that though he talked with her, his eyes would not leave it.

"I don't think your friends will be leaving with you. We've already seen to their commitment to the faith." The man's eyes broke away from the chalice to look deep into her own. With his lips now curling into the same smile she had seen him with the previous evening, he lifted his robed arms and pointed off toward the walls of the church. "Just take a look for yourself, see how a devoted member gives all they have to their one true master!"

She didn't want to look, but with everything going on, she couldn't help turning her head slightly to the wall on her right. There, seated in one of the chairs along the wall, was 'Righty'. Even in the soft candlelight, it was easy to see that the man had passed some time earlier, his arms stretched out along his sides, large slits cut into his wrists. The horror of it stopped her in her tracks as she took a closer look and saw that he was not alone. All along the wall there were people lined up in the chairs, each drained of their life's blood, all of it pooled onto the floor below.

"You monst…!" She tried to scream at him as she turned to face him, but in that moment of distraction he had come for her.

Large and seemingly too bulbous to move, the man showed a speed far greater than she had expected. The chalice was the only thing that saved her as she threw the contents into his face as he raced forward; dagger raised high over his head.

"Bitch! You will pay for this!"

The contents of the cup turned out to be blood as it covered his face and eyes, creating enough of a problem that his stab with the dagger missed wide and grazed her in the shoulder.

As the preacher's momentum carried him forward, she was able to step to the side, but not enough to get her braced leg out of the way. Hitting it with his foot sent a lightning bolt of pain up her leg as he tumbled face first down the aisle between pews. Quickly she picked herself up the best she could and stared down at the man as he tried to make his way back to his feet.

The anger he felt toward her was unquestionable as he tried burning a hole into her with his eyes. That look of pure malice did nothing to her, as she stared back with a determination she didn't know she still had. Using his unexpected speed, the man dove to one of the pews nearest to him, grabbing for the fallen dagger.

Injured leg or not, she was on him faster than he had expected as she swung the chalice with both hands and sent the blade out of his hands and flying across the room. Reversing her swing, she screamed as it crashed into the side of his face and drove him to the floor. Blood flowed freely from a severe slash across the man's temple and forehead that opened when the metal dented on his head.

With her assailant out cold, and probably bleeding to death, Charlie made her way to 'Righty' along the wall. She hadn't known him in life, other than the hours they spent running for their lives, but what she did know was he didn't deserve to end up like this. They had dressed him in some servant type robes and tied him to his death chair. The thick rope that looped over his belt didn't look like it had been strained much, as he probably couldn't have given much of a fight.

"I'm sorry my friend." Tears welled in her eyes, as looking into the dead man's hollow face brought thoughts of Will to her mind. "Why is this happening? How can I be the only one left?"

She cried to herself for just a moment before making her way along the wall. At the end, she was not surprised to see the 'Quiet' one also strapped to a chair. She found there was nothing left to say, but in her heart, she knew he had been at death's door when they had arrived. Maybe with him, they had done more of a favor than they had realized.

Making her way to the entrance of the church, she could see that it was deep into the night and snowing. Reluctant to find herself frozen outside after having survived the horror inside, she slowly made her way back to the quiet one and removed the robes used to dress him. Scavenging a pair of shoes from one of the other victims, she knew it wasn't great, but it was the best she could do. Holding the robe closed with one hand and the dagger in the other, she stepped outside the church and into the cold.

"Hey! Who are you?" The young man must have been standing off slightly in the shadows created by the light that burned over the doorway.

Glancing to the side, so he didn't see her face, she allowed him to approach as she kept her face to the ground. Even though he carried a rifle and kept guard outside a church where people were sacrificed, the man's voice gave him away as particularly young. He approached her slowly, rifle poorly held toward the ground as he eyed the door for anyone else that may exit the building.

"Did you hear me? I said who are..."

He was close enough, so she wasted no time. Slapping the barrel of the rifle away with her free hand, she completed a spin by pivoting on her braced leg and slashed out with the dagger in her other hand. The blade tore the young man's throat and coated the front wall with spray. Not wanting to draw any more attention, she quickly grabbed the hair from under his ball-cap and drove the blade through his chin and into his head. His limp body slowly slipped to the ground as she slowed his descent to prevent any noise.

She wanted to drag him out of sight, but with her busted leg, she had no choice but to leave him. Making her way down the roadway, she hoped against all odds that what she looked for was still there. Entering the alleyway a building down, much to her surprise the ATV she had ridden on sat untouched. A fresh inch of snow covering it. Stopping for a second, she realized only one ATV remained. Not wanting to stay any longer, she worked the starting wires as she had seen Fiddler do using the light cast by the oil lamps on the street.

Within moments, she had the ATV fired up and moving. Having no other option, she turned the ATV back toward the route they had come in on and headed back to the only place she knew; Fort Frozen Heart.

Chapter Seventeen

0121 Hours, Avos 4, 2258
  Fort Frozen Heart, Northwest Azhana

THE COLD BIT tirelessly into her legs as she stopped the
ATV on a small hill overlooking Fort Frozen Heart. The
robes and boots she had taken from the dead men had only
been sufficient to keep frostbite at bay for now. Rubbing
her hands under the robes and over her bare legs, she knew
if she didn't get to somewhere warm and soon, she would
be in trouble.

Following the path back to the fort had been easier
than she thought it would have been, especially at night.
The route had remained mostly clear and the full moon
this evening had provided enough light when mixed with
her headlights that, despite the temperature, she had made
it back. Now, what was she supposed to do?

Gingerly making her way off the vehicle's seat, she
wrapped the cotton robe around her body as tightly as she
could as she leaned heavily against the tree line. Below, the

fort was alive with soldiers moving in and out, completing whatever task they were given. The blast that had torn through the front wall of the base had been cleaned up. Now only noticeable from the large black crater in the ground and the large portion of the wall still missing. All the debris and remains of men, women, and machinery were buried or removed.

Anger, frustration, and sadness all worked their way through her mind. Somewhere down there, her one true friend and the man she loved either laid dead and buried or if he were alive, he was too far away for her to reach.

A stiff breeze made its way through the trees and brought her emotions and thoughts to the present. Scanning the work below, and shifting her now numb and strength-less leg, she realized she only had two options. She could go down there and give herself up, or take a wide turn around the base and maybe if she were lucky, make it past any scouting parties. Heading southeast from the base would put her no more than a full day's ride away from Fort Steel Heart's outer posts. There, she could get some help and report all she knew.

Another breeze swept up some snow behind her as it filled her robes and caused her to pull them tighter. She could barely move her toes, everything was stiff from the excursion and her injuries. The chances she could make it there were slim at best. Looking back at the ATV, she didn't even know how much gas it had left in it. Sighing and shuffling forward, she had to try her best. She was the only one left who could.

"Where do you think you're going this late at night there beautiful?" Charlie crouched and spun the best she could to the voice behind her.

Stepping out from around her were six armed men with rifles pointed at her. All she had on her was the dagger within her robe and the rifle. Well, the rifle was still on the ATV.

"Not too often we find such pretty Sergeants walking around in evening attire."

A man, his face painted a mix of black and dark green stepped out from behind the circle of men, he smiled as he tipped his white camouflaged hat toward her.

"Captain. Is that really you?"

She couldn't believe it. Here she thought she was the only survivor left, and now she wasn't.

"Of course it is, Charlie." He lifted his hand and the men around her lowered their weapons. "By what work of magic has gotten you out here at night in such a small amount of clothing anyway girl?"

Waving a signal to one of his men, a jacket from a supply bag was offered to her. She graciously took it and wrapped it around her shoulders.

"I'm not sure I exactly know sir. I will report everything I can to you, just, I don't think I'm in condition to stand out here much longer."

"Of course not, we shouldn't be standing around here much longer ourselves. Those bastards down there have patrols that sweep outward for two miles." The officer put his arm around her shoulders and let her shift some of her weight to him. "It looks like they are playing for keeps now. Their patrols are even random and unpredictable. Something has them stirred up."

"How were you able to find me, sir?"

The eight of them found their way back into the shadows where they led her to their stash of vehicles. Each equipped for silent travel at night.

"That was the easiest thing we've done so far since we lost the base." The captain helped her onto the back of his seat. "We've been scouting their outer perimeter to look for openings and weaknesses. Stumbling upon your tracks was easy. We couldn't imagine someone just wondering around this area."

"So you followed me?"

"Had to. If we had found you to be a scout, we wouldn't be talking right now."

The man's reasoning was correct. She had been lucky they were suspicious enough to follow her but also lucky they didn't just kill her to protect their cause.

"Where are we going, sir?"

She held on tightly as the group began to move.

"To a small encampment a few miles out of the danger line, due south of here. We'll stay there for a while. Get you fixed up."

Holding on tightly to the Captain, the remaining soldiers of Fort Frozen Heart quickly sped off into the night.

<h1 style="text-align:center">Chapter Eighteen</h1>

<hr>

0710 Hours, Avos 4, 2258
Fort Frozen Heart, Northwest Azhana

THUMP, thump, thump. Will struggled to open his eyes as the pain in his head pounded with the regular beat of his heart. However long he had been unconscious, hadn't helped the rest of his body recover. Just lifting his hand to his forehead ached his entire body. His vision started clearing as he tried to sit himself up.

"Looks like sleeping beauty is finally awake." The words came from a dirty, roughed up soldier who sat across the room from him.

Dirt and grime covered his skin. Where it didn't, was just as discolored from severe bruising.

"What's going on around here? Where are we?" Will's mouth was as dry as cotton as he lurched forward from dizziness.

"Already starting with the stupid questions I see. Well, we are in the brig. I'd say at least those of us left."

One or two of the others gave the man a hard look, but no one said anything. Everyone else tried to act as if they didn't know anyone was talking.

Will tried to take in what was around him the best he could. They were in a square metal room, only one door in or out and it was steel like the walls. At least whoever was guarding them had the decency to leave them with some light from the single bulb above his head. Joining him in the room were six other men. Most of them had their uniforms in tattered condition, so rank and position was difficult to determine. None, including Will himself, seemed as if they were in any condition to fight.

"Who are you anyway? Seems you're the only one willing to talk around here." Will tried to look the others in their eyes, but most looked in any direction but his.

"I'm Sergeant Walker. I was with the east flank mobile artillery run. The squirt sitting beside me is Private Ben Teller. He was the second in here after me. The rest, well aren't talking a whole lot. Who would you be?"

"I'm Sergeant Will Coffey. I was on the west tower when it toppled to the ground in the blast. I tried making it out when they breached the wall, but somehow ended here."

Talking seemed to ease the pain in his head.

"Ah, you're the one with that one hot chick, what was her name?"

Will's chest began to heat at even the slightest mention of her. He didn't know if she was alive or dead, but deep down he continued to fight the voice that said she was gone.

"Her name was Charlie, I believe." Private Teller finally spoke up, lifting his head revealed a narrow and gaunt face covered in freckles. Under his hat, bits of his carrot top hair poked out showing its non-regulation length.

"Yeah, it IS Charlie. She was with me when the tower went down."

For a moment, Will couldn't force himself to look the men in their faces.

"She wasn't with you when you got up? The best thing for her will be if she's dead somewhere under all that rubble."

The Sergeant leaned back with the slightest hint of a smile on his face. Will's eyes flashed red as it took all the injuries that wracked his body to stop himself from clearing the small room and choking the man to death.

"What the Sergeant means is, we've heard rumors of what these guys do to female prisoners. I've heard people talk about what she meant to you, but if they find her, well maybe for her comfort, you'd prefer her not go through that." The private seemed to sense the tension between the two men and shifted himself closer. "Of course, we hope she is alive and somehow found a way out of here. Maybe even found others and got out before the Fort was lost."

The Private was right, maybe both were, but Will wasn't ready to accept that yet.

"Anyone have any idea if there is anything we can do, or what to expect?"

Will looked around, someone had to have something so they could change the subject. All the other men sat there quiet and defeated.

"Not much we can do there, lover boy." The man seemed determined to keep digging the pain in deeper. "These walls here are at least four inches thick, and, from what these cry asses came in saying, those pricks are killing us all one by one. They say it's some game to them.

Fuckers come after us preaching about their gods and their righteousness, yet they are the worst kind of enemy. Fuck!"

None of that sat well with Will. There had to be something they could do. Being stuck in a cell with no chance of escape was one thing, waiting to die, was another.

"Anyone know exactly how long it's been since this all started?"

"You mean how…" Walker started.

"If you count how many meals we've gotten since me and the Sergeant got here, I would say it's been about a day and a half since the fighting started. Could stretch it to two days." The Private cut the Sergeant off to stop the bickering the man was determined to start.

"Two days huh, and they've fed us so far?"

"Yeah, I made sure I ate your rations for the day while you were still laying there getting your beauty sleep." A smile stretched across the man's face.

"Look, if you have a problem with me, just say it. We are all in this situation together, and I haven't been awake that long and I am already tired of your shit." Through the aching and pain, Will got himself to stand right in front of the man.

The man's face quickly turned from the sneering smile to hard rock. Standing, he looked Will right in the eyes. Surprisingly, he was just as large as Will was. Not many men in this remote station could say that.

"Yeah, I've got something to say to you. We know how you carried that little girlie of yours around." He looked at the other men in the room as if they were going to agree with him. "You were too busy keeping your eyes on her ass, maybe if you'd spent more time on your job we wouldn't be in this mess."

"Don't you for one second think our problem here has anything to do with Charlie! She gave her life just like the others in this fucking shit-hole, frozen wasteland, and you're gonna stand here and dishonor what she and the others did!"

There he had said it, no more denying it. Somewhere in the cesspool deep within his heart, he knew it was true. He had lost her forever.

"I'd send you through that door if I weren't already certain even your thick, shit-filled head wouldn't break it." Will threatened.

Squeezing every muscle in his body, he was ready to go.

"Hey now, take it easy you two. We have enough trouble as it is. Don't need to go starting stuff between each other." The Private tried, but didn't have a chance.

"Sit down, you lightweight, green neck recruit. If I meant for you to be in this conversation, I would have started yelling at you, too."

Will wanted to look at the others in the small room to see if any of them were on his side or the other. He knew he was hurt. He knew Walker was too, but with their emotions this high, both men were just as lethal.

"All right you goat-loving, sons of bitches. Sit your asses down and keep your hands on the seats." The voice was overconfident, high pitched, and barely less irritating than the sound of nails scratched over a chalkboard. Three men entered when the steel door to their cell opened.

Turning, Will tried to size the men up before deciding whether he was going to listen at all. Speaking and looking right at him was a middle-aged, pale man, who'd make Charlie look husky. Will had carried travel packs heavier than him. The two behind him though, big brutes, each standing with rifles at the ready and eyes that begged for resistance. The fresh air that blew behind them was a welcome feeling, even if it carried an overwhelming tone of cologne, probably from the half-a-man leader in their presence.

"And who would you be? So, I may have the privilege of knowing who I'm talking with, or talking down to." Sergeant Walker broke out into a laugh meant more for the others in the room than himself.

Even with their current situation, Will had to admit he smiled. The Sergeant's chuckle was cut short when the meaty fist of the man closest to him connected with his jaw and sent him to the floor.

"You may address me as General Saliander Beamen of the High Churches Second Regiment." The man had the audacity to bow just the slightest.

"So General Sally it is."

A quick boot to the ribs proved effective in making sure Walker wasn't going to say anything again.

"Now, is there anyone here a little more, how can I put it? Well-behaved? Or are you people all like this uneducated buffoon praying to the gods of the dusty floor?"

"So the rumors are true. The Church truly does lead the Graon's Army? I thought they fought behind the declaration that they were free countries, not a single Church state?" Will didn't know where this was going, but leaving it to Walker would put them all on the floor.

"Good, someone who at least feigns as if they understand anything past the nearest tree. Who might you be my large, dark friend?" Will wanted to rip the smile right off the man's face.

"I'm Sergeant Will Coffey."

"Do you speak for the men here?"

Will looked around, every soldier was wide eyed and clueless. Sergeant Walker looked seven grades past pissed.

"I speak for myself, sir. But if you require someone to speak, I will do it."

"Very well. To show that we are not too above you all, I will answer your question. It is true. The armies of the Republic are free countries, yet we fly under the honored belief of The God and His Church. This regiment, which found its name from our honored tradition handed down by The Church for centuries, works to put our true faith right where it belongs. At the tip of the spear that brings you heathens to your knees." Smiling down at Walker, who was still on the floor, the man looked like a thieving little devil.

"Then what do you want from us? It looks like you have already gotten everything you came for."

"Oh no, my slow friend. We are only at the beginning of what I, and my superiors want. Only the beginning. As for you gentlemen, your assistance is required outside with the others. Even though it took little sacrifice to take such a position from you, we did make a rather large mess that needs to be cleaned up. You look like a sturdy man yourself. I think you may want to talk these others into joining you at the front. Return to what you do best, working with your hands and the dirt." He snapped his fingers as he turned to leave. The two men with him never stopped eyeing Will and the others. "You have until morning to rest."

Weren't they alone? There were others still alive? Will didn't know which he wanted to do more, jump for joy, cry, or squeeze the General's neck until his little head popped. Whatever lay ahead, he would survive. If there were a chance Charlie was out there somewhere, he would find her. Now, all it would take was some backbreaking work and a plan.

Chapter Nineteen

0700 Hours, Juin 28, 2258
Miavlaco, Azhana

TWO SIGNAL BEEPS sounded from a small device within Brett's watch as the faceplate changed from a red to a green circle. Ed and Kris had made it to the library and were set up. Brett checked the chamber of his rifle as he visualized the kid positioned on top of the bell tower. Squeezing the grip of his weapon, he knew it was now or never. He positioned himself behind the closed door of an abandoned boutique shop as the red wood of the door made for perfect cover while the shoddy boarded front windows gave a wide view of the park ahead. The land sloped slightly downhill to the west, while sparse trees grew unattended along the overgrown pathways.

The park itself was empty of all life other than a few thriving squirrels and birds that joyfully sang in the midday sun. They hadn't seen a single person the entire way through the city. It worried him, and he had already answered the question about it three times to David. Damn that man was stubborn. David and Witch were positioned in the next building over, ready to move forward the second he and Dickie broke from their cover. Something felt strange about this entire situation. Everything was out of place, but he and his men had made it this far, and they would see it through. Now or never, it was time to go.

Stepping through the red door, he made a quick sweep of all available directions and began moving up the street. His target was the large temple only a few hundred feet ahead. It looked empty with boarded up windows, and a roof in bad need of repair as it peaked high above the surrounding buildings. Structurally, the building was nothing more than a rectangle, with a double door main entrance on the east side, and a single door entrance on the south side. The stained glass windows were busted, only shards of the artwork remained within the iron window frames. Now behind them, cheap plywood was in place to keep everything from people and animals, to the sunlight out.

The Sergeant moved slowly, keeping himself slightly crouched as he walked forward, rifle at the ready. As he passed the first building, Witch and David stepped out and filed in directly behind them. Their approach was bringing them up to the face of the building on the east side, allowing them direct access to the main entrance of the building.

Even though they hadn't seen a single person, their reports had said to expect heavy resistance unless they approached quietly. Did we get here too late? Is this the right temple? The feeling that something was amiss was building in his stomach with each step they took.

Nothing but a few pieces of trash and a curious field mouse had made its way in front of them as they stepped to the side of the door. David and Dickie stood on the far side as Witch and Brett covered the opposite.

Nodding the response quietly, David reached over and gave a small tug on the front of the door while keeping himself away from the center of the entrance. The entrance moved an inch as he pulled but quickly stopped as the lock held it in place.

With saying anything, Witch removed a small satchel from around his waist and pulled out a few lock breaking tools. Normally, they would burn it out with an automated antilock, or bust it down manually, but being quiet as long as possible seemed more appropriate. Witch was back on his feet after only a moment's work on the lock. Moving behind Brett, the rest nodded as the man gave the thumbs-up.

Preparing to try the door again, David reached over and squeezed the door handle just as a man walked around the corner behind Brett. A look of shock crossed the man's face as he hesitated with his weapon just before his head exploded into a red mist. The sound of the shot, inaudible to an untrained ear, could barely be heard as the body dropped to the ground. The sound of his rifle clanking onto the concrete was the only out of place noise in the area.

"Well, there goes getting in nice and clean." Brett looked at David who chuckled at the amusement of his own comment.

"Guess the boy actually can hit a deer at a thousand yards. Now help me move this guy David. Witch, lead us in."

Brett grabbed his feet while David lifted him from under his arms. The guard's now headless shoulders were resting against David's chest. The only evidence that anything had been there was the bloodstain quickly drying beneath the heat of the sun.

Inside the building was a different story. The second the men stepped within the walls, the putrid smell of death hit them faster than the enclosing darkness. The main doors led them to a narrow walkway, designed so worshipers could greet their priests as they walked in. The soft glow of candlelight was all they had to see by as they walked farther into the building. Only a few feet ahead, the path opened into a vast audience ground that once held seating for a few hundred civilians. Now it was mostly vacant in the center with a few sitting stations along the left and right side of the building. Staying in the shadows, the men moved forward.

Chanting could be heard coming from somewhere ahead, but the dimness of the candlelight only illuminated the other end of the room. The small wall of candles was only strong enough to cast enough light to see that there was a large altar in the setting area. Brett and Witch moved along the left wall, as David and Dickie blended into the shadows of the right.

"Bodies, there are bodies all along the wall," Witch whispered as he stepped around the first seating area.

Here there was a man sitting in a chair; head leaned back as his dead eyes gazed up at the ceiling. His arms stretched along his sides, and two-deep slits cut deep into his wrists. The blood had recently finished draining out as it was still pooled slightly on the floor where it spilled into a groove cut into the marble floor. The channel allowed the blood to flow into a deeper stream that led forward to the altar ahead.

"What the fuck is going on here?" Brett asked himself.

The idea and plan of the mission was gone as things seemed as though they were going from bad to worse quickly. Figuring that David found the same on his side, Witch and Brett continued to move forward. The chanting grew louder as they moved past three more sitting stations with men and women in the same state as the first they had found.

The front of the room began to narrow as they closed in on the altar. As they approached, it was easier to see David and Dickie on the other side of the room, moving parallel to them along the opposite wall. Just as the chairs that lined the walls to the building, a body laid spread on the altar. Her nude form, pale and unmoving, was displayed front and center in the candlelight.

"Holy shit, Boss. What did we walk into the middle of?" Dickie whispered aloud.

The horror of everything around him threatening to sink in too fast.

"Shut up!" David waved him down as he also shouted a whisper back at him.

No one would have thought it was possible as Dickie's eyes grew larger as he pointed ahead.

"Seriously, what the..." Dickie struggled to get the words out as everyone looked forward.

The woman was moving and had turned her head to them. She had flowing red hair that contrasted with her porcelain white skin. Across her face, from her hairline to her chin, there were markings either drawn or tattooed on her skin. She only hesitated a moment before she started to scream. It wasn't a sound of fear for where she was, or what happened to her, but it was a cry of anger for the four armed men now staring at her.

All four of them stood there frozen as the woman continued. The chanting itself grew louder as it struggled to drown out her voice. Brett was trying to run all the options through his head, but this was something they would not find in the situations manual. The men they came for were not here, but now they were surrounded by a bloodbath, and a naked woman was wailing while being sprawled out on an altar. His feelings had been right; things were going to hell, fast.

The combination of the shouting and the chanting pushed out all other sounds. Everything echoed off the walls of the temple, the vibrations suffocating even thought itself. From behind a bronze organ, two men came charging out, rifles at the ready.

The volume and intensity of the noise did not affect them as they quickly fired rounds off toward Brett and his team. Barely able to connect anything in his mind, Brett released a few bursts himself as Witch dropped in front of him. The man in front dove to the side as Brett's rounds missed high and clanged into the pipes of the organ.

Grabbing Witch, Brett fired a few more wild rounds to distract the man, as he tried dragging his fallen partner to the corner where he could provide some cover. Before he could get his setting, the man came charging around, bayoneted rifle held forward and ready to strike. Acting on instinct alone, Brett used his weapon as a shield and deflected the charge to the side and lost his weapon in the process. The man stumbled forward as he tripped over Witch's booted foot and crashed into the candle-lit wall. Removing his sidearm from its holster, Brett quickly sent two rounds into the man's chest as he turned around. A third split his face in two as his body slumped to the floor.

On the other side of the room, David and Dickie stood over their assailant. Who, judging from the holes torn throughout his clothing, must have walked into a wall of bullets. Rushing to Witch, it was a relief to see him moving.

"You OK, Witch?" Brett asked as he found it difficult to see anything particular in the hazy candlelight.

"Yeah, looks like the first round got me in the vest, the second took out my flashlight." The small lens over his left shoulder was shattered and dangled from a wire.

"You guys OK over there?"

David held a thumbs-up as they checked their man.

The attack had happened so fast that no one realized the woman on the altar was still yelling. The reality of the situation quickly came back to them as they turned to her.

"Sergeant, the chanting has stopped." David was right, the woman's high-pitched scream still echoed as they moved in on her, but the overpowering chanting had stopped.

She didn't try to move as the four men stepped up to the altar; she just sat there staring and howling at them with a look of hatred in her eyes.

"Hey bitch, calm the f..." Dickie was going to grab her face to shut her mouth when a larger set man in deep-red robes came charging from behind the organ.

The man never had a chance as the remarkably agile Dickie, spun two full circles in what seemed to be one movement. The large intruder dropped to his knees as dark blood came pouring out of a gash across his neck as he looked down at his chest. The hilt of Dickie's blade was resting firmly against his chest, held in place by the metal now struck directly into his heart. Unable to sound a word, the man toppled to the ground dead.

"Damn it, Dickie, how the hell are we gonna find out what's going on if we kill everyone?" David asked as he looked down at the dead man's robes.

"At least it shut this wench up."

He was right, she had become silent the second the man charged into the room.

"Roll him over." Brett wanted to see if the man had anything that could shed some light on this mess.

David and Dickie bent over and rolled the large body onto its back. There wasn't much to see, the man was obese by most standards, bald and his face was shaved clean. The robes he wore were peculiarly simple except for the orange flames that flowed from the lower half. His face was what held Brett's attention. This man had the same markings on his face the woman on the altar did. Looking up, he realized she was no longer there.

"Where did she go?" Brett asked.

To all of their amazement, she had slipped away leaving the altar bare. Stepping out from behind David, there was no way to stop her as she knelt and picked up the dagger the man had run in with. She started chanting something none of the men could understand. David went to grab the blade from her hands as pain lanced through Brett's forearm, but she was too quick. She drove the tip directly into her own chest as her chanting barely altered in the slightest. Looking at them with widening eyes, she slowly fell to her knees as the strength in her legs drained out. Blood ran down her bare legs and pooled at her knees before her head finally dropped and she fell silent.

"OK, now that is some crazy shit." David took a step back as her body no longer moved. "You OK, Boss?"

Brett looked at his men and then his arm, the pain was already beginning to dissipate as he flexed the fingers of his hand.

"Never mind me. We need to figure out what is going on around here, and quickly." Brett looked back at his men as he said it. "Witch, you take David back around that organ and see what you can find. Dickie and I will stay here and see if there is anything in some of these books on the floor."

All the men nodded as they turned to go, when suddenly a deep laugh began to come from the woman's body. At first it was only a chuckle, then it became a full-out roar as her head lifted and looked at them. Light flashed through Brett's vision as a fire erupted beneath the skin of his forearm. Dropping to one knee, Brett grabbed his arm as the building itself began to shake. Dust and bits of paint and wood began to rain all around them as the sounds of wood cracking mixed with her laughter. Her face had changed as the markings were no longer there, replaced by black veins that ran all over her face to the black holes she now had for eyes. It began to speak in a language more disturbing than her chanting had been as she lifted her hand and pointed directly at Brett. All four men were now crouching, trying to keep their balance as the world seemed to shake around them. Her voice began to rise as her face contorted in anger. The yelling began to echo so loud around the room they could feel the vibrations mixed with the tremors of the floor as her body began to lift off the ground with no aid from her arms or legs.

She was almost back on her feet, now shrieking loud enough to shatter glass when the left side of her face exploded and her body dropped to the floor. Witch quickly put his revolver away as the woman's face slowly returned to what it had originally been. Without saying another word, Witch and David broke off to see what they could find in the back of the building. Brett and Dickie began rummaging through the books scattered around the altar. All four of them moved as quickly as they could, each visibly shaken by what they had already found, and disturbed by what else may lay ahead.

Chapter Twenty

1454 Hours, Avos 8, 2258

Outpost Gamma, Ten Miles Southeast of Fort Frozen Heart

RELAXING ON A REAL BED, with real medication, and surrounded by real allies for the first time in what felt like months was a welcome feeling in Charlie's mind. The harrowing events of the past week were not quick to leave her dreams, but the drugs used to calm the pain in her leg were doing the trick.

"How's that leg of yours feeling now?" The Captain slid a small fold-out chair next to the bed she was laying on.

The man, before all this happened, already had years of military stress drawn on his face. Now he looked aged a dozen years in a few days. Dark circles surrounded his eyes. His hair, she would swear was an entire shade grayer, but his eyes had a determination in them that wasn't there before.

"It feels better, Sir. Thank you."

The other men who had accompanied the Captain were each busy with various duties. Some were studying maps and writing notes. Between bouts of sleep, she figured she had counted at least three men on guard, running on three shifts.

"Where exactly are we sir? I know we are south of the fort, but how, in such little time, did you guys set this up?

"That's an easy one, Sergeant. During our time sitting on our thumbs, waiting for the Republic bastards to come to us, I had these vacant outposts set up." The man sat back in his small chair and crossed his arms over his chest as he looked at the ceiling of the room and sighed. "At first, I wanted to set up scouting patrols that extended farther than just our protection. When the shit hit the fan, well, I realized they worked great for escape outposts. Far enough and secluded enough that there is no reason for them to come looking for us, but close enough for those who knew about them to make it, if they could."

It sounded as though it made sense to her, but any lingering doubts she had, she would have to stow away for later. These men had saved her, and it was her duty to help them in any way she could.

"Now that we have given you plenty of time to rest up, tell me what happened to you after the attack."

The Captain had all his attention turned to her now.

"Yes, Sir. Well, I was pulled from the rubble by a maintenance man who called himself the Fiddler."

Her gut sank, and a ball caught in her throat as flashes of the last memories from the top of that tower drove her mind away from the present.

"Hey, Charlie, you okay?" The Captain had a worried look on his face as she realized she wasn't talking anymore.

"Um, yeah. Sorry, Sir. Well, after I was dragged out,

me, the Fiddler, and two others escaped out a maintenance door on the western side. We tracked over the river to a hidden alcove where they had stashed the ATV you saw me ride in on."

"Those must have been the ATVs we lost over the last several months. Interesting, bastards. Continue."

Over the next several minutes, she recollected everything she could to the man of her assault at the hands of the pastor and his patrons. After working through all the story, the Captain had one of the men bring a map so they could establish exactly where it was, and who may be up there.

"Are you sure this is where you were?" The Captain pointed to the hill not far from their fort.

Looking at it now on the map, she was surprised at how secluded that village had been.

"Yes, Sir. I wouldn't forget it for the world. I'm just lucky that I got out alive."

The Captain rolled up his map and took a long breath as he sat pensively in thought. A look of concern burned creases into the man's face.

"We are all glad you made it out. Tell me though, are you sure the others are dead?"

"Of course, Sir. They had been drained of all their blood before I even woke up." She thought about her answer one more time. "Now that I think about it, I don't remember seeing the Fiddler there among the dead, though. He could have been somewhere. I didn't look for that long before getting my ass out of there."

The memory of only one ATV still being in that alley returned, but she decided she would keep silent, for now.

The Captain got up and started a short pacing in front of her bed.

"Looks like there are wolves at the door and wolves at our back. What are we going to do about this?"

"Are you asking me, Sir?"

The man looked down and gave her a smile a father would a child who said something silly, yet adorable at the same time.

"We've already made contact with the officers at Fort Steel Heart, and they are readying plans for our recent neighbors. As for those freaks sacrificing our men to some unknown 'being', I think maybe we should pay them our due respects. What do you think about that, Sergeant?"

"Sounds like a plan to me, Captain. I'm not sure how much help I will be."

She looked down at her knee and knew it would be a while before it was at full strength. Flexing it enough to move, she was amazed at how much the medication kept the pain at bay.

"Don't worry about that. There are enough of us here itching to get back into the action. I can't think of a thing these men here would rather do than teach a few blood hungry priests a lesson or two. As for you, we need someone to point out to us who to shoot and who to, well use your imagination."

With that statement, she could hear life return to his demeanor. She doubted that she would be useful on a mission into the hills, but he was right about one thing. The images of 'Righty' and the 'Quiet one' still burned behind her eyes. Someone had to punish these people for what they had done and she would make sure she was there to see it.

"I'll be right by your side, Sir. Every step of the way." Just saying that brought strength and resolve to her body, even if it was going to be short-lived.

"I count on it, soldier. We all count on it." The aging

soldier turned and started to make his way to the men going over the maps. "Plus there, Charlie, no one is allowed to make sacrifices out of my men, other than me."

She watched him walk away as his words made its way through her mind. Was this entire war nothing but a large sacrifice for nothing in return? Was it going to be nothing but a giant stalemate built on the graves of millions of men and women? Damn the gods if they thought she was going to let that happen. She would make sure they paid for it a thousand times over, one battle at a time.

Chapter Twenty-One

0709 Hours, Juin 28, 2258
Miavlaco, Azhana

THE SILENCE that followed the shot was astounding to Kris' ears. The image of the man's head exploding as the lead slammed into it, seared into the back of his eyes. The guard's body had dropped to the ground instantly, and his teammates had made quick work of disposing of the remains. A small nod in his general direction from the Sergeant was the only indication that he had done well, and probably the only one he'd ever get. If he had done well, why did he feel so wrong?

Looking down at his hands, it was surprising how white they were. A tingling like little needles trickled through as the blood rushed back, returning them to their original color. Had he been squeezing the rifle that tightly? Why can't I stop them from shaking? Kris looked down at his still clean palms as holding them steady seemed impossible at the moment. He knew that joining the military to fight in the war would put him in this situation. Few people in battle could return home with their hands clean. Did he think he would be that lucky?

All through his childhood, he had been taught the good work of the true God. Wasn't he supposed to make peace with his fellow man and lead a good life? Here he laid, looking down the scope of a rifle, ready to take the life of another human being. Was this the work that he was meant to do? Cautiously, he put his one free hand into his shirt and felt for his medallion.

"God gives me the strength to do what I have to," Kris whispered to himself.

There wasn't anything else moving around the temple or the streets that led to it. The whole city seemed dead and empty. He wondered how the others were doing inside. Did they find much resistance, or was that man just the remnants of this city's last defense? Was there anything he could do if they needed his help? Taking a deep breath, he knew he had to trust in the fact that they had done this a hundred times. Each of them was a veteran of more than one hundred missions and had the blood of a thousand men on their hands. Now he was one of them, with a body count of one. How high would that number go? Would he become a stone cold killer?

A barely noticeable vibration rattled his watch as the face of it turned red. The men inside the temple were ready to exit. Moving his scope up and down from the streets to the rooftops, he could not see anyone in sight. With a return signal sent, the faceplate went back to green, and he started packing his stuff. Heading down the stairs and clearing the second-floor room, he was finishing the trek down when he met with Ed guarding the front door to the library.

"They are on their way out; we gotta go."

Ed turned to him and nodded as he finished coming out of the stairwell. Checking both ways, Ed stepped out, and Kris followed as they turned down the street and headed to the rally point. They were to the second building down the block when a stream of smoke flew past them and blew the concrete wall apart. The concussion from the blast sent them tumbling out into the middle of the street where debris and smoke filled the air.

Gunfire mixed with the ringing of the blast as it pounded in his eardrums. Looking as hard as he could through the dust and smoke, Kris could see Ed kneeling in the street and firing down a side road.

"You alright?" Ed shouted as he fired off a few more rounds and got up and ran to Kris.

The shock of the blast bounced around the inside of his skull as the world spun before his eyes. Dirt scratched at his teeth and the taste of iron filled his mouth as he pushed himself to his feet. Finding his footing took a few steps as Ed helped brace them both with an arm around his back. With a few stumbles, both men raced their way toward the library.

"What's going on?" He knew he was shouting, but he could barely hear himself.

Everything sounded distant and muffled as they struggled to keep moving. The front door to the library was only a few dozen feet ahead.

"Ah!" Ed screamed as he toppled over, almost taking Kris with him.

Reacting on instinct, the fear for himself and his teammate unable to stop him, Kris spun, leveled his rifle, and started firing. The realization of what he was firing at didn't hit him until he saw the man on the top of the jeep fall and hit the ground. Buying them a few seconds, he reached down and grabbed Ed under the arm and started dragging him the rest of the way.

Turning into the building, he pushed Ed behind the front wall. He grabbed a grenade off the front strap of his backpack and hurled it at the approaching vehicle. The new gunner fired off a few rounds that hit the top of the doorway before the explosion shook the ground.

Looking down at Ed seated on the floor, he could see he was in bad shape. He had taken two rounds. The first looked like it tore through part of his left leg, halfway up his thigh. A second round had struck him behind his left shoulder. The pain stretched across his face as he tried to reach down to his leg.

"How bad is it?" Kris asked.

His mind had frozen. Here in front of him, his team-mate was bleeding out on the ground and no matter how much he tried, he could not concentrate on the next step.

"I don't know; I can barely reach down to see my leg you stupid fuck. Help me tie it off!"

Ed's calm-under-pressure demeanor was quickly spilling as fast as his blood pooled under him. Kris reached for Ed's uniform and pulled on the tourniquet attached to his leg. Time was going to be running out soon. Would the others be able to help?

Grabbing a square bio-cloth, he leaned his partner over and applied it to the opening in his left shoulder. Using some quick-drying sealant, he temporarily closed the wound.

"Fuck, that's going to sting for a while. Did you get those bastards with that grenade?"

The pain in Ed's face seemed to fade just a little bit.

"I-I'm not sure. I didn't get a good look before I came back to you."

The sudden thought that he hadn't looked hit him like

a slap in the face. Seeing the look of annoyance on Ed's face, he grabbed his rifle and made his way out the door.

Smoke and dust still hung in the air from both explosions as he tried to find a target or any sign of hostiles. Through the haze, he could see the front of the jeep burning as it laid on its side. The grenade must have rolled under and exploded near one of the tires. A man laid dead and mangled against the sidewalk having been tossed from the vehicle as it turned over. As Kris got closer, he could see the driver was still inside. At least what remained of him as his upper body pressed against the front windshield and the rest was behind the front seat. His body count was now up to four.

Slowly backing his way out, he made it back to the library where Ed remained seated on the floor.

"Looks like I got them all, you going to be able to move?"

He looked down and could see his teammate's face was becoming paler the longer he remained there.

"Doesn't look like I have a choice. If we don't get to the Sergeant and the others, I'm a dead man." He lifted his good arm and with help made it to his feet. "Better get a move on, we have a lot of ground to cover."

With Kris leading the way, they stepped into the doorway and looked around. The dust still made everything hazy, but it was fading. A searing pain tore through Kris' arm as he tumbled sideways and crashed to the floor. Using his good arm, Ed returned fire as he fell to his knees and shoved the door shut. Bullets crashed through the wood and shattered the glass that filled the windows. Looking at his left arm, Kris could see where the bullet had entered and exited. Damn, it hurt a lot more than he thought it would. He was doing better than Ed was though. The man, a fierce determination on his face, looked as white as the ghost he was soon to become.

"Get your ass up those stairs man! I'll hold them as long as I can. Make it to the roof and find the others." He started coughing and struggled to set himself against the wall. "The mission is over, get out of here!"

"I can't leave you like this. It's not right." Fear and sadness was filling his heart as more bullets tore through the front door.

"It hurts doesn't it? Never thought it would be me, but I'm not the first who didn't make it home. I'm sure as hell not going to be the last." The strength in Ed's face wasn't fading at all. "Don't make this the end for both of us. Get out of here son. Now!"

Kris got to his feet and crouched as he turned to head up the stairs. Looking back at Ed, he couldn't believe what he was about to do. Even more gunfire erupted outside the door. This time it didn't tear into the building. The bullets didn't seem to hit the building at all.

"Hey, you two lovebirds in there, you haven't started without us yet have you? Dickie here doesn't have the camera set up yet!" David's voice could have been the sound of the God itself for the relief that fell over Kris as he crashed to the ground.

Chapter Twenty-Two

1125 Hours, Avos 9, 2258
Fort Frozen Heart, Northwest Azhana

THE COLD BIT hard into their hands as they picked up razor-sharp stone after razor-sharp stone. Snow swirled around in circles as the wind swept down from the hills across the river making it feel so cold that they may freeze if they stopped working.

Will stole a chance to look around as he caught his breath from the heavy lifting. The six of them who shared a cell together now joined a dozen more battered soldiers turned prisoners. Some he recognized by name, some only by sight, but they weren't Charlie.

That dreadful feeling of sorrow was trying to sink in deeper with every rock he lifted. Taking a deep breath before lifting, he was at least thankful it smelled fresher here. Inside their cell, the body odor of the men was becoming overpowering with days of hard labor. At least their captors had taken the liberty of removing all the bodies to prevent the smell of death taking hold of the fort.

They had succeeded in removing most of the rubble from the battle and explosion. A few men had even been pulled to work on reconstruction, repairing where the weakened wall threatened to fall.

"Ah, fuck these god-toting bastards. My back hurts so much; my hands can barely move. Fuck!" Sergeant Walker's mood was deteriorating hourly. Will was glad his smug face wasn't trying to pick a fight with him as much anymore. "What the fuck are you shaking your head at big boy?"

"Nothing. Now keep your mouth shut." Will whispered as loud as he could. Two of the guards had turned to look at them but didn't make a move to check things out, yet. "Things are bad enough as it is, we don't need you running your mouth."

Will tried to end it by going back to work and moving another stone. The weather and forced labor hadn't done anything to help his injuries. His shoulder still ached as it limited most of his movement, and his joints felt eighty years old.

"You think these cry ass, religious zealots are going to do anything to us? They can't do anything without first getting some divine intervention. Why else would we be alive?" The madman was now looking around with his arms held wide, just asking for a fight. "I'm not the only one who's tired of this horseshit, am I right?"

All the men just tried to survive; now they were trying to distance themselves from what was probably a clear death sentence. The two guards, who had noticed Walker's first outburst, were now swiftly making their way over. Everyone moved as far as they could away. All eyes were on

Walker and his two new fans. Surprising even himself, Will didn't move at all.

"Ah, did I hurt someone's feelings? Maybe we should sit and close our eyes. Maybe if we listen hard enough…" He couldn't finish the statement as the butt of a rifle drove straight into his gut, dropping him to his knees.

"Shut that mouth of yours, wild man. Many things can happen to a prisoner out here." The guard looked around to make sure everyone was watching. Quietly, Will had made his way closer to the men. "Harsh weather like this has a way of tragically cutting men's lives short. We wouldn't want that to happen, now would we?"

Much to Walker's credit, all he did was return a toothy grin to the man as he worked his breath back into his lungs. Some joked that he had a smile only his mother could love. Knowing how angry he was making their captors, Will even found a place in his own heart for it.

"Whatever you say, sir, wouldn't want to impede on your afternoon prayers with my ramblings. I'll get right back to my chores."

The guard turned, but not without slamming the Sergeant across the chin with his elbow. Still, the man could do nothing but laugh. Moments later, they were all back at work.

"You crazy metal head, you trying to get yourself killed?"

Will helped the man pick up another piece of rock as his breathing returned to normal.

"Nah, just wanted to show these others what I suspected from the beginning. As I said, they can't do anything without orders, we could practically stand here and pick our noses. Until they get some divine order from above, they are no more dangerous than kids with pop guns."

Will wasn't sure he agreed, but looking at the man with only a bloody lip from two days of mouthing off, maybe there was a method to his madness.

"Look here Will. You and I are the only strong ones here." For once, Walker was whispering so only they could hear. "I'm not only talking about moving these fucking rocks. If anything is going to get done around here to help our situation, it's going to happen because of us. If you're with me, then we have to start looking for a way out of here."

"Help should be on the way soon. Word has to have made it to the capital. They'll send forces to help push them back." Even saying it made Will think it wasn't going to be that easy.

"Let me tell you a secret. No one is coming for us, Sergeant. The other gunners and I had been keeping tabs before these fucks came; we haven't gotten resupplies in more than three months. They aren't coming for us; we've been written off."

"Are you sure?" Will didn't know to be worried or angered. Probably both.

The look in Walker's eyes told him enough. They were alone, and it wasn't looking good. He might be a loud mouth and aggravating, but if it came to a fight for their lives, he was a man you wanted on your side. Will wasn't so sure about the other survivors. Most of them were young, and after the events of the last several days, most looked a step away from death. If things didn't improve, they would all be halfway into the ground soon enough.

"OK, we need to come up with some plans." Will whispered. Both men stayed within whisper range as they continued their work. "The weather isn't going to get any better, and I sure as well don't want to die out in the open just as easily as I can in here." Will tried to keep one eye on the guards as he continued to conspire with his newfound partner.

Sergeant Walker nodded his agreement but stayed quiet. They had a lot to consider and not much time to do it. Would they try to get them all out? Who would they leave behind? How would he return to look for Charlie? Lost in the world of his thoughts, Will never noticed the motorcade that approached until all the soldiers of the fort started yelling and straightening their appearance.

"Hey, shit for brains, snap to!"

Walker grabbed Will by the shoulders and pulled him back with the rest against the nearest wall. Whoever it was, seemed important.

Ten vehicles in all pulled into the opening that used to be the barricaded front gate. Three light armored personnel carriers with their mounted roof guns led three luxury black cars. The styling on them reminded Will of the ones used by politicians when they came to the city trying to buy the people's votes. Behind the black cars, four heavy armored war machines followed. If anyone tried to interfere with this motorcade, they had better bring some large firepower.

"Who the fuck are these assholes?" Walker asked the question on everyone's mind.

"No idea, but whoever it is, definitely has everyone's attention." Will watched as several armed guards opened the door to the middle vehicle.

Surprisingly, the person who stepped out was not dressed to match the importance brought about by their appearance. Emerging from the vehicle was a man or woman, impossible for Will to tell from this distance, dressed in a simple black cloak with a white sash around their waist. The hood of their robe was pulled over their head, revealing nothing to any onlookers standing more than a few paces away. Watching how the soldiers reacted, signaling some prayer motion with their hands, Will figured it was some high ranking church official.

Within moments of this official's surprise arrival, General Sally arrived at the front of the fort, rushing and looking all the worst for it. Imagining what the man sounded like, winded and embarrassed, brought a slight chuckle to Will.

"Ah, look, our pretty little General is getting all bent out of shape. Maybe he will want Private Teller to sing him a nice little lullaby to calm his nerves." For once, the private showed a bit of personality as he punched the Sergeant in the shoulder. Even amid all this, Walker was still trying to bring life to these men.

It didn't take long before whatever conversation they were having near the motorcade, turned sour. The General was now pacing back and forth, yelling, or at least speaking loudly enough that Will could almost make out what was going on. Whatever it was, Will wasn't sure he wanted to know. First the Church was involved, and he didn't like the thought of that, second, whatever the Church wanted, it made an esteemed follower angry enough to argue back. These must be some bad orders.

Just as quickly as the motorcade had arrived, the robed man and his armed escort began filing back into their vehicles.

"Well, that was damn short. I was hoping I'd be subjected to some Holy Conversion tonight, being that I've never been in the presence of such a holy man before. Sounds kind of fun if you ask me." Walker puffed his chest out and imitated the hand motions of the men below as the other captives began to disperse back to their work.

"Don't wish too hard, with our luck, you never know what we are going to get," Will replied to the Sergeant.

The show was over, and Will figured he had a lot of thinking left to do. If they were going to get out of here, whatever they did, it would have to be perfect.

"Hey, big guy!" Walker whispered loudly. "Trouble at two o'clock."

Will looked up, and walking right toward him was General Sally. The man looked pissed: cheeks red, his eyes were squinted right at Will, and if the man had a gun he looked willing to use it. Will put down the rock he had lifted and waited for the short man to arrive.

"Alright, you pile of godless inbreeds, make yourselves useful and file back to your holding cells." The man pointed off as if they didn't know where to go.

"I thought you wanted us out here, day and night until we fixed this little mess we created, or am I forgetting something?" The little man's eyes shot daggers at Walker as the big man poorly held in a chuckle.

"You will not talk back to me, you will do as I say!" The General's face was now completely red, matching his eyes. Without warning, his tone changed as a smile slowly raised from the corner of his mouth. "If you would prefer it, I could omit you from the list of available prisoners. I've heard it's a long fall after a short walk off these walls. Any volunteers?"

"No, the Sergeant is just a bit loose with his tongue when he gets tired after a day's worth of work. Thank you for letting us rest early today." Will stepped back and tried to place himself in front of Walker, to hopefully keep him quiet.

"Oh, you'll be thanking me later." General Sally's face softened as the corner of his lips began to curl up. "Soon, you'll be wishing you were still moving these rocks. Now get out of my sight, or I'll start changing my mind."

The others followed Will's lead as they headed back to

their cells. Something big had happened, and this might be their only opportunity.

"What are you doing, Will?"

"You didn't figure it out? Whoever that was from the Church just ordered the General to send us somewhere. We might have a chance out of here." Will whispered the best he could to the men, his heart was pounding as plans started going through his mind. "Trust me on this one. Just tell everyone to get ready and keep quiet."

Will hoped he was right, the General had told him enough, and he bet the man didn't even know it. Will just needed to be right, for once.

Chapter Twenty-Three

2217 Hours, Juillet 3, 2258
Fort Forward Trinity, Edge of Republic Territory

THE NIGHT HUNG like a thick wool blanket on the base as men seemed eager to stay undercover and drink their night away. Normally, the barracks and rows of cafeteria benches were lined with soldiers. Those who were coming off day shift quickly finding enjoyment among their squadmates over games of cards and refreshments that would make them regret what they did that night when they awoke the next morning. This evening though, everything was eerily quiet, but none of it mattered to Brett.

On the night they had arrived back at the base, the only thing that concerned him was the safety of his men. Medics rushed Ed and Kris to the surgical tent where each went into surgery immediately. Kris had come out quickly, shaken more by the reality of things than the new stitches that adorned his left arm. Ed, on the other hand, had been under the knife for a couple of hours.

While he waited for word from the medics, Private Erickson had come and requested that he report for debriefing before the night was through. Accordingly, Brett had told Erickson where the General could shove his debriefing, and that, if he had issues with the reply, he would know where to find him. No one had come to see him the rest of the night.

Tonight was a different matter. Once the sun had gone down, and his men were winding down for the evening, Brett began making his way to the General himself. Private Erickson was halfway to him when they ran into each other on the street.

"Sergeant Brett sir! The General…"

The look on Brett's face stopped the Private in his tracks.

"I know he wants to see me, you stupid dimwit. Where do you think I'm going?"

He stormed right past the now frozen man, who after a second, turned and followed. The General's quarters were just ahead, and nothing was going to stop him from discovering what in this world was going on.

Entering the three stall hangar the General called his quarters, Brett wasn't too surprised when he saw men scurrying between stations. It did stop him for at least a second when it looked like the number of "church" representatives had doubled. Most of the men didn't notice him enter until Private Erickson accidentally let the door behind him slam shut. Everyone stopped and stared at the two men. At first it was a look of annoyance for disturbing their duties, then most of them didn't stop looking at the Sergeant once they saw who he was.

The looks were a mix of horror and shock. What the hell were these guys problem? Ah, fuck'em. Brett turned and stormed up the stairs to the General's level. Barging in, he wasn't surprised to see he was in the same company as usual.

"You have a lot of nerve calling me to see you after the shit you pulled!"

The state of the General's face didn't change as Brett charged in, not waiting for the private to announce his arrival.

"Sir, General, sir! I give you Sergeant..." The private forgot to think before getting into the middle of the conversation.

"I know who he is Private. Now get out of here. I don't want to see you again, and next time, I won't be so easy if it takes you two days to get my men in front of me."

The Private swallowed hard, saluted, and ran down the stairs.

"Now, where were we? Oh yes, you're angry about something it seems Sergeant."

"You bet your ass I'm angry." Every second he stood in front of the General, and his lackey from the church made him want to unload every round he had on him. "The mission was to get behind enemy lines, locate a well-known temple, capture or eliminate high-ranking targets, and get the fuck out."

"And did you succeed?"

The General had a smile on his face again. The overwhelming smell of alcohol filled the room.

"Succeed?" Brett was furious. "We walked into the middle of a fucking bloodbath! The city was half empty; the temple was practically unguarded, and why was this? Everyone was already fucking dead! There was some mass suicide or ritual." Brett didn't even realize he was pacing back and forth. "It looked like they buried half the fucking city in an unmarked grave outside the temple. Then on the way out, I almost lose two men because reinforcements came out of nowhere. Fuck!" His blood was boiling in his veins. Squeezing and releasing his hands wasn't helping.

"Did you find any more evidence similar to what you've found before? Was there any way to tell if the people were brought there by their will or forced into submission?" Father Rondeau asked before he sat back, crossed his legs, and relaxed as he stared at Brett.

"How the fuck should I know? Most of the bodies we found were long dead before we ever set foot into that hell-hole. The ones we did run into did their damnedest to complete some sacrifice and take us out with them." The memory of that young woman stabbing herself in the chest, then rising and causing an earthquake under their feet played through his mind. Brett hesitated a second as his eyes met the holy man's unblinking yet relaxed stare. How much did he want to reveal to this man? "All I know, is there were a lot of flames drawn everywhere, tattoos or drawings on the people's faces, and a shit ton of bodies."

Father Rondeau didn't even seem surprised at the information.

"Well, maybe we'll have to check our sources better next time. I do hear your men are going to make it, no?" The General got up from his couch to look out his front window into the night beyond.

"Next time? Check out your sources? We are lucky there is even going to be a next time for Ed and Kris. How the fuck can you be so wrong to send us in, and every bit of your information is 'incorrect'?"

Brett slammed his fist into the nearest end table to further bring the attention to himself.

"Watch how you talk to the General!" For the first-time, Father Rondeau rose his voice and tried to talk above Brett.

"Watch how I talk? You little piece of shit. Don't you

go telling me what I can and can't do. I have more blood on my hands in the name of your fucking church than you will ever understand. Don't get me wrong, I'm willing to get more on my hands right now." The look in Brett's eyes went red as he reached to his belt.

"Hold on there, Sergeant. The church is only here to offer guidance. No reason to take your frustration out on him. I'm the one who sent you in; you can be angry all you want with me. You're lucky I allow these little tirades of yours." Something was different in the man as he left the window and picked up his glass of wine. "Just don't you start forgetting that I am in charge here. You answer to me, not the other way around."

A silent message passed between Brett and the General as they looked at each other eye to eye. He was right, and Brett knew it. There wasn't a thing about it he liked, but what could he do? A few options flashed through his mind, most of them ending badly for everyone.

"The Church will continue to look into this my General. There is evil at work here. We do not know how deep it runs, but it is our mission to stamp it out no matter how far it goes, or where." The man's snake like grin appeared for a second as he looked at Brett, then his look softened as he went back to kissing the ass of the man in charge.

"Now that we all have something to think about, you may want to head back to your men, Sergeant." The General started pouring himself another glass. "Give your-selves time to rest. You're going to need it as we are almost complete on collecting a last bit of intel on a better target."

"More lies you mean?"

Anger flashed in the General's eyes but quickly disappeared.

"Again, rest yourselves up, but I wouldn't plan on leaving the base or finding yourselves alone out there."

The General tipped his glass toward Brett, and Father Rondeau had an ironic smile on his face.

"Why? You gonna arrest us for not giving two shits about you or this piece of filth's lies?"

That took the smile right off the Father's face.

"Oh, it wouldn't be us you'd have to worry about." The cocky voice came from behind him. Turning it was a man he recognized instantly, Trevor Rilinger. The only man Brett knew with more blood on his hands than his own. He enjoyed it way too much as well. "You know, you shouldn't have made such a show when you killed those men entering the temple, and then all the people inside. Just because you hate their religion doesn't mean woman and children needed to die."

"What the fuck are you talking about? That's not what went on, who told you that bullshit?" Brett asked, but in a room full of human filth like this, he was quick to put the answers together.

"It's all over the news. A rogue squad of men resembling your team, but of course denied by us, entered a sacred Temple in the city and slaughtered everyone in it. Upon leaving, they burned the whole thing to the ground. It was all caught on video too." Trevor sat in a chair opposite the General, grabbed some cheese and started chewing on it. "The news won't stop playing it. Both sides are calling for an investigation and hanging of whoever did this."

The anger was getting so built-up in his chest, Brett hadn't even noticed that his hand had moved to his sidearm and knife until the eyes of Father Rondeau went as wide as dinner plates.

"Now Sergeant, think about this carefully. No one

knows your team was there. There are rumors that you were gone and returned around the same time, but there is no proof." The anger in Brett's face must have come across clear, as the General had his hands up in defense.

"For now at least," Trevor's smile never left his face for a second as he continued to eat the cheese.

"Go to your men. Check on the injured. I'd keep this bit of information quiet if I were you. You'll be hearing from us soon."

Brett turned and left without looking back. He hoped soon would come later, and before then, he'd figure out a way to get them out of this mess.

Chapter Twenty-Four

———————————————

2015 Hours, Avos 9, 2258
  Small Unknown Town, Northeast of Fort Frozen Heart

CHARLIE and the rest of the Captain's team rolled to a stop about half a mile from the first building within the village's boundary. In total, there were eight off-road ATVs each equipped with two soldiers a piece. Charlie rode on the back of the Captain's seat and looked around as he turned toward his men.

"Alright, you all know the drill. Fan out and follow us in." All his men locked their dead serious eyes on their leader. "Once we are in walking distance, me and the Sergeant will go in alone to check things out. Each of you comes in and secure as you move along. At the first sign of danger, target and destroy. We'll sort what remains after if we have to. Any questions?"

Charlie had a few, but at this point it was time to keep quiet. Remembering what she had seen of the town a few days before didn't give her a good feeling about returning.

'Righty' and the 'Quiet One' deserved better than they got, and who knew what happened to Fiddler. She was alive because of what they did. Now it was her turn to return the favor.

The Captain tapped his shoulder once and pointed forward as the ATVs roared to life and moved forward. Each vehicle broke off quickly and made their way into the woods. The studded tires were making easy work of the uneven ground.

Traveling with the Captain on the main road was far easier for Charlie than it had been before. Fully dressed now in white camouflaged battle gear, the biting winter air only bit at her cheeks as the rest of her felt warm and comfortable. Reaching down and massaging her knee, she was glad for where she was, even if it was front and center.

"The town is just ahead. It becomes congested with buildings quickly. We may want to slow down!"

She tapped his shoulder hoping he could hear her over the sound of the wind and engine. The Captain didn't turn or change the speed at all; he kept them moving forward, like a hound sniffing out its target.

It wasn't until they reached the first building that their vehicle reduced speed. Just as the village was when she had left it for the first time, the only thing present was a constant fog that hung low over the ground. An early-morning snow shower had blanketed everything with a fine coating of white powder, which showed no signs of movement within the village at all since the snow had fallen.

"Are you sure this is it? It doesn't look like anyone is here."

The Captain dismounted from the vehicle and allowed Charlie to slide forward to control the ATV. Unharnessing his rifle from the back, both soldiers moved cautiously forward.

"I'm sure this is it, Sir. Very few people were around when we showed up the first time. Mostly small kids until we entered the church."

For a town occupied by people who at first rushed to save her, and then tried to kill her, everything felt too quiet. The fog wasn't helping any either. With every step the two took, it seemed to grow thicker.

"It sure is damn foggy up here. Doesn't seem natural." The Captain whispered.

He was right. Charlie could barely see more than a building ahead. What sunlight came through the clouds above was choked out by the fog. Only the burning oil lamps along the side of the road let her know they were moving at all.

Without warning, the old soldier put his hand on the front of the ATV, and she hit the brakes quickly. He was looking around, sniffing the air like an old dog catching a whiff of something in the breeze.

"What's going on, Captain?" Her nerves were on such edge she was ready to jump at the slightest of sounds.

"Sssh."

Before anything else could be said, the familiar ping and echoing sound of gunfire bounced around them as a bullet slammed into the handlebars of the ATV. On instinct, the Captain opened fire on where he felt the shot came from as he moved to shield himself behind the engine block. Charlie, not able to move as fast, did the only thing she could, she rolled sideways off her seat and crashed to the ground beside him.

Screeching pain shot up her leg as she laid on the ground for a moment, flashing white lights sparkled in her sight as she gritted her teeth and pushed herself up.

"Fuckers, let us walk right into an ambush," The

Captain swore before three more rounds exited his rifle, and he ducked back down.

"There weren't that many here with rifles last time, Sir. What are we going to do?"

Just as if she had asked the wind, gunfire from all around the village erupted. Echoes bounced left and right, short bursts, long bursts, even a few screams filled the air.

"Our ticket out of here just arrived. Let's get you to some better cover shall we?"

Sliding his arm under hers, they were able to get her on her feet and to shuffle toward the nearest alleyway. A few bullets exploded as they hit the wood siding of the building next to them, causing them to shuffle faster.

"What do you want me to do Captain?" She had drawn the sidearm that he had given her, using the alley wall as a support; she stood there waiting for her orders.

"Stand right here is all I want you to do. Stay low and into the shadows as much as possible. The boys and I will clear this up. Can't be too many of them." An explosion from across the street, somewhere, got her to duck and regret it the second she did.

Wanting to say something about how she could help got lost as she opened her mouth just in time to see the man turn the corner, rifle up, and looking for targets. The gunfire continued its constant echoing as it made its way farther up the street. With each passing moment, the sound seemed farther and farther away. She wanted to see what was going on, get out there and make these people pay, just as she had promised. For now though, all she could do was listen and painfully edge her way to the building's corner. One painful step at a time.

Just as quickly as the gunfire had started, it stopped. The fog remained; it seemed worse now that a fire at the end of the village helped make the air that much thicker.

At times like this, she wished she had a radio. She had never liked being alone.

Peering around the corner of the building revealed nothing but dancing shadows in the lamp light. She felt if she stared hard enough, she could make out a building or two farther, but failed to recognize anything. Her patience was wearing thin as she decided that it wouldn't help if she stood here waiting.

Taking a cautious step out, back to the building's front, the next alley she swore would be as far as she would go. If anything had happened, she wanted to make sure she was not a sitting target. Slowly and quietly, she slid each foot side to side, wanting silence to be her friend where speed was not.

"You're only back a few days and already disobeying orders again, Sergeant?" His voice came from the fog, and without thinking, she stood stiff as if being inspected.

"Sir, no, Sir! Well, I didn't know how you were all doing, and I didn't want to be a sitting duck. Sorry, Captain. Hard for me to get used to not being in the fight."

"There will be time for that when we can finally get that leg of yours fixed up. For now though, everything looks clear." He turned and signaled for the man next to him to head back the way they had entered the village. "No one is hurt. Only about a dozen dead crazies. Let's keep moving. We need to see what's going on with this church of yours."

Charlie, the Captain, and two other men slowly made their way up the side of the street. For a village filled with the sound of war a moment ago, it now was eerily quiet. Smoke lingered in the air as the four crept along.

"There it is, sir," Charlie pointed to the central building ahead but stopped as if frozen.

"Something wrong, Sergeant?"

The others stopped as well and waited for her to answer.

"I'm not sure, Sir. Just did any of you damage this building?"

"Shouldn't be more than a few holes that plaster wouldn't fix. Speak your mind, Charlie."

Nothing was as she remembered. The structure looked to be on its last legs. Large fissures in the hard-pane ground stretched like the legs of a spider. The front door cracked at its center where the pressure from the frame crushed it as the front of the building sagged toward the ground.

Stained glass littered the ground at their feet and mixed with the recently fallen snow. The rear of the building itself sank partially into the ground, giving everything the appearance of leaning backward.

"You mean to say it wasn't like this just a few days ago?" The look on the officer's face was just as evident as the sound of his voice. "Are you sure about this Charlie?"

"I'm positive, Sir. I mean it was standing perfectly straight last time."

She couldn't figure it out. Could she be wrong? No way possible she could have dreamt the whole thing up. She had to take a look. The four soldiers moved forward, slowly and cautiously approaching the structure ahead.

Nothing in the front of the building gave evidence that the church had been in any better shape in a long time. With a nod of his chin, Charlie and the Captain held guard as the two others worked the broken door open. The second the two men pulled it free from the frame an unmistakable smell overcame the four soldiers.

"Oh my god, where is that coming from?" The younger of the two soldiers coughed as he spit up into the snow.

"That's it!"

Without waiting, Charlie lifted her pistol and flashlight

and entered the building. Crouching under the sagging frame, the smell of death grew stronger and stronger with every step she took. Dust and dirt kicked up as the four of them moved deeper inside.

Everything was the same as Charlie remembered it, except the floor sloped horribly toward the altar now, and a large fissure cracked its way through the center of the aisle. Flashing their lights to the side where Charlie pointed, the others could see the bodies of those killed either still seated, or sprawled out on the floor.

"Shit, it's just like you said, Charlie." The Captain stayed right behind her.

At the altar, the crack in the floor ended as it split the center rock table in half. On top of it laid the young woman, her lip split from where Charlie had struck her while trying to get away. Her fist had left a cut on the woman's upper lip, but the new ornate dagger buried to the hilt in her chest was what had finished her off.

"Did that priest you were talking about do this?" The Captain was still right behind Charlie as she looked down at the young woman.

"That's a negative, Sir. Unless you're not talking about this guy."

Turning, they could see one of the other men pointing at a pair of feet sticking out from between a set of pews. Even in the dust and dirt, the elaborate blue of his robes stood out. Charlie turned back to the dead woman and noticed who had finished the job. Sitting against the back of the altar was one of the older men from the night before. Half his head was caved in from a rock that laid by him, but he was the only one close enough to have helped.

"This is worse than what I expected, Sergeant," The Captain stood wide-eyed as he absorbed the situation.

"Sir, I think there is something else going on around here," Charlie said.

"That I can agree with, and we are going to find out."

The four soldiers made their way back out the front after it was evident there was nothing left they could do. They had found the bodies of 'Righty' and the 'Quiet one', but whatever had destroyed the building, their bodies had suffered greatly and were no longer in a condition to move.

"Did anyone else see anything?" The Captain asked.

Most of the men that had accompanied them to the village had checked in at the church. The men looked quiet as if something had them spooked.

"Sir," one of the men shrugged as all attention turned to him. "There is something just outside the town you should look at."

"Speak up son, what is it?"

"I think you should come look, Sir."

Charlie couldn't imagine what could cause these men to act the way they were. Dread filled her stomach as the Captain nodded his agreement. Somewhere under this fog she knew the secrets just waited to be uncovered. As the remaining men turned to lead them to whatever it was they had found, a small tremble began to shake the ground under their feet. Earthquakes this far north? Something didn't feel right.

Chapter Twenty-Five

0630 Hours, Juillet 10, 2258
  Fort Forward Trinity, Edge of Republic Territory

"HOW ARE YOU FEELING THERE, ED?" Kris looked down at his bandaged comrade.

Morning had come early for him today as he fought the burning sensation of fatigue that clouded his mind. Most of the base was still moderately quiet, and no one had seen him make his way to the medical tents.

"Uh, I've been better."

He looked pretty roughed up though he was still one-hundred percent better than he was when Dickie carried him in. The doctors had been able to patch him up well. They saved his leg and said his vest and shoulder blade had stopped the bullet in his back from tearing through his heart or lung. Both of them were lucky to be still breathing. Just another minute and he would have left Ed in that house and run for his life. Did Ed know he would have left him? Did he care?

"That was a pretty bad scrap we were in back there, wasn't it?" Kris tried to fake a smile as he sat uncomfortably next to Ed's bed. His left arm was held up in a sling, and the doctor said it would be another day or so before he could put it back to some good use.

"Ha, we've seen worse as a team. Talk to David or Dickie. They'll let you know how bad things have gotten. If you get them going too much, they'll have you believing they've died and come back several times." Ed got that out just before coughing shook his body. "Ugh… It sure does hurt though, I always seem to forget that part."

"Well, I just wanted to come in and check on you. Make sure you were alright." He started to stand, his emotions slowing him as if he had weights tied to each of his limbs.

"No, you didn't. Sit your ass back down and tell me why you're really here." Ed tried to sit up, but couldn't. The look on his face sure said it didn't matter if he sat up at all. Time to spill it.

"Um, back at the house, you know, just before the others showed up." Kris was seated in his chair again, now that he was finally speaking, he wished he was anywhere but right here. "You told me to leave you. Make my way up to the roofs and find the others. Well, I just."

"You would have done it. Another minute and I would have been in that room by myself." Ed was right, and Kris couldn't find the words, so he looked down at his feet. "Look, kid, don't get yourself all worked up wondering if it would have been the right choice. It's a war out there past that fence. Once the bullets start flying, each man has to make his choices. I can tell you I'm not proud of every one I've made. Shit, every man on this team has made more mistakes than they can even remember."

Kris thought about it. The whole team had years of

fighting behind them. Each had hundreds if not more deaths on their hands; maybe he wasn't alone in this. Would they have all made the same choice though?

"In the end, Kris, we are both alive and soon will be back out there to catch another bullet or two. No one on this team will fault you for a decision you never even got to make. What happened in that room is between me and you, and I'll let you in on a little secret." With his good hand, Ed waved him closer. "These docs got me on so many meds; I'm lucky I remember my name."

Sitting back, he noticed Ed's level headed and relaxed smile. He wasn't sure this talk made him feel any better, but no reason to not at least try.

Kris relaxed and retreated into the back of his mind. The more he thought about that few minutes of his life, the more he regretted it. But Ed's voice kept pushing back, repeating itself in his head. Ed dozed in-and-out of sleep as he tried to watch reruns of some show on the television. Neither of them noticed when the perfectly dressed Private Erickson stepped into the room.

"Sergeant Kris Bowman, I am here to escort you to the audience of the General. Please come with me." The man stood there at attention, his hard-set eyes trying to burn right through Kris. Ed awoke when the man started talking.

"Oh, the General. Moving up the ranks are you now, Sergeant?" Ed just smiled as if he made the best joke he'd ever heard.

Maybe the medications really were affecting his mind. Kris got up from his chair and followed Private Erickson out the door.

Chapter Twenty-Six

2149 Hours, Avos 9, 2258
  Small Unknown Town, Northeast of Fort Frozen Heart

A SMALL BREEZE whistled through the trees carrying with it small wisps of snow. What remained of the sunlight above, was fading as the soldiers stood in a circle, stone-faced and silent. After leaving the center of the village, Charlie and the Captain were led to a large hole dug in the thick growth of trees that surrounded the town.

"For fuck's sake, what happened here?" Most of the men wanted to look away, but the Captain seemed to grow angrier by the minute. "Anyone have a fucking clue?"

Nothing but silence moved between the soldiers.

"That has to be the entire town down there." Charlie could barely hold in the contents of her stomach as she looked into the pit.

Even in the darkness it was easy to see more than fifty naked and mutilated bodies left to the elements, to rot where they laid. Women, children, and men found their final resting place with their family and loved ones, but in a way no one would have ever imagined.

"Why is there no smell, Sir? Shouldn't there be a smell or something?" The outside air was cold and blustery with the newly forming breeze, but the soldier's face was as pale as a ghost. The man struggled to stand there and hoped for an answer that would comfort him.

"They are all frozen, private. Frozen Popsicles don't rot." The Captain started pacing behind the men.

Charlie could see him squeezing and releasing his hands as he chewed on something, anything he could think of, that would explain what laid before them.

"Sir, I think we need to report this as soon as we can." The officer stopped and looked at Charlie as she spoke. "Someone needs to learn about this. Maybe something can be done, find out who did this."

He started pacing again.

"It's easy to see who did this. Those crazy religious touting loon bags which are now laying in their own waste inside that damn church."

"But what happened to the church, sir? I swear it wasn't like that when I was here earlier."

"Good question. We'll get to that once we find someone who can tell us something about this whole shit-storm mess here."

He stopped to look down into the pit one more time.

"Fuck!" Bellowed one of the soldiers as he bent down and lost his lunch from earlier.

"OK, anyone have any ideas before we get out of here? Anything?"

The look on the soldier's faces told more than any of them could put into words. Each of them wanted to leave, and leave quickly. They knew death; they had seen it first hand, but when faced with the reality of such brutality, it was too much.

"Sir, there has to be another way out of here. If this village had been here for as long as it looks, then we would have known about it back at the base. They had to have gotten support from somewhere if we find that, we might find some answers," Charlie replied.

The Captain nodded his agreement but looked his men in the eyes. Half of them looked as if they were ready to go. Anything to get them away from this area. Looking around, the Captain worked every possible route out of the hills through his mind. South would lead them right back to the base, everything north was a sheer climb back up into the hills, and the trip east ended no more than a mile or two with a drop back to the river.

"Alright, Stevens and Markus, you head back and meet with the others. Get back to the outpost and start making contact with headquarters. Let them know you need to come in and get them this information. Tell them they need to send us a team or two to finish a sweep of this area. We can't leave a fox in the henhouse just because there is a wolf at the front door." The last bit he whispered to himself as he turned to survey the forest around him.

"What about the rest of us, sir?" Charlie figured they were going to be looking for something, and she did her best to hide the pain in her leg as she took a step closer to the man.

"Somewhere out here to the west that support of theirs is hiding. I say we go find ourselves a little more trouble. What do you say about that, Sergeant?"

The last comment seemed to brighten the mood of the Captain and the men around him. Charlie wasn't going to lie and say it didn't bump up her attitude as well. To show her agreement, she withdrew her sidearm and racked back the slide. The familiar sound of the metal locking into place echoed in the rest of the men as each prepped their weapons, and the team of soldiers started looking for whatever answers lay ahead. The question burning in their minds was, if what they had found was just the beginning, what else was in store for them?

Chapter Twenty-Seven

0745 Hours, Juillet 10, 2258
   Fort Forward Trinity, Edge of Republic Territory

KRIS HADN'T BEEN in the General's quarters since the night he learned of his first assignment. Nothing had changed other than there were more members of the church present. These men made him feel a bit more comfortable as if there were people around whom maybe felt the way he did. Without stopping, he was led upstairs where he found the General, Father Rondeau, and a man dressed in black battle attire. Something didn't feel right about the last one.

"Sergeant Kristofer Bowman, as you requested, sir." Pain shot through Kris' left arm as both men saluted.

"That will be all Private Erickson. Ah, good to see you, Kris. Come take a seat." The General seemed in a delightful mood as he swung his arm around and pointed to a plush leather chair.

The morning had just begun, and the man was

drinking already, but who was Kris to judge. Father Rondeau sat a few feet to his right and looked at him intensely, his gaze narrowed making Kris feel as if the man was trying to see what was inside of him. The third man seemed bored, yet after spending the last couple weeks with the others, he wasn't going to be fooled, he knew he was being watched.

"The God is glad to see you are doing well my son. I hope you know it was he who made sure the bullet did minimal harm as you fought hard for him." The look on Father Rondeau's face looked genuine.

"I'd call it shitty aim, but if that's what passes for the God nowadays." The third man looked pleased with himself, but the sudden look of anger on Father Rondeau's face showed differently.

"Ah, the plight of nonbelievers. Oh, that reminds me. How is that friend of yours, I think his name is Ed?" Surprisingly quick, the man's voice went back to soft and concerned. How did he know his name was Ed?

"He's doing well. Doctor said he was a lucky man. They are doing what they can for him. Thank you for asking." Kris looked around and could see all three men's eyes locked on him.

"Well, that's great to hear!" The General was quick to finish his glass of wine. "That is just terrific to hear. Your team is why we asked you here today. How are you liking it among some of our, let's say, most effective soldiers?" The General emphasized the last word as he poured himself another glass.

"Soldiers? I'd call them amateurs at best. Shit, that fat one is lucky he can roll himself out of bed every day." The man in black looked particularly pleased with himself.

"Please forgive Lieutenant Trevor Rilinger here. He has a bit of animosity toward others who give him and his team a challenge." The General got up to walk to the windows.

"Challenge! My men could kill an entire platoon of targets before these…"

"That will be enough, Lieutenant." The General raised his voice as his hard pressed eyes bore directly into the man. "Well, back to matters at hand. So how are they treating you there, Kris?"

"They are treating me well, Sir. It's a great team to work with; hardworking, loyal men, Sir. I couldn't be prouder to be with them." Pride tried working its way up his chest, but something told him this wasn't going to be a pleasant conversation.

"Ah, good, but I want to ask you about one thing you just said. Loyal. Do you know what it means to be loyal there, son?" The General was looking out at the runway in front of the building: watching men and women performing their daily routine.

"Loyal, sir? I'd say it is doing what you are told to do by those who you swore your allegiance to."

"Are you loyal to your God, Sergeant?" Father Rondeau moved in closer as he asked.

"Uh, I believe I am, sir." The sudden image of the man outside the temple, his head exploding rushed to Kris' mind.

"That's a good answer there, son." The General turned back to him as he spoke. "Let me tell you something you may not know about this 'loyal' team of yours. Now, I think in the pressure of the last couple weeks, and the heat of your first battle, this 'loyalty' you feel is misplaced. Do you know what happened during your mission that got you and Ed hurt?"

"Yes, Sir, I do. I filled it out in my field report." A strong urge of doubt and nausea was building up in his stomach as he tried to replay the whole mission in his head.

Was there something he missed? What are they trying to say?

"I'm not going to beat around the bush with you, son. I've received reports that what you saw from your position in the library may not contain the whole picture. I know you were up there, I read the other reports. The thing is Kris, a lot of people died in that Temple. It's all over the news that innocent woman, children, and men were all butchered and burned by a 'rogue' group. Did you see any of this?"

Nausea in Kris' stomach almost overcame him as he pictured an entire building of people burning. They didn't burn anything; that wasn't part of the mission. No one had told him anything about it. Wouldn't they have?

"No sir, I have no idea what you are talking about."

"That's what I thought my boy." The General stood silently and took a few more sips of his wine.

"I heard that an international committee is demanding the heads of the men responsible for this. They don't treat those convicted of war crimes nicely." Trevor smiled as he slid one finger over his throat from ear to ear.

"A true child of the God would never do something like this of his own free will, now would they, Kristofer." Kris turned to Father Rondeau as he spoke.

"Oh no, Sir. I wouldn't. But really, I know nothing of this. The temple was fine when I last looked at it before we left the library, and the others haven't said anything at all." Realizing he could be in extreme trouble had Kris' hands shaking just as bad as they did that day up in the clock tower.

"That's why we have you here today, Sergeant. None of us wants to believe you had any part in this." The General was now standing by the couch looking down at him. "The thing is, son; we don't want to believe anyone in our army could do that. In the end though, we need to know if we have a rogue team among us. That Sergeant of yours though is one stubborn son-of-a-bitch. He has his men, as they say, loyal to a fault. We need someone on the inside. Someone who will keep an eye out for us, and report anything that they think we should know."

Kris knew what the General was asking. He wanted him to spy on his team. Could he do this to them? What if they found out? What if what the General was saying was true? Did he want to be part of a team that would kill innocent women and children?

"Your God wants you to be truthful, Kristofer. Isn't doing the right thing the reason you joined the Army?" The soothing voice of Father Rondeau had its desired effect on him.

"I think I can do that, sir." He had his doubts but did he have the option to say no? "It may take me a bit to find out anything. They aren't going to be so open about secrets like this."

"We have faith in you, son. I will periodically and privately have a messenger come find you when we would like a report. Remember this needs to stay between you and us. We don't need the Sergeant learning about this and you becoming the tragic victim of some field accident. Now do we?"

The General was right. If they discovered what he was doing, he'd be a dead man. The General pushed a speaker button next to the couch to call Private Erickson.

Kris stood and saluted the General when the Private arrived to escort him out. Father Rondeau stood as well and took Kris by the shoulders and placed their foreheads together.

"The God will protect you, my son. He takes care of all those who obey." Kris tried to feel some comfort in those words.

"Thank you, Sir," Kris turned and walked out with the Private.

The men had been right: he was a spy for the General and his men. The thought of people burning alive in that temple, screaming with fear and pain, echoed in his head. Could they have done that? He didn't know, and the General's orders or not, he was going to keep his eyes and ears open.

Chapter Twenty-Eight

2314 Hours, Avos 9, 2258
   Unknown Temple, Northeast of Fort Frozen Heart

IT HADN'T TAKEN LONG for the team to find the trail. Not far from the burial site, but still moderately hidden by the tree growth was a distinct path that led west into the forest. The path itself was barely big enough for a standard ATV to fit through with the thick brush of pines and other leafless branches itching to fill in space.

Not wanting to waste too much time, the Captain decided it was better they make the trek on foot. Returning to get their vehicles would both delay their search, and make it easy to be spotted in the darkness. Each member of the team was well trained at night travel, and over the last few days, they found themselves in the dark more than the light. The only one in the group struggling, as they moved forward, was Charlie.

"Can you keep up there, Sergeant? We don't know how far we have to go." The man stopped to watch her limping forward as the other men continued moving along the trail as it grew steeper with every step.

"I don't think I have a choice now, Sir. Unless you want me to roll myself back down the hill, I'm staying with you." Gritting through the pain, she tried to smile at the man. She wasn't even sure he could see it that well.

"Your choice, soldier."

He threw her arm over his shoulder and helped her take some pressure off her knee as they moved forward. She knew she was a liability for the team, but she had to have answers. Why did all those people have to die? Who was in charge of all this? How come the others were strapped to chairs while they were willing to make a sacrifice of her on the altar? Too many questions and hundreds more unbelievable possibilities bounced through her head.

The group continued to move forward through the night. Between the cold weather, the dark sky, and the now constant wind, it felt as if they had been walking for hours. That, of course, couldn't be true as the Captain hadn't called for their first rest yet. No way, not in weather like this, right? She tried to put the thought out of her mind as she struggled along, now on her own as the Captain had moved forward to the front.

"Charlie!" The older man whispered as he tried to wave her forward.

The movements of the men at night were so coordinated she regretted not practicing it more when she and Will had worked together back at the fort. A few memories of the time they spent together flashed in her head and sank into her heart. The emptiness filled with a burning sensation as the sight of "Righty" and the others lying dead or dying, filled her mind.

"What's the matter, Captain?"

All her fatigue and exhaustion dissipated as she moved up to the front as fast as her busted leg would allow.

"Looks like we have a clearing just ahead. Large stone building is all we can see right now. Frankie says there are a few lamps burning inside, but not much else."

"Why are you telling me, Sir?" His sudden need to clear things with her confused her, but if he wanted her to say anything, it was that they needed to keep going.

"From his best guess, he says it looks like a large temple of some sort. You think maybe that priest man of yours was taking orders from someone up here?"

"Man didn't sound like he took orders from anyone, but the voices in his head, Sir. To me, I'd guess he thought he was saving everyone in the world with his words, but your guess is as good as mine." She looked at the men beside her, they had lost their hollowed looks from down in town and replaced it with an expression that said each of them was ready to go to work. "What's our next move, sir?"

She watched as their leader shifted on the balls of his feet as he thought it over for a minute. They still had a couple of hours before the sun would rise and at this point they didn't believe there was a chance any knowledge of what they had done below had made it this far. Maybe they didn't know anything about what happened below though she doubted it.

"Alright, we rest for ten, then split into two groups. You three go to the west of the building, the sergeant and Frankie will go with me to the east. Stay within the tree line and look for a way in." Each man kept their eye on him without a trace of questioning on their stern faces. "Keep the radios silent, but tap twice on the transmitter if you find anything. Meet back here in one hour if we haven't found a way in."

The next ten minutes were a mix of emotions for

Charlie. Her gut told her that entering that building was the last thing she should do, that nothing but horrors beyond what she had already been through, waited through those doors. Fighting within her mind was an internal burning that said if she didn't go in, all those innocent people had died for nothing. Maybe this would help avenge the loss of her beloved Will. Deep down she knew that wasn't going to happen. The monsters that took him away from her were back at the bottom of the hill. They would have to wait until she finished up here. She would return, and they would pay with their lives.

Chapter Twenty-Nine

1710 Hours, Avost 1, 2258
Fort Forward Trinity, Edge of Republic Territory

THREE WEEKS HAD PASSED, and the others were getting anxious. The team never had to wait long for assignments, but now the more time that trickled, the more each man's nerves grew edgier and short. Of course, this was slightly different with Ed finally out of bed and at least on his feet. Not exactly one-hundred percent, but on the road to recovery. Kris had recovered physically though the effect on his personality seemed to distance him even more from those in the team. Ed was the only one he was willing to chat with most of last week, probably because of a bond formed during their brush with death. That's at least what Brett thought as he entered the sleeping quarters of his men.

The rain fell in sheets from the sky above as it raked against the roof of the army building, waves of echoes chased themselves along the length of the room as Brett made his way to his team. Witch, who rarely seemed to let anything bother him so long as someone told him what the plan was, was furiously writing in a journal on his bunk. Turned to the last few pages, Brett wondered how much he could keep going as the man had filled all of it since they had returned from Miavlaco. Dickie was meticulously cleaning every knife he owned. A supply of a bunk and half worth of arms.

David was pacing, mixed with calisthenics, which, of course, was irritating an already angry Dickie. Ed and Kris sat lounging and silent. It seemed they remained in the world shared between their minds. Ed had his leg stretched in front of him, bandages still wrapped around his upper thigh.

"Alright, enough of this silent bellyaching between you all. Someone is going to spill the beans, or I'm going to be spilling something else." Brett meant every word of it, especially when he found himself eye to eye with Kris. "Now start talking."

"I'm just keeping myself nice and fit, Boss." David didn't even bother to stop doing his jumping jacks to talk. "Women love men with abs and scars. We all know that." The smile on David's face disappeared the second he saw the Sergeant's face.

"The boys are just getting a bit, how should I say it 'claustrophobic', and I'm getting a bit hungry, Sergeant." Dickie looked up to meet Brett's eyes, but his expression was dead serious.

If that wasn't enough, the knife he held reflected the shine of the overhead lights on its sharpened edge. The others remained quiet though Witch refused to turn his attention away from his studies at all.

"Plus, we've heard a few rumors there, Sergeant." Ed positioned himself more comfortably as he sat up. "Something about us not being allowed to leave the base. Word is passing around there might be a bit of a bounty on our heads from what we did back a few weeks ago."

"I've been checking on that." Brett pulled up a chair and sat among his men. "It is true what you hear, at least part of it."

He had tried to keep this from them as long as he could while he made plans for what they could do next. Too much time had passed for his liking, and now it was time to get them brought up to speed.

"What part of it is that?" David now decided his attention was better served talking with them.

"Leaving the confines of this base would be a bad thing for any of us." The memory of the General's veiled threat burned into the back of Brett's mind. "What we saw back there in that temple, is being blamed on us."

"Wait! What? We didn't do shit to anyone in there except those two who attacked us!" Dickie was quick to get back to his excited, angry ways.

"I know that's what happened, and that's what we put in our reports. It is what we put in our reports, isn't it?"

Brett looked each of his men in the eye as he let the statement hang. Kris had a difficult time holding his sight, so Brett let it sit for what felt like forever.

"My report contains only what I saw, Sir." Kris finally broke down and spoke. "Mainly, what happened to Ed and me, Sir. Neither of us knows what happened to you in that temple. Other than you went in and got out, and then we ended up getting ambushed."

"Who bailed your ass out of that little hole of yours, huh?"

Brett silenced Dickie with a wave of his hand; the large man had become too quick to anger as of late.

"That's what I thought there, Kris." Turning back to

the others, he took a deep breath before he spoke again. "First, I guess we should fill you and Ed in on what happened back in that building."

Ed and Kris listened in silence while Brett filled them in on the specifics. He didn't hold back as this affected them as much as the rest. After relaying the story of the sacrifices they had found within the temple, he recanted the horror they had discovered hidden within the shadows.

Witch and David had gone to clear the rest of the building as he and Dickie searched the blood covered altar. When the two men returned, they had been in a rush to get Brett and show him what they had found. If the remains of killed citizens and the peculiar acts of the demon tongue woman was enough, none of them had been prepared for what was outside. Recounting in all its gory details, the Sergeant told them of the mass grave that held rows upon rows of bodies. Each victim, man, woman, or child, was half buried and left to rot. Their blood pooled within the temple. He could tell by the look on the faces of his two men that this was a lot for them to digest. With a pause, Brett decided to leave out the veiled threats and games being played by those above them.

"Then why are they blaming us? We didn't burn the building, much less kill all those people." Kris appeared to relax as he now knew something of what was going on.

"I'm not sure, but I intend to find out."

Brett sat back and quickly flew through a few options in his mind. None of which seemed to end well for any of them.

"We aren't completely in the dark," Witch finally decided to get in on the conversation.

With his notebook now placed next to him, it was easy to see all the mystical drawings and calculations he was doing on the paper.

"Speak up there, Witch. We almost forgot you were even here. Lost you in all that old man's white hair." Dickie couldn't help but smile with that.

Witch just flashed him a look before chuckling to himself.

"As I was saying, at least at this point, we know more now than we did back then. I've been looking into a few of the books and drawings that we found scattered around the temple." Witch removed a few from his bag, which he must not have reported when they arrived. "Whoever it was that we walked in on, their purpose seems pretty clear from these books. They are trying to summon some demon god to aid in their cause."

"A demon? Like a devil or something?" David looked confused as he imagined the bedtime stories of his childhood.

"Well, if I'm reading these texts right, it's not a demon the people are following. There is an old belief; it goes back about 2,700 years to a time before the world was civilized. Monks and priests have written accounts of cults spread far across the known world that worshiped a god named Xabione. He was supposedly the master of all that fire and heat brought to this world. People believed when the world was at its weakest, a man with a soul strong enough for the passage, would open a doorway to this other realm. Doing so would bring forth the god to our plane, giving him total control of all mortals of this world."

Ed and David sat and looked at each other. The ideas are running through both their minds. Dickie just leaned back and chuckled.

"So you think this silly god of fire shit, is what we found back at that temple. Really? If it was so simple, then why are we sitting here? Wouldn't they have brought forth the apocalypse already?" Dickie could barely hold back his amusement as he asked.

"The references do not mention anything about the cults ever being successful. The only thing I can find is references to a war where men fight and die for reasons that make both sides innocent, yet guilty at the same time. This part, I'm not entirely sure, but it's some demon god by its description. I wouldn't be surprised if they think they can bring one about and control it. Maybe even use it against us." Witch sat back and looked at the faces of the men in front of him. A mixture of complete disbelief, confusion, and in the case of Dickie, the face of a man who thought his best friend just lost his mind stared back at him. "Look, if you don't believe me you start doing all the reading!" Witch uncharacteristically shouted at no one in particular.

"Okay, now that we have that out of the way." David looked over at Brett. "So what we gonna do, Sergeant? Sit here like captives until someone shows up with the balls to arrest us for real?"

"I don't think it will come down to that there, David. First, Witch I know you've come up with some crazy things before, but you've never been wrong. That is why we need more information than what you have been able to stow away in your bag."

Witch shuffled around and took an inventory of what he had.

"What do you have planned, Boss?" David sat and leaned in close.

"Well, the reports describe us as a rogue military group. No information that I've heard says who or how many. Kris, you and Ed will be missed if you try to get off the base. The doctors will notice the minute you don't show up for an appointment. Dickie, you and I will stick around to make people believe we are still here. David, you and Witch, will need to go out and see what you can find."

"And where are we going to do that?" Witch now sat forward, putting his notebook into his bag.

"There is a city just down the river. It's about three days ride into enemy territory. It's been all over the TV that they are planning a festival hosted by the local church to celebrate their 'Night of Ghosts'. After, they are throwing a media event to celebrate the reopening of its new 'holy' library. We need you two to get there, mix in, and see if you can find any more of these texts. Let's see how widespread this 'demon' theory of yours goes."

The men sat there looking at their leader silently for a minute. The rumors bouncing around the base now held some truth, the reality of it sank in as they pondered their next move. They had spent the last several years fighting shoulder to shoulder with one another. Now, hidden inside the books that only they knew existed, held the possible truth about what remained hidden within the shadows of this war. If anyone caught them, their allies or the enemy, they could lose everything. Even the usual jovial mood faded from David.

"Good luck to you two then." Ed tried to sit up straighter. "I'd say I would like to join you, but I think I'm going to have to sit this one out." The man shifted his leg as he smiled at his friends.

"We won't need luck, we'll need a fucking miracle." David stood and began to pace. "This all we have, Boss?"

Brett stopped scratching the rash on his arm that now circled halfway around his tattoo.

"You have any better ideas? Would you prefer to sit here and wait till someone finds something else to blame on us, or maybe the General finds another mission for us full of bullshit information? At this point take your pick."

Brett stood and looked down at his men. "Unless someone else comes up with a better idea, Witch and David get yourselves ready. I want you guys out the first chance you get, morning if possible. Just cover your ass, we all know what is at stake here."

Brett turned and left his men there with their thoughts as he struggled with his own. How had they gotten into this mess? All of them had done what they were asked, all of them were good men. Now outside these walls, they were fugitives, and he couldn't tell them he had a suspicion it started in this very base. Plus whispers of demons? He thought he had heard it all, of course until now the problem was always as easy as killing the first available target. Now, they had no idea who they were fighting.

Chapter Thirty

0113 Hours, Avos 10, 2258
   Unknown Temple, Northeast of Fort Frozen Heart

THE OUTER WALL of the large temple was a blank slate with the stone reaching high into the air. Ornate stone sculptures stared down at the team as they stayed in the shadows of the forest. Each creature appeared at regular intervals, and though they kept moving, the open eyes of the beasts never seemed to leave their direction.

Going along the tree line around the building, the thick blackness of night could not hide the depth of the massive wall that stretched all the way to the face of the hilltop. There had yet to be any signal from the other men as Charlie began to wonder whether sneaking into the building from a side entrance was a lost cause.

"You are almost there. Follow the darkest shadow to the deepest point, within you will find the key to your answer." A voice shattered the silence as the three soldiers crept along the brush and snow.

"What did you say, Sir?" Charlie wanted to make sure she didn't miss anything the Captain had said.

Both men turned to her, a look of confusion on Frankie's face, and a mix of anger and frustration on the Captain.

"By the God's woman, what are you talking about?"

Doubt stabbed its way into her mind as she swallowed back the realization, maybe her nerves were getting to her.

"Sir, I thought you said something."

"No, I didn't say a damn thing. Now keep quiet! We can't have you get yourself caught again, now can we?"

Already feeling like an idiot, she shook her head no. The response must have been enough for the Captain as he turned and continued to lead them along the path. Questions and doubt swam through her mind, unwilling to let her concentrate on the memory of the voice replayed in her head. Did I even hear anything?

"Follow your instincts, the darkness will see you through."

There it was again. It wasn't a voice she recognized from the two men with her, but there was something familiar about it. She had to be going crazy. No one else was here but them. The stress of the last few days and the pain in her leg had to be getting to her. Confident in her reasoning, she shook her head to clear her thoughts and pressed on.

"The others are blind, yet you hold the key to their success. Do not follow, but lead!"

She reached out and grabbed the Captain by the shoulder.

"For fucks sake, Sergeant!"

He turned to Charlie but became silent as she pointed toward an unnoticeable crevice within the stone wall. The entrance seemed only a single person wide, and within the first few feet the shadows drank up all the light leaving only the absolute black of nothingness in its wake.

"I don't know how you saw that Charlie, but good job."

The Captain reached down and quickly chirped the receiver of his radio two times to signal the others. No response returned, but the officer did not appear to be affected and moved them forward. Dashing from the tree line to the building was quick for both the men, but a slight struggle for Charlie as her leg hindered her more now than ever.

"You OK there, Charlie? Can't have you go lame on us now."

"I'll be fine, Sir. Just keep moving, I have your back covered."

As the three soldiers entered the walkway, the blackness swallowed them whole. Something in the darkness prevented their eyes from adjusting as they continued deeper. Within several feet, they were moving more by feeling than sight, hands stretched forward along the smooth, cold wall.

It felt like several hundred yards, yet the group had only moved several meters before the path ended at a wooden door. Charlie looked back and could not think of a thing that could cause what she saw. Behind them was nothing but a veil of black shadow. Their path had felt straight and didn't seem to deviate at all, so why couldn't she see the end of the tunnel?

"Well, isn't this convenient, an open door at the end of a dark hallway. I say we pay our new friends a visit." The Captain whispered as they waited at the door.

It had taken Frankie a moment, but he found a handle on the wooden door that ended the path. The knob creaked with age; the hinges rang out as the door slid open with moderate resistance.

Light from inside the building spilled out as the door opened. Slowly, they stepped in as their eyes adjusted to the sudden addition of color. Upon entering the building, the first thing that hit them was a sudden gush of warm, comfortable air. Within the wall of comfort, was the unmistakable smell of incense and fresh wood smoke. All the aches and chill within their bones melted away in seconds as they stood there and took in their surroundings.

Before the three of them, stood a hallway that opened above their heads into a high arched ceiling. An elaborate floor-length rug, decorated with masterfully rendered pictures of unknown figures adorned with halos battling grotesque demons, stretched as far down the hallway as they could see. Along both walls of the hallway, torches burned evenly, brightening the path that moved toward the center of the temple.

"My question awaits your answer. Do not delay, your strength is at hand!"

The voice returned and was now so loud she could not mistake it for a figment of her exhausted mind. Turning around in a circle, Charlie could not see anyone but her companions standing before the door.

"Did you guys hear that?"

"Sssh, hear what?" The Captain didn't bother looking at her as he assessed the hallway before them, though, Franky arched an eyebrow in her direction before shaking his head.

"I swear I keep hearing someone talking. Are you sure you didn't hear anything?"

"Look, I know this isn't your first go-around, so pull your shit together. We can't have you going all mindless on us. Get your mind straight, and let's get moving."

The man was right, but something felt wrong. She couldn't tell what it was, but there was something she was missing about all this. How had she located the door and dark passageway hidden so deeply within the shadows? She knew she couldn't be losing her mind, but she couldn't ignore the new voice within her head. Closing her eyes tightly, she tried forcing everything out but the job at hand.

Taking point, Frankie moved first down the hallway. Other than the elaborate carpet and torches along the walls, the hall remained mostly bare. The three soldiers stalked forward, weapons at the ready as they moved.

When they reached the end of the hallway, their path split into opposite directions, left and right. Both ways led down paths filled with torch light, but still too far to see what lie ahead.

"So which way, Boss?" Frankie continued to sweep left and right with his rifle.

"That voice you hear tell you anything, Charlie? Your guess is as good as mine."

She didn't like the idea that they were going to trust a voice only she could hear, nor the fact that they appeared to be joking about it at a time like this. Looking both ways, neither gave her the faintest feeling of which way was the best way to go.

"Well, sir, Will always said the right way is the right way to go, so..."

He nodded his agreement, and Frankie led the way. Just as the entrance hallway had been, their current path was straight with little furnishings other than the rug and bare walls. As they approached the end, they noticed doors begin to line the walls on both sides. At the end stood a ceiling-high, arched, wooden door that swung open from the center. Pristine bronze handles and hinges held the door in place. The size of it was big enough for all three of them to walk in side by side.

Frankie slowly approached the door and placed his ear

against it. There wasn't a thing that any of them could hear other than the sound of their hearts and the breathing of those standing beside them. Stepping away from the door and with a quick nod of the Captain's chin, Franky reached down for the handle. The metal was cold in his hand, ice flakes fell and melted on the carpet as he removed his hand to blow a quick warm breath onto his skin. No matter how much he tried, it would not move.

"Looks like this is as far as we go, Boss."

Frankie turned back around to see Charlie and the Captain already looking at him.

"Then we turn around and go back the other way. Maybe we'll get lucky, and those slackers have found their way around. Let's see if they will meet us back along the way."

The thought of making their way back didn't sit well with Charlie. She didn't know why, but moving forward was the only thing keeping her nerves at bay. Frankie moved past them to take point and began heading back down the hallway.

They were approaching the first set of doors when a loud and ominous creaking came from behind the wooden frames. The group stopped as Frankie lifted his hand and waited to see if they would hear it again. Cold sweat covered Charlie's hands as she squeezed the grip of the handgun she held by her side. The sound of her heartbeat thundered as she tried to calm her breathing.

"Are you ready to make your choice?"

The voice tore into her mind with a vengeance as she jumped onto her toes in surprise. Eyes darting back and forth, there was no one in the hallway but them.

Without her realizing it, a large black shadow had crept up behind her, as both of the others were too concentrated on the doors that stood just a few feet ahead to notice anything. Hardening her resolve, she adjusted her grip on the weapon and turned to see her target.

She had only enough time for a glance, but the dark figure behind her stole the breath right out of her lungs. She had to look straight up to see where its head laid upon its massive, black shoulders. In that quick second, all she could see was a shadow. The firelight that illuminated the room seemed lost within whatever stood before her. Even had she wanted to, she never got the chance to fight back as whatever the figure held, it struck her across the side of her head. A bright flash of light burst in front of her eyes just before she gave way to the shadows of the night.

Chapter Thirty-One

2327 Hours, Avost 2, 2258
  Fort Forward Trinity, Edge of Republic Territory

THE STORMS HAD PASSED. The base and its soldiers dried up as they returned to the everyday duties of the military. A few skirmishes and a whole lot of standing around was making the base itself feel like a room full of high school athletes anxiously waiting to burst out onto the field. Two nights had passed since the Sergeant had come to them with the news that they were prisoners within their own base, and it wasn't sitting well with Kris or any of the others. If they accused him as well, why had the General told ordered him to spy on them? Could the Sergeant be lying and the others covering for him? Thoughts like that didn't sit well in his stomach and mix that with dreams of Witch's demons made for a couple of sleepless nights.

The third night seemed as if it were going to be like the others. Tossing and turning while listening to Dickie snore until Ed threw something at him. He remained motionless into the night as every detail of what had happened until now played through his mind. Finally able to close his eyes, dreams brought visions of all the people in his hometown lying in a mass grave to the world of his nightmares. Fear and sweat finally drove him from his rest once he noticed that the last body was his own. Twisted and torn in death, he would watch as his body laid there waiting to decay with time.

Sitting up, he could feel the fine layer of sweat covering his body and sticking his shirt to his shoulders and chest. With a look up at the moon in the sky, he noticed it was later than he had thought it would be. Maybe he got a little sleep this time. The others were fast asleep, and Dickie was on the verge of snoring once again. Kris quickly slipped his feet off the edge of his bunk and placed his bare feet on the cold floor. If the nightmare wasn't enough to wake him, the cold shock sent through him was. Getting up and making his way to the nearest door, Kris hoped a breath of fresh air would do him good.

Opening the door and looking out, the base itself looked as empty as it was quiet. The cool breeze blew into his face, bringing a smile as it helped his nerves relax.

"I hope you're not looking to go too far, my son." A familiar voice came from the darkness just outside the door.

Thinking about it, he could almost place the man's voice, but his name or face would just not come.

"Not really planning on it, just looking for some fresh air." Kris couldn't anyone. He peered into the shadows the best he could, but he still felt alone. "And who am I speaking with?"

"Oh nobody, and just somebody very interested in what you have been up to." A man cloaked in the pure black robes of the church, minus the white belt, stepped forward and into view. "It would seem that someone who hasn't slept well in several nights has something on his mind. Is there anything you want to talk about?"

It wasn't the pastor he saw at the military church; this one was shorter with fewer lines on his face and less girth around his waist. With so many from the church around now, he couldn't recognize them all. Pausing to think about it, something about this man marked him as familiar, his presence made Kris feel as if the man had always been there.

"I'm not sure I understand your meaning. I couldn't sleep because one of the guys in here snores like a freight train."

He was lying, and he knew it, but he also didn't know who this man was.

"If that is the case my son, how about you come walk with me a short while. Let us see if the night air can clear that mind of yours."

"Wait, I never."

The priest didn't wait for a response and turned to walk down the footpath that led away from the door. Not really knowing why, Kris followed him, ignoring the fact that he wasn't even wearing his boots.

"You know, I find time like this peaceful, even if I'm surrounded by thousands of armed soldiers and enough weapons of death to make the gods weep."

The priest seemed to be talking to Kris, and no one, at the same time. Kris didn't know what to say, so they just walked in silence for a few minutes.

"I'm sorry here, sir, but I still don't see the point in us walking about this time of night."

Kris stopped and looked the man in the face as best he could. Even though in the darkness, with his hood, it was kind of difficult to make it out.

"Haven't figured it out yet, have you?" Amusement echoed in the cloaked man's voice. "Just listen to your heart and feel for a minute, let the freedom of this open space sink in."

The man was right, the two had walked to possibly the most remote area in all the base. Here in this place, a man could forget where he was. Kris let his words sink in, closed his eyes, and took a few deep breaths. Behind his closed lids, the sudden image of the firefight in the city played before him. The sight of his first kill, the guard's body as it fell in front of his teammates and the vision of the temple sitting there as he and Ed waited, filled his thoughts. He couldn't understand the accusations that followed, or Witch's reasoning behind what they had found, nor would he forget the look on the Sergeant's face as he told them what they faced. All of it flooded into his mind, and it hit his tongue like floodgates opening into an overfilled dam.

"What am I supposed to think, Father? The men I'm with seem as if they are capable of anything. I watch as they kill men without even the slightest of hesitation." The words came out with no ability to stop them; he only had the strength to hold back tears as his emotions threatened to take him over. "But, I just don't know, Father. I can't see them doing anything like this. There is honor behind what they do. Behind the rough faces, the stories of amazing and horrific battles, and personalities larger than life; these are good men. I cannot for one ounce of me, think they had anything to do with what happened."

The robed man stood silently and listened. Putting his hand on Kris' shoulder, he turned them, and they began to walk again.

"The loyalty among men, teammates who have faced death together, is beyond what someone who has never seen it can comprehend my son. Just do not let that blind you."

Walking felt good as Kris began to feel his emotional strength return.

"I know that, Father, I just can't put it together. There has to be another explanation." He meant to hold it back, but he couldn't stop himself. "Father, Witch thinks he figured something out. Something that might be important."

They stopped, and Kris tried hard to find the man's eyes in the shadows.

"What is it, my son?"

"There was something about a demon. Inside the building, they found symbols, artifacts and writing about some monster." It felt stupid just to say it, probably as much as it sounded. "He's not sure about the specifics of it, or what it means, but that's what he has figured out. I know he is still looking into it."

Surprisingly, the priest didn't laugh directly into his face.

Before he knew it, they had come up to a building that Kris recognized immediately. Both men stood silently looking at one another, just as quiet as the empty church that their path had ended at was.

"Have they any plans to continue this search? How is this Witch going to keep looking?"

The man's voice was so soothing Kris felt as if he could tell his deepest, darkest secrets to the man, even if he couldn't see the man's face. Kris had taken a deep breath before he decided to speak.

"Witch and David are going to find a way off the base. There is a festival a few cities south of here. I'm not sure what they plan, but they are hoping to find some information there. Once they get back, they'll discuss it with the Sergeant, and go from there."

A weight lifted off Kris' shoulders. Had the knowledge of that weighed down on him? The holy man didn't say anything for a minute. He stood there, the blackness within his hood burning deep into Kris.

"That is something the Church will have to consider my son. Any information that can help us complete our mission works to better our cause for God."

"You mean the General, right, Sir? You came to me, after being instructed, correct?"

"Of course." The man placed his firm hand on Kris' shoulder. Even if Kris had to look partway down at the robed figure, his presence made Kris feel like a child. "The General is the God's chosen leader. Anything that we deem important for our mission will go directly to him. We always see to that."

"I just want to help, Sir, but I feel torn in half."

Kris took a seat on an empty bench beside the church doors.

"Now that is a better answer, my boy. Let me tell you a little secret." The pastor talked in hushed tones as he sat by the young soldier. "If you want to know the men you are with, each one will show you who and what they are if you stick with them. You can't hide who you are forever. Trust in what you feel here." The man placed his hand on Kris' chest. "Let that decide before you use what is up here." The holy man finished by tapping the top of his hood, and Kris finally nodded his understanding.

Before Kris could say or think of another word, the darkly dressed holy man reached over and opened the door to the military chapel. Entering, Kris could see that it was empty, the darkness within only broken by the soft candle-light that burned at the end of the room. Turning back to the door, he took notice that the man he had been sharing all his feelings and internal worries with, did not follow him in.

"Father, why aren't you joining me?"

"There are other things I must attend to, my son. I feel that some time alone, with your thoughts, may help you more than to listen to the ramblings of an old man. Father Jacobs will be here shortly if you are in need of anything."

With that, the man shut the door behind Kris. Still feeling like a ball of emotions, Kris made his way to the front pew. A man could do a lot of thinking while sitting alone with nothing but his mind to keep him company. Why did it feel as though no matter he did, he wasn't going to find the answers?

Chapter Thirty-Two

1900 Hours, Avos 10, 2258
Unknown Temple, Northeast of Fort Frozen Heart

PAIN, thunderous pounding, confusion, and cloudiness filled Charlie's mind. Opening her eyes did not help make things any better. She couldn't move. Her wrists hurt. Her legs couldn't move, and any attempt to move them sent harrowing pain through her body. All she could see was a large mural of a robed man standing before an army of demons. With his one hand extended, he held them at bay with a blue fire. The demons seemed frightened, fearful of what the flame would do. The land itself seemed to change from that of death and rot, to green and clean as it passed the flames of this lone man. She hadn't spent too much of her life learning about the various religious people of any faith, but nothing about this painting seemed familiar to her.

As her mind began to clear, the pain subsided only enough so she could feel around at what had happened to her. They had tied her hands over her head and her feet at the ankles, leaving her leg in a position that throbbed even if she didn't move. If being tied up in such a position wasn't enough, the fact that she was barely wearing any clothes didn't help the matter.

Whoever or whatever had taken her from that hallway had removed all her clothes, but seemed to have at least a little decency, and left her underwear on. Even stranger was that all along her body, little black markings were drawn all over her, from her feet to as far as she could see her chest. She could not understand any of the writing, and taking a deep breath, figured she didn't want to know.

Giving up on the "why," she decided maybe "where?" was a better question to ask. Turning her head gently to the left and right, she could see what looked like a large oval cathedral room lit with candles and torches that circled the entire open area. From what she could make out, she was in the direct center of it. All along the walls were empty chairs, each marble white with a matching pedestal and unsecured ropes that dangled to the floor.

Nothing else seemed to occupy the room as she lied there tied to a stone table. In the silence, the only thing she could make out was the faint sound of moving water. Inside a building? She looked around, but there was no fountain or source of water she could see. Concentrating, she did her best to locate it, but the only place she couldn't see well was directly under her. Straining to see what it was, she shifted her weight enough to lift a shoulder and get a look at the ground near the table.

"Oh shit! What the fuck!" She screamed as she slapped herself back on the table.

Excruciating pain ripped through her leg. It had only taken her a second to recognize it. The table rested over a pool of blood. The waves of black and red liquid slowly shifted left and right as she was forced to lie there, unable to move.

"Why does this keep happening to me?" She whispered to herself as she struggled against her bonds.

The ropes on her wrists were tightly bound and gave no slack. Her leg was still too busted to make much effort for escape. Images of all the dead villagers came ripping into her mind. It was all of them! The entire village reduced to nothing more than a frothing pool of gore, and she was lying right above it! What kind of sick and perverted idea is this? She could barely keep her thoughts coherent as the fear threatened to overwhelm her.

"So, our prized possession finally stirs awake, I see."

Turning to the right, she watched as a large man, robed identically to the priest from the village, entered with a line of hooded figures behind him. Unlike the cocky, fat, and bald man of before, this one was tall, broad of the shoulder, and much darker skinned. Even with the thick layer of blue and golden robes, it was clear from how the large robes clung to his lean body that he was a man built by hard labor. Now, with his dark-brown eyes, shaved head, night-black skin, and golden marking of a flame etched into his forehead, he was the last person she wanted to see.

"Who the fuck are you, and what have you done to me and the others?"

Just for good measure, she struggled against her bonds, but there was no helping her situation.

The man smiled as he clasped his hands in front of his lips. Silently behind him, the progression of followers began taking seats at the chairs that surrounded the room. Every other body took a seat in a chair while the person before them stood and waited by the marble pedestal. Shadows filled their hoods so she could not make out a single person's face in the entire room.

"You don't know how glad I am to see you, my child. We have been waiting a long time."

The man was now up to her table. He reached down to softly stroke her cheek. Fighting the basic urge to turn and cover herself, she instead did the next-best thing and snapped her teeth at his fingers. Much to her dismay, she missed by only a hair length.

"I don't know who the fuck you people are, but let me go! Whoever it was you were waiting for, you've got the wrong woman."

With every struggle and argument, the man's smile seemed to grow wider. Over the next several minutes, her captor circled the table, careful not to trip in the pool of blood but never taking his eyes off her. She felt as if she were being studied. Hunger burned behind his eyes, an excitement that remained barely in check.

At first it started with a slow hum, then as it seemed to recycle itself, it grew louder and louder. The others in the room had begun to chant something. It wasn't anything she had heard before, nor could she understand any word of it. Even then, each new word and syllable caused the pit in her stomach to grow deeper, and the pressure in her chest to rise. If she didn't figure out what to do, and fast; she was going to end up in a hole like the others. Things didn't get better as the leader began an echoing, maniacal laugh as if he could read her mind and found it amusing as she ran possible ways to escape through her mind.

"You were born for this, my beautiful. Every step you have taken has led you to us."

"What?"

Was this man crazier than he looked? Again he just smiled back.

"Your choice is upon you, think clearly and choose wisely."

The voice returned once again, from the deep shadows of her mind. She quickly looked in every direction she could to confirm, but no one was talking; other than the now constant chanting, and the crazed fool with golden etching stuck in his skin.

"What choice do I have? I don't see many options here."

At this point, talking with a voice in her head wasn't the weirdest thing in the room. The sudden change in the dark man's face showed her that talking to herself seemed out of place, even for him. Nonetheless, the smile returned, and he walked to one of the chairs located around the room.

"I believe the time has finally arrived, the coming of our Lord begins tonight."

Reaching down and grabbing a hood, he tore it back to reveal Frankie bound to the chair. From the bruising and cuts on his face, she could see he hadn't come willingly.

"Pick soon, you can't save them all." The voice was as clear as day in her mind, no matter how loud the others got.

"Pick what?"

She looked around, but could not figure out what any of it meant.

"Oh our Lord, Voros, we give you a willing soul, one who comes to join you, and with his blood, bring you forth."

Frankie didn't move or struggle as the hooded aid brandished a knife from the pedestal and quickly slit two gaping slashes across both his wrists. The only sign that Frankie gave that he knew what was going on was when he started to cough as more and more of his life's blood drained to the floor. There it pooled and began to flow down a small duct that led to the flowing mass underneath Charlie's table.

"Fuck you! You crazy son of a bitch!"

Charlie struggled with her bonds, but only succeeded in sending pulses of pain from her leg through the rest of her body.

She watched the smile on the cult leader's face grew larger as she gave up struggling against her bonds and sighed as her back pressed against the cold stone of the altar. One by one, the man's assistants removed the hood from each man seated around the room. Shock, horror, and a thousand other feelings rushed into Charlie's mind, and soul as each member of her team was revealed one by one. Somehow these bastards had gotten every one of them. The men looked battered and defeated though the Captain remained steadfast in his anger and defiance.

"Oh Lord Voros, we have another soul for you to add to your great army. Bring forth your power, so we shall stand by your side in glory!"

As the man continued his chanting, every member of her team was one by one drained of their life as Frankie had suffered only moments before. Anger and pain racked through her body as she watched each die slowly and pointlessly. Between bouts of holding back tears, she struggled against her bonds. There was nothing she could do. The ropes would not give. No amount of pleading seemed to change the mind of these crazed killers as they single-mindedly went about their duties. Her time was running out, how could it end like this?

"You are stronger than he is. It does not have to end like this." The voice began to pound on the back of her head.

Tears filled her eyes as every bit of energy she had was spent fighting against the ropes that held her tight. Only a few men remained alive as she laid back and felt herself drain away. Nothing but anger filled her. Anger toward the bastards killing her friends. Rage against an enemy that had taken the only man she had ever loved away. Nothing remained but her tortured memories. With all the anger built inside, the fire in her chest threatened to burst out of her skin as tears and perspiration covered her body.

"The time has come. Do you give in, or do you fight?"

She didn't know what it meant but using what energy she had, she stretched to look at the remaining man who sat staring his captives in their eyes. There, defiant as ever sat the old man. His bonds stretched to their maximum as he pressed forward, trying to tear into the killer that brought his doom.

"Oh lord, I have for you another."

"Give it a rest will you? Whatever fucking god you pray to isn't going to help you any. If I get off this chair, you're going to need every god in the heavens to stop me from tearing you limb from limb." The fire burned behind the Captain's eyes as he snapped his teeth together, trying to get a piece of the man.

The priest only smiled as he nodded to his assistant, who, like the others, opened up large gashes over the Captain's wrists. Refusing to give up or flinch, the Captain turned and met Charlie eye to eye. No fear hid behind those eyes, even the anger that she expected was missing. Instead, she found behind his deep brown eyes was a look of acceptance. His time had come, yet he fought but was not angry. The change in his eyes stopped her for a second; the acceptance froze all of her fear before she turned to her team's killer. His big, shiny, white teeth, practically glowing in the candlelight of the room, stretched across his face. The anger inside her rushed forward as she could not handle it any longer.

"I choose to fight!"

With those words, a burning sensation scorched through her body. Pain unlike anything she had ever felt tore apart her skin as her back arched uncontrollably, lifting her partially off the table. Through all of it, she tried opening her eyes against everything she felt. Fear crushed her as she looked down at the symbols written on her body. The ink began to glow and rearrange itself on her skin.

Her mind was frozen, unable to comprehend the pain as she slammed back down on the stone altar. She tried desperately to regain her breath as the burning suddenly stopped. Before she could begin thinking, spasms and pain rushed into her from her fingertips and toes as instead of burning, it felt as if she were suddenly freezing to death.

Every muscle in her body cramped as she tried to force the feeling away. No matter what she did, the icy fingers of death crept further and further up her body. Once it reached her chest, she could see it begin to open, the bones broke, and the skin parted though no blood rushed out as her body lifted off the table. The beating of her own heart began to throb in her ears. Each pounding second became slower and slower as each pulse became weaker and weaker. Finally, her heart and everything else slowed to a final halt as her body crashed down to the table.

Opening her eyes, it took a second for her to orient herself. Had all that really happened? What had happened? Lifting her head from the stone, she looked down at her half-naked body and saw that all the markings that had been there were gone. Was it a dream? Turning to her left and right, the sight of her fellow soldiers dead in their chairs pushed reality back into her mind.

She could hear some movement behind her, but paid no heed to it as she fought against her bonds. Moving her leg ever so slightly, she realized there was no pain, and that the rope that tied her down seemed as light as a feather against her pull. Taking a deep breath, she jerked her body and ripped all four ropes from the table as she rolled off and splashed into the pool of blood beneath the altar.

Still standing next to the Captain, whose head now slouched like the others, was the priest who had just torn her world apart for the second time in the last few days. Joy and excitement filled her as she stalked toward him, blood dripping onto the cold marble floor, her feet leaving small prints as she moved forward. The smiling fool even had the tenacity to giggle like a little schoolgirl as he clapped his hands together. Charlie couldn't help it, but she smiled too.

"Ah, there she is. A miracle brought to the flesh."

Charlie was now standing in front of the murderous man. She kept her eyes on the floor as she fought every urge she had to not laugh in his face.

"Please, let my assistant dress you in something more befitting a child of our Lord."

He opened his arms and waved the assistant standing next to the Captain forward. Stepping close to her, they unraveled a glorious blue robe, like the one the leader himself wore. Charlie looked up at the person presenting the robe, their face still hidden in shadow. Before any of her captors could do anything, she snapped her hands forward and around the assistant's head. With a quick tug, the hood was no longer looking forward as she now stared at the back of the cowl and the sound of shattering vertebrae echoed from the walls of the room.

With a glance, she watched the smile disappear from the man's face, replaced by a look of fear as she slowly, but surely, revealed the smile that now adorned her face.

"You? No! This can't be! I have been nothing but a faithful servant!"

The man stumbled back, tripping over the leg of the Captain's chair. Reaching out, Charlie caught his hand and held him half fallen to the floor. Muffled sounds came out as he tried to scream in protest, but Charlie would have nothing of it. Squeezing, she could feel every little bone in the man's hand crush under the pressure of her grip. Echoes of pain and bellowing bounced around as she lowered him to the ground slowly. His weight tearing at his broken bones.

"How?" The man gurgled as he slipped into a panic.

"You don't know half of what you truly deserve, you wretched piece of dog shit. I will make all who have done this to me, pay!"

The man barely got a scream out as she slammed the heel of her foot into the base of his nose. The force crushed his head, leaving him there to rot on the floor.

Looking around, the other hooded assistants tripped over each other, trying to get themselves out the door and as far away as possible. Fantasies of chasing each one, hurting them in every way possible, flashed before her eyes as she began to feel the excitement build up in her again.

"Charlie!" Weak and wracked by coughs, the Captain's voice broke her trance and turned her back to where he remained.

His skin was pale and ashy. Every breath was shallow and forced as the man tried to keep himself alive. Rushing over to him, she could see that it was too late and there was nothing she could do.

"Captain, Sir!"

All her anger and excitement for death faded into the face of the last man in this world she could call a friend.

"What has happ..." Coughing refused to let him get anything else out.

"I'm not sure what is going on Sir, but it's over now."

Lying, she still tried to look the man in his eyes. He was still there, but his eyes were looking elsewhere. The end for him was near.

"It's never over. Not until the last man."

The Captain, her last beacon of hope, slumped as he took his final breath.

She pulled the ropes that bound him to his chair away and laid him to rest on the altar where she had found herself. Between all the dead men in the room, she was able to rummage through and find enough clothing to cover herself for the trip outside.

Once outside, she was startled to see the foundation of the great building had crumbled and cracked from what could have only been a massive earthquake. It didn't matter to her anymore; nothing did. She now had a mission, a purpose, and she would see it done. Bending down to the ground, she lit the line of fuel that lead back into the building. Within minutes, she could see flames lighting up windows as the fire took hold and began its work.

"It's never over. Not until every last one of them is dead."

With a smile, she began her long walk back toward the village.

Chapter Thirty-Three

2039 Hours, Avos 6, 2258
   Purgh, Azhana

HELL HAD COME to the world, and David knew it. The streets streamed with monsters, ghosts, men and women wearing robes and swinging swords at the demons that stalked the streets. Sounds of children laughing, screaming, and preachers calling out mixed with organ music and the sweet smell of incense as it settled over the street.

"How the fuck are we going to find anything in all this?" David bent in closely as he whispered to Witch, who led the way.

"Keep quiet, there is nothing out here for us to find anyway." Witch looked around at people in the midst of partying or prayer. At this late hour in the day it was difficult to tell. "Just stay behind me and don't get yourself lost."

David took a step closer to the man as they moved through the crowd. Normally, he was comfortable and confident in the biggest of crowds, but this was something different. Religion put him on edge. The fact that the army was practically run by one didn't help. Now, he was surrounded by strangers, who, being lost in their religious celebration, he couldn't tell whether they were enemies or not.

Both men moved as best they could through the pulse of bodies filling the streets. Three days of hard riding had found them at the city line just hours before dusk. Getting off base had been easier than they thought. Regular caravans of supplies left at predictable hours. Most military police stationed there were too used to stopping people coming in, not going out. Hitching a ride with the last transport got them inspected by the ending-shift checkpoint. The two burly men stationed were more interested in having their night relief arrive than starting something with the final truck carrying two extra men out.

From there, they had stayed to side roads and hidden paths as best they could. They hit enemy lines on the second day. From there on out, they found themselves looking over their shoulders every minute. Everyone could be looking for them now, and who knew how much time they had.

"Alright, here we are. Looks like the party hasn't made its way here just yet." Witch stayed as close to the shadows as he could when he approached the building.

The church wasn't at all simple. Oddly shaped, the building was three stories tall and shaped more like an octagon. Large solid entrance canopies extended from double glass doors on the three entrances that looked out onto the main street. Not knowing this was a place of worship, one would probably guess it was a conference building, maybe even corporate headquarters of some international company.

"How are we going to find anything in a place like this?" David asked as the two entered through the first set of glass doors they found.

"If anyone asks, we are looking for the 'library.' It will be easy to believe we are here looking for guidance and understanding among these people. Nothing makes it more convincing to them than putting it into a book."

The glass doors led them to a large lobby. In the center sat a circular island desk with a large television displaying messages of the holy celebration, upcoming events, and prayer times. Sitting behind the desk were two young men, their backs straight, shoulders back, and their attention held steady as Witch and David approached. Both wore tailored black business suit attire covering over muscled bodies that spoke of years of hard training and not a career behind a desk. White shirts and flame red clip on ties finished out the outfits. Each man was clean shaven with military buzzed brown hair, and their desk was meticulously clean with each item laid out in perfect order.

Smiles of perfectly white teeth greeted Witch and David as they approached. Both men squared their shoulders to their approaching guests, the furthest one slowly inching his rolling chair around the corner to remove the furniture from his path.

"How can we help you two this glorious evening?" The taller of the two asked as they approached. His welcoming smile slowly faded when they reached the desk.

"Uh, yes. We'd like to do some research in the church's library. My friend and I are from out of town and don't know our way around." Witch patted David on the shoulder, a pleasantly fake smile on his face.

The two men looked David and Witch over. Both men wore simple brown robes, aged from years of use, and the slight smell of horse or donkey radiating from it. David had protested the second Witch had devised their plan, but now that he saw how quickly people looked away from the two, he realized maybe Witch was full of more good ideas than he thought.

"Are you two here for the festival? You know most people are finding it delightful to stay outside and watch the festivities. Bless the gods we couldn't ask for a better night."

The man motioned toward the second set of glass doors that opened to the street. Staying silent, the man's partner never took his eyes off them, while the taller man's smile returned.

"Of course, the gods blessed us with such great traveling weather. We will be sure to join in once we have satisfied our need for knowledge. See my friend here is new to our faith, and he is interested in learning some of its storied histories." Witch leaned over the front counter, his white hair falling over his forehead as he tried to widen his smile just that bit more. "I figured this was the perfect time to bring him. Once he has his fill of the great stories, the festivities will mean so much more to him." Quickly Witch's face turned to all business. "Or am I incorrect, and the Church has now decided to turn back those seeking help and understanding? A little time with my young friend here is all we are asking for."

David stood there, trying to not look stupid as he kept his mouth shut. Both guards looked at each other. The taller one then straightened his tie before shuffling the papers on the desk before him. The second still sat there silent, measuring both men up, now having pushed his seat slightly backward from the desk.

"No, no. Please forgive us. The Church always welcomes those who seek understanding and knowledge. Just pardon our curiosity. The city has seen an influx of thousands of people in the last few days. While open to everyone, there are many precious and unique items found here. As much as we would like for it to be true, not everyone is of a pure heart." The young man stood and began leading them to the first hall on the right. "It is our job to protect the word of the gods for our people. As for your question, please follow this hallway down to your second right. There, you will see a stairwell that will lead you to the second floor. Feel free to sit and learn as you so desire, but do remember that open hours end at 11 pm. The festivities outside will be going on all night if you should choose to join."

Courteously the man smiled and began walking back to his post. The sounds of the partying could be heard echoing through the walls. They only had till 11 pm, it wasn't going to be much time. Both men made their way upstairs as quick as they could, both hoping they find the needle they were looking for in a building lined with haystacks.

Chapter Thirty-Four

2153 Hours, Avos 10, 2258
Fort Frozen Heart, Northwest Azhana

THE WIND WAS HOWLING and bitter cold as she stopped the engine of the ATV. A storm, growing since she left the temple on the hill, was now at full strength. Snow whipped across through the trees, carried in all directions as the wind seemed to swirl everywhere and nowhere. The temperature had dropped to a deathly freeze, yet that did not bother her.

Surprisingly, nothing about this storm bothered her. Looking down at her over-sized boots, baggy pants, and blue hooded robes she couldn't understand how she hadn't frozen to death already. Instead, she felt warm inside as if she were finally in her element. Wiggling her toes, she knew something about her was different, something was off.

It no longer mattered, she hadn't felt this confident and strong in a long time. Whatever it was, she liked it. She was going to take every advantage of it. Unstrapping the rifle she had collected on her way back to the base, she hunkered next to a tree and peered through the blowing snow.

The fort below was still in repairs, but in just a few days, the workers had made a good start on clearing everything. With the sun rising to the east, its first rays breaking over the tops of forest trees, those workers would soon be back to their jobs.

Gripping the rifle tighter, images of the horror that she had gone through at the hands of the men below flashed into her mind. His face, wide-eyed and shocked, his hand reaching out to her burned deep in the pit of her stomach. Where have you gone, Will? The angrier she got, the less she felt alone. But that wasn't true. After she had left the temple, something or someone had been following her. Several times she had tried to turn quickly, maybe catch a glimpse of whatever was back there, but every time nothing but shadow and snow laid in her wake.

Now, looking down at her intended target, she had to shake that feeling of being watched and focus on what gave her strength, her anger.

The long shadows were now stretching along the side-walls of the fort as the sunlight finally made its way to where a few men now gathered, preparing for a hard day's work. Quietly, she slipped away from the tree she leaned against and moved along the shadow line toward the maintenance entrance she had used to escape only a few days before.

Men were stationed up along what remained of the wall. She had seen a couple of them walking, trying to keep themselves warm, but now it was a shift change. The men who had been up at night were tired and looked for a warm bed. Those just waking were damning whatever gods they worshiped that they had to get up and stand in the cold. She smiled as the thought of them praying for mercy to those same gods as she ripped their life from their bodies. That thought alone brought a warmth to her belly as she moved swiftly through the snow, staying as hidden in the dark as she could.

Reaching the last of the tree line, she stopped and caught her breath. Looking up, she saw that the west wall was clear. The shadows were still heavy on this side. In the swirling snow, she couldn't see anything or be seen herself. Taking one last look at her weapon to make sure there was a round in the chamber, she took a deep breath to calm her excitement. She had always been nervous before a fight, maybe sometimes describing it as excitement, but this was different. She hadn't fired a shot yet, and already her blood burned, her palms itched, and she shivered with anticipation.

Closing her eyes one last time, she turned and bolted as fast as her newfound strength would propel her toward the outer wall. She cleared the snow covered ground in a few seconds and planted herself flat against the wall. Nothing moved. The only sound she could hear was the wind as it whined and growled against the heavy stones.

Staying alert, Charlie slowly inched to the maintenance door. Extending her hand down and twisting the handle, it surprised her when it opened without hesitation. Fiddler had been right, not many people knew about these hallways. The fort's new occupants must not have bothered to look.

Smiling at her luck, she stepped in and closed the door behind her. The lights that had once shown her the way out now laid dark leaving her in a hallway unable to see through the blackness. Gripping her rifle tighter, she sidestepped to her left until her shoulder found itself against the cold, damp wall. Using this as a guide, she slowly moved forward.

Within moments, she stopped and caught her breath. Whatever had been following her was here and it was close. Maybe if she stayed quiet and didn't move, whatever it was would be unable to see her as she could not see it. Seconds felt like minutes. Minutes felt like hours as she stood there waiting. Still, nothing had changed. Steeling her resolve, she moved forward. Whatever it was would have to make its presence known, and when it did: she would be ready.

The sound of the wind, beating itself against the wall, echoed in the dark. Each vibration sent strength through her body; the growing storm was pushing her forward. Tingles moved up and down her skin each time she heard the sound. An excitement continued to build within her chest. Along with this feeling, a strong familiar odor began to fill the passageway. With each step, the noxious fumes became stronger to the point of being unbearable.

"Oh, shit. What is that smell?"

No one there to answer, but the words felt better voiced than in her head. The second she opened her mouth, she regretted it, as she would swear she could now taste it. Creeping further down the tunnel, she tripped as her lead foot slid into something on the floor. Her momentum sent her forward. Catching herself, she pressed her back against the wall and slowly slid till she was sitting on her heels. Reaching forward, she felt for what she had hit and recognized it the moment her fingertips touched the hard rubber. The standard boot moved loosely in her hand. Even with no light, she could see it clearly in her mind.

"So no one has found you yet? Poor bastard." The smell from the body worsened as the boot slid off in her hand. "Don't worry, I'll make them pay."

Still lying just as he had died when she last saw the unknown soldier, she knew she was close to the door that would get her inside. Standing, she stayed pressed against the wall and extended her arm to feel for the exit.

Cold metal and the tiny droplets of condensation touched the palm of her hand as she found the entrance bar. Charlie stepped forward and strained to hear what she could through the thick metal door. She knew she had no idea what was there, no idea how many now faced the wrath of a woman scorned, or what she was going to do the second she made it through that door. It didn't matter. A rifle loaded with ammo, and fire in her belly craving vengeance was all she needed.

Confident that all she could hear was the continued wind, she pushed the long bar handle of the door and tried to ease it open. At first it would not move, but with a push, it started to slide.

Fresh air was a welcome feeling as it flooded through the crack in the door. A hazy light and wind-driven snow quickly followed as it splashed into her blind face.

Seconds of blinking later, she could see out into the field. A fine layer of fresh snow covered everything and more was falling every second. During her time in the dark, the storm must have picked up more as flakes fell in blinding sheets. No soldier was in sight as the wind whipped snow in all directions. Thankful for the streak of luck, she stepped out and looked for a target. Nothing presented itself, so she bolted over to the remains of the tower she had once patrolled.

Most of the rubble was gone, but the base remained. Hunkered down, she looked for something to target, something that would help her move forward. The Captain's quarters! Any officers left here to lead these bastards would have taken shelter there, leaving the grunts to bear the storm. Best to cut the head off the snake first; the rest can die after.

Having been stationed in the fort for so long, Charlie made her way to the rear of the camp while remaining hidden from anyone that happened to be out in the elements. Moving from building to building, the fort itself felt empty as the fierce weather was her only companion, its wind a beckoning voice that moved her forward. Within a short time, she could see the Captain's quarters and the lights that burned inside.

The wind raged in her ears as she prepared to make her way across the small road that separated the building she hid next to, and the building she meant to enter. Each time the storm surged forward, she could swear there were voices in the wind. The voices weren't human. It sounded as though dogs were howling. She shook it out of her mind as she knew storms could play tricks with the mind. This one was no different.

Taking a deep breath, Charlie pushed forward and ran across the road. Her robes ballooned up as the wind pushed into her face, yet she didn't feel the cold at all. Something felt right as the ice-cold air hit her skin, soothing the fire that burned inside of her.

Making it to the small alley outside the front door, she ducked into the shadows. Looking down at the rifle in her hands, she bit her lip in frustration as it was not the right tool for the job. A familiar taste of metal tingled her tongue as she realized she bit her lip to the point of bleeding. Shrugging, it would have to do. Inching forward, she prepared to make her move.

"Ha-ha! Good one, Lieutenant. I'll make sure to pass that on to the new recruits!" The man stumbled out with a can of beer in his hand. "The God be damned, it's cold out here. This storm fights better than these heretics! Ha-ha!"

Charlie saw her chance coming right to her. She slipped back into the shadows as the drunk man made his way to her. Just as he reached the front of the alley, she grabbed him from behind and wrapped her forearm across his neck. He was a head height taller than she was and looked as though he weighed twice her weight. Those drinks cost the man everything he had as she squeezed with more strength than someone her size should have had. She felt the bones in his neck separate and crack. The man's olive eyes glassed over as his final breath expired.

Watching his life slip out of him, she dragged the body back into the alley. A search of the dead soldier netted a handgun and a good field knife. Slipping back to the front of the alley, she took one last look around to make sure no one was there to see her. In the raging storm, it would have been difficult to see her from only a hundred feet away. Pulling the hood over her head, she stepped out and knocked on the front door. Looking to the ground, she hoped the low light and snow would hide her identity long enough.

"Come on, Sergeant! You've only been outside a minute. Already looking to come in and warm your girlie hands up?" A slurred yet growly voice called from behind the solid door. Without checking who was there, the large bellied man opened the door.

"Oh bother come..."

The rest of her enemy's words gurgled in his throat as his windpipe opened, and blood decorated the door and his opened uniform shirt in seconds. Stumbling back, he tried to grab the wound to stop the flow, but the attack was relentless. Charlie stabbed her knife forward into his abdomen and between his ribs as fast as she could. Falling, the man crashed into a table, sending playing chips flying across the room. Lost in her blood-lust, she fell with the man, tearing at his innards as they hit the floor.

"What the fuck!"

A short young man stood as the table crashed at his feet. Much to his credit, he quickly pulled his sidearm and fired at the robed attacker now tearing the man in front of him apart. The bullet missed wide and only grazed her shoulder as she rolled off the fat man. Without having to think, she pulled out her new handgun and unloaded three rounds into the young man's chest. He fell backward over his chair as a red mist of blood remained in the air before falling to the ground at his feet.

Everything fell quiet in the small room as searing pain shot through her shoulder. Cupping her hand over it, she could feel where the bullet tore through. There wasn't time for her to be slowed by an injury. She tore a piece of the fat man's shirt and tied it over her shoulder as quickly as she could. Someone would have heard the shots, she didn't have much time.

Securing her knife, and two new handguns, she made her way back out the front door. Before she had entered the building, the weather had been as bad as she could ever imagine it being. Stepping out, somehow, it had become ten times worse. The wind roared to a deafening howl. Snow was coming down so fast it resembled a monsoon rainstorm. Nothing Charlie had ever experienced would have prepared her for this. The whole fort was threatened with snow that could bury it.

Hesitating only long enough to brace herself for the wind, Charlie began making her way to the armory. Now it was time to start taking out as many as she could, as fast as she could. Hopefully before the storm did it for her. She could move freely now as if she belonged, visibility no more than a couple of feet. Anyone who saw her would be in danger long before they knew who she was. A smile stretched across her pink cheeks as the wind blew across her face.

The armory was one of the largest buildings in the rear of the fort. Evidence of heavy fighting peppered the front metal walls as she approached the entrance door. The high arched, half circle roof had light spilling through the windows that created the glass wall up at the top. Boards covered most either from the storm or damage, but a few remained. The recent snow piled up against the wall; the new storm now quickly adding to where it began to reach the low windows. Just as the other buildings remained, the front door was unguarded as some new soldiers felt it was better to stand inside where it was warmer than at their post. Bad decision.

Confidently, she strode up to the door and knocked on it. Stepping to the side, she waited till someone answered. Sounds of a few voices grumbling from the inside blended with the constant wind. The sound of locks being undone scratched at the metal before the door opened.

"Yeah? Which of you crazy bastards is out in this damn storm?"

The older soldier never saw what hit him as the butt of Charlie's rifle struck him square in the nose. Before the man could react, she grabbed him and used him as a shield in front of her. Stepping inside, she could see rows of munitions and tables lined up all the way down the building's long walls. Several men stood at various places along the open area, each of them frozen in the realization of their current situation.

"You crazy son of a bitch! What do you think you are doing?"

The anger of the man was evident as he tried to struggle against her hold. In return, she squeezed harder around his neck, his knees buckling slightly under the pressure. Each man just stood there looking at the old soldier. His nose bleeding down his face and shirt, and the blue robed intruder holding him hostage.

"Will you lazy bastards do something? You're soldiers, aren't you?"

A couple of pairs of eyes turned from a look of confusion to inspiration.

"I was a soldier once too," she whispered in the man's ear as she pushed him forward and kicked him with the heel of her boot.

The man turned to catch several rounds to his chest as she opened fire on the men in the armory.

The old soldier and two others fell quickly as the fighting began. Once their comrades began falling, the four others quickly snapped into their training and dove for cover, grabbing whatever weapons they could. As the men started returning fire, Charlie dove through an open doorway to her left. Bullets crashed into the wall and through the windows of the office. She was outgunned and almost flanked, yet her mind was a cloud of confusion.

Each round fired began to fade in her mind as the only thing that seemed to fill her ears was the sound of the storm. The wood boards used to cover the broken windows began to shake as the wind and power of nature crashed onto the exterior of the building. Snow was pouring through the open door as fast as it could push through. Her gut sank as more bullets crashed through the windows and the sudden feeling of being watched surrounded her. With all the confusion in the fighting, it felt as if there were eyes watching her from every direction. The sound of the storm was now threatening to burst her ears as pain lanced through her skull.

Panic and pain flashed through her mind as the storm

raged, and glass shattered around her. Dropping her rifle, she cupped her head in her hands and began to scream. Anything she could do to relieve the pain and the overpowering feeling of being watched. Just as she reached the top of her lungs, everything broke loose. The room fell into a world of thunder around her as the boards on the walls shattered, and the wind and snow barreled into the building. Looking up from her position on the floor, she couldn't believe what she thought she saw.

Inside the snow, as it entered in a tidal wave, were wolves with fur made of snow. Grayish with dark specks of dirt speckled through their frozen coats, the beasts rode the storm surge. With blue-tinted claws, and bearing black teeth as smooth as polished glass, they jumped in from the windows near the roof. They slipped and tumbled as they stormed into the building through the open front door. Their eyes glowed with a bright blue flame, a power that deep down inside she recognized. Dozens filed into the room as fast as their lean bodies could squeeze into the armory.

The men inside turned their weapons on the new enemy as they entered. Bullets tore through the beasts' body just as if they were ice and snow. For every one that fell, three more came through an opening in the building. Charlie listened as the men began fighting for their lives. Their enemy was relentless as each beast fought to be the first to find their way to one of the men.

One of the monsters stopped in front of the door that led to Charlie's position. The beast was larger than the other creatures; its fur was as white as newly fallen snow unlike the other's grayish mix of ice, and dirt. Each hair sculpted to perfection, yet when the wind moved, each flake would shift across its body. Muscles rippled beneath its radiant coat, moving with such grace, the monster was the pure essence of power, the storm itself not willing to disturb the space around it as the other wolves kept their distance.

As the magical took two steps into the office, its eyes settled on hers. The beast looked angry, yet she didn't feel it meant her any harm. She could see the blue flame in its eyes, yet when she looked deeper, she almost lost herself in the blackness behind it. The feeling of a deep winter surrounded her with warmth, and a resurgence of strength flowed through her muscles. She welcomed the feeling, smiling as she let it embrace her. The beast was the first to turn as it broke eye contact and howled. Unlike a wolf, the howl had the power of the storm behind it, the roar of a hurricane rattled the roof of the aluminum building, its rafters above shaking against the violence. With a look of recognition, the monster turned and joined the others making their way to the men that remained.

The sound of screams replaced the rapid gunfire as the men were quickly losing their fight with the wave of beasts as they continued to storm the building. Standing, Charlie didn't bother with the men behind her as she walked out the front door. Reaching up to her shoulder, she was surprised it no longer ached. Removing the bandage revealed her wound was crusted over by a scab of blue ice. Touching it sent streams of cold down her finger, but no pain in her arm. Shocking as that was, the sudden sound of howling stole her attention.

The storm continued to grow stronger. Now within the streams of snow that circled, she could see the forms of snow beasts running freely across the open fort. Now and then, mixed with the wind and howling of the wolves, she could hear the scream of a man or woman succumbing to the monsters that had found them. She didn't know where they came from, or why they didn't bother her, but it didn't matter. They had helped her achieve her first goal, and now it was time to move on to the final step of her plan.

She looked up at the sky above as she walked straight through the fort. To her, the storm was a gift, the clouds above ordered to move with her, ready to follow her every footstep. Her power and confidence surged as the idea of the storm and what it contained brought a terrifying smile to her face. The world of the Republic had yet to see all that she was capable of doing.

Chapter Thirty-Five

2145 Hours, Avos 6, 2258
  Purgh, Azhana

PAIN like this only came to David's mind once every few years. Usually, it was preceded by a nightly bout of drinking Dickie under the table, or the result of finding himself doing something he was never fond of doing at all. Reading. Which at the moment, he had done more than three years' worth for him in the last forty minutes.

"Fuck this, Witch!" David, out of habit, whispered to the man sitting at the other end of the table. "It would take me years to understand any of this ancient history stuff. You found anything yet?" David slammed down the cover of the dusty old book he was reading and flicked his fingers at the cover of another.

Witch, who remained quiet across the table from him, had already sped through four dozen books. The pile of discards sprawled at his feet as the newest one had gathered his attention for the last fifteen minutes.

"Witch, you hear me?"

David could see the intensity in the man's eyes, back and forth they went as they skimmed page after page.

"Sssh," Witch put his hand up to quiet his partner.

David, the impatient man he is, got up and walked over. Reading over the deadly scholar's shoulder, he noticed the text looked particularly old even for a library full of old books. The text was hardly legible. Squinting, David realized that even if the ink were still fresh and dark, he couldn't read it. The language was beyond anything he could understand.

"Come on man, we are running out of time!" David reached down and put his hand on Witch's shoulder.

"This is it, look here David."

Witch shifted over in his chair and presented the open book.

Witch's finger pointed to where he wanted David to read, which didn't matter in the slightest. Right beside the passage though was something David could understand, a picture. Drawn in faded black were illustrations of ceremonies, things that looked like sacrificial deaths. Witch flipped the page when he figured David had understood what was before him. Over the next few pages, he recognized drawings of rivers, all flowing toward what looked like convergence points.

Upon these spots, illustrated light rained from the sky, and at each location robed men emanating power came forth. They looked like gods coming down from the heavens. Images of men and women following these figures continued through the pages.

"Look, I see these pictures you're showing me, but what have they to do with us?"

David looked down at his friend who was back to reading the book.

"See, I told you if you read more, you'd actually come in handy in a situation like this." Witch shook his head gently from side to side. "Look, reading these passages tells the story of a blood ritual. These rivers you see, that's not water, and it describes the sacrifice of hundreds if not thousands of people. For within their life, the power of some god or gods can be restored."

"So, we have some nut jobs killing innocent people by the truckload, to bring back some ancient god, for what though? To win the war?"

"That would be my guess, plus it mentions the first chosen receiving blessings that bestow rewards and unimaginable power to their followers."

"There it is! Why is it always someone who wants to rule the world? I thought that only happened in the movies." David looked up as he spoke, the library had been empty when they entered, but he swore he just heard a door open and close.

"It seems that sacrifices aren't the only things needed. These last few passages speak of something else, a dark decision made at a dark time." Witch had to bring his face closer to the writing as it faded, the single bulb lamp on the desk not clear enough for the age of the text.

"What the bloody hell does that mean?"

"The library will be closing a bit early tonight, you two." The voice of the guard down at the front broke the silence of the room.

David turned around. The man was approaching them from the stairwell entrance that they had used. The same smile on his face, same overconfident walk. Looking down at his watch, it was only 9:45.

"Thought you said we had till eleven? Something wrong?"

David stood straighter as he pressed his back against the table.

"Just got word things are changing, the whole celebration outside and all. Orders are what they are, you know."

David wasn't sure, but he swore he could 'feel' the eyes of several others behind the bookcases that lined the room's walls. Approaching, the man was alone, his black jacket undone in the front and his red flame tie held firmly in place.

"Well, we were just finishing here, my friend is almost to the end of this great book. Just a few more minutes, and we'll be out of your hair. Any chance you guys have a loaner program do you? I think I found a few books on how to approach women you might want to read."

The comment didn't seem to faze the man one bit as he continued to smile and stepped up to David. Standing side by side they were about the same height and build, pretty different from a lobby guard of a city church. David concentrated on the man's eyes; they didn't waver even for a second. The man didn't even try to look at Witch, who was still engrossed in his reading. Enough was enough as David snapped his fist out into the man's gut.

A cough billowed out as the man bent forward. Reaching under the man's coat, as he figured, David grabbed the man's pistol and removed it. On cue, four other men stepped out from behind the ceiling-high bookcases as David slid behind the man while holding the pistol to his head.

"Where do you plan to go? We know why you are here." The man's voice was harsh as he fought to get his breath back.

"Who are you? Who are you working with?"

David tried pressing himself closer to Witch, who still sat at the table, his attention buried in the book.

The four men started to circle them. Each of them had a pistol of their own drawn, Witch and David were going to lose any path of exit in only a few more seconds.

"Witch, you may want to put that book away now!"

In one fluid motion, Witch flipped the table he was sitting at on its side, sending books and paper up into the air. As his hands lifted, shots rang out and the two men in the front screamed before they fell to the floor. David didn't hesitate as he pushed the man he held forward and fired several times at the man off to their left.

The fourth man, caught off guard, was only able to squeeze a single round off into a bookcase across the room between David and the guard from downstairs. Rolling to his right, Witch quickly sent three rounds into the young man's chest as he looked up at him from the ground. His last breaths were gurgling as blood poured from his chest and mouth while he fell to his knees and toppled to the floor.

"Where do you think you're going?" David grabbed the unarmed one by the shoulder and forced him into a chair. "We have a few questions to ask you?"

"You will get nothing from me. Take your worthless lives, whatever is left of them, and get out of here. There is nothing you can do to stop us. We are everywhere, and when the time comes, we will rule this world."

"Looks like we really do have some nut jobs here, don't we Witch?"

Witch was quickly packing away several of the most important books he had found. Through all the commotion, the men had forgotten the celebration outside. Voices and music could still be heard coming from the streets below.

"We could take you with us and show you exactly how

we treat crazy like you." David put on his greatest smile as he breathed each word into the man's face.

"Ah!!!" The music stopped as a woman's scream echoed above it. David and Witch looked at each other as sirens could be heard approaching, and flashing lights bounced around the shadows.

"Looks like you're just in time for the roundup. Wouldn't want you to miss the real show; see what this celebration is all about."

David had enough of the man's toothy grin. He slammed his fist across his jaw, sending him reeling to the floor.

"Alright, now we have to go." David turned as he and Witch started heading to the door.

With a shout, the man dove forward as he tried to reach David. His right hand was raised high above his head, a small blade extended as he intended to bring it down on David's back. Barely able to turn in time, David watched as the man's face exploded, and his body fell inches short. A small amount of smoke exited the barrel of Witch's pistol as he looked down at the man.

"Let's get out of here." Witch holstered his weapon and led them out.

1951 HOURS, Avos 9, 2258

Fort Forward Trinity, Edge of Republic Territory

THE CHAPEL WAS EMPTY, quiet, and hazy from the candle smoke. Even with all its simplicity, it was a comforting thing for Kris. Something had broken within him over the last few weeks. Being stuck on this base, the looks of the other soldiers, the memories of what he had seen and done played through his mind daily. Was this what he was meant to do? This war? Was it for a good cause, or were there hidden secrets that used him for cover?

He looked up at the paintings of all the sacred men and woman of the church. Recalling all them from memory, he envisioned what they went through. The tests and trials they faced on their way to finding their true path in life. Why didn't the world seem as easy as it did in the holy book? Good versus Evil, good men did good things while they banished the evil from this world. How did he end up on the wrong side of that equation?

"Can I take a seat next to you?"

The familiar voice was so startling that Kris practically jumped from his seat. Looking up, he found himself staring right into the eyes of Sergeant Brett. Not exactly the man he was looking to talk to, remembering he was in the chapel brought up the question why the Sergeant was even here. The man wasn't much of a believer in religion, or faith, or anything outside his existence and desires.

"Well?"

The Sergeant's voice was calmer than Kris would have expected.

"Oh yeah, please sit." Kris slid over making room for the man on the pew.

"I hear you've taken to this place lately. Can't say I blame you."

A distant look glazed over Brett's eyes.

"You can't, Sir? I thought you despised places like this."

The Sergeant smiled as he leaned back and chuckled to himself.

"There are many things you don't understand in this world, boy. Just because a man hates religion; hates everything there is to do with it doesn't mean he's going to fault you for the way you feel."

Kris pressed his back against the wooden seat and looked back at the paintings. The officer's words bounced around in his mind for a moment.

"Why did you join the army, Kris? Does it run in your family? Couldn't afford school or a worthwhile trade? You're not, how should I put it, bred for killing."

Kris thought about the man's question for a good minute. How much did he want to share with him? Wasn't it his choices that put them in this situation? Kris didn't even know if the man was even honest.

"I felt a calling, Sir." The words had slipped out before Kris realized he was saying it.

"A what?" The Sergeant sat forward, a deep look of interest on his face.

"There was this pastor at my community church. At the beginning of every day, my family and I, we'd go and listen to morning sermon. Well, something he said about becoming the men we were meant to be struck a nerve in me. I wanted to find what God had in store for me. Thinking about it, Sir, lead me to joining the military. We'd heard horrific stories in school and the news about all the terrible things done to innocent people. How could a man, which follows a god that preaches protection of others sit and let this happen? I just, well it felt right, Sir. That's why I'm here."

Tears welled up in Kris' eyes. His mind said that everything that had brought him here was just as stupid as it sounded. Somewhere in his heart though, it still felt right.

"That's a pretty good reason, I guess. Here is the real question. What's your plan now that you've seen what war is like?"

The Sergeant didn't press the issue. He didn't try to

stare down an answer or see if Kris would admit having a change of heart. He just sat back and gave the young soldier some space. Kris looked around the room, empty as it always was when he was around. This question had wrapped itself around his brain almost every waking moment of the last couple of weeks. Did it even matter what he thought about war now that he was here? Could one-man change anything at all? Kris took in a deep breath, let it flow through him, and then let it out.

"To see this through I guess, Sir." A smile came across Brett's face. "I've come this far, I now realize that one man can't change anything at a scope this large. War is what it is, but it's about those around you who you can affect with your actions. The team, you and the other guys, believed in me out there in the field." A feeling of pressure coming off his shoulders helped Kris relax. "I can't believe for a minute what has happened to us since we returned. The rest be damned if I'm going to sit and let others think otherwise."

Brett patted Kris on the shoulder. He let the silence in the room set in again, just to make sure Kris didn't have any lingering doubt that he was holding back.

"That's what I wanted to hear, Kris. To be honest with you, I wasn't sure you had it in you. This church here, the whole religion thing can do some strong things to a man in your position. It will either cause you to run and hide or stand and fight. I'm glad you're standing with us."

"You are? I wasn't so sure you would be. After last time, now that we have the world searching for us, I figured if we ever find ourselves back on the field, you'd want men you trusted out there."

"That's the thing soldier. You are one of us now. Plus, speaking of the field, your next assignment is to be ready and geared up by 0200 in two days. Is your arm feeling up to it?"

Kris rotated his shoulder; it was stiff and sore from not using it, but he knew better than to say no.

"Better than ever, sir." They both knew he was lying. "I'll be ready for what is ahead of us." Kris paused for a moment. "Um, what is ahead of us?"

"I got word a few hours ago. Witch and David are on their way back. Should take them another day to get here. David says they are coming in hot, looks as if they found something or someone."

Kris didn't know how he should take the news. The idea that they found what was behind these mass-killings, and the talk of demons? He couldn't tell if this was too much for his mind to consider, but he would have to roll with the punches until he could decide what was going on.

"Orders are coming from up top. I have a sick feeling that I won't like what I hear, but you'll know more when the time comes. Just be ready to get your feet wet again, and be prepared for the worst. I'm not going to lie to you; this one is going to be tough. Whatever it turns out to be."

Kris' stomach clenched up. Something in what the Sergeant said sent a shiver down his spine. Was he ready to go back on the field?

"Thank you, Sir, I will be ready and I won't let you down."

"I know you won't, because my orders still stand. Do what I say, when I say, and you'll make it home. If you don't, well, I'll keep that to myself here in this holy building of yours."

The Sergeant went to stand.

"Sergeant Brett, before you go. Why did you join the military?"

The question stumbled the soldier for a moment as he

remained halfway between standing and sitting. For the first time since had joined the team, Kris found himself with a chance to learn more about the men he wanted to consider his family.

Slowly sitting, the officer placed his hand on his chest before he began to speak.

"You have anyone special at home, Kris? Anyone waiting for you?"

"Me? No Sir, unless you count my ma and pa, Sir."

"Do you remember the first bombs that went off? The ones in the subway inside Rylen City?"

"Yeah, the Free Azhana Militants claimed responsibility. They said it was retaliation for bombings some fanatical religious followers had done on their side. To be honest, I never thought any true follower of the faith would ever do something like that."

"Well, it's what people claimed started all this. See the thing is, I used to call Rylen, home. My wife," Brett coughed before he could continue. "She and the boys, they were out shopping that day for my birthday. Big one too, damn 3-0. They were on that fucking train."

Kris felt like his jaw was on the floor. He tried to say anything, something to end the feeling that rooted in his stomach as he realized what he had asked. The man in front of him, probably the deadliest thing he had ever met, and he had done the one thing that made him look human. Now he looked fragile, his shoulders slumped, and his eyes glossed over. The moment lasted only a second as the man shrugged and straightened himself.

"That day, I swore that I would see that every person responsible found themselves buried in the ground. If they were lucky, they'd die before I got my hands on them. Some have been; some haven't."

The Sergeant flexed his hands back and forth.

"Things have changed though, haven't they?"

Moments passed, and Kris wasn't sure the man had heard him.

"Nope, things never fucking change around here." The Sergeant stood and began to make his way to the exit. "No matter what happens, things always seem to stay the same. In the end, the only lucky ones are those who don't stick around long enough to realize that."

Sergeant Brett made his way out the door leaving Kris alone again with his thoughts. The idea that his commanding officer wasn't a stone-cold killer brought some relief to Kris' heart. Maybe the priests were right. Maybe there was some good in all men, even if they buried under layers of hatred and death. If Kris was going to do anything with his time here, he finally knew where he was going to start.

Chapter Thirty-Six

0757 Hours, Avos 12, 2258

Road South to Koplaitin, Republic Prisoner Concentration Camp

THE TRUCK RATTLED LOUDLY as every bump, hole, and rock on the road shook the prisoners seated in the bed of the vehicle for the second straight day. Bits of light made its way through openings and poorly welded seams all along the metal walls and roof that held the men inside. Body odor, gaseous fumes, and at least the smell of one person's soil, filled the truck making it feel as if suffocation was a better choice.

Will looked around at the men seated around him. Sergeant Walker sat patiently examining the bonds that held him. Private Teller watched the sergeant at work. The look of worry returned to his face, and the others a mix of horror and disbelief. He wondered if he looked the same in the eyes of the other men, he hoped not, but at this point, it didn't matter. Just as the other Sergeant was doing, he looked at the bonds that held him in place.

Iron cuffs locked his wrists a few inches apart with a metal chain that attached to another chain extending to the link between the metal cuffs closed around his ankles. A last lock was used to connect his ankles to the metal of the truck bed.

Most of the restraints looked as if they had been around a long time, probably not used either. Flecks of rust and old paint came off as he twisted his skin under the rough edges. When he had realized that the General's orders were to send the prisoners off-site, the golden opportunity for escape had flashed into his mind. Having only a short time to think it through, he had passed the idea to Walker, but neither of them could produce any specifics as too much was left up to chance. The often rowdy sergeant had agreed that if they were going to have any chance of getting away, this trip would be their only shot.

"Where do you think they are sending us? Some fucking reforming camp, show us the salvation we need?" Walker never could let the enemy's strong belief in religion go.

"Doubt it. Probably some large concentration camp, no way they'll waste their time on converting us. We've sold our souls to all kinds of demons remember." Will watched as the big man across from him smiled.

"Oh, I've sowed my oats more times than I can remember, cost me a pretty penny over the last few years." Private Teller found it difficult to stifle a chuckle as Walker gave him a small punch to the shoulder with what little he could reach. "Now here is a man who knows what I'm talking about!"

The Private's smile disappeared as his cheeks brightened red.

"Good, now you're finally coming back to us." Will knew it was better if they could keep the other men at ease, instead of frozen solid with fear. "Walker, any luck with those chains of yours?"

"Not a damn chance. Shitty things are rusted through, but going to hold. If these bastards made anything right, it happens to be these damn things." Walker even gave a good tug with his large arms and not a single sign of budging. "Damn things are probably a couple decades old."

"Mine aren't any better either. Fuck! I have no idea how far we are going, but if we can't get out of these before we get there, we won't be in any better situation than we were before." Will shuffled on his metal seat as he continued to examine the locks between his wrists.

"Uh, any of you guys good at picking a lock?" The two sergeants snapped their look at Private Teller. The little man looked as if he were about to shit himself, again.

"Speak up Teller, what do you have rattling in that empty head of yours?" The younger man looked at Walker as a child does when finally showing they've been hiding something important from their father.

"Well, the whole time we were holed up back in the fort, I found a way to edge out some of these metal filings from the bed frames." He reached into his boots and hidden within the padding, he pulled out two sets of metal bits. Neither of the pieces was more than a couple of inches in length, but anything was better than nothing. "I didn't know if it would be useful at all, but I've read in a few books that prisoners can do many things with just a little bit given the right motivation."

"Any gods out there be damned, our man here just proved himself worthy there Sergeant Coffey. I think we might just have a field promotion on our hands. What do you say?"

Will reached over and grabbed the metal from the man whose smile damn near reached his ears.

"I think you may be right there Sergeant Walker, maybe right up to your level, sound about right?"

Walker's face went serious and angry for just a second, then returned with a smile.

"Hey now, no need to rush these things. Can't have the boy growing a big head." Will was already working quickly on the lock that held his feet together.

The metal filings weren't great, flimsy and oddly shaped especially for picking locks, but as Teller had said, something is better than nothing. Maneuvering the best he could, Will tried desperately to feel for the small piece he was looking for to trip the lock. It had always been so much easier sitting in his room, practicing while watching all those spy and war movies with Charlie. He never thought he'd have to use the skill. His mother had always told him movies were a waste of time. He would prove her wrong.

After a few minutes, he found the right angle and with a twist the shackles fell off his left ankle. Having done it, removing the other took half the time.

"Hurry up there boy. We don't have all day." Walker's voice carried with it excitement.

Shuffling to keep his balance as the truck bumped and shook, Will started on the locks that held the Sergeant's wrists.

"Either of you two know how to do this?" Blank stares answered his question quickly. "Well, once I have you unlocked Walker, head to the back and get an idea where we are. Teller, I'll get you fixed, and then I'll show you how to finish me. We don't know how much time we have, and I don't wanna get stuck with my hands still all tied up."

Within minutes, he had Walker released and headed to the back of the truck, and was busy working on Teller. By the time he began working on the Private's second wrist cuff, the process had become natural.

"I'm not sure what else you got planned but whatever it is, it better have something to do with a lot of angry men!"

Will looked over at Walker trying to peer through an opening between the back doors of the truck. His face was stone cold and a bit angry, but his eyes, deep inside, hid that longing look of desperation. Something had the man frightened.

"What is it? I just finished clearing Teller, what do you see?"

"I can't tell how many there are, but just back here I see three sets of armored trucks. Whoever wanted us, definitely wanted us there alive. Shit, that's going to be a lot of men."

"What are we going to do, Boss?" Teller was already visibly shaken again.

"I'll figure it out once you get me unshackled, now concentrate."

The order seemed to straighten the young man up as he went to work on Will's wrist. He looked as if he had been paying attention as his restraints were removed, because Will barely sat down before the young soldier went to work on the locks.

"Looks like I almost have..."

Screeching of tires and the sudden force of momentum sent everyone in the back of the truck slamming to the front. The three free men had it worse, as standing and unchained, they slid and crashed into the metal wall that separated them and the front compartment. Several of them coughed and moaned as they tried to find their way back to their seats. A couple could be seen bleeding where their bonds had torn into their skin as they shifted forward.

"You guys alright?" Will seated himself upright from where he had landed on the floor. His hands were still locked together, preventing him from having the chance to brace himself for the shock.

"Yeah, fuckers need to learn how to drive." Walker now had a good cut over his left eye. It made the man look twice as mad as he did before.

"I guess I'm alright, don't think I see those metal filings though." Teller started pawing at the dark floor of the truck.

"You're shitting me, right?" The Sergeant's eyes got wide as he started checking the floor by his feet.

Will watched as they shuffled between the other men's legs. Possible other routes of escape flashed through his mind as he tried rolling his shoulders, both of which were horribly sore and locked from strain and injury. Even if they did find the metal pieces and got his hands unlocked, there was still the problem of the men outside the truck.

Hollering and doors opening could be heard just outside the metal frame of the truck. So many men outside were trying to talk at the same time; it made it hard to hear what was even being said.

"Wait guys, listen. I don't think this stop was planned." Will shifted forward and tried to get his ear as close as he could to the wall.

Ping, Ping!

Several dents banged into the wall just above Will's head as he fell to the floor. Explosions rocked the truck, and the sound of commands mixed with the screams of agony filled the truck's compartment as every man tried getting as close to the floor as they could. Several times over the next few moments, bullets tore through the metal framing sending streams of light through the stagnant warm air. One of the men laid screaming as a bullet bounced around before it became lodged in his leg.

"Fuck! What is going on?" Walker screamed as he started picking himself up.

More bullets tore through the wall sending him back to the floor.

Everyone was slowly getting up off the ground as the sound of gunfire began to die down. It had only taken a couple of moments, but everything seemed almost peaceful outside their metal prison. The only sound was the heavy breathing of the man trying to stop the bleeding in his leg.

"I have no idea, maybe some of our own found the convoy?" Will wasn't going to keep his hopes up; their luck hadn't been that good so far.

"We better hope they are. Whoever is out there sure has some balls to take this train on."

Will slid closer to the door as everyone else tried to shift back into their seats. The ringing in his ears had hardly calmed, but outside their mobile cage, it was silent as if they were all alone in the area.

"Hey, you see anything out there?" Walker whispered, but was quickly silenced by a wave from Will.

Was that the sound of footsteps crunching in the snow? Will looked out a crack in the door, straining to hear anything.

The doors were pulled wide open. With all his weight against them, there was nothing to hold Will back as he tumbled out of the truck and hit the ground hard with his injured shoulder.

"Will!" Walker screamed as Will quickly turned himself over.

The familiar sound of rifles and pistols being raised

and prepared to fire quickly stopped any sudden thoughts of fighting back.

Staring back at him past the barrel of a rifle no more than a few inches from his face was the face of a young soldier. His cheeks were red, eyes blue, and under his white and gray helmet tufts of brown hair stuck out longer than normal regulation.

"I'm alright. Everyone just take it easy, no reason to get something started, now is there?" Will tried to pick himself up, but the man wouldn't move the rifle enough to allow much movement.

"That's OK there, Lieutenant. Let the man get up, can't you see he is one of us?"

This young recruit is a lieutenant? The young man looked to whoever was talking and with a quick motioning of his weapon, he moved so Will could get up. Orders or not, the man did not take his aim away from Will's head.

"I'm sorry for such a rude welcoming my friend. You all must be pretty shaken up after that." Stepping from around the truck, the leader of the group came forward.

He was an average sized man with streaks of gray hair coming out from under his helmet. Dressed in light gray and white camouflaged armor, counting him, Will could see at least twelve surrounding their truck. The man seemed overly confident after such a firefight as he lit a cigar. He blew out a ring of gray smoke that lifted slowly into the air. Placing the cigar back between his teeth, Will noticed the large, badly sewn scar that went from the left side of his lip up to his left ear.

"Who the fuck are you?" Sergeant Walker asked.

With rifles still trained on him, he tried moving toward the end of the truck but quickly stopped as the two closest men seemed a bit too jumpy as they prepped their rifles to fire.

"Oh, where are my manners? I'm Corporal Vincent LaCleur of Azhana's Second Regiment. We are out of Tarlington Fort. We got some leaked information that there would be a prisoner transport coming through this neck of the woods." The man walked around examining the dead men stiffening on the ground, blowing smoke circles as he moved. "Looks like, for you guys, we made it just in time."

Something about these men didn't seem right. Everyone was still jumpy, it was clear they were prisoners, but not a one had put their weapons down. Each looked ready to kill. Tarlington Fort? Why did that sound so familiar to him? Will tried shaking the thoughts from his mind.

"We are sure glad to see you guys. Any idea where they were taking us?" Will looked around to get an idea where they were and to get a better picture of the group that had "saved" them.

"From what we have learned, there is a concentration camp of prisoners of war, about another half a day's ride south of here. Right in the middle of the city of Koplaitin."

Some men in the truck started whispering as the news became a reality. Will wasn't as certain as he tried drawing a map in his head. Charlie had always been better at directions and open world travel. She could find her way in the woods in the dark with no map and only the stars if she had to. Without a radio or a positioning unit, Will was lost but now was better than anytime to remember.

"So if we are a half day's ride from Koplaitin, coming from the North, that puts us right on the border of the Slein River."

Will could see the frozen river not far off into the distance, but the man's face quickly went from welcoming to hard.

"That would be correct, but enough of that. You guys must be pretty beaten up, and ready for a good rest. Plus, we can't be sure there aren't more coming up behind us."

Something was bothering Will, and he wasn't going to let it go.

"What's wrong Will?" Even Walker could sense there was something missing.

"Which fort did you say you were from again? If I remember correctly, Tarlington Fort was lost over a summer ago."

"Ah, fuck. You had to go and make this difficult for yourselves."

The older man nodded to the Lieutenant. Will had only a second to react before his world blacked out.

Chapter Thirty-Seven

2120 Hours, Avos 9, 2258
  Fort Forward Trinity, Edge of Republic Territory

THE GENERAL'S quarters were busier than Brett expected as he entered on the heels of Private Erickson. Spread across the first level, logistics officers had their aides running in and out of the central room in what he hoped was organized chaos. The more each officer shouted, the louder the next person had to be to get their message noticed. Brett couldn't understand out how anything ever got done at this level. If you could get past the tremendous amount of ass-kissing that went on, you would find yourself in the middle of a cookie jar with thousands of greedy little hands all reaching in at the same time. Too many hands and none with an arm long enough to reach in and get the job done.

"Keep me in the field and away from this craziness. It's deadlier in here than it is facing the enemy." Brett whispered to himself as they headed to the stairs that led up to the General.

"What did you say?" The private turned back to Brett.

"Nothing, just keep us moving. We don't want to make our General wait, now do we?"

The private hesitated for a second as his face crinkled in thought. Giving up, he turned to lead once more. Oh, some people are meant to lead, and others will do their best to follow, Brett thought as he knew which Erickson fit into perfectly.

Bringing his attention back to the commotion around him, it struck him by surprise that he didn't see many church 'advisors' around. Over the last several years, he couldn't recollect a single decision made without the church's advice. But now on the cusp of what was rumored to be the deciding battle of the war, they acted as if they were never there. Of course, as rumors are, this was probably going to be the thirtieth deciding battle since Brett enlisted. No way was he going to hold his breath thinking anything would be different this time. Nothing ever changes, everything always stays the same.

"Right inside, Sir. They should be waiting for you."

The private ushered Brett through the door, but unlike all the other times, he did not follow him in. That little change in routine put the Sergeant on edge. Something was different, and he didn't like different, especially when it involved upper-level brass and his team.

"Sergeant Brett, I am so glad you could join us. Thank you for answering my summons so quickly. Please take a seat right over here." The General, dressed in full combat colors of tan and brown minus any real field gear, called from the window overlooking the runway below.

For the first time in years, the man did not have a glass or bottle of alcohol in his hand. Looking into the man's eyes, added to the forward slump of his shoulders, gave Brett the impression something was weighing heavily on the man's conscience.

"I think I would rather stand for this."

Brett always thought better on his feet. If this was going to turn out badly for his team, he had better have every moment he could, to think it through.

"Very well, have you informed your team to be ready? I know it's been awhile since you were last out."

"They will always be ready when the time comes, Sir. But, nothing has been ordered yet or have I missed something?"

"Good," the General scratched his head as his eyes widened at the question. "We'll need all we can get for this. We may only have one shot at this."

Almost on cue the door opened and shut behind Brett. Turning, he found himself looking right into the eyes of Father Rondeau and Trevor. The priest looked hard-pressed and concerned, his eyes darkened with shadow and red as if from a lack of sleep. Trevor, on the other hand, had his normal ear to ear, shit-eating grin plastered to his face.

"I'm sorry we are late, General. I was off collecting the last bit of information I could before we convened today."

"That is alright. Did you find what you were looking for?"

The General seemed in a rushed mood more than he normally was when he was sober.

"Some of it, yes. I'm afraid it's not as much as we wanted."

The priest sat across from the General, who had found his normal spot on the office couch. Trevor made his way to the back wall, his eyes never leaving Brett.

On the coffee table between the two couches, the priest

spread a map and held down the corners with empty glasses. The Sergeant didn't recognize it from the ones hanging downstairs with the other officers. This one looked far more detailed, yet older judging by the yellowed corners.

"See, our focus point needs to be here. The temple will is hidden, and probably heavily guarded as well."

"Wait, what is going on here, Sir? Another temple? My team has already seen enough of these forsaken 'temples' for a lifetime."

"And we saw how well you handled it last time, didn't we?"

Red flashed through Brett's mind as he snapped his head toward Trevor, who was leaning against the wall. The soldier had a white tooth grin from ear to ear as he tossed up an apple, caught it with the tip of a knife and took a bite out of it.

"Fuck you! You know as well as I do we had nothing to do with anything that happened back there."

"Not exactly as I hear it. News still plays about the maniac team of killers and what they did to all those women and children. Almost brings a tear to my eye every time I see a report."

Brett could swear he heard a chuckle in the man's voice. It took every ounce of restraint he had to stop himself from jumping the couch and throttling the man to death where he stood.

"That's enough!" The General was on his feet and his bloodshot eyes were dead serious. "Quit your fucking pissing contest, or I'll throw you both into the brig and get two officers who know what the fuck they are doing. Now listen up!"

"As you can see here, the temple is in the southern tier of the city. Expect it to be heavily guarded inside and outside." The priest looked up at Brett as he tilted his shoulders to show more of the map.

"What city is this? I don't recognize it." Brett asked.

"This is Obrathe. Azhana's military capital." Rondeau replied without looking up.

"That isn't how it looks. I've seen a dozen maps. I think your information is wrong again."

The priest let out a sigh but showed no other emotion than being tired. Grabbing a new map he placed it on the table, overlaying it with the previous map. They were identical on the outskirts of the city, but things changed as you got closer to the southern end.

"It is the same map, but what you don't realize is once you get past the main part of the city, there is a hidden section most people don't see."

"What do you mean don't see?" Brett moved closer and finally sat next to the priest.

"It's underground, Sergeant. We've never known it was there until we got word from some men on the inside." The General replied as he pointed down on the map and moved his fingers on a route that looked like a clear path to the center.

The whole idea made sense to Brett. Leaving your most important assets visible and vulnerable, even in a 'holy' temple never ended well. Underground left you virtually invisible and protected. Maybe they were smarter than they looked.

"Let's cut to the chase here. Your team is one of the best I have for this type of work."

"I'd like to differ on that one, General." Trevor stepped forward, a challenge behind his words.

"As I was saying," the General gave the man a look that Brett thought the officer never had in him. Trevor backed himself up to the wall again. "We need you and your men to get inside, find out what's going on, and end it. Everyone inside is considered expendable. There is more at stake than anyone wants to admit."

"Another mission where everyone dies, and we take the blame again? Is this the same 'inside' information that we used last time? I'm sorry, Sir, but I think my team and I will have to pass." Brett went to stand again. This conversation was over.

"You talk like you have a choice there, soldier." The General's eyes had a sternness behind them, yet they looked far more tired than Brett had ever seen.

"My team is already a walking target. We took the heat for whatever horrible chaos went on last time. We are not going to walk into the same mess again. I almost lost two good men!"

"Maybe your team would have been better off."

The priest was able to grab Brett's arm before he threw himself off the couch to get at the bastard behind him.

"That is enough!" The General was back on his feet. "The information is as good as we are going to get. Add that to everything you have brought us until now, whatever is happening in that underground temple cannot be left unattended. From the information we have, the city itself has been cleared of most civilians."

The General sat on the couch, his face inches from being buried in his cupped hands that rested on his knees.

"Can you give me any certainty that the civilians will be gone?" Brett still wanted nothing to do with this.

"No, we can't, Sergeant." The priest ruffled some maps to draw his attention. "Our worry is that the same thing you found before is happening again. From the reports we have seen, whatever unholy beliefs they have is ten times worse here. The only people you should find within the confines of the city are defenders who most likely will offer heavy resistance. Everything that we have is telling us that the civilians..."

"What about the people?" Brett demanded.

"Well, they probably have already fallen to the same fate, or will be soon, that you ran into last time."

Brett sat back into the couch, thinking about the idea of an entire city again wiped out. For what? What kind of evil would slaughter so many people? He could feel the fire beneath the skin of his forearm beginning to warm as he thought of what they saw in the last temple and scratched at his forearm.

"It has to end here, Sergeant." The General sat back, a little resolve built behind his words. "That is why we are sending your team. This mission is too important for us not to."

"How are we going to get inside? Not like my team can just walk in, and that's way too far to go under cover of night."

"You're not going alone. The whole base is being mobilized. Our main battery will come in from the west, draw as much attention and defense to us. For all they know, we still believe we are fighting this war with Azhana. I've seen other reports surfacing that these 'mass killings' have happened worldwide. Even on our side." The old soldier took in a deep breath before continuing. "All we have is this chance for a diversion, throw all we have at it, and see if it's enough."

"Will this be enough?"

"I'm not sure."

The General began toying with an empty glass on the stand next to him. His eyes were longing for what wasn't there.

"Once we are in place, your team and others will come from the east, take out any defenses you find, and get to that underground temple as fast as possible." The priest etched a path with his finger as he spoke and drew Brett's attention. "Hopefully, we are not too late."

"Others, sir?"

"Yep, we couldn't let your team ruin everything again. My team will be going in to make sure you don't miss anything. That way when you fail, we'll be right there to clean it up." Trevor flicked off the strap to his sidearm to send home his message.

Brett did everything he could to hold his restraint. This man had some serious issues and seemed only interested in pressing every button he could find in Brett. He couldn't think of a thing that he had done to the man or his team. Jealousy was a bitch.

"Whatever happens, the job must be done." The General got up and paced again in front of his windows overlooking the base. "This won't end the war. Shit, we aren't even fighting the original enemy. Whoever the fuck these people are have become far worse than anything the other bastards could even think of." The General let his head down for a second, looking at his feet.

"General?" Brett rose to his feet. "Anything else I should know before I get my men ready?"

"I just hope they remember what we did here and why."

"What sir?"

"Oh, nothing Sergeant. Just make sure they know, this CANNOT fail. Everyone is expendable, even you and I."

Brett nodded as he left the room. Now there is something he never thought he would hear that man say. Whatever laid before them must be so important that the most self-centered man he'd ever met was risking everything to accomplish it. Too bad that included their lives.

Chapter Thirty-Eight

2210 Hours, Avos 10, 2258
  Fort Forward Trinity, Edge of Republic Territory

THE STARS TWINKLED BRIGHTLY over their head as Kris sat and ruffled through his bags one more time. All his gear was stowed away, extra ammunition, medical supplies, and a holy book that he no longer went anywhere without. He needed to keep everything to a minimum. The Sergeant had said they were going in fast and heavy. Supplies for a sustained battle would not be needed, everything else he kept a secret for now. The sound of engines roaring to life and officers barking orders carried with the slight breeze that made its way to where he seated himself on a small grassy knoll that overlooked the exit to the base.

Something about this mission felt different. An urgency followed the movements of every man and woman he passed, pushing them into their work as they followed the orders of their commanding officers. The whole base was up in arms and doing something to move them forward.

He hadn't been stationed here that long, but he knew it had to be something bigger than he could ever imagine as the entire base moved at once.

Putting his hand on the dewy grass made him realize that his throat was drier than he thought. Nerves he guessed, it had to be nerves.

"Hey, Kris! Get moving. The Sergeant is here. He wants to see all of us." Ed waved him over as he walked his way back to the single command tent lit by fluorescent lamps.

Kris got up, grabbed his bags and made his way to them. As nervous as he was, something about seeing the men of his team; ready, professional, and calm, gave him some relief, fleeting as it was.

"ALRIGHT, I'm going to be brief and to the point. I've got some important information to go over, and I don't have much time to do it. David and Witch have returned and delivered some disturbing news to me."

Kris looked over at the two men. Both looked slightly haggard and weary from the days of travel.

"You two go ahead and relay to the rest what you already told me." Brett had nodded to both men before they recounted their story.

Everything from what they saw when they got there, what they found inside the library, and what happened when they tried to leave. Did those men say they knew they were coming? A ball knotted up in Kris' throat as he knew what that meant. Both men finished talking before everyone looked up at Brett.

"Looks like we have a rat among us here, Sergeant." Dickie put his meaty fists on the table before them.

All of them looked right at Kris. Even if he tried, he

wasn't going to be able to say anything to make what he did any better.

"There is no rat among the lot of you." The General's voice brought all of them to attention. The Sergeant stood there, arms crossed. "The young man only did what I instructed him to do. He was under direct orders from me to relay anything he felt I should know, even if it meant breaking your orders."

The veteran leader and Sergeant Brett now looked at each other eye to eye. At first it looked as if daggers were about to fly between the men, but quickly the General softened his tone.

"I'm glad the information did get to me. It proved my theory correct."

The General sat on a small folding chair and stressfully pulled at the collar of his battle uniform.

"What theory was that, sir?" Brett's angry eyes now shifted from the General to Kris.

His arms remained crossed against his chest.

"We have traitors within our rank. Could be one, could be a dozen, hell could be half the men here. I wasn't told about your little assignment for these two here until late last night." The man looked up at Kris. "And I wasn't the one he told, Father Rondeau relayed the message to me himself. Seems you told one of the priests more than five days ago. That's plenty of time to get the message out. I'm sorry to say this, but I believe this whole operation could be compromised."

"We are still going, General?" Brett leaned forward, half addressing the man, half looking at the maps on the small card table.

"We have no choice. There are very few men I still trust, and you six here are among them. Father Rondeau has assured me the information they have is still trustworthy, but even he doesn't know how deep the treachery goes."

"You trust that religious bastard? You already said the information leaked from one of his own." David crossed his arms, his boot tapping the ground as he waited impatiently.

"The man has been by my side from the beginning. He has nothing to gain with demon massacres and ritualistic sacrifices. Again, we don't have a choice. People are dying out there, and it will only get worse unless we stop it. Is that understood?"

"Yes, Sir!" The team answered together.

"Then I need a private word with the Sergeant here. Take a few moments to finish getting yourselves ready."

The men grabbed what they could and stepped away from the area. Each of them trying to stay within earshot the best they could.

"I know you don't like this and neither do I." The General didn't bother meeting Brett eye to eye as he looked off into the distance, watching as hundreds of soldiers prepared for battle.

"This could be another trap. The worst part is it will snare us all this time."

"I know that and you know that. Damn even they know that." The older man took his hat off and ran his hand through his hair. Streaks of gray now finally showing through. "That is why everything is riding on you and your men. Get in there, and do what you guys do best. No matter what I've said before, you've never failed me. Don't make this a first time."

"We won't, Sir," The most sincere thing Brett had said to his commanding officer in a long time.

The General put his hat back on as he took in a deep breath and exhaled it in a sigh. Nothing passed between the two veterans for a few moments. Both knew the stakes on the line. Maybe, just maybe, this battle would be the real end to all this.

"All right then. Good luck to you all. Make us proud, and one more thing, Sergeant." The General walked right up and looked Brett in his eyes. "Go easy on the kid. He was only following orders, I set him up for it. He'll surprise you before this is all over, trust me on this one thing. It's not the first time someone with a good heart made a decision with dire consequences. You'll thank me if you get the chance."

The General saluted and walked away. Brett didn't need to do anything. By the time he took his eyes off the departing officer, his men were already coming back to the tables. They had a lot of work ahead of them, and he hoped they were ready for it.

"Well, here it is." Brett looked into each of his men's eyes one by one and proceeded to ask them to follow him into what he knew was the gates of hell.

Chapter Thirty-Nine

1110 Hours, Avos 13, 2258
  Hiowell, Keiola, Northeast Republic

BONE SPLITTING PAIN, ringing, and the taste of metal mixed with blood. All these were the last things Will wanted when he awoke. Groaning, it took all he had to open his eyes, made more difficult with one partly swollen shut.

"What the fuck happened? Ugh."

His throat was dry, and the smoky air tickled the back of his mouth the second he opened it.

"Looks like they didn't crack open that thick skull of yours, did they?" Walker's voice called through the haze.

It took a second, but Will could see Walker tied up to a chair across from him. Turning his head and trying to concentrate through the pain, Will looked to see if everyone was there. All of them were individually tied up and looking groggy or scared shit-less. The room felt more like a closet, it couldn't be more than ten feet by ten feet, but there were more than twenty men crammed inside. Candles burned on pedestals at each corner, filling it with a smoky haze and casting a yellow light on everything.

"Where are we?"

Just the sound of his voice sent pain through his head. He wanted to reach up and see how bad the damage was, but he could not move his arms an inch.

"Hell, as far as I can tell. Look at the walls. We have to be in some fucking church." Walker was correct as Will squinted for a better look. The walls had pictures of what had to be religious figures fighting demons, or at least that's what he could figure out. "I told you they were going to try to convert us."

Of all things, Walker always seemed more worried about religion and church than death.

"As I can remember it, these guys killed the Republic's men. Whoever they are, I think we are in a whole different pile of trouble." Will tried to look around, get any bearings he could about their surroundings.

"Why do you have such a problem with religion anyway, Sergeant?" Private Teller looked worse in the candlelight. His eyes were so shallow and blacked out, he looked dead already.

"Did I say you could ask me a personal question like that? Remember who your senior officer is before you speak again." The Sergeant's eyes carried with it a veiled threat.

"Now I think it's coming back to me. Didn't you give him a field promotion to Sergeant, Sergeant?"

Walker went to open his mouth and say something but hung there silently. Even with the help, a smile did not find Teller's face.

"Anyway, enough with that. Is everyone here? Did I miss something?"

Who knows how long he had been knocked out?

"Only one didn't make it. After they had taken you out, it wasn't much to stop our advance. The only ones untied were me and Teller, and there wasn't much we could do against twenty armed men. When they went to move us to their trucks, they decided Specialist Rogers wasn't worth the effort." Walker took a few seconds as he sighed while looking into his palms on his lap. "They dragged him into the woods and finished him off like a fucking dog. With his leg as bad as it was, he couldn't fight back. Fucking cowards, shot a man who couldn't even walk."

Will could still hear the sounds of his screams back in the truck. Unlucky bastard. The bullet must have done some terrible damage to his leg.

"So what's the plan, Boss? Any more big ideas?" Walker was now looking at him, waiting.

There it was, everyone was going to wait and see where he would lead them. Since when did I take the lead? With a look at the others, there wasn't much any of them could do. Each was tied securely to a chair, no finding metal bits to cut the bonds loose this time.

"Anyone notice anything we can use to cut these ropes? Maybe a…" Will couldn't even finish the question when the one door that led into the room opened.

Three tall robed individuals stepped in without a word. Their faces lost in the shadows of their cowls. The robes in the candlelight reflected a minor shine with a clean blue exterior, embroidered into the cloth was a golden flame. Without saying anything, they made their way directly to Will. Two of the men grabbed his arms while one released his bonds.

"Who are you? Where are we?" Will demanded of his captors.

Will tried to struggle as the men forced him onto his feet. Their grips were surprisingly strong, even a man his size had a difficult time resisting. He thought he caught a glimpse of one of their faces; it looked paler than Teller.

"Answer me damn it! Who the fuck are you?" Even though it was fruitless, Will tried fighting back. He felt like a child being dragged by his much larger parents.

"Hey, you pajama-wearing bastards. Let the man go!" Walker tried kicking, but all he was successful doing was making a grunting noise, even his chair didn't move.

Just for his effort, the men stopped, and one effortlessly shot out his arm and slapped the Sergeant across the face. The sound of the crack and the look of daze across his face told how hard that blow was.

Without waiting for any further resistance, the men escorted Will out of the room.

The men led him down a long candlelit hallway, closed doors on each side all the way down. The only sound in the hallway was the sound of their feet as they progressed down the carpeted path. Each time they got close to a door, Will swore he could hear faint crying coming from behind. When they reached the end of the path, a tall glass case stood with two single-handed axes crossed over two single candles. Something was different with the candles. One burned a bright yellow and red flame while the other burned a light blue. No smoke rose from the fire that lit the candles as they flickered behind the glass and shined off of the engraved blades of the axes.

Passing the display, the men led Will to the right and through a set of large, curved, double doors. On the other side, the building opened into a large gathering area lit with even more candles all along the walls. The surrounding floor rose gradually the farther you got away from the central floor that was marble and shined with gold laced between the stones. Will could imagine if used for another purpose, this room would be full of rows of seating. Faithful believers hurrying in weekly to hear the word of their God's faithful preachers. This room was not being used for that purpose.

The center and front of the room where he entered were empty. The only furniture in the area that he could see were chairs spaced evenly apart all along the walls. Both men moving him along stopped as they got closer to the center.

"Hello my child, I am so glad that we could finally meet. I did wish it could be under different circumstances." Coming from the shadows beyond, a man not much different in size from Will slowly stepped into the light.

He was dressed similarly to the men who had escorted him to this room; flowing blue robes, yet this man did not cover his face. He was young, clean-shaven, with neatly trimmed brown hair. What struck Will as odd was the sky blue eyes that now looked him straight in the face. A fire burned behind them, something like a drive he hadn't seen since Charlie.

"Well, I'll accept your apology once you explain who you are, where this place is, and what you want with us. Also, for fuck's sake, haven't you all heard of electricity?" Will looked around exaggerating. "How am I supposed to see what you all look like when I kick your ass if it's so damn dark in here?"

"Ooh spirit, I like that. I can tell why she picked you."

"Who picked me? Again, who the fuck are you?"

The man laughed and waved off Will's comments as he

walked by them. The two men escorting him made sure he kept up.

"Who I am, no longer matters. Maybe years ago, when I was younger, it would have mattered, but not today." The man turned, and Will noticed his eyes were brighter than before. "But maybe, just maybe, it will matter tomorrow!"

Will struggled against the men holding him. His head hurt, his whole body ached, and now he was stuck listening to the ramblings of someone who had clearly lost it.

"Do you know how many years I've been looking for you two? How long it has taken me to set all this up?"

The man spun with outstretched arms as if he had built this whole place with his bare hands.

"Let me guess, five months? I'll maybe believe eight if you promise to let us go."

The man's smile disappeared for a second and with it, Will lost the breath from his lungs as a fist rammed into his stomach.

"Fifty years, I have been waiting fifty years for this!" The man's smile was back. "It wasn't until halfway through that I learned I would one day meet you two. Once I knew," The man shivered and giggled as if something ran down his spine. "Oh, it's been a glorious twelve years of hard work, and soon it will all be worth it."

"What work? What two? I count only one unless these two mutes of yours are as half brained as I would guess. Maybe that makes it two."

"I guessed you wouldn't know, how could you? You probably don't even believe in the petty gods your adversary worships. How could you know the truth?" The confident man now tapped Will on the face as if he were a child. "Ah, but she will come. When she does, the decision will be made, and my master will arrive. Oh, the power he will bestow on us all will be spectacular!"

She? What she? No way he could be talking about Charlie, could he? Will looked around, there were more of the hooded men now entering the room. They worked quietly and without command, getting little tables set up with the chairs that lined the room.

"Now for the reason you are here. I would love to keep bantering with you, it has been such a long time since I've had a good laugh. You are right though. These mutes, as you call them, can be rather dull. Nonetheless. I have a very important decision that I will need you to make." The man made his way to one of the chairs and removed something from the little table near it. Coming back, it was a sharp knife or dagger of some sort. "Those men you came with, what are your opinions of them?"

"Each one is a fine soldier. More than I can say about you."

"Oh, terrible. It will only be harder on you then. My question for you is, which should die first?"

Even with such a dreaded question, the man had a smile on his face as he flicked some dirt from under his nails. Will couldn't tell how to feel, angry or scared. His blood was boiling, but his legs lost all their strength.

"Fuck you! How about you go first, tell them to let me go, and I'll make sure it happens!" In defiance, he spit on the man's face, which remained unchanged.

"It's not that difficult a question my boy. They are all going to die, and there isn't much you can do about it. The only thing you can change is the order at which they die."

Will's fear gave way as his anger continued to build. The men holding him could tell as they squeezed his arms tighter. They were a lot stronger than they looked.

"And what makes you think I'll even help you with that?"

"You don't have much of a choice. I'll start selecting at random, and I'll make their deaths last even longer. They will go one by one slowly if you don't choose. If you do play along, I'll make sure it is fast and as painless as can be."

This madman didn't look as if he were playing a game. The faces and names of everyone he knew in that room went through his mind. Could he pick who died first? Would he be sending them to their death?

"Me, I will go first."

A smirk stretched across the man's face.

"I'm sorry, we can't have that. You're supposed to die later, and I promise one thing." The man stepped closer so he could whisper in Will's ear. The strong smell of garlic filled Will's nose as the man's breath blew warm on his cheek. "All these men will die in this building, but you will make it out alive. In the end, though, you will still die."

Will thought about the man's words as he stood there. He was going to die last, but not here in this building? What kind of game is this?

"I told you, FUCK YOU!"

"That's okay. I will give you one hour to decide. These men will escort you back to your friends one last time. Just remember, when they come back you will all be coming here. Have your decision made, or you will watch each die slowly and painfully. Think on that for the next sixty minutes of your life."

The man turned, and Will was pushed back out the curved doors. What was he going to tell the others?

1210 HOURS, Avos 13, 2258

Hiowell, Keiola, Northeast Republic

. . .

SHE COULD SEE the first snowflakes fall from the clouds above as they made their way to the buildings and city below. The storm that had aided her back at the fort now made its way to the city at the bottom of the hill. Looking down at it with her ever-growing strength and confidence made her feel as a giant would about to devour a small village of farmers.

Before her sat Hiowell, a city that had been fortified and occupied by more armed troops than she could imagine. The citizens of the city relocated themselves when the army moved in. Fortifications were built-up, and the infrastructure designed around making this location ground zero. It would take days if not weeks, to surround and overtake such a bunkered and well-armed base of troops. They had never faced the wrath of someone like her, and she was ready for the challenge.

It had taken her two rough days of travel by jeep to get within ten miles of the city. When the engine finally quit, she walked the remainder of the way, reveling in the cold that followed her. All notion of distance lost to her. By the second day, she no longer needed to rest. The cold no longer bit at her skin. The ice and snow warmed her skin, and the howling wind soothed her body as it blanketed her in its embrace. Her arm no longer ached, though the blue scab of ice remained as a reminder of the changes coming over her. It was a small price to pay for what she was given.

Looking down at the city, now covered by a gray and black rolling mass of storm cloud, the snow was coming down in waves. At its heaviest, the snow could reduce visibility to a mere few feet in front of one's face. Waiting and anxious with anticipation, she knew then would be her time. Their end would soon be upon them. She smiled, as a snow wolf walked over and sat on its haunches beside her. Looking down at the beast, both predators hungered for more destruction and death. Turning their eyes back down to the target below, lost in the shadows of the storm, two sets of bright blue flames burned with desire.

FORTY-SEVEN MINUTES HAD PASSED, and there was nothing they could do. All twenty men struggled with their bonds and searched for anything that could show them a way out. Some men cried; some swore, others just sat in shock. Will had told them what was going to happen the minute he returned. At first, Walker and Teller figured it was some game, but he had assured him there was nothing about this man to say he was lying.

"Fuck! Anyone think of anything yet?" Sergeant Walker was soaked from his collar halfway down his shirt from trying to tear his bonds free.

"Maybe, if we all fight at the same time when they come, we can overpower them. It will be pretty hard to fight all of us at once." Teller suggested though he was quick to put his eyes back down to the ground.

"If only it was that easy, Teller. Those two who came to get me were as strong as oxen, and there is no telling how many there will be. Plus, I have a feeling it is not going to be that easy." Will didn't want to worsen the hopes for the struggling soldier, but no reason to lie at this point either.

He didn't know what the endgame was, but he doubted brute force was going to get them out of this.

"Then what you do you have, big shot? Either enlighten us with your plan or start thinking of one quick." Walker spat as he spoke, the veins in his neck bulging as he pulled harder on his restraints.

He hadn't told them the part where he would be the

one to pick who died first. Giving them that bit of information would have made this last bit of time worse than it already was.

"I told you, I'm doing the best I can. If we can't come up with something, better go with what Teller said." He looked at the men. Mixed looks of terror, sadness, and anger looked back at him. "Give everything you can, and fight until the last man drops. No holding back. I doubt they will hold back on you. Better to die fighting to get free than to sit and die in whatever way they have planned. I can promise you that."

Great set of last words he had in him. He could remember great speeches given by men of both history and fiction in the movies he watched growing up. If any of them survived this, would he be remembered for that? Better to be remembered for saying something than to have let everyone go down quietly.

"How much time do we have left?" Teller, who looked surprisingly calm, asked as he sat still in his chair.

Almost seemed as though he was accepting the situation and wanted to face something like the man he was meant to be.

"No idea, they gave us an..." Will's words stopped as the doors to the small room opened.

Just as before, the same two large men walked in, their faces still darkened out by their hoods that held back the candlelight. They didn't say anything, didn't even move their heads as they walked straight to Will and began removing his restraints.

"So you're gonna kill us, you pussy little pieces of shit? Untie me and we'll see who kills who." Walker spit on the closest man, his face as red as a ripe tomato. The man didn't even flinch to acknowledge the Sergeant. "Come on you fuckers!"

Will kept his eyes on Walker as the men released him. The only hope he had was to remain calm for the moment he was free. The pressure of the bonds released quickly. Giving all he had, he snapped from his chair and crunched his fist right into the chin of the man on his left. The man stumbled backward and fell to the floor as he tripped over the lap of the prisoner behind him. Turning to the guard on his right, Will raised his other fist to swing, but a bright light flashed before his eyes as a fist connected directly with his nose.

Blood flowed freely over his face and down his chin as he came to his senses sitting on the floor. Lifting himself into a seated position, Will tried to piece it together. How had he reacted so fast? The one he had hit was now standing over him. His hood was pushed back revealing a white as snow face, and eyes pink as the skin of a pig. Both men didn't say anything, just reached down and forcibly picked Will off the floor and began moving him toward the door.

"You won't kill me you bastards! You think Will hits hard? Just untie me, and you'll see how a real man fights!"

The slamming door quickly cut off the voice of the screaming Sergeant. The silence in the hallway was as horrifying as the knowledge of the death that hung over Will's head. The two men quickly led Will back to the center room of the temple. Just as before, the area was completely vacant except for the one man waiting for his answer.

"So here is the guest of honor. I do hope you had enough time to think long and hard about your decision."

The man had changed into even more elaborately lavish robes: blue silk encrusted with gold, diamonds, and jewels all shaped into the pattern of flames. When the bastard moved in the candlelight, the reflection moved up the fabric like fire.

"Fuck you and your decision. You can't kill us all. You need us!"

"Need you? Well, I guess you're right in that. I do need YOU, but the others, well, let's say I consider them like lambs to the slaughter. There are always more, and yet, you think I care about them in the least? Valiant my son, foolish, but valiant." The man circled the room looking pleased with himself. Will tried everything he could to break loose and attack the overconfident son of a bitch, but his two guards were like stone statues with a vice-grip of iron. "I'll ask one more time. Have you come up with a decision? We are running a bit short on time."

"Yeah, fuck off you bastard. I've got all day."

An expression of exaggerated pouting crossed the leader's face, but he quickly replaced it with a smile. Above them, all the rafters began to creak as a strong wind from outside battered the exterior of the building. Moaning and struggling against the storm, Will could hear rattling as something rolled itself across the shingles above.

"Ah, but you hear that? The time for us all is quickly running out. She is almost here!" His robes bounced up and down as the man jumped like an excited child. "Soon, you will behold the strength of a true god, and for once in your life, you will fulfill what you were meant to do!"

Will didn't understand a thing this man was talking about, but whatever it was he was pretty sure he didn't want to know. Giddy as a child, the leader clapped his hands and his servants, mostly hidden in the shadows, filed out of the room.

"Your friends will be joining us in a minute. I'm in a good mood; this will be your last chance. Decide or their fate will be far worse than anything you can imagine."

Will waited and listened for any sound that made its way from the hall. Hopefully Walker, Teller, or any of them would be able to put up a fight. Maybe something that would let him know they had a chance.

"Oh, by the way, if you think their little plan of fighting back was going to work, don't strain your mind trying to find out. Once we pulled you out of the room, we filled it with a little bit of nerve gas. Our guests would be lucky if they knew what was going on by the time they reached this room."

His laughter echoed through the room as he made his way to each seated station and made sure the preparations were ready.

The moments that passed felt like hours, but soon the soldiers who had been tied up with him were filed into the room one by one. Will tried looking into their eyes. Staring back at him were looks of complete disorientation. Each man drugged temporarily to the point of compliance.

"Walker! Teller! Wake up!"

His two friends marched into the room. Teller looked as if he was barely awake, using the servant that led him in as a crutch to carry his weight. Even the big man Walker was nothing but a glossy pair of eyes. Both men looked directly at each other, but nothing passed beyond the chemicals that clouded his mind.

"Guys, come on!" Will screamed as he strained to fight, but no one answered.

The only person who seemed to notice was also the only bastard with a smile on his face.

"Ah, isn't this lovely. All of us together at last."

With his robes flowing out around him, the church's leader now stood right in front of Will, facing the men who had entered. There wasn't anything in this world that made Will angrier than he was at this moment. Every muscle strained as he tried to reach for the man only two feet in front of him. The sound of wood bending to the will of nature echoed far above in the rafters. Maybe if he were lucky the whole roof would cave in on him. Possibly even crush this monster right where he stood.

"OK, so who goes first, my boy? She is almost upon us, so the ceremony must begin."

The man swept his arm out like an advertising model would as they presented a row of lavish rewards.

"I told you, go fuck yourself!"

Crashing could be heard from the roof as the wind began finally tearing some shingling off.

"As you wish, seven. I have always liked the number seven. We'll start with him."

Will watched in terror as one of the youngest recruits was selected and brought to the first chair along the wall.

0617 HOURS, Avos 13, 2258
Obrathe, Azhana

THE SUN WAS INCHING over the eastern horizon as Brett and his team slowed their jeep to a quiet stop in a small opening in the brush of the forest outside Obrathe.

"I don't remember the weather guys saying it was going to get this hot out here. Damn, I wish I had their job." David wiped the sweat from his brow. The top of his undershirt was already soaked all the way through. "Only people I know that can be this wrong or forget to tell anyone and still have a job. What would happen if we made mistakes as much as they did, huh?"

"We'd be dead." Brett lifted his small backpack, shouldered it and began moving forward.

No reason to waste any more time.

"What are you crying about there, ladies' man? You always said they liked you for that dark skin of yours. All this sun will just make you damn near irresistible, won't it?" Dickie poked him with the butt of his rifle before quickly following the Sergeant.

"They already do!"

David was quick to follow.

The team moved forward. Staying as deep into the shadows as they could, they made their way to the first few buildings. The entire city stretched out in front of them, over one hundred city blocks before they reached their intended target. From the information they had, militarized roadblocks had been set at every major intersection. Each one located at regular ten-block intervals.

Motorized and personal travel was controlled to section the city off into wards, making it much more manageable for the leaders to handle. The poorest and most likely to be unruly were on the far outskirts of the city. As you moved deeper inside the limits, the prosperity of the population grew. From everything they heard, the military was just as present there as it was in the poorest regions.

Here in the slums, the buildings, or what remained of what could be called buildings, stood close together. Other than the main streets that all traveled toward the center square, alleys were used as paths of travel and homes for the unfortunate. Brett kicked at the trash and cardboard pitched together for a cover that was abandoned sometime in the past.

"Holy shit! People live out in places like this?" David pinched off his nose as the putrid stink from the trash grew just as fast as the heat index.

"Not everyone lives a life of prosperity. This war has taken casualties outside the military on both sides of the fighting." Witch was taking up the rear guard, making sure they didn't miss anything as they moved forward.

"But that's not why we are here, is it? Whoever this 'demon cult' is has taken over this city." David swallowed hard as he thought about what it would be like to be in a situation like this; not having a home or meal to eat.

"Our mission is to take out whoever is behind these murders and stop whatever they think they are starting. It doesn't matter if it's some 'cult', the Azhana Army itself, or our men doing it. They all deserve more than we are going to give them, but a bullet will have to do." The whispering ended as Brett checked to make sure there was a round in the chamber and ready to go.

He was serious, and everyone knew it.

The team had made it through the first ten blocks, slipping from alley to alley. Just as they had been led to believe, there hadn't been a soul to stop them. To the surprise of all of them, there hadn't even been any wild animals: no dogs, cats, or even birds. Just as the city before, this city seemed dead.

Brett poked his head out from around the corner of the alley between two mudbrick buildings. Both had boarded up windows, and the roof of one caved in at the front corner. Opening before him was a main artery road, three lanes of traffic in each direction. In the center stood a small rectangular building. Looking at it, it would be lucky if it held more than one person at a time. At its base were piles of sandbags that extended partially into the first lane of traffic.

No one appeared to be inside. The only movement he could see was a swirl of dust and dirt that came off the concrete in a small swirling cyclone. Across the other side of the highway, buildings quickly rose from the small amount of brown grass that separated them from the road.

"Not much of a checkpoint, is it?" Ed's face was within inches of Brett's ear. He could feel his breath on his neck.

"All of them must have been pulled into the battle."

Listening Brett could hear explosions and echoes of gunfire. The sounds had started not long after the team had started moving through the slums. He wondered how many would lose their lives today, on all sides of the fight.

Lifting his hand, the men made ready to make their way across the road. Once they were on the other side, they were to start their sweep of the buildings. The poor area they had decided would have been the first place abandoned and didn't need much attention. Squeezing his hand to push back the fire that now burned constantly under the skin of his forearm, Brett waved them forward. All six jogged as fast as they could, yet kept their eyes open. They were in the open and vulnerable to any attack that came.

Approaching the solitary checkpoint, Brett took a quick glance to reaffirm that it was empty. It was. The outer glass was dusty from what seemed to be a lot more than a morning's worth of abandonment. No time to stop and think about it. They had to keep moving.

"I have awaited your arrival; I am glad you are here, my child." The voice crashed into Brett's mind so hard his vision blurred and he stumbled to his knees, yards before he got to the end of the highway.

Without missing a beat, David and Dickie scooped him up under his shoulders and supported him the rest of the way.

"So much work awaits us. You are strong. There is no better choice." Brett pressed his palms against his temples as the pain in his head, and the fire in his arm thundered down to his bones. Wherever this voice was coming from, the pressure was too much as he sank to the ground and sat with his back against the first building approached.

"Boss! You alright?" It was David.

He was kneeling as the others kept their guard up in all directions. Looking at him, Brett could hear the man, but his voice echoed as it came through an invisible tunnel between them. "Sergeant!"

"I know it hurts, but in the end all will be yours. The time is coming faster than I anticipated." The pain ripped through his mind.

"Guys, I think we need to turn back. Dickie, help me get him up again." David reached down and started pulling on him.

"No! We keep moving forward." The pain left just as fast as it appeared. His vision cleared, and the only sounds he could hear were the men near him and the battle in the distance. Too much was at stake for them to turn back now.

"But Boss? Something is wrong." David's look of concern echoed in the faces of the other men.

"Nothing is wrong. I am fine, let's keep moving." Brett gave them the strongest look he could.

The pain was gone, the voice was gone, but he had no idea where it had originated. Shaking his head, he accepted the assistance with getting up from the ground and quickly moved to take the lead again. He couldn't let his men see him weak.

He wanted to say something to them, make sure they still had the confidence in him they needed, but no time for that now. They were trained soldiers. They were a team. In the end, they would still follow him. The end. That thought echoed in his mind.

Moving them forward, they began their sweep of the second ward of the city. The buildings, a mix of mud brick and metal were a higher class than they had seen coming in. Small businesses and simple apartments were the majority of what they checked. Just as before, the buildings were empty. The dust and garbage that filled the streets and buildings gave the men little hope they had arrived early enough to save anyone in the city.

Chapter Forty

1346 Hours, Avos 13, 2258
  Hiowell, Keiola, Northeast Republic

"WHATEVER YOU CHOOSE, you can have. All you have to do is take it." The unknown voice had returned to her mind.

Sometime not long after destroying the men in Fort Frozen Heart, she had begun hearing it once more. She still didn't know where it came from, but over the last seven days, she had grown accustomed to it to the point of wanting it there. It soothed her; it beckoned her to continue, to destroy more and craved the power that she also craved with every fiber of her body.

The storm over the city was a full-on blizzard now as she approached the outer limits. Snow fell around her in a wall of white and gray. She knew she was invisible to anyone who wasn't close enough to touch. Everyone would be running for shelter if they hadn't found themselves inside already. To her, the storm was home. She basked in its glory, reveled in the power, and craved more. Walking beside her was her new companion, the alpha snow wolf.

Words did not need to pass between mistress and servant, as she knew from the look in its eyes, it followed her command just as the storm above did. With a nod of her chin, the wolf reared its head back and howled. Only a second later, other howls could be heard echoing through the storm. Looking deep into the walls of white that surrounded her, she could see hundreds if not thousands of white beasts racing forward into the city.

She continued moving farther into the city. The storm poured snow all around as inches began accumulating on everything and the world was a sheet of white. It wasn't long before the sound of the storm began to mix with the sound of gunfire and screams. The beasts were tearing their way into buildings and ripping apart anything they could find.

"Our greatest triumph will soon be before us! Feel the power that pulses through you. Embrace your calling!" The voice brought a smile to her face.

Whoever the voice belonged to, was correct. She could feel an excitement run through her body. She flexed the fingers on her hands, and she looked for anything to tear apart. She wanted blood; she craved it just as much as the beasts at her control did. A fire tore through an upper window of the building ahead.

Ah, time to have some fun.

Approaching the simple looking square building, she could hear men screaming inside. Beasts from every direction started to converge on the exterior doorway. Whoever was inside was giving one hell of a fight.

Oh, if only they knew their end was approaching.

Entering, she could see holes torn into the wall as bullets shredded the wolves when they approached. Piles of furniture and household items were built-up at the top of the single set of stairs that led to the bedrooms on the second floor. Snow began building up in front as the bodies of her wolves fell apart as they died. For each one she lost, three more would come in. The beasts parted and stopped charging the stairs as she approached.

A couple of rounds crashed into the wall beside her as she took her first step upward.

"Is that how you plan to help a woman in search of help?"

She wrapped her robes close around her body, trying to hide her face.

"Stop where you are! There are demons all around us! How did you get here?" The man's voice sounded strong yet wavered with fear of the unknown.

"These beasts ran to find something easier to kill. Whatever you did seems to have scared them off. I was barely able to make it in alive."

The cowl of the robes hid the smile she had, but she knew it would not be much longer.

"Well…Well, stay where you are. If you approach any closer, we will be forced to shoot you as well."

She did not stop as she walked up to the fortified wall of junk. The familiar sound of a rifle being reloaded and the whispered words of prayer echoed through the hall.

Oh, they still pray to their useless gods, I'll show them what a real god can do!

She giggled at the thought as she pulled at the storm from within her mind. She could feel her soul reach out and grab the wind and snow as if they were physical things to touch and move. Following her command, the storm tore through the windows that remained behind the men. A roar erupted as the wind rushed in.

The men turned to the attack from behind as she reached one hand up and tore down the wall in one quick motion. Before her stood two armed men, one woman, and a child in an unfurnished single room lit by a solitary oil lamp. The woman cradled the child in her arms as they huddled in the corner and screamed. All four of them looked ragged, their clothes torn from the fighting and dampened with blood and tears. Her lust grew as she closed the distance between her and the two men.

The larger of the two turned just as she grabbed his right arm. She wrenched it toward the other and used her free hand to squeeze the trigger. Half a dozen rounds burst through the young man's chest before he toppled to the ground near the cowering woman. Horror and fear struck the remaining man's face as he finally saw the look on her face as the cowl of her robe fell back. Her eyes burned with a magnificent blue flame, her skin was a shade under that of her blue robes. She smiled as he dropped his rifle and her hand wrapped around the front of his throat.

Snow and wind blasted through the windows; the sound drowned out the screams of the others as she lifted and pushed the man back toward the open window.

"What…Who…?" He gurgled as he struggled for breath.

She had his life in her hands, every breath he was to take from this point on were hers to decide. With a thrust, the man found himself free falling outside the building. His screams fell silent as the storm swallowed him, and he soon found the ground.

"The God protect us! Why has he forsaken us? Please leave my child alone you demon!"

The woman's voice scratched at her ears, but Charlie could no longer understand the feeling behind them. Her child in her arms, the mother's face was wet and streaked with tears, snow from the storm was now accumulating on her as the two cowered in the corner. Her child, a boy, held his eyes closed, and he squeezed harder into his mother. Looking at him, he had to be no older than ten, scared and full of fear.

"Weak," was all she said as she turned and walked out of the room.

A whole pack of hungry wolves waited at the bottom of the stairs. She met each with a look of agreement as she passed, and they continued up the stairs. Within moments, the screams of those who remained in the room could be heard over the ever-increasing howl of the storm.

"This is a good start, but we have so much more work to do." The voice in her mind beckoned.

The voice was right. She wanted more, and there was an entire city ahead of her. Only these weak-minded people didn't know what had come with the storm…

SCREAMS MIXED with the sound of the roaring wind as it beat against the walls and the roof above. The young man made a noise like nothing Will had ever heard. One of the church's servants slowly pulled the soldiers entrails out, inch by inch. They had tied him to his chair; arms spread wide with cuts that slowly dripped to the floor. Unlike the others, once the cutting started, he regained his full consciousness and was still somehow awake through the pain. Watching as the servant worked on the man almost brought the contents of Will's stomach up.

"Stop! Oh shit, what are you doing to the man! Don't you have any mercy? Stop!"

Will fought but could not move at all. His handlers had

vice-like grips on his arms, and no matter how much he tried, they held still as if he were a child pulling on his parents.

"You want me to stop?" The leader walked up to Will's face and slapped him to where his knees buckled. The fury in him reignited as he renewed his fight. "I gave you a chance to stop this. I told you to make your choice. This is what YOUR choice has brought. Each of these men is going to die here; YOU had the choice to decide if it was going to be slow and painful, or fast and clean." He now grabbed Will by the chin and forced him to look at the man as he took his final breaths. "We all have choices to make. Look at what your choice has done. Don't you dare try to get angry with me. You could have changed all of this."

"Fuck you, you sick bastard. How can you do this? You fucking monster!"

The man ignored Will and pointed at another dazed and drugged soldier in line. Quickly the servants led him to a chair and started preparing.

"A monster? You think I am a monster? Oh, how little you know my boy. You haven't seen a monster until she gets here. Then you will see true power!" Almost on cue, the rafters above rained more dust down on them as they sounded on the brink of breaking in two. "Don't you worry. It won't be long before I find a friend of yours mixed in with this group. Then you'll decide. Just think of what you've done to these fellow soldiers. Just because you won't DECIDE!"

Waving to the servants with the back of his hand, they began to cut. First they started with the middle-aged soldier's wrists. Only small cuts to start the bleeding, so it dripped and pooled on the floor. Will looked back and forth between the dead man and the soon-to-be dead one.

The leader was right. He didn't know these two well, but it wouldn't be long before they stumbled on Walker or Teller.

Once they started working on the new man's abdomen, the screams started again. His voice, like the other, started echoing across the room. With each harrowing scream, the storm outside answered with a roar of its own.

"Ah, isn't the power of the storm exciting? Ha-ha!" The man was in his glory as another soldier sat screaming as he his bowels was torn out. "Behold, we are upon the start of a new age! Just think. You are at the center of what will become the new world. In the end, you will be part of the catalyst to our lord's beginning!"

"What the fuck are you talking about? All I see is a crazed fool, killing defenseless men for his own gruesome purposes. Nothing you can do will change that!"

"What we do here will be remembered for generations! We will be the first servants of our gods. People will worship at our names!"

Nothing Will could say would stop these monsters. He was not going to give in, no matter what they did.

With a flick of his wrist, the killing continued. Each soldier screamed louder than the last, and as the shouts grew with the pain, the storm outside grew stronger. The leader danced and twirled as he tapped his fingers in front of his smile with each and every kill. Will knew he was running out of time.

1849 HOURS, Avos 13, 2258
Obrathe, Azhana

THE HOURS PASSED, the temperature continued to rise, and the team made their way forward and closer to the center of the city. All along the streets, garbage and debris moved with the wind that picked up as the day passed. Unusual even for this time of the season, the wind did not carry with it a coolness. Instead, it was drier than the air, making them wish it wasn't there at all. After twelve hours and four rests, the men had consumed almost all their water supplies. Each of them could feel the effects of dehydration setting in.

"There's the next checkpoint. Looks just as deserted as the first." Ed again was right up behind Brett as he took a quick look out to the stand-alone structure on the road.

Unlike before, marks could be seen in the asphalt where large military vehicles had been pulled out from their stationary positions.

"Yeah, we still have a long way to go. How are you guys doing?" Brett looked back at his men, most of them had their backs to the wall of the alley they were using to stay in the shade.

They were tired. The temperature was getting to them. Sweat soaked Dickie from head to toe, and he looked as if he were using the wall as his only way of standing. David and Witch didn't seem to fare much better as they squatted on the ground. Their faces, red and pasty from a day of sweating. The only two who looked any different were Ed and Kris. Kris had a white look to his face, but a concentration that seemed to say that he was ready to keep moving. Something was driving that boy forward. Ed, as calm and driven as anyone could be, would do whatever it took to make sure he looked the same now as he did when they were resting at the base.

"Shit Sergeant, no one told me this was going to be a pressure cooker. Fuck, it's hot out here." Dickie tried wiping the sweat from his brow, using his already soaked sleeve.

"Conserve what water you can. The temperature should break as the day closes in on the night. We are already well past the midpoint; it will be downhill from here." Brett knew he was lying. They knew he was lying, but they had to keep moving forward.

The sounds of battle rang out even louder now: a constant drum in the background of their minds and the walls around them.

The men each took final pulls from their canteens and got up to move. Too much waiting would threaten them with cramps, and none of them wanted that. Just as before, the men waited for a signal from Brett, and they moved as a team across the divided highway. Approaching the outpost, Brett turned to take a quick look, expecting to see the same as before.

Spider web cracks ran across the front of the protective glass. Two holes punched closely together were surrounded by brown blood and fingerprints dragged across the glass toward the bottom. Just as Brett recognized the carnage in the window, his vision blurred, and his mind went elsewhere.

"Your followers have already worked so hard to clear the path for you. Each step brings you closer to your destiny." Brett could hear the voice, but the pain did not follow.

Instead, he was standing in front of the same check-point box; a young, clean-shaven soldier stood with a small smile on his face.

Looking up, it appeared the boy recognized Brett as he stood a few yards in front of the structure and saluted. Within seconds, another soldier dressed in an unfamiliar military suit decorated in black and red stepped up next to Brett. Most of the uniform was black, black as a starless night, but the red stuck out in various spots on the ankles, knees, elbows, and neck. Looking closer, he could see it was fashioned, so it appeared to have red flames working its way out from behind the black.

His attention is returning to the boy in the checkpoint box as the young soldier's face changed from the welcoming smile to a look of horror and fear. Without warning, the man standing next to Brett raised his pistol and quickly fired two rounds straight through the protective glass. The young soldier never had a chance as the rounds tore his life way, dropping him to the ground. Anger welled up in Brett as he turned to grab the man beside him, but he was already walking away. The man didn't even turn to acknowledge he was there.

Running up to the stranger, he grabbed him and spun him to look him face to face. No fear in the man's eyes, no look of anger, or concern. The only thing he saw was a look of recognition as the man eyed Brett up and down. Doing the same, Brett could see he was wearing the same uniform, black with elegantly designed red flames.

"God damn it Sarg! Are you OK?" The man finally spoke, but it wasn't his voice. The voice was coming from further away.

"Fuck this shit, someone get him some water, we need shelter and evac out of here quickly." Dickie's voice was loud and clear as Brett's vision finally came back.

He was seated again against a wall facing the highway they had just crossed. This time, his face felt scuffed up and looking down at his forearm, blood seeped out from burns that had bubbled beneath the soaked bandage that covered it.

"What the fuck happened? Why am I on the ground again?" Brett's mind was trying to clear itself; something had his thoughts cloudier than when he was drunk.

"Boss, you face-planted as we ran across the street."

David again knelt in front of him. "Your eyes were practically rolled into the back of your head. We had to carry you halfway across. What's going on?"

Honestly, Brett didn't know. The images he saw and the voice in his head was as clear as day. Could the heat be doing this to him?

"I have no idea David, but I think I need to rest before we move on. I'm not feeling right."

"You're damn right about that." David went to pick their leader up.

"Hold on, contact on the left!" Witch's reaction had them all moving on instinct.

Without waiting, the team moved forward, the renewed adrenaline surging through Brett had him on his feet quickly.

They had entered a new section of the city. Here the buildings were built with an eye for luxury, steel and hardwood decorated the industry headquarters and larger homes for those who could afford it.

The building that had their attention was a five-story steel square, most windows were boarded up, but closer to the top some remained intact. Witch led the way, the rest of the team in a tight line behind him. Brett held the rear, keeping up the best he could watching their back as they approached a side metal door.

"How many contacts Witch?" Ed whispered as the team spread evenly around the closed entrance.

"I saw one, possibly two. They were on the second floor; the boards shut down tight the moment I spotted them."

"Civilians or soldier?" David looked at the rest of the team as he made sure there was a round in the chamber of his rifle.

"Doesn't matter. We go in and find out. Our instructions are to make sure this city is cleared building by building. David you breach the door." The men nodded to him as Brett gave the orders.

Whoever this was could be their first contact since they entered the city. Things would only get trickier from here on out.

Without hesitating, David reached over and tried squeezing the vertical handle of the door with the tips of his fingers. Just as he expected, they didn't move at all. The building and been locked from the inside.

"Looks like this isn't going to be that easy." He muttered.

David reached down to remove his lock cutter. Placing it over the handle, they could hear the small hum followed by a slight hiss as the small device cut the steel bolts of the lock. In less than a minute, the light on the control panel went green, and the device fell off the handle and into David's hand.

"Now time to get inside and make sure we aren't too late." David smiled at the others as he stepped back and with a quick motion, hit the door with his shoulder. Taking one step quickly into the first room, he dropped to his knee and swept the room with his rifle.

Witch and Dickie quickly followed to the left and to the right covering everything they could see.

"All clear!" The others followed as David sent out the message.

The doorway opened to an empty office building. Most of the furniture had been removed. Dust and paper laid scattered on the floor. Broken tiles and tattered gray sheets hung loosely from the drop ceiling above them.

The team made quick work as they searched the room looking for any signs of the contacts that Witch had seen.

Nothing they found inside told them definitively that anyone was there.

"Sssh," Kris put his hand up and everyone fell silent.

The whole group held their breath as they waited for any sound. Within seconds, between the pounding of their heartbeats, the soft pattering of footsteps could be heard above them.

Without saying a word, Brett signaled them to the stairway sign over the door to the west corner of the room. Witch, still leading the way, found the stairway door unlocked and proceeded to make his way to the second floor.

The silent stairway wound its way up all five floors of the building. Large numbers marked the entrance doors to each floor. All six men stood in front of the one marked number two. David, using only his hands, made the suggestion that they separate to cover the rest of the floors in pairs.

Brett knew it was a good idea, but something was uneasy in his stomach. Maybe it was still just lingering effects from the heat. Thinking about it, he could not get the images of that young soldier dying at the hands of a man who had "cleared" the path for his arrival. Whatever that meant, it felt better if he kept his whole team with him.

Shaking his head, he signaled for them to prepare to breach the building one floor at a time. Floor number two, unlike the entrance door below, had a horizontal pressure handle for a lock.

Knowing their entrance was going to be loud, the team prepared for a quick and decisive entrance as they all stood back. Dickie stepped forward as he set himself up before the door. With an inhale of breath, the man let forth a kick directly into the center of the release bar. Rather unexpectedly, the door gave away easily and was accompanied by the grunt and yell of a man from inside.

"Contact!"

David led the way in as he stepped around Dickie and made his way to the back of the door. Lying crumpled on the floor and holding his shoulder was a middle-aged man in tattered, dirty business style clothing.

"Leave him alone!" The young voice of a little girl came screaming around the corner as she ran to throw herself at David.

Swooping her up in his arms, Dickie picked the little girl up as he swept the room with the rifle held in his other arm.

"Coleena!" A frail woman, blond like the little girl in Dickie's arms, came charging from the same corner that the child had. Moving quickly, Kris stepped to the side and grabbed her around the waist as he picked her up and stopped her momentum. Putting her down and placing her against the wall, he put one finger up to his lips. Noticing the situation she was in, the woman complied, but fear sank deep into her eyes at the sight of six armed men, one holding what had to be her daughter.

"All right, how many of you are there in here?" Brett stepped forward and looked the woman in her eyes.

Tears ran down her cheeks as she tried to speak, but her lower lip was trembling too much. With a quick nod to Dickie, the large man put the girl down, and she ran into the woman's arms.

"You have nothing to fear from us. We are not here to hurt you, but we need to know how many of you there are."

The woman looked at Brett with a blank stare. Brett sighed, he knew they were scared, but they didn't have time to waste trying to convince them to speak.

"Boss, this one is waking up." David stepped back as the man lying on the floor began to move again. The jarring from the door looked like it roughed him up pretty good.

"Daddy!" The girl tried to run from her mother's arms, but the woman held tight.

Brett saw his chance and knelt in front of the little blond girl.

"Hi, little one. What is your name?"

She looked at him for a second as the mother tried to pull her closer and turn her away. The little girl resisted.

"My name is Coleena."

She had a strength within her voice. She wasn't scared of them as her parents were.

"Coleena, I like that…"

Brett's vision went blurry again as the pain in his head returned tenfold. He fought to keep his balance, the whole room seemed to swirl around him as the sheer pain in his head threatened to split him in half.

"See how weak they are. You are not like them. That is why I chose you. You could snuff the life right out of them at any second that you wanted. Why don't you?" The voice was as clear as day in his mind.

"You know you want to, I can feel it in your soul. The power you have over these people, these little inconspicuous bugs. Show everyone who you are, start with that little girl."

The voice beckoned him to do things straight from his worst nightmares. He fought it with everything he had, but he knew down inside there was this strange feeling. It started in his belly and found a stronghold deep in his chest. A strange enjoyment in listening to the voice, a desire to follow its orders that he knew if he didn't fight, it would swallow him whole.

"Are you alright, Mister?" The little girl's voice shattered through the pain and the visions racing through his mind.

No fuzziness, no confusion, she spoke and instantly brought him back from the depths his darkened soul.

"I'm alright little one." Brett tried to give the little girl the best smile he could.

Ed already had one hand on his shoulder; the rest must have seen what had happened to him again.

"You don't look alright, Mister. Are you sick?"

"I'm going to be okay there little Coleena; I just have to ask your mommy here a few questions." Brett stood to look the still-terrified woman in her eyes.

Tears freely ran down her cheeks. The hold she had on her child was the only thing that held her together.

"She won't answer you. She doesn't speak as you do."

In the chaos of everything that had been happening, Brett had forgotten that not everyone in this land spoke the same languages. Shit, they were out of luck here.

"I might be able to help you. They taught me in school how to talk with people like you."

A proud and confident smile grew on the little girl's face. Looking down at her, he knew that if she had the chance to grow up, she would grow up into something special. She had that look children have when the world is nothing but a limitless number of possibilities.

"Sounds like a deal then. Are you and your parents the only ones here?"

"Yep, the others were taken away by soldiers over a week ago. We hid on the top floor. I had daddy and mommy crawl into this really small space behind the wall with me."

"You're a brave little girl for saving your parents like

you did. Do you know if there are many others out there that hid like you?"

For the first time, sadness slipped behind the little girl's eyes. Even before she spoke, Brett already had his answer.

"Not that I know. Mommy and daddy don't tell me much anymore. It takes daddy longer each time he goes out for food. He says the fighting outside is why we can't leave. Is that why you are here?"

"Yes, but we are here to help you. There are a lot of bad people out there, the ones that took all the others away. Those people they took need rescuing, and we are here to do that." Brett reached over and put his hand on the little girl's bony shoulder. "Do you happen to know where they have taken all the people?"

"Only the six of you?" She said it so sarcastically David had to stifle a laugh. "Mommy whispers when she thinks I don't hear her. She says they are taking them to the temple. It's somewhere in the city. I peeked out one night and saw lights heading that way into the city."

The little girl pointed in the same direction that the team had mapped out. That was all the information that they needed.

"Thank you very much, my brave Coleena. Now it's time for you to stay here with your parents. Explain to them that we are here to help, and that once your father is feeling better that you three should try to leave the city as fast as possible."

"Why? Where should we go?"

"The fighting is going to get worse, and we don't want to see anyone else hurt. I'm not sure where you should go, but make them understand it is no longer safe, even in this section. Can you be strong and tell them that? Make them believe you?"

She shook her head yes, but doubt was in her eyes as

she looked up at her trembling mother's face. Brett wished there was more they could do, but there was still so much left to accomplish. The sun was going down, the heat somehow was still rising, and they had hours of work still ahead of them. All that, and he still had whatever kept bursting into the back of his head just itching to come forward again.

"Sergeant, look!" Ed was over by the window pointing toward the military battle.

Lights flashed up in the sky as the sounds of explosions and gunfire still echoed throughout the streets. The familiar reddish-yellow glow formed a half sun between and over the buildings at the edge of the city. From his best estimate, it looked like their forces had made it to the second districts of the city. At this pace, the team was running out of time. If this 'cult' had anything planned, they would use it before they became completely overrun by the army. Their mission was still crucial. Exhaustion or not, time was running out.

"All right, you guys. Let's get a move on. We are running out of daylight, and the cavalry is approaching. There are a lot of areas still to cover."

The men didn't question his orders. They checked their gear and made their way to the building exit. Over the next couple of hours, they checked building after empty building. They found no more scared families hidden within the discarded trash. The little girl had been right, whoever had lived here before had been taken away some time ago. Other than the life he saw in her little blue eyes, this whole city seemed as dead as that soldier from his dream.

"Sergeant, the center of the city is around the next block." Ed held a small map in his hand while shining a small flashlight over it.

The sun was only a sliver over the horizon, and with no electricity keeping the street lamps lit, they would soon be working in darkness.

"Alright then, we move cautiously from now on. No more sweeps. No more hope to find people we can get out of here. The only thing left is our primary target." Brett looked back at his men.

They looked tired, but he hoped the look he saw was one of determination behind everyone's eyes.

"Sir, I have some final things you may want to see." Witch was seated on an overturned trash can as the others began getting up from their final rest break.

"What is it, Witch?" Brett walked over and looked at the small leather bound book the man was holding.

Even with the little time they had for a rest, Witch still used every second he could to keep his research going.

"I've finally been able to decipher more of this text. 'After the rivers fill with the blood of the unworthy, one strong of heart, strong of body, with a soul longing for retribution will turn the blade on what his heart truly desires. For once the choice is made, the deed cannot be undone, and the doors will open. Our lord's champions will come forth, and of the worthy, their generals will be chosen to lead the cleansing to the ends of the world.'" Witch looked up at Brett as he closed the book.

"That makes me feel all warm inside there, Witch." Dickie was putting the last of his knives into his belt.

"It's not supposed to. Whoever this cult is, they are trying to bring forth these 'champions' to cleanse the world. Just look at what we've seen. There are at least three cities now emptied of people. Can you imagine how much blood drained from all those we saw back at the first temple?"

The whole team wanted to forget what they saw back

there. Everyone fell quiet as the memory haunted each of them differently. Even thinking somewhere in this city, another mass grave was filling with the blood drained from thousands of people shook them to their core.

"We aren't going to let that happen here. Everything ends tonight. One way or the other, we stop them here." Brett shouldered his rifle, checked his clips of ammo, and looked each of his men eye to eye. "Let us see if they have what it takes to sacrifice men who know how to fight back, and let's make sure we send them to their dark lord."

Every man in the group felt a resurgence as they stowed the last of their provisions and began making their final push toward the center of the city. When they cleared the final city block of emptied office buildings, they stopped when unlike the other roadblocks they found this one well-guarded.

"Finally, I was tired of all this talking anyway. Time for some action." A smirk stretched across David's face as he looked at the bunkered building ahead.

In the middle of the four-lane highway was the same one-person glass building they had found before. This time there were four men, two on each side with sandbags piled up to waist height. Across the street on both sides were two armored war machines whose entry covers were open. A small amount of light escaped the inside letting them know that they were operational and had someone inside ready and waiting.

"What's the plan, Boss?" David squatted as he pressed his back against the dumpster he was using for cover.

Brett took another look at the men a hundred yards from them, then back at his team. They needed to be quick, but silence was secondary. The fighting on the other side of the city now raged to a point of deafening.

"Two teams. We smoke them, divide them; and then

we finish them." David nodded his agreement. "Ed and Kris you're with me. Dickie and Witch stay with David. On my signal, take them out."

Each man silently gave their agreement and before they split. Using the last bit of fading light, David and the others broke off down the road. Once they were concealed enough by the shadows, they would find their way across the highway and to the cultivated pines that lined the innermost section of the city.

Brett waited the three minutes he knew it would take for them to sneak their way across the empty road. Checking his communicator on his belt, he was confident when the light went from red to green. Time for them to make their move.

Putting on night vision and gas masks, the three soldiers backed into the corner alley they were using as Ed stepped out and fired two gas canisters at the unsuspecting men waiting. Just as they expected, the men turned their lights toward the alley, trying to catch a glimpse of the enemy before the area filled with smoke. On cue, two more cans lifted into the air from the opposite side and landed behind them.

The momentary seconds of confusion had them turn the lights away from the alley and to the trees shadowed across the street. The distraction gave the smoke the precious time it needed to spread and reduce everyone's visibility to mere inches.

Just as they trained, Brett and his men stepped out and moved forward. A couple of shots rang out as the overhead lights burst sending sparks glittering to the ground. Knowing they were under attack, the cornered men of the roadblock opened fire on everything they believed was a target. Using everything they could as cover, Brett and his team ducked and moved as bullets, though threatening, were never truly aimed correctly.

Two screams broke over the gunfire, as rounds fired by David and his team found their mark. Looking at Ed and Kris, Brett signaled for them to advance. They only had moments to get to their target before someone in the vehicles ahead finally got the smart idea to make a move.

Darting ahead, Ed sneaked up behind the war machine on the right as Brett and Kris made for the men still bunkered behind the sandbags. Getting closer, Brett could hear the familiar gear grinding of the tank's guns being turned toward them, followed by a magnetic metal clink and zip tie of wire. Before the machine's guns were armed, a bright flash and bang ignited the top of the war machine as the metal crumpled down on itself. Climbing back on top Ed dropped in a grenade and dove into a roll to get away.

The inside of the vehicle exploded, sending shrapnel into the air and further confusing the bunkered men remaining. Ducking and moving up as fast as they could, Brett and Kris made it to the sandbags and rounded the corner.

Both men crouched in fear. One still held his rifle but was too scared to use it. The other had already put his on the ground and was covering his ears as he coughed away the gas. A similar explosion that tore apart the first machine destroyed the second as Brett and Kris approached the two remaining men. Through the smoke, the two who remained could barely know who approached them.

For a mere second, Brett considered what to do. The smoke from the canisters was as thick as a storm cloud on the ground. Both men were practically defenseless; one wasn't even holding a weapon. It would take nothing for his team to disarm the last one and take these two out without violence. The weight of his rifle finally registered in his hands. Sweat collected on his palms as he squeezed the grip tighter. He would have to make his decision quickly before one of the two men made a stupid mistake.

Stepping forward, he could feel the presence of Kris standing right next to him. The young soldier, whose ideals would always lead him to mercy whenever possible, for some reason trusted him. *Am I the right person to trust? Could I be the one to save so many and stop such evil when sometimes I feel evil within myself?*

Only a dozen feet separated Brett and the two crouching shoulders when the one thing Brett didn't want to see flashed before his eyes. Both men, crouching in fear for their lives, were dressed in black uniforms. Even through the smoke, it was now possible to see the red flame markings sewn into the fabric. Anger filled within his chest so fast he didn't have time to think.

Those eyes filled with fear and anguish stared right back at him as he watched the young soldier die inside that roadblock post. These men, these two very men were the reason for all this. The cult wasn't just one man, wasn't just one idea. It was all of them. The evil that the cult bore pumped through the very men that fought for its cause. Nothing would stop him from erasing this black spot on the world from the pages of history. When he finished with them, only old books in dead libraries would have any records they even existed. Without even noticing it, the weight of his rifle was like a feather in the wind. Each round he fired, each explosion of sound, the flames erupting from the barrel of his rifle brought relief to his heart. They would all die, by his hands, they would all die!

"Sergeant!" Kris was grabbing at his rifle. Reality snapped back into Brett's mind.

He was screaming just as Kris and the others were. Except, he was screaming at nothing, and they were screaming at him. Loosening his grip on his weapon, he realized he was still squeezing the trigger over and over, the clip long empty of bullets. Before him, both soldiers laid dead on the ground, sprawled in a pool of blood. Their bodies torn from more than a dozen rounds fired into them from only a few feet away.

"Holy fuck man, are you okay?" David grabbed him by the shoulders.

Both men looked each other in the eyes. David's were filled with concern while the only thing Brett could feel anymore was exhaustion and emptiness.

"Yeah, I'm alright." Brett shrugged the big man's hands off. "Everyone else alright? Any injuries?"

None of the men looked harmed, but each of them showed signs of concern as they looked their leader in the eyes. Kris in particular looked angry and distant. Turning quickly, the young man brought his attention away and to the rest of the city ahead.

"Look, Boss, it's dark out now. We've had a long day. I know you said more rest was out of the question, but I'm going to have to insist. Something isn't right here." David was right, and Brett knew it. "Ever since we entered this city you have been acting strangely. I'm not saying we rest all night; there is still too much to do, and the dark will help us. Just think about it for a second. We can't go on if you're going to lose it like this every time we get involved with something."

Brett looked at the rest of them. Not a one looked as if they were going to argue with the suggestion. Kris didn't even turn to acknowledge anything was going on.

"What do you say, Boss?" Ed stepped up and asked again.

"One hour tops. Witch, you scout us a good place to rest. I'll try to find something to clear my mind out."

Witch nodded and headed toward the darkness within the trees. The rest checked their gear, supplies and grabbed anything they could from the men who they would leave behind. After a minute, they headed in the direction that Witch had gone. Brett had no idea where to start. Something told him he would need a lifetime to figure it out, but he wasn't sure they could even afford one hour.

Chapter Forty-One

2132 Hours, Avos 13, 2258
   Hiowell, Keiola, Northeast Republic

THE CITY WAS HERS, and she knew it. Each new building, each new defense fell as she approached. Men, woman, and children lasted only minutes before her fury and the storm she carried. She now walked barefoot through the snow that would reach the height of a man's knee. She glided effortlessly over it.

The beasts at her command grew stronger and hungrier the more and more they destroyed. Reveling in the fury of the storm, she watched as the land changed around her. Snow piled and swirled as the wind whipped it between buildings and vehicles. Entire blocks within the city fell to the white death that rendered them unrecognizable. Looking at her arms and legs, she was unrecognizable to herself. Blue scabs made of ice peppered her entire body, the only reminder of the injuries sustained, yet they healed instantly. Her power was growing. It surged through her veins, and she loved it.

"We are almost there, my child. These weaklings run before you. Watch as they fold and die at your feet. None of them can stand before your power!"

The voice was always right, and she was always willing to listen.

"Keep going until you get to the temple at the center of the city. That which you seek is there. The glory that will be ours is waiting for us. You can taste the vengeance that will be yours. The very reason you have suffered will be within your grasp. All you have to do is decide to take it, and destroy it!"

She felt all the pain that she had suffered over the last couple of weeks sink its way into her gut. She couldn't remember what caused it, or who caused it, but she didn't have to. The feeling was something that drained at her power, something that she couldn't allow to take hold. Everything was different now. Everything was within her control. Whatever was inside that temple would be hers, and she would crush it. Only a few more blocks to go…

SIX MEN HAD ALREADY DIED, and Will could barely stand. His strength almost drained from fighting, from screaming, from trying not to feel the pain, as he watched each man die slowly. Every new prisoner was going slower than the last. The smell of the room now made him sick to his stomach. The stench of lost bowels and candle smoke hung thick in the air. The only people who didn't seem bothered by what was going on were the two monsters they used as guards holding him upright. Their stamina and concentration were inhuman.

"Starts wearing down on you, doesn't it? Death, pain,

the feeling you can't do anything about it. Of course, there is always something YOU can do about it if you would only make your decision." The leader pranced on his toes as he clapped his hands in front of his lips.

The bastard giggled louder with every scream, and his smile widened as the body count grew. Or was it the raging storm outside the temple that made him happy? The power of the storm had grown so strong that the building swayed on its foundation.

"I will not become like you." The words scratched at the back of Will's throat as he forced them out.

He wasn't sure how long it had been, but it felt as if he had been yelling for hours now.

"Still so much fight left in you, good." The man's deadly smile reappeared. "It will make things all the better when she gets here."

Will wanted to spit, kick, cry, anything, but nothing would come out. His energy was gone; his strength drained as his body ached for him to rest. A sharp whistle blew out as the wind came swirling in up near the rafters. One of the stained-glass windows up in the rafters had broken two murders ago.

"See how our friends here are starting to come back to reality? What a good time for them to join us."

Will tried to ignore what the man was talking about, but he was right. The remaining men's eyes were no longer as hazy as they once were. Some even pulled on the holds that the servants had on their arms as they stood and waited their turn. The sluggishness caused by the drugs stopped them from gaining any true resistance as the exertion quickly exhausted them.

"Let us see if we can finally find someone that will strike the right nerve with you. Um, how about this rather young man right here. Given the right circumstances I'd guess he could be an officer one day."

The bastard walked right to Teller and patted the young man on the shoulder. Teller looked up into the man's eyes but gave no resistance as the robed servant lead him to the seventh chair along the wall.

"Please don't, just stop. Why are you doing this?" Tears had found their way back into Will's eyes.

"Don't you see, my son? It has to be this way. You are part of a bigger plan. Our god requires sacrifices from us all: special children like you most. Who are we to deny their requests, and at such a momentous occasion?"

Will gave another fruitless tug with his arms, but had no luck better than the thousand times he had tried before. The man in blue just shook his head and nodded.

Just like the others, the first cuts were delicate yet deep enough along the wrists to get the blood flowing. Only this time, Teller was awake the second the cutting started. His screams echoed through the room, for a second, loud enough to drown out even the roar of the storm.

"What the fuck is going on?" Something in Teller's scream had awoken the large Sergeant Walker from his drug induced state.

Everything seemed to stop as the man looked and saw what surrounded him. Death was everywhere, and if anyone was not going out without a fight, it was Walker.

Will had only a moment to see the fire rage in the man's eyes before he flexed his large arms and lifted both servants holding him off the ground. The men didn't have a chance as Walker quickly grabbed one by both ears and ripped so hard that his head almost popped off as it spun. The second was barely back to his feet when the adrenaline surged soldier of death grabbed a handful of hair, turned and smashed the man's face into the wood beam next to him. Blood splattered to the ground as the man's head split in half.

The room was now echoing screams from everywhere, but for the first time it was death coming for men on both sides. Will watched as robed men of all sizes threw themselves at the crazed Sergeant. Each who got close found themselves face to face with a demon straight from hell.

Using the few moments of chaos to his advantage, Will slumped in his two captors' arms as much as he could. For all the concentration they showed during the slaughter of the first six men, Will could feel them give as they itched to join the fight in front of them. Feeling that they had given him enough, Will lifted his right foot and brought it down directly into the man at his right's knee, buckling it into an unnatural angle, toppling him over.

As the first guard screamed and fell, the second turned to react. But Will, using reserves he didn't know he had, threw a punch as hard and fast as he could into the man's throat. A crunching feeling accompanied Will's fist as the large guard stumbled backward and toppled to the ground. Not wanting to hesitate, Will ran two steps forward and kicked at the side of the man's head. Another familiar snapping sound came as the man's head now rested sideways on his shoulder.

"Will!" Walker yelled to him as he backed into a corner, as a half-dozen servants with knives tried to flank him.

Reacting on pure instinct alone, Will ran to the nearest seat and table, grabbed a knife of his own, and slid behind the first servant. A quick wrench back and a yank of the knife sent blood spurting everywhere from the new opening in the man's neck. That couple of seconds of lost concentration was all Walker needed as he revamped his efforts and crashed right into the nearest three sending them all to the floor.

The remaining two didn't know who to keep an eye on, Will with the knife before them or the crazed Sergeant now tearing into their friends on the floor. Both men chose wrong as they looked to aid their friends. Will moved quickly and sent his knife directly into the neck of the closest and ripped it out toward the last one. Surprised as blood covered his face, Will quickly rammed the smaller target against the wall and jammed the knife deep into the man's shoulder and neck.

"Will, we have to check on Teller!" Walker yelled from across the room as Will realized he was still stabbing the man.

So much damage was done his head almost rolled right off. Releasing him, the body slouched to the ground, its robes soaked through in the dark-red blood. Around him laid the corpses of over a dozen men and one large guard still screaming in pain about his knee. The bastard could rot where he was laying for all Will cared. Where did that monster of a master go? Somehow in the confusion, he had disappeared.

Teller was almost no better than the men the Sergeant and Will had killed. During what was only a few moments of fighting, the young soldier had been trying to stem the flow of blood from his wrists but had failed. His already pale face was now a ghostly white, and his breathing was shallow and labored.

"Fuck man, we need to get him out of here. Fuck!" Even through his hard outer shell, anyone could see how much Walker cared for the young Private as he did everything he could to keep him alive.

"Tie off his arms, stop the blood in any way you can. I'll get the others moving and get us out of here." Will knew it was easier saying than doing, but at least they were alive.

Turning to the others, he saw that most of them had awoken but remained mostly confused. They didn't have time to wait for them to finish coming around. Running over he grabbed the first he reached and started shaking him by the shoulders.

"Hey, you guys remember me?"

His voice, and forcing them to move, got them turning faster.

"Look you guys, grab anything you can and follow me. We are getting out of here."

Several of them shook their head in agreement, the others seemed well enough to follow him.

Will supposed going the only way they knew was their best chance. He moved the group toward the door that they had entered. The noise as the wind outside the temple crashed into the building made anything short of a shout impossible to hear. Wave after wave of snow broke against the exterior wall, shaking the very ground the soldiers walked on. The idea of going into the cold unknown didn't feel any better than staying inside, but their time was running out. They had no idea how many remained guarding the temple.

Going partly down the hallway revealed a path empty of any living souls. That was good enough for him.

"OK, you guys. Continue down the hallway and try to find a way out. I need to get back and help the others. Stay quiet. We'll be right behind you."

They had gone as far as he knew. He couldn't leave Teller and Walker, so they would have to do without him.

Returning to the killing room, Walker had gotten Teller to his feet.

"How is he doing?"

"Shit dude, I don't even know how he's still breathing.

He's lost too much blood. This kid has some real fight in him. Wish I had even half that in me."

Will threw the injured man's arm over his shoulder to help keep him moving.

"We all wish we did. Now, let's get everyone out of here!"

The three men stumbled as fast as they could. Will tried listening for any signs of the group he had instructed to go ahead. Straining, it sounded as though he could hear yelling, maybe even some fighting. All of it was lost when the windows high above them exploded inward as a stream of snow blasted through. Glass shards rained as the snow began falling in.

"Now this shit? If these crazed bastards don't kill us, the damn weather will. I'm starting to think I should have stayed in school." Walker grumbled as he hoisted Teller higher onto his shoulder.

If they weren't trying to run for their lives, Will would have stopped and stared at the big man with probably the dumbest look on his face. He couldn't imagine the big Sergeant doing anything but fighting to kill.

The three continued as they made it through the large doors and entered the hall. Shouts and commands muffled together as the others who had gone ahead turned the corner and were slowly backing up with their hands raised. Some of them were arguing with whoever was standing in front of them. Whatever it was that was stalling them, they didn't have time as Teller started coughing and buckling at the knees.

"Oh, fuck this!" Walker didn't stop to ask.

He moved Teller's arm off his shoulder, and as gently as he could, he put all the man's weight on to Will.

Just as if it were a switch he could turn on or off, the man gave out a roar that would make a demon shake in the knees and charged forward. The soldiers who stood in front of him, hands in the air didn't know what charged at them, but also whoever was in front didn't know either.

Friend and foe tumbled as the steaming train that was Walker rolled through. With everyone crashing to the ground, two armed guards laid sprawled on the ground, their weapons skidding across the floor. Walker was quick to jump on the first man he could grab and began pounding the life out of him. The second died as one of the rescued soldiers grabbed a dropped rifle and shot the man dead.

"Anymore?" The adrenaline was still pumping through Walker as he bellowed the challenge to everyone around him.

Will moved forward with Teller as those who had fallen began to stand and began moving again. The Sergeant made his way back and helped remove some of the dying soldier's weight from his shoulder.

"That was subtle." Will could see the adrenaline surge dropping from the Sergeant quickly.

"Shit needs to get done, and we don't have time to waste. Now shut up, and keep us moving."

Right as always, the remaining soldiers made their way down the hall. Not long after they passed the door, Will recognized as their original cell, the group stumbled on two men sprawled on the floor. No one said anything as they passed, but looking down, Will saw two of the surviving men weren't lucky when they had run into the guards. Unlike those they had left back in the other room, these men had died quickly, their chests opened from several rounds of gunfire.

No time for sentiment remained as every minute that passed, Teller's condition worsened. His breathing was barely audible and all his strength to even help carry himself was gone.

"Have any idea how to get us out of here?" Walker shifted more of his friend's weight onto himself.

"No idea, but keep listening for the sound of the storm. If we hear that, we are close."

Two of the most alert soldiers kept them moving as they searched down every hallway. No guards popped up to stop them as the train of survivors moved through. The dim thump of the storm raging outside began building louder as they moved on.

"Oh, shit!" Teller's voice gargled as he vomited on the floor.

All strength dropped from his legs as they buckled, and he fell.

"Will!" Walker knelt by his dying friend.

"He's alive, but can't keep moving." Will could barely register his breathing.

"Then we move for him."

Using some of his last reserves, Walker picked the man up and started carrying him like a child.

"This way. I think we found the way!" One of the men up front called.

Moving as fast as they could, Will and Walker followed behind. Another torch lighted hallway ended with a set of double arched doors. The horrific sound of wind and storm surges could be heard crashing against the frame. The brass hinges holding the doors in place and the frame itself shook with each gust of wind.

"What are we gonna do? We can't go outside in something like this!" One of the men started losing his nerves.

Honestly to Will, he was surprised the soldiers hadn't lost it already. The front two men looked back at Will and Walker, indecision written across their weary faces. Outside that door, they faced a storm of immeasurable strength that, by the sounds of it, threatened to kill them if they even attempted to go outside. Inside this horrible place remained an unknown number of enemies who already showed their willingness and a need for murder.

"I, for one, don't want to stay inside this building one more minute. I'll take my chances out there. Has to be somewhere we can hold up till this passes?"

Walker was right. Will couldn't think of anything better as he knew the crazed man who led this temple would show up eventually. Nodding his agreement, the men in front didn't argue as they went to open the door. As they got closer, the roar of the wind grew louder, and the shaking of the frame grew in intensity tenfold.

The lead man closed his eyes as he pressed his hands on the frozen push bar and prepared to use his entire weight to open it. Just as he was about to start, the entire hall fell into silence as the wind and noise from outside stopped completely.

"What the?" The surviving men started whispering as something strange was going on.

"Oh just get done with it, and get us out of here!" Walker, covered in perspiration from carrying Teller, yelled to keep them moving.

Coming back to his senses, the lead man pressed his weight against the door. For a moment it wouldn't move, frozen with a layer of ice that cracked against the pressure.

Boom!

1940 HOURS, Avos 13, 2258
Obrathe, Azhana

· · ·

"KILLING those men was easy wasn't it? They were weak. Hiding like cowards, hoping you wouldn't find them, but you did. With only a fraction of the power I can give you, you ended their silly, worthless lives. The cowards didn't even deserve to breathe the same air as you. They were nothing but bugs. Ready to be stomped under the boots of the righteous."

Images of men in the black uniforms dying in waves flashed before his eyes. They ran from him. He could smell their fear and taste it as it flowed through the air. The cowards fell by the dozen before him. He was a god to them. They were unworthy to stand before his presence. The sight of each of their deaths, screaming in pain brought a yearning to his heart. Their terror filled a void that he carried every day with him since he had lost the only thing he cared about in this world.

Here it was. For the first time, he had something that could fill that missing space. Bodies piled up as he walked among them. Their hollow stares reached out to him, and he smiled back in return. They deserved it. He'd cut each and every one up if he could. He'd take one of Dickie's knives and carve them all into little pieces. Watch them all scream, cry, and bleed out without anything they could do to stop him.

No! He wouldn't cut them, that wouldn't do. He had something better in mind for them; something more fitting for vermin like these. Burn them! Yes, he would burn them all! He would burn the world to rid the land of such disgust and rotten disease. Yes…They would burn.

"Ah!" Cold sweat dripped down Brett's face even in the excruciating heat as he sat forward quickly. His eyes darted in every direction.

"Sergeant, are you alright?" David leaned in and took a closer look into his eyes.

The team was sitting huddled in an abandoned waiting room. They had taken shelter on the first floor of the last office building before they reached the center of the city.

"Yeah, I'm alright. A bad dream is all it was."

He knew he was lying. The voice still echoed in his mind. The worst part of it was he could feel it gaining control. Already there was a longing deep within him to feel that power again. Joy and excitement had filled him as he watched all those men die, and he wanted it back.

"Seems as though you've been suffering a lot of those lately." David offered him the last of the water from his canteen.

The heat was still rising, even after the sun had gone for the night.

"How long was I out? It feels like hours."

"Forty-five minutes at best. You went out the second your ass hit the ground. Toss and turned the whole time. Thought I was going to have to come over there and slap you around a bit." A wide grin found Dickie's face as he held up the knife he used to clean his fingernails.

The light from a flashlight reflected off it and into Brett's eyes. Even in the dark, that man's blades looked razor sharp and perfect.

"Well, that's enough of that. We need to keep moving."

Gingerly, Brett picked himself off the ground. His whole body ached. They had been moving and searching all day, but this felt different. He was worn out as if he had been fighting for the last several days straight without a chance to rest. He was surprised he had any reserves left.

"Are you sure about this, Boss? The General should be overrunning this area in a matter of hours. We could, you know, say we didn't make it in time." David looked around to see if there was any support from the others. "There are many ways to get lost in a city, especially when working with maps that aren't 'updated.'"

There wasn't much consensus among the men. None of them wanted to give up on the mission, but he could see their concern for him in their eyes. All of them except Kris and Witch.

"Where's Witch gone off to?"

"He left about fifteen minutes ago. Said he was going to scout for a quicker route to the entrance to the temple. Something about possible traps and things we've never seen. Old man's lost it if you ask me. Should have retired years ago." Dickie put away his last knife as he stood.

"And what would he have done then Dickie if you know so much?" David slapped the man on the back.

"Fished. Like other retired, OLD men."

David did what he could to stifle his laugh, but Brett ignored the two. Kris was by one of the exterior windows looking out into the night.

"You okay, Kris?" Brett asked as he swirled the last of the water in David's canteen.

"You seemed as though you enjoyed it back there." Kris did not turn back to look him in the eyes.

"Those two always joke like that. Keeps them from losing their minds." Kris turned and looked him dead straight into his eyes. He knew what the young man was asking, he had hoped he could deflect it with a joke. "Look, I'm not sure what came over me back there. The truth is, son, sometimes even the best of us lose ourselves in the bloodlust. It doesn't make us bad people, just normal. Killing isn't easy, no matter how many times you do it. Just someday, it catches up with you."

"Is that what it is? It's catching up with you?" The man didn't look convinced.

"Something is. Gods know if I have any idea what it is.

It doesn't matter really. We have our mission. You have your orders. We have people to save. If it means a bunch of murderers die in the process, then, so be it. I'm sure as hell going to do what I can to make sure it isn't us. I promise you, though, those men deserved it, and those who come next do as well. Now grab your gear and give me a little more faith. A bigger problem awaits us here, and we need to find it."

Brett could feel the words choke in his throat as he spoke them. The same fears that ran through the young man resounded deeply within his own heart. Was he losing it? Did all these years of fighting and killing finally find a way to catch up with him? In the end, the only thing he knew was that the danger was larger than any of them thought. The voice in his head kept telling him so.

"Ready whenever you are, Boss." The others called out.

David, Ed, and Dickie were set up at the door. All their gear was collected, and they were leaving the room as if no one had been there. No reason to be so covert about it, but better to be safe than sorry, just in case someone happened to be following them.

"Lead on, then. Let's catch up to Witch."

All five soldiers exited the building in a single file. The starless night would have been as dark as ever, but the glow from fires and fighting deep within the city gave everything a yellow and reddish glow. If someone didn't know better, it would be easy to mistake it for dusk with the sun setting to the West.

The central part of the city was not very different from the previous section. Upscale business offices and expensive houses lined the streets. Large yards, overgrown from neglect, stretched between buildings. Deep within the center, the rounded dome top of the city's primary temple rose over all the rest. Alongside it stood government buildings and courts, yet, for people not known for their religious convictions, the temple rose above them all. Its bronze top reflected the firelight even at this distance.

The dry wind shifted as the team moved forward, carrying with it the smoke and ash from the distant fires. If the dead, dry heat wasn't enough to make it difficult to breathe, this newfound nuisance began to tickle the back of all their throats. Only a couple of deserted blocks filled with brown lawns separated them and their primary target, the main road that led into the very center of the city. Once there, they would begin their search for whatever was below the city.

"Well, look who it is. Our guests of honor have finally arrived."

Bright lights blinked on and blinded the five of them as they rounded the corner four-story brick building that opened to the central thruway of the city. It took a few seconds before their eyes could adjust enough to see. Two transport trucks were turned sideways across the two-lane highway. Between them was a tripod mounted searchlight, with two stationary guns at its base. Both weapons were manned, and with their eyes still burned with the glare of the light, an unknown number of enemies were stationed behind the vehicles ready for any move they made.

"What the fuck is going on?" Brett was shielding his eyes the best he could, he wanted them to retreat, but there was no chance they would make it back around the corner in time.

Where was Witch?

"Sadly, we've been stuck here waiting for you. Took you and your sorry lot of losers here a long enough time to get here."

His eyes adjusted enough to see the man who stood out in front of the blockade. Just from his cockiness and voice,

Brett had known, seeing made it worse. Trevor leaned against the front vehicle, his hands on his hips and a smile on his face.

"What the fuck do you think you are doing here, Trevor? This isn't your assignment." Brett could feel the tension in the air between Trevor's men and his own.

"Ah, the assignment. Oh yes, sweep the city of all bad guys and save the innocent. I remember now. Have you ever asked yourself, who is ever really innocent?" The man's smile repulsed Brett in every way possible.

He stepped forward, closing as much of the distance as he could between them.

"I can think of a few, the people of this city do not deserve the fate that these monsters have in store for them."

"Monsters? You look at everything you've done over the last decade, the atrocities on both sides of the fight, and you're going to call them monsters? How can you, of all people, be the chosen one? Shit, you can barely understand what's right in front of your own fucking eyes!"

Brett did not like how this was going. He was the chosen one? What was he missing, and why was Trevor talking like the voice in his head?

"Chosen one? Say something that makes sense, you jealous piece of shit, or don't speak at all."

Brett didn't need to hear the answer, the weight of the world fell into his gut as his chest filled with fire when Trevor finally stepped close enough to reveal himself. Brett could not mask the reaction on his face.

"There we go men, it finally looks like our slow friend here is catching up. Like the new uniform, I think it suits my complexion rather well."

Anger welled up so fast in Brett's chest he thought he may explode right where he was standing. Dressed in all black, red flames bursting out as they etched into all his joints, Trevor smiled like a schoolyard bully starting to draw the crowd he wanted.

"You're behind all this? All these people? This whole mission?" Brett could feel his hand itching to draw his sidearm, but his team was still too exposed.

They had to see what was going on; there was nothing he could do to help them from here.

"Ha-ha, you give me too much credit. I may be smarter than you by leagues, but alas this mission was brought about by someone so powerful, a mind like yours can't even start to comprehend. I still can't understand why they picked you. God, it's like asking a child to lead an army."

"But how? How could everyone have missed this?"

Buy time, it was the only thing Brett could think of doing, other than shooting the man where he stood.

"Everyone missed this? For fuck's sake man. We are so deeply involved on both sides of the fight; I'm surprised it hasn't been labeled a civil war. We have had a hand in everything that has happened so far. The bombings, the gas explosions, the hostage situations, and every move each side has taken; we have been there. This world needs the filth that pollutes it cleansed down to the last man. Everything will start anew, and only those strong enough to see it through will survive to take advantage of the spoils."

His words vibrated in his ears, echoing as deep as the voice he carried within his mind. That voice. It beat against the back of his mind now constantly, begging to be allowed to come forward. Trevor was repeating it as if he heard it himself. The fire in Brett's blood was boiling, all the deaths he had seen, all orchestrated by people on his side. How were they going to save these people and stop this war if neither side knew who the real enemy was?

"But, I am sorry to say, it will all end here for you and

your sorry bastard friends. I have my orders to take you alive. They say you are some 'special' instrument needed in the final stages. I don't see it, though, when the power of our Lord is released back into this world, it will be the strong who he grants the blessings to, not idiot meat bags like yourselves. Of course, they never said anything about your team." The man's smile grew bigger as it stretched across his face. For a second, Brett thought he saw the man's eyes glow red. "Maybe I will get to have some fun, after all."

Images of his team sprawled dead on the ground behind him flashed before him; the entire city cried to him as legions of dead, their soulless eyes stared him in the face. There wasn't any more he could take. Ignoring all the pain and fire that burned beneath the skin of his forearm, his hand snapped down for his pistol.

Trevor, moving faster than Brett could realize, grabbed Brett's arm as his right hand drew a weapon and fired directly into Brett's chest. The world silenced as the force slammed into him. Everything grayed in his eyes as he stumbled backward. First, seeing Trevor's face go from smiling to shock, and then his vision lost focus as he looked up to the sky when he fell to the ground.

Gunfire erupted around him, but everything sounded distant, almost unreal. Within seconds, he was lifted by the shoulders and dragged backward. Looking up, it was Kris, the man had dropped both his pistols as he grabbed Brett and started dragging. Two explosions tore through the sides of the trucks and flattened the overhead lamps. The men behind them were scattered. Some fired up toward the rooftops while others tried to fire at Brett and Kris, but quickly found themselves turned away by cover fire.

"Don't worry, Sergeant. I got you." Determination and anger burned behind the young man's eyes.

The pain in his chest was excruciating. He had been shot several times before, but never at that close a range and never directly in the chest. Breathing was becoming harder and harder as his dead legs dragged across the street. Trying to look down sent convulsions through his lungs and sparkles through his vision. The only thing he could see was black that now covered the left side of his shirt.

"We've got you, Sir..." Kris dropped quickly as a bullet struck him.

"Kris!" Brett's voice choked out as he tried to turn toward the young man risking everything to save him.

He couldn't see where the bullet hit Kris. All he could see was his arms reaching up trying to stop the bleeding in his upper body.

"Two down! Cover me!" Dickie's voice roared over the sound of the gunfire.

The man barreled forward and using a feat of strength not seen before, he grabbed both men by the underarms and started dragging them back to the corner of the building.

"Don't you two die on me now!" Bullets slammed into the wall behind him. "You fuckers, I said cover me!"

Grunting, the man heaved and sent all three of them stumbling around the corner. Quickly, Dickie sat up and laid both men out where they could see how bad it was.

"Sergeant, hold on." Using one of his knives, Dickie started cutting into his shirt.

"No! Check on Kris!" Brett coughed out as his back arched in pain.

The only response they got was gurgling coming from the young soldier. The large soldier's eyes went wide and white as he turned to the other injured man. Brett couldn't tell how bad off the kid was, he could only feel the pain in his chest. The words that Dickie was yelling became incomprehensible as he gingerly reached down and touched the hole in his uniform. The blackness of his shirt now spread from his chest down to his abdomen.

Applying pressure with his hand sent waves of nausea to his stomach as the pain hit him like a truck. Something was wrong. His breathing was difficult and moving was the worst feeling he could imagine, but it didn't feel as though he was slipping away. Death must be different from what he expected. Hundreds of deaths he had seen with his own eyes, and this was not what he expected.

Lifting his hand, he wanted to see the reddish black smear of his life draining away. If he were going to die here, the last blood he wanted on his hands was going to be his own, or his enemies, not that of the innocent or the men that followed him. Years of the blood of others would be washed away in a river created from his bottled up regrets. Maybe if his team completed this, with or without him, it would all be worth it. His hopes would not be a reality as his hand was not what he expected. The black liquid on his fingers and palm was not warm and thick as blood, but oily and thin as it dried instantly to his skin. It was ink!

He reached further into his shirt as the pain again radiated through his chest, forcing dry heaves and coughing. Feeling more with his fingers than his mind, he grabbed at his undershirt. With a slight tug, he pulled out wads of paper now pinned to his vest armor. A single copper bullet flattened, stapling the folded letters over his heart, and pieces of a shattered pen tumbled to the ground. Looking down at the contents of his hands, every letter he ever wrote to his wife came back to his mind. Instead of the torn messages and quickly drying black ink, all he could see was her face smiling back at him. His children were running in the background as she held up a vase of flowers she had picked from the garden. A yellow sundress waved gently in the wind as she smiled on the porch, waiting for him to join her.

"Thank you, my love, for giving me this one last chance," Brett whispered to himself as he forced himself to sit.

"Sergeant! Someone check the Sergeant!" Dickie was feverishly working on Kris.

"I'm alright! Just help me up. How is he holding on?"

Brett reached up as Ed grabbed him beneath his shoulders to get him to his feet. The fighting had stopped, David was still guarding around the corner of the building and looking up, and he could see Witch scanning the area from where he had joined the fight from the rooftops. Shuffling over, Brett looked down at the young soldier, and the blood smears on Dickie's face.

The injury was bad, and he didn't even need to ask. The bullet that hit Kris had found the small opening in his vest armor between his shoulder and neck. The man was bleeding out; there was nothing they could do without a surgical unit.

White pasty skin covered the boy's face. The pain was etched in the muscles of his neck as he tried to hold it in. Dickie had worked as fast as he could to stop the flow, but all he could do was delay it enough to give the man a few more moments. Reaching over, Brett placed the letters that had saved his life into Dickie's blood covered hands and dropped to a knee next to the one who had risked everything to run in and save him.

"Kris it's me, I'm alive. You saved me."

The only response he got back was a few gurgles as the young man tried to speak and partially filled his throat with blood. There wasn't fear in Kris' eyes. Instead, acceptance and determination peered back at him. Brett saw in those few moments, any anger between them, any resentment had passed away, and they were now brothers. Kris had seen what monsters they truly faced, how deep this danger was, and sacrificed all to keep Brett and the others alive.

"We'll get these sons of bitches for you, Kris. I promise you with my last breath I will do what it takes to finish this job. You are, and will always be, one of us." With that he felt Kris squeeze his hand, the strength in it almost gone. "Thank you so much my friend."

Before he could even stop talking, a convulsion of pain passed through the young man's body, and his eyes glossed over as his life passed on. A fire burned in Brett's chest so intense that it threatened to boil out the tears now built-up in his eyes. He didn't know which he wanted to do more: scream, explode, or cry. Everything was so bunched within him; he wanted to make everything in this world disappear. Looking down at the body of such a young man, given up so he could live that much longer, was too much. It had to end now.

"Shit," was all Dickie could say as he lowered his head to the ground.

Blood covered the man's arms, upper body, face, and the letters still in his hands.

Ed remained silent and motionless as he also looked on. His friend now long past anything they could do. Brett got to his feet, ignoring the pain that streaked across his chest, and forced back the coughing that tried to come up. He gripped both hands so tightly into fists they were white behind the ink and blood now staining them.

"Boss, what are we going to do now?" David stepped forward as he asked.

A look of sadness hung heavily across the man's face.

"I am ending this here," was all Brett said as he stormed past his men.

Grabbing a razor-sharp dagger from Dickie's belt, he made his way out of the alley.

Laying with his back seated against one of the toppled over trucks was Trevor. He had dragged himself through the streets and finally lost the energy to keep moving when he had reached the now destroyed barricade. Blood pooled around the man, draining from two holes, one in his chest and the other in his shoulder. Brett looked down at him, the man still had a smile in his dirt and grime covered face.

"Kris was the first to fire when you went down. Looks as if he made his shots count." David said. He was behind Brett looking down at the dying traitor.

"Doesn't fucking matter." Coughs of blood and spit made their way through Trevor's smiling teeth. "We'll still win in the end. Fuck, it should have been me. How can our god need anything with a man like you?"

Brett, through all the pain, squatted in front of Trevor, looking at him face to face.

"It doesn't matter what your GOD wants with me. I will kill every last one of you, and if I meet him, I will kill him as well. You can tell him that when you see him!"

With everything he had, he thrust the dagger right into the side of Trevor's abdomen. He wanted to make sure the man felt everything as he gripped the knife as tight as he could and tore it sideways. Screams of pain echoed out of the man's throat as it quickly filled with blood, and he toppled over, his insides spilling onto the ground.

By then, the surviving men of his team were standing behind him. The echoes of the man's screams bounced around the metal buildings that surrounded them. With each echoing wave, the sound grew louder. Soon it was no longer a scream; it was a loud moan mixed with a growl.

Tremors shook the ground beneath their feet as the sound of the earth struggling to hold itself together echoed through the city. The men braced themselves as pieces of the buildings around them began falling to the streets below, and large cracks started tearing through the concrete and grass. Something was trying to tear itself from the ground. Each of them looked around, no one could see what was going on. All they knew is, it no longer mattered. Whatever this was, it was bad.

Chapter Forty-Two

2232 Hours, Avos 13, 2258
  Hiowell, Keiola, Northeast Republic

THE DOORS BARRING her entrance into the temple burst open to her will, just as the storm and everything around her did. The alpha wolf, her companion, slowly marched his way through the doors. His confidence, his desire for more, rippled through her. They connected like two bodies sharing one spirit. The bond between them was like something she hadn't felt in a long, long time. It gave her strength and power, and she wanted more.

Through those doors, our destiny awaits. Inside you will come face to face with what you desire, and soon we will have everything!" The voice was like an unending stream of motivation.

It whispered promises and anything she wanted to hear. As her strength grew, its influence grew.

She wanted everything, and through those doors, whatever was inside, she wanted it. If anything were in her way, she would destroy it, just as she had everyone who had crossed her in this devastated city. Smoke and ash filled the air as it mixed with the snow and wind of the powerful storm that followed her.

Excitement grew within her as she entered through the broken doors. Her companions had feasted yet again on the lives of the weak. She could feel it even before she saw the carnage sprawled on the floor and walls before her. Several men, dressed in weathered military gear, were torn lifeless on the floor. Something about their uniforms, their color and design nagged at the back of her mind.

"Continue inside, and you will soon have it all. More will try to stop you. Some will even try to join you, only you can decide who is worthy. You have the power!"

The voice was right, it always was. Shaking the absent memory away, she followed the bloody trail of her companions. Blood smears were easy to follow, but now the air was not only filled with the sounds of her storm's fury but the voices of arguing men. Who dares to treat their arguments and differences more important than her?

Turning the corner, the weak excuses for a weaker god's children stood before her. Two men, dressed as the others who laid dead on the floor stood in front of a dozen men draped in simple robes with rifles held at the ready. Such pitiful excuses for weapons. If only they knew real power!

Charlie was quick to dismiss most of those in front of her. They were nothing more than mere bumps on her path to her destiny. Two of them though struck a chord in her mind that she could not ignore. One of the men wore robes similar to the others, but they shined with the illusion of power and wealth. Blue with golden flames that rose from the ground decorated his trim body. His smile, a sense of strength in a situation where he had none, irked her.

The second man, a large soldier with dark skin, stopped all thoughts in her mind. Even the voice that had led her this far was silent in his presence. She tilted her head to the side, she could not think of what was different about this man. His eyes gave her a sense of strength, courage, and a fight that none she had encountered until now had held. He made her curious.

"Charlie, is that you?" The dark soldier looked shocked as if her appearance surprised him.

Who is this Charlie? Who is this man? How dare he speak to me like this!

"Ah, our beloved guest has arrived. She looks better than anything I could have imagined." The robed man opened his arms as he approached her like a friend.

"Your fate is upon you, my child. Make your choice with these men. Some will try to stop you. Will you let them?" The voice returned.

It didn't have the strength it had before, but the closer she let this robed man get, the louder it got.

"Didn't I tell you, Will? She has finally arrived and the hour of our ascendance is upon us."

The man turned his back to her as he spoke to the soldier directly. Will? The thought of the man's name silenced the voice again. What is different about this one? She could feel her strength draining the longer she concentrated on him.

"Well my child, we have one more step for you to take. Soon we will be gods among men!"

She looked right into the man's eyes. Deep inside, she could see his soul, it was weak. Men followed him out of fear, out of promises that deep down he didn't know if he could deliver. He desired the strength to be a god among men. He would soon learn that true power comes to those who have the will to take it.

Tilting her head to the left, she considered the smiling man and his dozen armed guards. He continued to talk, but she was no longer listening. She had already decided that he was not worthy. None of them were acceptable, only that dark soldier made her question.

"Come, we have preparations to complete."

He put his hand on her shoulder and waved cleared a path through his men with a wave of his hand. With a quick swipe of her arm, she smashed the man against the wall beside her. He struggled to catch his breath. Liquid could be heard filling his lungs as coughing overtook him.

"But!… I was supposed to be his chosen one." The man struggled to cough out the words as his mouth and lungs filled with blood.

Kneeling, she looked into his eyes once more. His life was draining, his soul cowered with fear. He was not worthy. With a twist of her wrist, his neck was shattered.

"Holy fuck, Will!" The second soldier, just as large as the one named Will, began backing away.

Fear filled the man though he had an inner strength of his own. He was still unacceptable.

She stood as the twelve men with rifles all hesitated though they readied their weapons. Oh what weak vessels, useless against a power they don't understand. With the simple thought, several wolves followed her command and charged forward. Cowards, just as she had known. They never got a shot off before their death was upon them. Screams and the sounds of her wolves tearing them apart filled the air. She smiled as she approached the two remaining men.

"Charlie? That's you isn't it? I know it's you. Please, come back to me. It's me, Will. Don't you remember?"

The dark skinned one pleaded with her. Even in this desperate attempt she could sense his strength. He wasn't afraid, she felt him searching, searching for something, just as she was. She stepped closer, with every inch that disappeared between them; more power drained from her body. She fought it, but there was something drawing her to him.

"Come on Charlie, tell me you remember. I thought you were dead. I was beside myself with grief. I have stayed alive in the hopes I would find you again."

She was inches from him. His eyes were swallowing her. Her legs began to wobble as more and more drained out of her. What was this he held over her?

"Will, it's not Charlie. Look at her! She looks like a monster!"

The other man brought a cool fire back to her belly. His fear was overtaking him; she could smell it. He was not worthy. Her eyes moved from the second man to her Alpha. She could still feel his mind, he wanted more, and he could have it. With a nod, the beast stepped forward.

"No Charlie, don't! You don't have to do this. Stop!"

The dark skinned man grabbed her as he shouted. His hands were warm, her skin fought against it as it began to burn. Her Alpha went to lunge at its target, but to her surprise the large man attacked first. A new strength flowed through him as he fought a foe he could not hope to beat. Blows struck beast and soldier. Her Alpha fell back as the large solder struck it over and over, but she could see the life draining from the soldier. He was flesh and bone; her wolf was pure power. The beast could be harmed, but it could not be killed.

"Charlie! Stopped this, now!"

The dark soldier squeezed her arms, sending burning a burning heat that seared her flesh. She almost dropped to her knees as more power drained from her.

The warrior fighting her Alpha finally slipped to his

knees as his blood pooled on the floor. He fought with a strength that she hadn't seen in any man.

"Walker, no!"

The dark skinned man released her arms as he went to aid his friend. The moment his hands released she could feel her strength surge back. His friend was going to die, and there was nothing he could do about it.

"Kill this one, he is the only one left to stop you!" The voice returned stronger than ever. It filled her, her cravings returned, she would have her revenge!

Reaching out, she grabbed the man before he could get more than a step away. Spinning him around, she slid the knife she carried on her belt deep under his ribs. The look of shock in his eyes filled her with sorrow.

"Charlie…Why?"

The man used his remaining strength to talk as she lowered him to the ground. He sat there and looked deep into her blue eyes, never turning as his friend fought to the last against her Alpha. She could see his soul fighting, trying to understand everything around him. He didn't fear death; he wasn't afraid. Sadness filled him, yet he seemed confused.

"Why Charlie, I love…"

The man's eyes glossed over as his life faded. Even in death, he was strong, he was worthy.

"We have done it, my child. He was the key to our glory! Rise, my soldier. Rise for a glory that will be ours!"

The voice no longer only filled her mind, but echoed around the room. Her power surged, and a terrible pain tore through her back as her Alpha howled next to her. She dropped to her knees as the ground began to shake. Cracks broke across the floor and stretched themselves up the walls. The ceiling began to crumble around her.

"The final choice is finished! All our strength is

complete! You will be my first warrior. Your general awaits!"

The voice tore through her mind, as the pain in her back intensified. Looking up at the crumbling roof above her, she arched her back and began to scream. She screamed as her skin burned, her mind cracked, and the world shook…

2237 HOURS, Avost 13, 2258
Obrathe, Azhana

"WHAT THE FUCK IS GOING ON?" David tried to scream over the sounds of falling rock and the ground tearing up around them.

All of them stood there, arms and feet out wide as they tried to balance through the shaking. Standing in the middle of the road, the falling pieces of metal and rock smashed against the asphalt of the highway, mere feet from where they stood.

"Is this some kind of earthquake?" Dickie struggled to keep his balance and slipped to one knee.

"I doubt it. Maybe we are too late. Could they have a weapon that would level a city?" Any possible idea that he could think of, passed through his mind as Brett spoke and tried to keep his balance.

Large fissures cracked open down the middle of the highway. Steam burst from the water pipes below as the water rushed to the top.

"I do not like this one bit." David was trying to help Dickie to his feet.

From somewhere deeper within the city, toward the Temple and their mission's destination, a moan like wood beams ready to snap carried through the wind. The team of five soldiers all looked on as the ground itself rose from beneath that part of the city. Right before their eyes the whole city was shifting upward. Buildings farther from the center started falling and crumbling backward as if the hands of a god tore the carpet of the earth from beneath them.

"Whatever that is, doesn't look good. I say we get the fuck out of here, Boss." Dickie back on his feet started to tug on Brett's shirt.

All thought of their situation had left Brett's mind. Watching the ground start to rise felt like hypnosis and he refused to turn his eyes away. Something within the destruction wanted him to watch. A power drew him closer; he wanted to run to it, to be there when whatever was below ground, finally, pulled itself free.

"Ah, my time has come. Finally! The time of reckoning for the insects of this world is at hand. Behold my true power!" The voice, until now pressed deep into the back of his mind, plowed forward again and sent Brett back to his knees. The pain threatened to tear his mind in half. "My General awaits, are you ready to take your command beside him? Submit to me, and power beyond your belief will be yours. How did it feel to cut the life out of that worthless scum by your feet? I can give you that and a million more. The weak and useless will run before you, fear will have them tremble at the very thought of your name. Join me now, and we will watch the world burn!"

The words tried to grab a grip on his soul. Everything they said, every vision it tried to press before his eyes begged him to comply. Why not? So many people out there deserved death. His mission was still not complete. Every cult soldier and member needed to die; he had promised Kris. Wait Kris? What had he said?

Memories of the young man, the conversations about what they did and why they did it broke through the voice's grip. Reality sank in as his men pulled him back to his feet. Before them all, the temple and surrounding buildings had lifted dozens of feet into the air. Sounds of crumbling buildings and the destruction of the city echoed in waves.

"Brett, we need to move now!" The men shouted as they tried desperately to pull his attention away.

They did everything they could to turn him. All his attention, all his being was focused on this one event. They had to clear as much distance as they could from whatever was ripping up their world. The hold the event had in his mind and vision would not give up. Then, just as they stopped to try to spin him around, everything changed.

The ground, the buildings on top, and everything within the distance of the risen earth crashed back down as if dropped from the sky. The force of the wind and flying dust knocked each of the men down to the ground. Everything before them lit up like a midday sun as flames and smoke shot straight up into the air. A flow of fire like nothing they had ever seen streamed straight up into the sky. Anything that the fire touched was incinerated instantly: buildings made of rock, wood, and metal liquefied or burned the second it touched the flames. Heat radiated from the funnel, so dry and strong, the men could see the steam coming from each other's body.

"Oh shit! What the fuck is that? What the fuck!" Dickie was already trying to scramble away.

Each of them was going frantic as they scrambled to get back to their feet. The wall of flames now reached only a couple of blocks from them. Ash rained from the sky as molten rocks crashed down, crushing anything they hit. Then, burning as they broke open, they spilled their hot molten liquid onto everything around.

More fissures broke from the earth as the team finally scrambled back to their feet. Steam burst from the cracks as the ground shook, and fiery death rained around them. None of them tried to speak as Ed and David quickly took the lead. The team scrambled among buildings, around rocks and fallen debris as the world around them took on a gray ash-colored appearance.

Brett followed closely as the team ran on. Something in the back of his mind could hear a different sound mixed with the wind and destruction around them. If he listened closely enough, he swore he could hear screams, not of pain, but of enjoyment. These screams weren't coming from people; there was a bestiality to them. Was there something in the ash cloud that now covered everything around them?

Their world was a mix of thick gray smoke, bright light from the still streaming wall of flames, and bouncing shadows threatening to overwhelm them at every corner. The obstacles, the constant ground shaking, and almost zero visibility had them running blind. It no longer mattered what direction they ran in, so long as it was away from that wall of fire and death.

"Sergeant, what the fuck is going on?" Dickie yelled back as the team continued forward.

"Hell, if I know. Just keep your ass moving. Let those murderous fuckers burn in the fire of their creation for all we care."

Brett wasn't certain the cult had done this, what kind of thing can create a volcano in the middle of a city? A God! He didn't want to say it, but the world was fucked.

Their movement was slower than they wanted, and in all the chaos, time seemed to slow as the men continued to move. They had made it to the third section, each of them breathing heavily between coughs as the ash and smoke began to choke out the air for them to breathe. By the time they got to the second dividing highway, their movement could no longer be called running; a forced march was a better description.

"Shit, we aren't gonna make it like this." David bent over, hands on his knees as the others caught up. Each of them only wanted to stop and catch their breath, coughs, and heavy breaths riddled their bodies.

"Put on your gas masks. It will make seeing anything a real bitch, but at least we will be able to breathe." Ed pointed to all the others as he grabbed his own.

Once the air filters were on, breathing became simpler. They would have to watch their exertion. Breathing through these things was more laborious than normal, but it would stop their lungs from burning out from the inside.

"We need to keep moving." The others nodded at Brett; they needed no further explanation.

Just as they started down the first side street they found, a horrific scream erupted from the clouds above them. Something within that sound, echoing through everything around them had them flinching for cover. Just as the sound stopped, a shadow, cast by the still shining light of the volcano of flames, washed over them, and then disappeared.

"There is something up there!" David pointed up, but the clouds were too thick.

Black bulbous clouds of smoke and ash moved quickly above them rendering the sky void and depthless. After the black shadow had disappeared, large balls of molten rock started raining across the city. Only a few hundred feet from where the men crouched, one touched down crushing through the first few feet of the street's asphalt.

The sound was deafening. If their ears weren't ringing enough from everything around them, they were now.

Vibrations could be heard everywhere as these meteors of fire and rock smashed everything in their path.

"Fucking fantastic. Now this!" Dickie was pointing at the nearest opening in the ground as he passed.

Before Dickie could get too far, his jog slowed to a few dragged steps. The large soldier's eyes, now the size of full dinner plates, would not leave the smoldering hole.

"Dickie, keep moving!" Brett went to kick the man right in the ass when he took a moment to look as well.

The steam rising from the ground started to fade. At first the hole was covered in shadows, then those shadows began to move. An arm stretched out of the hole, its skin as dark as molten glass, cracks within the blackness revealing the bright orange-yellow glow of melted rock flowing within it like blood. The creature's hands were all glass-like claws, strong enough that when it gripped the asphalt of the road, they tore right through the solid road and began lifting itself out of the ground.

When it finally pulled itself from the crater, the whole team could see it for what it was. Large tree trunk sized muscular legs led to a large barrel chested body of muscle made of rock. A broad set of shoulders fanned out wide as it stretched its arms and extended its deadly claws. Each of its feet carried three molten glass claws the size of crane hooks; its face was something straight out of a nightmare. Red flames burned deep within its eye sockets, each movement of the demon's face created cracks that oozed the molten rock inside.

"Fire!" Brett ordered.

Whatever this thing was, Brett and his team had to deal with it. They were too close to run. Just looking at it gave the impression it would tear after them in a heartbeat.

All five men had rifles up, on target, and firing as metal projectiles crashed into the beast's body. Bright yellow and red liquid sprayed as openings in its rock exterior tore open, a roar of anger erupted from the monster's throat.

The succession of quick firing drove the thing backward, toppling it back into the hole from which it came. Brett looked in, horrified by what he saw. Whatever the thing was laid sprawled out on the bottom of the crater. The wounds in its chest still open, molten liquid flowing out, but as it did, the fiery rock hardened and cooled.

The beast was healing itself. He could see the clawed hands begin to flex, the blood solidified as new skin to cover the openings. Since they weren't going to kill it by simple means, he reached into his pack, removed a grenade and tossed it in. Everyone backed away before the grenade blasted and tore everything inside apart.

"Try coming back from that you piece of shit." Dickie tried to sound confident, but he and the others were now seriously doubting the chances of their survival.

"OK, keep us moving! Just stay in the shadows as much as possible. Hell knows how many of these things there are." Brett ordered from the back of the group.

Brett looked back as the men started moving in front of him. Was the whole world ending? What were they going to do if the whole city became filled with these things?

The adrenaline from fighting that beast coursed through their veins. A renewed vigor helped them push forward, strangled breathing and all; they pressed on. Shadows stretched deeper and darker the more they moved away from the wall of fire that now seemed to cover the entire center of the city. Somehow, whatever caused it, provided the flames an unending source of fuel. The heat, the flames, the smoke, and the light continued up into the sky without wavering. The whole world was going to burn, and they were only the start of it.

"Everyone stop!" David waved backward to get the others to stay behind him.

Looking around the corner, he squinted to see into the smoky air and shadows. Within moments, the dark head and burning eyes of one of those demons could be seen slowly coming around the corner of a building a couple of doorways away.

"What's going on, David?" All the men were close, so Brett only had to whisper for the front man to hear him.

"Another contact, two buildings over. Looks like just one."

Brett didn't like this. They had no idea how many of them there were, and they still had a good distance before they were out of the city. They could drop this one and move on, or hope it passed without noticing them. He didn't like the idea of it at their rear, always feeling like a shadow on their back, but their time was running out. He had to choose quickly.

"Let me see."

Brett squeezed up to the front. Looking for himself, he could see the thing had moved out onto the street. Stretched upright, the thing was clearly more than seven feet tall. Muscles made of rock covered its entire body, and with its face turned up to the air, he could only guess the thing tracked by scent.

"We have to drop it, looks like the damn things can track us like dogs." He looked at his men, each of them had a determination in their face, ready to do battle, but behind their eyes there was a weariness. The sounds of echoing thunder and the roars of unknown demons battered their ears while the world was crashing down around them. Even to hardened war veterans, this was a lot to take in. "Alright, concentrate your fire, drop him quick and let's get out of here. We will move quickly to the outside of the city."

Each man nodded as they checked their weapons. Taking a deep breath, Brett slowly turned the corner. Their target was still searching the middle of the street. Maybe if they were lucky, it was just as blind as they were in the shadows. Improved smell or not, no vision would give them at least this little advantage.

Taking a few steps out, he waited until he felt the other four prepare themselves. He only had to count three heartbeats later before all five opened fire. Just as before, the monster tore open as the bullets wrecked its body. A roar of defiance escaped its throat as it toppled to the ground.

"Frag it before it gets back up. Let's move!"

Brett could see Ed reach for a grenade of his own to toss at the body in the road. No more time to waste, they started to jog again.

"Contact!" Witch yelled as he fired a few rounds.

Brett and the others looked farther down the street. Barreling around the alley corner a whole mob of creatures came spilling out. Unlike the large things they fought before, these monsters were smaller. A wild shriek of rage pierced the air as the mob turned toward them.

They were stone skinned like their larger brethren, but as a mob they glowed a brighter orange. Running on all fours, they charged through those in front who fell to a wall of bullets. Those in the back stumbled over the fallen in a maddened rush for the men who now fired at them. No amount hesitation slowed them as their cries for bloodlust drove them forward.

"Move, now!" Brett ordered his men as he continued to fire.

More and more of them steamrolled from the alley. They didn't have enough bullets to stand and fight.

Running was their only option. All five of them darted as fast as they could down the nearest side street. Vacant shops passed as the men didn't bother looking back. Muscles ached, and joints creaked as they pushed forward.

"In here, now!"

David, the fastest of the group, ordered as he turned into a small passageway between two abandoned office buildings. Without slowing, the man crashed his shoulder into and through the first door he saw. The others followed as David recovered himself and stepped back out. Pulling the pin on a grenade he tossed it as close as he could to the corner of the building across from them. The explosion shook the foundation as debris fell into the alley blocking the way they had entered.

Each of them was breathing heavy as they tried to catch a rest for a second. The boarded windows provided some cover from the street while Witch and Ed worked on sealing the door they had broken through.

"What the fuck are we going to do now?" Dickie was pacing the room, sweat and grime running down his face.

"Did you see those things? What is going on out there?" David knelt to the ground, trying to catch his breath.

They were low on supplies, and they knew it. Each of them looked up at Brett, wanting an answer he couldn't give. What do you tell them when your best guess is that their only option is to fight to the last man? The world was ending, and there was nothing they could do.

"I have no idea, all I know is we aren't safe in here either."

The shrieks of the beasts vibrated through the walls. Their screams carried past as the thunder of their steps rolled down the road.

"There is a way out for you; you do not have to suffer as they do." The voice tore into Brett's mind again.

Pain flashed behind his eyes as he dropped to his knees. With all the excitement of running for their lives, the voice had finally been silenced.

"Look around you. Your options are running out. It does not have to end for you like it will for them. Accept my offer, open the door and end these fools' misery. My power can be yours, and so much more!"

Every time it talked, the muscles in Brett's body tensed. Looking at his hands through the pain, it felt as though they were no longer his.

"Brett, are you okay?" David put a hand under Brett's shoulder and lifted him back to his feet.

"Yeah, it's these damn flashes of pain. They started once we got here." He couldn't tell the men about the voices.

"Seems a whole lot of things have started since we got here." David walked to the boarded windows, putting his ears against the wood as the world outside fell silent.

"What's our plan, Boss?" Dickie stopped pacing, his hands on his hips waiting for an answer.

Looking around, he could see them waiting for something, anything that would get them through the next minute.

"Their fate is already sealed. Why join them, when you can lead an army of your own!" The voice tore through Brett's conscience, but he did his best to bite back the pain.

"We can't fight the bastards, that's for sure. They die easy enough, but unless one of you is carrying more ammo in your pants, our best bet is to go as quietly as possible. David, do you hear anything?" Brett tried to sound as confident as he could.

The man shook his head no. It wasn't a great idea. Hell, on a normal day, it was a shitty idea, but it was the best they had. If a man was going to die, better do it on his feet and fighting. The whole team had lived by that motto. None of them wanted to wait until death found them in an empty store.

"Alright then…" Brett began to speak as the building and everything around them started to shake violently.

High above them, the horrific sound of a roar echoed through the streets as something flew overhead. The men inside the building couldn't see it, but they sure as hell could feel it as dust and sheetrock pieces crumbled from the ceiling above them.

"That's enough of that. Anyone know of a way out of here?"

"This way," Witch pointed toward the back as he led the others out.

Through the back door to the shop, the team exited into a small grassy area hidden behind all the buildings. Children's toys could be seen scattered in the overgrown grass. A long time had passed since those things had brought joy to the children who owned them. Quietly and huddled the best they could, the team moved forward. Following back alleys and staying as deep into the shadows as they could, the five surviving men slipped between buildings, hoping the sounds and confusion of the still falling ash and rocks would hide their escape.

For the better part of an hour, they traveled through two sectors of the city unnoticed. The beasts were patrolling the streets in large groups now. The larger ones with their razor talons commanded as small mobs of the shorter monsters followed in their wake. They had to keep to the shadows. None of them carried enough firepower, or strength, to fight off an entire mob.

"One block to go, and then it's the slums. They must be searching for survivors. Unlucky for them, the cult took care of that before they got here." David was right as he looked out onto the highway that separated them from the last part of the city.

Survivors. That word brought back a memory to Brett's mind. This whole city had been dead before they arrived. If it hadn't, everyone inside would now be living through their worst nightmare. Silently, Brett ran the options these innocent civilians would have faced. Would the people have preferred dying at the hands of lunatic men, or at the hands of horrific monsters? Brett shook his head to rid himself of the thoughts as the image of a little girl echoed deep in his mind.

Hopefully, they had listened to her. If there were anything right in this world, she would have found a way to convince them to leave. Brett squeezed the grip to his rifle. If I've done anything right, let her live.

"Looks like the coast is clear. Let's move." David waved them forward as all five of them moved to run across the road.

"Your chance to choose is almost up. Leave this city without me, and you will die. Leave this city with me, and you will rule this world by my side." The voice grayed out Brett's vision and weakened his knees, but he pushed on. He had to keep up with the others.

All five of them were halfway across when a shriek rained from the ash cloud above. A shadow flew over them. Looking up, they were barely able to catch a glimpse of something large before it was lost again in the clouds. Did it have wings? What in the seven hells can fly like that? Questions ran through each of their minds as they turned to continue.

Just as quickly as the shadow had come and was gone, large molten meteors began to fall around them. Five crashed on the road with two directly in their path. Steam rose out of the craters as the monsters made their way to the surface. There was nowhere for them to run.

"Move! Move now!" Brett opened fire on the two in front.

No one missed a beat as they pressed forward at full sprint and full auto fire. As quickly as the front two climbed out, they fell back in. The rage roared from the other three, but at least the team had a small head start.

David ran in front; the others quickly fell in behind. The crashing footsteps of the demons behind them could be heard getting closer. They had to find a way to lose them, or anything that would help slow them down.

Ahead, past the start of a side street, was another alley. If they could get inside, they could focus their remaining fire. They were a few feet from the corner of the side street when the glass shattering howl of a mob came from around the corner.

An entire mass of blackness mixed with golden red magma crashed into David, Ed, and Witch. The first wave stumbled as the mass of bodies rolled into the streets. Shrieks mixed with screams, howls with fits of anger as men fought demons. Brett and Dickie opened fire as best they could. In the smoky air, it was difficult to tell friend from foe, and more of the beasts were coming down the street. In seconds, the large ones chasing behind would be on top of them.

Dropping his rifle, Dickie took out two knives from his belt and dove right into the mass of bodies. If the demon's clawed hands were made for tearing apart their prey, the knives in Dickie's hands made him a chef, and he was hungry. Moving with the grace of a ballet dancer, but with the precision of an assassin, the large man tore through body and limb with every swing, stab, and rip of his arms. Bodies and pieces fell before him; the creatures could not touch him. He was an artist at his greatest moment. The last two had fallen before Dickie scooped all three men from the ground while Brett now carried two rifles.

It had only been moments, but the damage was done. All three men were hurt badly, lucky to be alive, and already being pulled forward. Death was knocking on the door for all of them, but they were trying their damnedest to keep that door shut. The five men turned to continue down the side street. They had the big ones now nipping at their heels, the new mob charging right at them. That alley in front of them was their only option. Pushing as hard as they could, they ran for their lives.

"Get in there!" Dickie screamed as he pulled the three men he was dragging.

All three stumbled in as Brett quickly slipped in behind, handing Dickie back his rifle. Turning at the entrance to the dark alley, Dickie with everything he had roared back at their pursuers. Waves of little ones died at the wall of lead fired into them. Brett fired the best he could through the little room he was given.

"Get the fuck out of here! I'll hold them for as long as I can!" The man gave no room for arguing.

He turned and positioned himself to block as much of the entrance as he could. With every passing second, the horde of enemies drew closer, but with each step he made them pay. A couple got close, but without a second of hesitation, he cut them down and returned to firing.

Not wanting to, but seeing no other choice, Brett picked the others off the ground and pushed them forward. Nothing he could do would stop the man, the only way to help was to keep them moving. The four men stumbled into the shadows at the end of the alley. Echoes of gunfire and explosions shook the brick around them. In the darkness, the alley turned behind the buildings, and they continued their retreat.

They were a dozen feet down the rear alley when the shriek they had heard returned from the clouds. Struggling to look up, the four men tried to see anything as they struggled forward. Above them, the shadow returned, breaking from the clouds above, a beast, unlike anything they had ever seen swooped down. Silhouetted by the firelight still streaming into the sky, skin made of pure volcanic glass shone down at them. With its wings spread, the demon covered what must have been more than five city blocks. Massive legs curled into it as it flew. Its claws were as large as a man was tall. As massive as the beast was, it swooped with the grace of a hawk, its roar tearing through the night sky. Just as it approached the alley where Dickie was making his last stand, the beast gave out one last roar before thrusting his head forward.

From its open maw, a wave of flames burst out and filled the night sky. Everything it hit as it slammed into the alleyway burst into flames and melted instantly. The heat from the blast radiated all the way to the four of them still running. The thought of his friend's last moments sank into Brett's gut. They were losing each other, one by one, and there was nothing he could do. Pushing the others forward, he could see they were in bad shape. Witch was torn up, large gashes across his back and face, the blood seeping out stained his clothes a deep black and red. Ed limped and pressed most of his weight into David. The fighting and rolling around had torn his old injuries anew, and fresh bleeding wounds only hastened the matter.

David himself bled from several wounds, but the man's strength was unending. His right leg limped, but he bit through the pain as he carried Ed from under his shoulder.

Brett followed closely behind, every few seconds looking back, expecting the pursuit to continue.

"There! That's the straight alley back to our jeep!" Witch pointed a weak arm forward.

Before them, the same trash and filth covered stone alley opened. With renewed vigor, David tried to quicken their pace, but the others could only go so fast.

"Do you think I will let you get away that easily? Look how the others struggle, they are barely hanging on, yet you are still strong. Leave them. They are only slowing you down. You've seen what power I can give. Look how sadly that other one died. Do you want to share his fate?"

The voice was relentless. It rang so loud and clear, and it took everything Brett had to ignore it. Every time it was there, images of that young soldier, of Dickie, each of them dead, returned to his mind. Inside, his anger was building, he wanted to make those responsible for this pay, but who was it? These demons seemed to want to kill everything in their path. He could not do this on his own, the voice was right, alone he was doomed. He could feel himself growing weaker against its will. He tried screaming against it in his mind, telling it that he would rather die, but it did not seem to hear him. It just continued to tell him to make his choice, one led to certain death, the other to unlimited power. The more he watched his friends suffer and die, the closer he got to slipping away. He did not want this to be the end.

Shadows enveloped them as they entered the alley. Old trash and cardboard crunched under their feet as they stumbled on. By now, Ed and Witch's movements were more like forced labor. Their loss of blood was catching up to them. Even David seemed affected as his browned skin had a grayish hue to it, noticeable even under the ash.

"Come on guys, just a little bit farther!" David shifted Ed's weight and tried for one more push.

Above them, another roar erupted as the shadow swept by overhead. In the distance, the shrieks of dozens of demons howled like a pack of hounds who had caught their scent. Needing no more incentive, David and Brett shuffled the others at their fastest pace.

"We aren't going to make it like this! They will find us quickly!" David called back.

David was right. If they left Ed and Witch behind, they had a chance, but their friends would perish. With them, all four were going to die. Brett looked over and saw the same thoughts going through David's eyes as he wrapped Witch's arm over his shoulder and tried to help him along.

"Over here, quick, before they find you!"

A small door opened behind a pile of cardboard boxes. From it came a voice, one they thought they wouldn't ever hear again. Little Coleena stepped out just slightly and waved them in. Even in the depths of all this horror, this little girl had the courage of a hero. Her mother still clenched her from behind, but the little blond girl pressed forward, making sure the four men saw where they needed to go.

Falling inside the small room, Brett quickly shut the door as he looked around. They were in what was nothing more than a supply closet. A single candle wavered in the center of the small room where seven people now occupied. Ed and Witch quickly fell to the ground, both without any more strength to give. David grunted as he shifted his weight and moved to find his seat. Positioning himself, he pressed his back against the door, sighed and began looking for any medical supplies they had left.

Huddled in the corner was Coleena and her family. Her mother still clenched her tightly to her chest as she knelt behind the little girl. Behind both stood the father. A large purple and swollen red cheek failed to hide the fact that he stared at the four tired and injured soldiers with a look of pure hatred. He'd have to get over it. They were alive because of them, and neither his family nor the team had anywhere left to go.

"What are you doing here little Coleena?" Brett knelt to look the little girl in her eyes, the voice suddenly silent in his mind.

"I convinced them to get out of the city just as you said. We didn't make it far before the ground started shaking. That light burst into the sky, and now there are monsters everywhere." A sudden crash rocked the floors above them, a look of fear crossed her face as her mother squeezed her closer. "We thought some of them had found us, so we hid in here. We were about to leave again when I heard your voice come down the alley. I wanted to help."

Her words brought a smile to his face. It amazed him how much she reminded him of his kids, but they were only memories now. She was flesh and blood, and if it were the last thing he did, he wasn't going to fail her.

"We thank you and your family very much for the help. You did a very brave thing back there. We would be in serious trouble if you didn't help us."

As if her father had understood what he was saying, the man clutched his wife and child closer to him. Glancing quickly up into the man's angry brown eyes, Brett could see the proud man's shoulders slump as he released his grip on the two women.

"Sergeant, we've got another problem here." David's voice interrupted them.

Turning, Brett could see he was working on Ed and Witch. A strained look of pain was on both of their faces as they fought to keep their eyes open. Using what little supplies they had left, David had stopped most of the bleeding on both men.

"We don't have much farther to go, can they make it?"

David looked him face to face, and the answer was as clear as day, but neither wanted to say it. Brett took a long look down at his friends. All of them had been through some of the toughest times imaginable together. Nothing could make him believe it was going to end like this.

"It's okay, Brett. Can't save us all, every time." Ed coughed out the words; Witch remained silent, his white hair pasted to his forehead.

He wanted to argue, say something that would give them the ability to push on. They were only a few blocks away from their escape. David's hand rested on his shoulder now, and the big man gave it a squeeze as he forced himself to sit again. The sounds of the beasts howling in the distance could still be heard echoing down the alley.

"Leave us here, we are only holding you back. Take them with you." Ed nodded his chin toward the huddled family in the corner. "We came here to save people and end this abomination. Let's at least get half of it right."

Ed was right, they still had a chance to get something accomplished, even if it were the end of the world. Looking over at David sitting against the door, the man dipped his head in agreement and removed the pistol from his belt. Checking the remaining rounds in the gun, Brett removed his own and handed both to the dying men who would remain behind.

"Both of you, we will never forget what you did here. None of this will be in vain. I am proud to have served with all of you." Brett could feel the emotion building in his throat. Neither of the two said anything back.

Ed, his hand shaky with his blood drying on it, reached

out and grabbed Brett's forearm. The fire beneath his forearm no longer burned. The scars remained, and his friend's touch cooled his skin. Without words being spoken, Brett heard all he needed from them. Now it was time to finish what they had started.

"All right, Coleena, you guys are coming with us. We have a jeep just outside the city waiting, and it's gassed and more than capable of getting us out of here. Stay close, there is no telling how many are between us and safety."

With that, David got up and prepared to move them outside their hiding space.

"What about these two? Are we going to leave them?" The little girl asked.

"They have a special surprise for anything that tries to follow us. We need them to give us the time to get out of here. Now please, we need to move quickly."

Brett looked down at the little girl as she led her parents out the door behind David. Something in her look said she trusted him. She was scared, but no matter what, she would follow.

Before leaving, they positioned Ed and Witch on opposite sides of the alleyway. Both men armed themselves with as much firepower that the group could spare. If anything did follow, the toll would be high to get past those two.

"Final chance, if you do not choose to come with me, I will be forced to take things into my hands!"

The voice tried to fight its way back. For some reason, thinking about the family that followed closely on his heels helped push it away. The despair that had found its way deep into the recesses of his mind faded. These people needed him, and there was a chance life could still come out of all this disaster. He would fight to the last man to make sure it did.

"Just ahead, only another few hundred yards!" David called back to the rest of them.

Brett picked up the pace as best he could. The tree line was now visible as the tops of the trees poked over the buildings ahead. The five survivors stayed close as they ran forward. Only two more buildings stood between them and their ticket out.

Without warning, a roar tore from around the corner as one of the largest demons yet, charged forward and crashed right into the side of Brett. The impact knocked the wind right out of him as he was lifted off his feet and thrown into a nearby wall. All the energy he had was drained as he tried to get back to his feet, the beast already turning on those following him.

David was quick to raise his rifle and squeeze the trigger. One round went off, slamming into the monster's shoulder before it jammed and stopped firing. The black creature rose to its full height as it extended its arms. The thing was massive by all accounts, rearing its head back it roared in defiance as the wound on its shoulder already started to heal. Brett tried to move; pain wracked his body as his legs would not cooperate. With a final look at his last friend, their eyes met for a moment before David closed his.

Giving an almost nonhuman roar of his own, the injured soldier charged forward. The beast hesitated as David slammed right into it. Man and beast crashed to the ground, rolling as each tried to tear the life out of the other. Both fighters bit, tore, and squeezed whatever they could as they rolled on the ground. The thing was twice the size of David, but the man fought on. Streams of blood sprayed from newly opened wounds as the monster's claws found unprotected skin. Howls of pain echoed as the iron-like grip of David's hands tore pieces of black rock away, spilling the molten blood within onto the ground.

"Get the fuck out of here! Save them!" David yelled before he slammed his forehead into the beast's face.

Doing his best, Brett struggled to his feet. Little Coleena and her family made their way over and helped what they could. He didn't want to take his eyes off his friend, who now was visibly weakening as more and more blood found its way to the ground. The soldier still fought on, so Brett would try to do the same.

With his first step, horrible pain seared through his side and into his chest. Looking down, he could see blood quickly filling the right side of his uniform.

Reaching down, he could feel the metal that now protruded from his side. Blood soaked his stained hands as he tried to slow the bleeding, he didn't have much time left.

"We have to go now, quickly. It isn't much farther."

Fighting for the others, Brett pushed on. With every step the pain grew, and his exhaustion doubled.

"You have made your choice. Unlike the others, you will not die here. You possess something I need. You are stronger than they ever were. I will take from you what I want, and those you protect will pay the price."

The voice slammed into him stronger than he had ever felt. The tree line was right in front of them, and a path opened through the bushes leading to the jeep.

The pain in his mind and his side was too much. Dropping to his knees every breath he tried to take was labored. An explosion tore through the buildings a few blocks into the city, causing two buildings to collapse from view. He was the only one left, and he would be joining them soon.

"Come on! We are almost out of here!" Little Coleena tugged on Brett's shirt, trying to lift him back to his feet.

"The jeep is through that path there. You cannot miss it."

Looking up at that beautiful little girl, he could not help but smile through all the pain. Everything about a life he had thought lost reflected in her eyes.

"You're sick, aren't you?"

Brett looked down at his shirt; blood soaked through it, and it felt heavy on his shoulders.

"Yeah, I'm sick. I need to rest here while you and your parents keep moving."

The pain in his mind tripled to where he could feel it peel down his back. Gritting his teeth, he fought it the best he could.

"I want you to have this," Coleena whispered with tears running down her cheeks.

Reaching behind her neck and through her blond hair, she removed a tiny locket. She reached out and placed it in his blood-soaked hands.

He didn't know what to do; the pain was horrible. He struggled to stay on his knees and here she was handing him a gift. Doing the only thing he could think of, he reached up and removed the dog tags from around his neck. Where he was going, he wouldn't need them anyway. Reaching out, he placed them and the keys into her soft little hands.

"Now take these, and get your family out of here. Please, go now. There isn't much time left."

Tears streamed down her face; she knew what was happening, but there wasn't anything either could do to stop it. With sadness on their faces, her parents gently took her by the shoulders and turned her away. The father hesitated for a second as he looked down at Brett. He hadn't known the man at all, but at that moment he could see all the gratitude in the world reflected in his eyes. Just as quickly, the family turned and started running to the path. They were safe, they finished their mission.

Pain ripped through Brett's body as the skin of his back began to tear in two. He was down on his hands and knees, and blood filled his mouth as he bit down on his lower lip.

"All right you bastard. I'm right here. I told you once that I'd die before I joined you. Let's see if you have what it takes to kill me. I'm right here, come and get me!"

Brett yelled in defiance as the pain took over. His whole body was shaking as his vision started to fade.

"You will not die today. No, I have greater plans for you. My army needs a leader, someone already soaked in the blood of the innocent!"

That was the last Brett heard before a roar broke through the clouds. The shadow returned, casting everything around him in black as the pain finally took its toll and Brett collapsed to the ground.

Chapter Forty-Three

____

0137 Hours, Avos 13, 2258
Obrathe, Azhana

THE PAIN WAS GONE, nothing but silence remained in his mind. Was it a dream?

"Awaken my child, behold what your master has given you. Feel the power run through your body. You are born anew!"

Brett opened his eyes; he was still laying on the ground where he had fallen. Ash and smoke fell from the dark sky like the soft petals of snow in the winter. Howls and destruction echoed through the city.

"Why is there no more pain? What have you done?"

"I gave to you willingly what you chose not to have. Stand and take your rightful place at the front of my army!"

Brett could hear the familiar shrieks of bloodthirsty excitement and the beastly growl as the various demons made their way from the alleys. Sitting up, Brett could not figure out why they weren't attacking him. Where did all the pain go? Anger and rage filled his eyes as he looked at his body before he leaned back and howled into the sky.

His side was no longer bleeding, it was a volcanic glass crust. Razor sharp claws replaced the fingers of his hands, and the skin that covered his arms, legs, and body rippled and cracked as he moved. With each crack, he could see the molten liquid flow beneath the surface, as it reached air it would harden, giving him an ever renewing layer of skin. Fear and questions circled through his mind, then a small flash of light caught his eye.

In his right hand, a small silver chain hung loosely to the ground. A small heart-shaped locket remained unscratched between the sharp talons of his hands. The memory of the little girl, her tear filled eyes as she handed him this locket burned forever in his mind. His chest filled with a fire so hot, the molten rock beneath began to glow.

"Arise my son. More worthless creatures need to be exterminated, and there is no time to wait. In front of you comes just a fraction of the army you will lead."

More and more demons stepped from the shadows as they waited for him. They stood there, waiting for a command. Above them all, the beast that could block all the light circled in the clouds.

His anger continued to swell, he could feel the heat radiating through his body as he turned to face all the demons before him. The last images of her family before they turned to run for safety stuck in his mind.

"Come forward. You are the strongest of them all. They will follow you, and you will lead an army built to change this world. Let us rid this land of those no longer worthy to breathe!"

"You made a serious mistake, you sorry excuse for a god."

"What mistake is that? A God does not make a mistake, especially not in a world of such lowly creatures." The voice hesitated, then grew angry.

"This war has taken everything from me. My family, my friends, and the lives of more people than I could count." Images and the memories of the start of the war and what brought about this disaster filtered through Brett's mind. "Everything I have done has been to hunt down the ones responsible for all this; I have destroyed countless lives to find you hiding in plain sight. I told you that you would have to kill me before I joined your ranks. Now you have given me the power of the very weapons you use. I will fight you until I take every last freak you have brought to this world with me. I have lost everything, and now it is my time to return the favor!"

Extending to his new full height, Brett let out a roar that radiated in waves toward the front lines. The smallest demons backed as they shrieked like frightened animals, the larger ones roared back in defiance. Gripping the locket as tightly as he could with his clawed hand, Brett gave the little girl and her family one last chance. Barreling forward, he charged their front lines. He did not know how long he had been out, or how far they had gotten away. The only thing he knew was they would stop here. Using everything he had, he tore every demon he could grab with his claws. With his dying breath, he was going to take out as many as he could with him.

Coleena and her family would survive…

Epilogue

The last light within the city burned out as snow and ice covered everything. Sounds of ice wolves and new unimaginable ice demons echoed through the dead city streets. High above in the ever-growing storm clouds, a shadow circled the beginning of its new territory.

Her feet felt at home as they walked bare through the snow. Now measuring more than six feet deep, she gracefully glided over it, barely disturbing a single flake. Walking away from the quiet remains of civilization was easy for her. She found comfort in the power that surged through her body, and the thoughts that were no longer hers. Looking down, she could see her newly formed body. When her master had broken through, he had given her the power she so badly desired.

The cold frozen air kept her warm as her blue skin reflected the sunlight when it rose above the horizon. No warmth would come to this world today, or if her master had his way, ever again. As the storm moved on, the world itself froze in its wake. So much remained for her to do, so many things to destroy and conquer. She smiled as the idea tingled her very being, squeezing her hands into fists, she turned her eyes with their blue flame of power toward the south. Her job was not finished.

THE CITY BURNED into the morning hours. Coleena held her mother's hand tightly as they looked down to the city. Smoke still rose high into the air as a cloud of darkness spread outward toward the rest of the world.

No telling how many people would survive the awakening of demons. Her mother and father rambled on about how this was the end of everything, how there would be nothing left as these monsters brought nothing but darkness and death.

Coleena didn't feel the same. She was young, maybe even a bit naive, but six soldiers alone had stood against an army. She had joked when they had said their mission was to save people. Here now, the three of them stood miles away from a ruined city. Above, the beast circled through the storm clouds that covered the city.

The world would change, many more people would die, but in her heart she knew they would survive. In his eyes, she could see humans still had a strength in them. She didn't know why she gave him that locket, he was dying, and there was something else sick within him, but something told her she had to. Maybe it was her way of telling him she understood. He and his men had saved her from those monsters, and she would live because of them. The flying beast gave out a roar as it burned another line through the city.

Squeezing the soldier's tags in her hand, she could feel the tears running from her eyes. For them, she would survive. This world would find a way to survive. Even the smallest bit of hope started from somewhere. Turning her face to her small hands, she wiped away the last bit of blood from the shiny metal.

Sergeant Brett Giles
Our Lord's First Battalion, Second Division
Knights of the Vanguard
Born 2247

THIS WORLD WOULD SURVIVE...

About the Author

William J. Seymour is the author of Dark Fantasy which includes the titles Dark Choices, Merchant, and the upcoming Pestilence: Traveling Merchant Book Two. He lives with his family in southern Pennsylvania where he writes into the darkness of the night.

You can find out more about him at his website.

www.worldsbyroh.com

Also by William J. Seymour

Merchant: Traveling Merchant Book One